While compiling the present anthology of a new generation of Latin American authors, published from the early eighties to the present, I was struck by how far the literature has traveled, literally and figuratively, from such legendary landscapes as Juan Carlos Onetti's imaginary Santa María or Gabriel García Márquez's fantastical Macondo. The variety of styles, settings, and intrigues turned out to be wildly unpredictable: Santos-Febres's edgy depiction of the literally murderous pace of media living ("Flight"), the Chekhovian delicacy in Laura Restrepo's rendering of an elderly couple's adulterous reunion ("The Scent of Invisible Roses"), the hallucinatory precision of Ignacio Padilla's tale of British Colonial nostalgia and ruin ("The Antipodes and the Century").

So much has changed in the geography of Latin American literature since the "boom" of the sixties and the decade that followed. If the "boom" writers were less than comfortable with the very notion of a homogeneous cultural landscape called Latin America, the new Latin American authors have exploded it entirely.

**Thomas Colchie** is an acclaimed translator, editor, and literary agent for international authors. He is the editor of *A Hammock Beneath the Mangoes* (available from Plume) and has written for *The Village Voice* and *The Washington Post*. His translations include Manuel Puig's *Kiss of the Spider Woman* and (with Elizabeth Bishop, Gregory Rabassa, and Mark Strand) Carlos Drummond de Andrade's *Travelling in the Family*.

# A whistler in the nightworld

## SHORT FICTION FROM THE LATIN AMERICAS

EDITED BY

## THOMAS COLCHIE

A PLUME BOOK

PLUME
Published by the Penguin Group
Penguin Putnam Inc., 375 Hudson Street,
New York, New York 10014, U.S.A.
Penguin Books Ltd, 80 Strand,
London WC2R 0RL England
Penguin Books Australia Ltd, Ringwood,
Victoria, Australia
Penguin Books Canada Ltd, 10 Alcorn Avenue,
Toronto, Ontario, Canada M4V 3B2
Penguin Books (N.Z.) Ltd, 182–190 Wairau Road,
Auckland 10, New Zealand

Penguin Books Ltd, Registered Offices:
Harmondsworth, Middlesex, England

First published by Plume, a member of Penguin Putnam Inc.

First Printing, September 2002
10   9   8   7   6   5   4   3   2   1

LIBRARY OF CONGRESS CATALOGING-IN-PUBLICATION DATA:

A whistler in the nightworld : short fiction from the Latin Americas / edited by Thomas Colchie.
p.   cm.
ISBN 0-452-28358-2
1. Short stories, Latin American—Translations into English. 2. Latin American
fiction—20th century—Translations into English.   I. Colchie, Thomas.

PQ7087.E5 W55 2002
863'.010898—dc21                    2002022450

Printed in the United States of America
Set in Simoncini Garamond
Designed by Leonard Telesca

In memory of
**Emir Rodríguez Monegal**
critic, raconteur, mentor, friend

# Contents

# Acknowledgments

Editing an international anthology, especially of newer writing, is a bit like shooting a road movie on location. You don't know what you've got or how many people it will take to get you there—producers, writers, actors, extras, crews, technicians, friends, and strangers alike—until you watch the final cut. So this book must begin at the end: with my appreciation.

I'd like to thank Kathryn Court for her patience, as well as her lasting commitment to fine publishing, and for having introduced me to my savvy editor, Sara Bixler, who has also shown remarkable tact, wit, and understanding in handling my Neanderthal skills with respect to the computerized wonders of modern publishing. I also wish to acknowledge the cooperation and enthusiasm that a number of literary agents representing Latin American authors have brought to this project, including my dear friend Mercedes Casanovas in Barcelona; and my colleagues, old and new: Guillermo Schavelzon in Buenos Aires, Anne-Marie Vallat in Madrid, Antonia Kerrigan in Barcelona, and Susan Bergholz and Nicole Aragi in New York.

Without the work and skills of the translator, international publishing as we know it—not to mention the present anthology—would simply not exist. And so I wish to express a shared debt going back a good many years to gifted veterans like Edith Grossman, Dolores M. Koch, and Margaret Abigail Neves, who have quietly provided homes in the English language for so many

Latin American authors; and to newer translators like James Graham, Stephen A. Lytle, Amy Schildhouse Greenberg, and Natasha Wimmer; and finally a personal debt to the poet and master translator Alastair Reid, who long ago revealed to me the alchemy of friendship and language. Elaine Jabbour Colchie, my wife and fellow traveler, carefully edited all the previously unpublished translations, and was as unsparing as she was inspired in her suggestions about the selections, my introduction, and the accompanying biographical notes on the authors. But my greatest debt, of course, is to the authors themselves, whose works you are about to read.

*. . . and a whistler, somewhere, lonely in the nightworld.*
—"Deathwatch on the Southside," Jorge Luís Borges
(tr. Robert Fitzgerald)

# Introduction

In 1993, one of the great maverick editors of American publishing, Robert Wyatt, decided to take a chance on a virtually unknown Brazilian first novelist named Edgard Telles Ribeiro. All Wyatt had to go on, besides his own intuition and one chapter in English translation, was an outline of the novel in English. The following year Ribeiro's novel was published as *I Would Have Loved Him if I Had Not Killed Him*. In it Ribeiro deftly weaves his double tale of intertwining lives. The first, set in modern-day Brasília, concerns a briefly rekindled, slightly comic love affair between an ex-director with a rather sardonic view of himself and a former actress who had starred in his only film. The second story, set earlier in the century, revolves around the notorious life of the actress's recently deceased great-aunt. Critics loved the novel and, since it was written by a Latin American, more than one reviewer saw it as proof that "magical realism and murder can also work together beautifully." While that may be true, in Ribeiro's subtly nuanced novel the reader will find no amorous iguanas, no flying dictators, no metaphysical butterflies: its sole magic lies in the narrative gifts of a remarkable Brazilian writer.

While compiling the present anthology of a new generation of Latin American authors, published from the early eighties to the present, I was struck by how far the literature has traveled, literally and figuratively, from such legendary landscapes as Juan Carlos Onetti's imaginary Santa María or Gabriel García Márquez's fantastical Macondo. The variety of styles, settings, and intrigues had turned out to be wildly unpredictable: from Santos-Febres's edgy depiction of the literally murderous pace of media living ("Flight"), to Javier Valdés's mordant ribbing of Stephen King ("People Like Us"); from the Chekhovian delicacy in Laura Restrepo's rendering of an elderly couple's adulterous reunion ("The Scent of Invisible Roses"), to the hallucinatory precision of Ignacio Padilla's tale of British Colonial nostalgia and ruin ("The Antipodes and the Century").

A question *did* occur to me, however, while assembling this collection of delightfully iconoclastic authors: Were they going to be pigeonholed, however effusively, into that same exhausted category originally applied to the Latin American fiction of the sixties? Certainly the term "magical realist," even when fresh, had hardly served to describe the startling variety of authors (Arenas, Donoso, Fuentes, Lispector, Puig, Vargas Llosa, etc.) who had helped to launch that first, unprecedented "boom."

How, then, do our expectations and our preconceptions—cultural, intellectual, even political—color our reading of a text? In 1997, the diskette of a novel called *El tiempo que nos tocó vivir* ("The Time We Were Meant to Live") was sent out of Cuba, apparently by a relative of the author. The work's structure recalled the temporal experiments of Carpentier's and Cortázar's more audacious fictions, such as "Journey Back to the Source" or *Hopscotch*. An epic novel, it tells the story of a dozen or so teenagers who fought Batista on the streets of Havana in the years leading up to the triumph of Fidel Castro in 1959, and then went on to become the heroes or the *gusanos*, the martyrs or the bureaucrats, the powerful or ordinary citizens of the new Cuba. What was most striking about the novel, however, given the generally Manichaean attitudes of Latin American intellectuals toward that seismic historical event, was the empathy with which the author treated the personal lives of his characters, regardless of their political views.

In 1998, the novel was published in Spanish under a pseudonym, Jorge C. Oliva Espinosa, supposedly to protect relatives still living in Cuba. The author was apparently a hero of the Revolution who had died in disgrace, years later, in Miami. Except for a French and a German edition, most other publishers shunned the novel. It had become fashionable, despite the embargo and the poverty, to frequent Cuba. It was the cheap, chic, mildly daring thing for foreign tourists to do in the late nineties. People were learning about Cuban music, Cuban films. So publishers, too, wanted a taste of the real thing, not from disgruntled émigrés living in Paris or Miami, but from the authentic voices of Cuba.

Within a year, however, the three publishers of the work in question received a surprising letter from an author by the name of Jorge C. Oliva Espinosa. It seems that this name was not a pseudonym at all, and the author was very much alive and well and living in . . . Cuba. The mix-up involved a level of deception and mistaken identities worthy of a Le Carré novel. The effect for the real Espinosa, however, had been not simply the loss of the rights to his own work, but the erasure of his entire personal identity. His novel, as it turned out, *was* the real thing publishers had been looking for. Yet, because the book had been perceived to be written by an exile, and was enjoying a certain notoriety in Miami, it had never gotten published elsewhere. Politics? Or just another kind of "magical realism"? It makes you wonder: Doesn't anyone see the barn?

In Don Delillo's disturbingly deadpan novel *White Noise* (1985), Professor Jack Gladney at the College-on-the-Hill offers one day to take his new colleague Murray, visiting lecturer on "living icons," to see the most photographed barn in America. Along the twenty-two-mile route to the barn, they pass five signs announcing their approach to THE MOST PHOTOGRAPHED BARN IN AMERICA. Eventually they pull into a parking lot filled with cars and buses and make their way on foot to a viewing area cluttered with tourists and their Nikons. After silently taking in the scene for a while—the catatonic crowd intently photographing the famous icon—Murray concludes: "No one sees the barn."

Something analogous might be said, lately, of Latin American fiction. To paraphrase Murray, what was Latin American fiction like before *magical realism* became the most photographed barn in all of Latin America? And what is that literature like today? To consider some answers to the first question, the reader may want to turn to *A Hammock Beneath the Mangoes: Stories from Latin America*. That anthology of twenty-six authors examined the "boom" writers of the sixties (Amado, Arenas, Cabrera Infante, Cortázar, Lispector, García Márquez, Puig, etc.), their precursors (from Machado de Assis and Quiroga to Borges, Guimarães Rosa, Onetti, and Rulfo), and the generation of the seventies (Rosario Ferré, João Ubaldo Ribeiro) and early eighties (Isabel Allende, Ana Lydia Vega) that was, at least initially, so powerfully influenced by the "boom."

The present anthology is an attempt to address the second question: What is different about the new Latin American fiction? How has it evolved through the eighties and nineties and into the twenty-first century? And is it possible to travel across this startling literary landscape without following the same old signposts, which, still today, point so confidently from all directions to that sacrosanct cul-de-sac known as "the marvelous in the real"?

So much has changed in the geography of Latin American literature since the "boom" of the sixties and the decade that followed. If the "boom" writers were less than comfortable with the very notion of a homogeneous cultural landscape called Latin America, the new Latin American authors have exploded it entirely. Indeed, they have made us begin to think in terms, not of Latin America but of Latin *Americas*—or, at the very least, of *Latin* Americas. Not only is the United States the fastest-growing market for Spanish-language fiction, with one of the largest Spanish-speaking populations in the world, but the USA is or has been home to nearly half the twenty-two writers included in the present anthology. Two of them—Anna Kazumi Stahl, who now lives in Argentina, writes in Spanish, and translates herself into English; and Julia Alvarez, who writes in English and divides her time between the United States and the Dominican Republic of her childhood—were actually born in the States. Only ten of the authors anthologized herein currently live in Latin America. The others may be found in New York, Madrid, Paris, London, and even Wellington, New Zealand.

Exile, internal as well as external, is therefore one of the more powerful threads running through much of this anthology, from Alvarez's "The Blood of the Conquistadores" to Ernesto Mestre-Reed's "After Elián." At the same time, many of these writers feel at home with their wanderlust, which has less to do with national politics than the realities of global economics. Padilla has encapsulated the phenomenon fairly succinctly: "We are unrepentant travelers, accidental academics, authors by vocation, and rigorously urban."

That last quality calls to mind another distinctive aspect of the new Latin American literature. It is emphatically urban and cosmopolitan in outlook. And when it visits the jungle, it is closer to Conrad than to Macondo. As Restrepo has suggested regarding her generation's debt to García Márquez, "We were much more taken by the idea of learning from the terse and realistic author of *No One Writes to the Colonel* than from that equally brilliant author of the florid and fantastical *One Hundred Years of Solitude.*" An urban vision is fundamentally a darker one—although, for many of the writers you are about to read, a vision by no means devoid of lyricism (Pedro Juan Gutiérrez's "Nothing to Do," for example), or laughter (Carmen Posada's "The Nubian Lover"). Still, an underlying irony, often sly (as in Ángeles Mastretta's "Aunt Concha Esparza"), sometimes bitterly corrosive (as in Jaime Manrique's "The Documentary Artist"), seems to bleed through the surface and textures of much of their fiction. Hence, the title of this anthology: from a poem by that *other* Borges—the more elusive (but no less astonishing) one, bluffing the reader with those enticingly elegant labyrinths, while furtively nurturing his fascination and loathing for mirrors, entropy, and murder.

This seismic shift in the mental landscape is not without precedent in Latin American letters. (One has only to think of Onetti or Lispector, Cabrera Infante or the early Fuentes.) Nor is it all that surprising when, as Edmundo Paz-Soldán has pointed out, "More than fifty percent of the population in Latin America now lives in cities, with cable and all that." And at least in the United States, the Hispanic sector of the population is the fastest-growing market, for example, in the sale of computers. So the new realities are more likely to be virtual (as in Laura Esquivel's "Blessed Reality") or postmodern (as in Jorge Volpi's "Ars Poetica"), than magical. "The current homeland of Latin American literature," Padilla reminds us, "is literature itself." And the present authors are as comfortable taking their readers off to Egypt (Posadas), Alaska (Franco Steeves), the Gobi Desert (Padilla), New Orleans (Kazumi Stahl), Miami (Restrepo, Mestre-Reed), New York (Manrique, Vega Yunqué), or even Edison, New Jersey (Díaz), as they are bringing them back to Argentina (Andahazi), Bolivia (Paz-Soldán), Mexico (Mastretta), Cuba (Gutiérrez, Montero), Puerto Rico (Santos-Febres) or the Dominican Republic (Alvarez), not to mention the Amazon (Telles Ribeiro).

The international outlook of these writers has much to do with the vagaries, personal and professional, of an increasingly globalized world. Their journeys have taken them across language, as well as geography. Many authors from the Latin Americas now write in English, or translate themselves into English from the original Spanish (or Portuguese). A growing number of them have found U.S. publishers who are eager to bring out their fiction in both English and Spanish: an experience that can prove as schizophrenic as it is gratifying. Like some spanglified protagonist out of a novel by Paz-Soldán, these writers seem "intent on a kind of double life, which produces a lot of fissures." Yet they also enjoy the advantages of actually *knowing* a second language: that secret passage not just to some other culture but to an unexplored region of the self. Such duality may explain, to some degree, their love of irony and the self-deprecating humor to be found in so much of their work.

This is not to say these writers are any less passionate on the subject of our shrinking, troubled world. Mayra Montero's electrifying novel set in Haiti, *In the Palm of Darkness* (1995), has as much to do with the ecological destruction of amphibians as with the nature of obsession and desire. And in "Eight Morenos," Edgardo Vega Yunqué offers an uncommon meditation on the whole question of race, while remorselessly weaving the unconscious threads of his protagonist's evolving personal trauma into its final implosion at the family dinner table. However, as Rafael Franco Steeves rightly points out, their works signal "a departure from . . . sociopolitical themes [as] traditionally handled by earlier generations."

These new writers are, in short, a fiercely independent lot. The second of the four commandments of "Crack"—that group of wildly dissenting Mexican authors that includes Volpi and Padilla—in its opening manifesto, of 1995 (written by the novelist Pedro Ángel Palau), flatly proclaims: "Thou shalt not covet thy neighbor's novel." Obviously, there was a slapstick side to the manifesto. After all, who publishes manifestos anymore? Written in praise of *levity*, it turned out to be a wry vindication of *clarity*, *complexity*, and *precision*—cardinal traits of the best new fiction from the *Latin* Americas.

*NOTE TO READERS: To the extent possible in the biographies that follow—for the authors who write in Spanish or Portuguese—*

*the English translation title is cited when one exists; otherwise the original Spanish or Portuguese title is given. Unless otherwise indicated, publication dates for such works are given only for first publication in the original language, not for the English translations, whose dates would be misleading in terms of the writer's development.*

# Mayra Santos-Febres
## (Puerto Rico, b. 1966)

Mayra Santos-Febres was born in Carolina, Puerto Rico. Growing up in a family of educators, she early on developed a passion for reading. She recounts that her high school Spanish teacher "introduced me to Cesar Vallejo and sealed my fate. After a fifteen-year-old reads *The Sea and You* and *Trilce*, what else can she do with her life except dedicate it to literature?" Graduating from the Colegio Lourdes, in Hato Rey, she went on to receive various fellowships to pursue a B.A. program in Hispanic studies at the University of Puerto Rico in Río Piedras, and then to complete her master's and doctoral studies in literature at Cornell University.

By 1984 Santos-Febres had begun publishing her poems in various international newspapers and periodicals. Two collections of her poetry appeared in 1991, *Anamú y manigua*, which was selected by the Puerto Rican critics as one of the ten best books of the year, and *El orden escapado*, winner of the first poetry prize to be given by *Revista Tríptico*, in Puerto Rico. A third collection of poems, *Tercer Mundo*, would be published in 2000. In the meantime she began writing fiction and contributing, as a columnist and critic, to various newspapers: *Claridad* (1992–96), *Dialogo* (1995), and the *San Juan Star* (1995–97).

Santos-Febres's short stories won her immediate international recognition, including the Letras de Oro Prize (USA, 1994) for the collection *Pez de vidrio*, and the Juan Rulfo Prize (France,

1996) for her story "Oso Blanco." A selection of her often erotically charged stories, taken from that first collection and from *El cuerpo correcto*, was published in English as *Urban Oracles* in 1997. Her novelistic debut came three years later with a tale of passion—part tragicomedy, part cabaret—exploring the demimonde of an aging transvestite and her breathtaking protégée, the eponymous "siren" of the title. Published in nearly simultaneous editions—in English and Italian translations as *Sirena Selena*, and in Spain and in Mexico as *Sirena Selena vestida de pena* (2000)—it went on to become a finalist for the prestigious Rómulo Gallegos Prize the following year.

Recently, she has begun working in other media, writing for television and collaborating on Edwin Reyes's documentary film *Adombe: the African presence in Puerto Rico*. A second, comically *noir* novel, *Cualquier miércoles soy tuyo*, will be published later this year. Santos-Febres lives in Puerto Rico, where she teaches literature at the University of Puerto Rico.

# Flight

*To Luis Alcalá del Olmo*

*You escape in the very instant*
*That you reached your best definition.*
*Ah, my friend, you wouldn't want to believe*
*The questions of that newborn orb*
*That dampens its tips on an enemy star.*

—José Lezama Lima

Beep. Beep. Beep. Her pager. It's the editorial office. "Virginia. Call me—urgent. Front-page stuff. Pepe." She's on her way home in her new car. It's the latest model Montero, and has high monthly payments, which she can easily make now that she has a secure job at the newspaper. The car is a symbol of her salvation.

She stops at the supermarket. Buys pasta, rice, beans, milk, coffee, juice. She also buys some frozen dinners for the shattered nights, nights when she arrives home from work dead, with no time to cook, stricken with a hunger that tears her in two.

It's true, she hadn't counted on this life. Virginia remembers the trips from the old days, the photos of scenes of burning automobile tires in the middle of strikes, of old women watching the slaughter through the bars on the windows of their homes. She remembers running around after ambulances, police cruisers, to photograph some occurrence. When she was a dog hunting for images, a thief of light—one eight-thousandth of a second—and she with her multiple eyes casting a quick glance over the surface of things, giving her the whole picture, the light bouncing off the figures that were only flesh until a sudden flash mixed with them and converted them into a gold mine of something palpitating. Her multiple eyes all alert to a fraction of a second. Virginia remembers how she lived for that, hidden behind the fleeting aperture that was attempting to trap what is always fleeing. And her after it, like a dog, like a thief, like a being absolutely devoted to that crumb of reality. Later she arrived at her empty house, a naked house, without a man and without plants and without furniture, a house worthy of a monk who has renounced everything in search of delirious beauty. But still one has to live. So to arrive was to leave the cell to offer some photo to the news agencies, to become a slave to the telephone, to be able to charge something to later invest in more eyes, in more lenses, in zooms and tripods and in light meters to be able to collect the flashes of light bouncing off the surfaces of things. It's true, she had never been, nor wanted to be, what she now was. But now she has money for developing chemicals and, if she saves up a bit, she can even set up a dark room in the next two weeks; have her own lab, a scanner at her disposal in her home. She has already changed from being a hunting dog to a bird of prey, why not toss a little of the cadaver into her mouth?

Virginia unloads her purchases and her purse from the car. She unloads her beeper and her body from the car. She opens the trunk. Her body is still young, her flesh still firm. At the end of the hall a meowing is tangled in the shadows. It's the cats. They came with the car, with the furniture and a personal computer. The cell is turning into a home. Melusina needs water in her dish. Silvestre brushes against her calves and she smiles a greeting. The answering machine flashes its light on and off. Three messages. Mami, wanting her to come to dinner on Sunday, if she can find the time to visit her family. The condominium committee and its plan for repairing the building's façade. A blank message, with a fax signal. Who would have wanted to send her a fax? Probably a wrong number.

Virginia lifts the receiver and dials the direct number for the editorial department. The call goes through. Ring, ring, ring . . .

Finally, "Editorial . . ."

"Pepe."

"Virginia, *mi amor*, where'd you go?"

"Darling, I have a life; not like you who spends his stuck in that newspaper."

"Someday you'll see how the paper ends up sucking up your life too."

"Why'd you page me?"

"Why do you think?"

"Fresh cadaver."

"You guessed it. . . .Twenty-seven bullet holes, *mi amor*. The kid looks like a colander. But that idiot Gregorio took the photographs at too low an exposure and you can't see the puddle of blood very well, or the forensics guys lifting the body. How am I supposed to use that?"

"Didn't he take any more pictures?"

"Two or three. I'm telling you about the best one."

"So what's wrong with the guy? Didn't it occur to him to take his light meter out of his car?"

"*Pues, negra*, that seems to be the case."

"If you had sent me, these things wouldn't have happened."

"Okay, enough of that. . . ."

"Well, when are you going to get me out of the office and into the street? I'm tired of inventing photographs on a computer screen."

"Patience, Gina, your turn will come."

"Okay, okay, put the photograph on my desk. I'll be on my way over there as soon as I get something in my stomach."

"Make it light so you'll be able to digest it. The kid looks . . ."

"I'm used to it."

"You never get used to this."

*   *   *

Virginia opens the pantry door to put away the beans, coffee, pasta, rice. The milk and frozen dinners go in the refrigerator. One of the latter goes into the microwave. "Chicken with pasta. Remove cardboard cover, cook on high for three minutes, stir and cook for another two minutes. Serve hot." Virginia opens the refrigerator again. She takes out a Diet Pepsi, drinks water from a gallon jug, grabs a mango. Her hands tremble a little as she removes the skin from the fruit. Her hands always tremble when she's hungry. The hunger that always congeals in her blood when they take away her chance to lay her eyes on the real stuff. The people at the newspaper don't want her to go where the action is. As if she had never been there, hidden behind her metal pupils, with one of them copying everything that is about to disappear, she herself, her nerves, the pain from crouching behind a patrol car or the tear about to fall when the mother arrives to claim the bloody body of her only son. She too disappears, she too flees until only light is left. Then nothing exists but that instant of whole things vibrating; that fleeting moment when reality is condensed, like a twitching muscle.

"I can't believe it," Virginia sighs, chewing. "I have to drive all the way back to the newspaper. And who knows what time I'll finish working." She turns on the radio to shake off exhaustion, another muscle twitches, but she doesn't notice.

Ring, ring. . . . It's the telephone. She doesn't want to answer it. She doesn't want to hear anyone talk, to carry on a conversation with anyone, ask them how their day was. "Mine was great," she has no desire to say. "I'm working for *Última Hora*," she doesn't want to have to say. "I finally freed myself from unemployment. I'm getting used to the routine of work, you know? But, who knows . . . ? Maybe I'll surprise everybody with something of my own soon." She doesn't want to say anything. The answering machine takes the call.

"Virginia, it's Solá. I was calling to say hi. It's been so long since

I've seen you. I was cleaning out my files and found some of your old photographs, the ones we took of the fire at the lighthouse in Fajardo. I had forgotten how good they were. So I decided to call. You're lost, *mija*. Call me when you can. Okay? Hugs. . . ." Beep.

"Lost. I'm lost," thinks Virginia, but she shakes the thought from her head. It's the work of a photographer to be lost. To lose herself behind the potential image, behind the paper that captures it, the lens that probes, the light that bounces. Many were the hours she spent learning to lose herself. Entire afternoons looking at a ray of light fall upon bullet shells, the promise of a gesture that would reveal a whole life of fear or of frustration. Emptying her head, like now. That's how she learned to lose herself on the street. And she feels happy there, at ease, in a much cozier home than these four walls she's paying for could ever be, the aluminum sides that she pays for in sensible, fixed monthly installments. The street is the territory of everything that flees. And she is a photographer, a fugitive, a street dog after scraps. All of her an eye that wants to eat the world.

Now, from her house to her car, with her chicken with pasta in her stomach, she drives back to the newspaper. She gets out of the Montero, goes up to the graphic design department, sits in front of her computer. She turns on the scanner. Opens Photoshop. Scans the photograph of another eighteen-year-old boy, dead, with his tennis shoes lying across the sidewalk, his T-shirt pulled up on his back, dead, and she looks for the most impactful angle of that death, for front-page morbidity. She looks for the bloodiest close-up of the wound. Her eye lightens the glow of the blood by twenty percent. Virginia reproduces the photo, click, brings the body closer, moving it more to the center of the page. This way the open eyes are more noticeable, and the spurt of blood on the shirt, click, click.

## II.

It's true, she hadn't foreseen this life. The contact sheets from before, the close-ups of clubs falling on broken backs and of old women watching the melee between the bars on their homes. But today wasn't such a bad day. Today she was lucky. Today she was able to leave the office. They sent her to take some photos of the latest Miss Universe contest. Virginia actually enjoyed herself a little today. She found a way to make Miss Universe look even more ridiculous. She invented a new trick for turning the crown on the winner's head, adding a little dye to the eyeliner that was running down her cheeks and warping her Universal Barbie posture. The poor contestant was so excited about having been crowned the most beautiful in the world and here Virginia was converting her into a front-page fright on her computer terminal. She laughs at her mischievousness as she walks to the parking lot. Today she left work early. She's going to see her mother and then take a run on the beach. Maybe she'll have time for a little dip in the ocean. And, as always, she'll take her camera. She foresees a beautiful sunset.

## III.

Another fresh cadaver has arrived. "Brother kills brother, family vengeance." Another kid. Four bullet wounds. Four holes from which congealed blood flows in dark paste. The guy is wearing a Nike T-shirt and brand-name tennis shoes, expensive ones, and brand-name canvas pants, also expensive. And a white cap thrown on the asphalt in the airport parking lot. Also lying on the ground is a sweat-suit jacket that matches the shirt. Everything is expensive. Everything is ruined now by the four bullet wounds, two in the chest, one in the throat, another in the base of the nose. The cadaver shows a face exploded to the four winds, the body turned into a spring of powder and blood. The homicidal brother looks at the cadaver with empty eyes. His hair is dyed blond, with dark roots. He's wearing a cheap shirt and torn pants. The reporter is saying that the suspect was waiting for his brother, who was arriving from New York to attend their mother's funeral. The deceased was suspected of narco-trafficking, but no one had proof. His brother waited for him at the airport and killed him. He didn't know how to shoot. Some bullets hit a car window, another a lamppost. The four remaining ones reached his brother.

And again, Gregorio and his underexposed photographs. The colors in the photo aren't clear. The murderer's gaze has no color, for example. If it had been her, if they had removed her collar and let her loose with her hungry eyes on the street, she would have used another angle. There, at the back, the brother with those empty eyes, as if looking from the deepest recesses of his sockets at what his hate or his pain forced him to do. Luckily they had put the handcuffs on the guy under a streetlight. But she would have waited for another beam, another ray falling over his shoulders, a better shadowing of that relieved and absent gaze. He killed his brother for making their mother suffer. He killed him because his brother left him to take care of his poor sick mother who devoted herself to her criminal son, the one who lived the good life with cocaine and dollars while he, changing their mother's diapers and putrefying bandages, wondered when he would ever count for something, even if it were only to make the old woman's agony more real. He killed him, his own brother, flesh of his flesh, out of envy, relief, distance, escape, love. That is what the guy's eyes say, even in this poorly exposed photograph that fool Gregorio took. If they had loosened her collar just a little and let her, a loose dog in the street . . . But now her neck has an owner.

The rest of the image is dark, half of an officer's body is cut off at the edge of the photo. A policewoman gently pushes the murderer's arm, and he turns his head to see his brother's body spitting its last drop of blood on the pavement of the parking lot. He looks at the white cap stained with thick blood near the unrecognizable face. Virginia fights with the material. She clicks a button on the Photoshop screen to see if she can lighten the background so the death will look good on the cover page of the Sunday edition.

## IV.

Beep, beep. "It's Friday. I'm inviting you out for a beer. We'll be at Yahaira's, if you're in the mood. Pepe." Virginia's on her way home. Melusina must need water in her dish. That cat drinks so much water. She should learn from the cat. She should go for a drink. After all, she left work early today. She laid out everything she had to lay out. The head of design was thrilled. The head of editorial, delighted. The head of photojournalism heeded her technical suggestions, recognizing that she knew what she was talking about. He even suggested that next time maybe he would give her a more challenging assignment. He would pull her off covering social events, with old women drugged up on Prozac and Zanax at their latest fund-raiser for children with muscular dystrophy, or cranial fibroplasty or who knows what other fashionable illness. They would loosen the chain. Maybe they would let her return to being the street dog she always wanted to be, with that hunger in her eyes, her multiple eyes that want to condense that beating in the hearts of things. Of reality. The one she needlessly adulterated on demand in Photoshop on her computer. After all, it's just a question of carefully measuring the light of things. Light always reveals them under another density. It's a question of emptying yourself and not thinking, letting time, fleeting time that can't be measured, carry her off into the air, make her back paws agile, her front paws, and then, to force her to press the button at one eight-thousandth of a second and detain that which is escaping. Flight, the most faithful testimony of how life occurs. Maybe they would loosen her chain, even if they spit on the street, even if she's wetted and dragged along by the other dogs after the scraps. But free and with dignity intact. Even with a bit of money. It's time to celebrate.

"But I'm not going anywhere looking like this," Virginia thinks as she lights a cigarette at an intersection. Red light. Green light. Foot on the accelerator. "With this crazed witch look," she thinks as she sucks smoke. "I'd better go home, take a bath, change clothes. I'll pull together an outfit for Yahaira's. Yes, it's time to celebrate."

She takes her briefcase and her purse from the car, opens the front door. The cats are fine. Melusina has finished the water in her dish again. She takes off her shirt, her slacks. Turns on the shower. She looks at her nude body in the mirror above the sink. Her body is still good. The skin on her breasts is still taut. "I'm going to wear the black short-sleeved shirt, the low-cut one," she thinks as she steps into the shower. "And the black cotton trousers, and high heels," she thinks. "Tonight I'm going to dress like a femme fatale. The neon from the lights at Yahaira's will look good on my clothes."

On her way to the bar she counts the stoplights. At the second she turns left. She looks for a place to park. She parks the Montero on the street, gets out and walks toward the bar. She doesn't see any of the boys from the newspaper. Maybe she has arrived too early, or too late. She sits down. "A beer, please. Save the glass. Thanks." She looks around. In the back there's a guy who looks at her with gluttonous eyes. She lets the gaze slide along her body. She likes that celebratory gaze. Another dog already sniffing at the bone.

"It's two pesos."

"No, forget it, I'll pay for the lady's beer," comes the guy's voice. It's a warm voice, well intentioned. A voice that slides easily from his throat and pours over her refreshingly.

"Thank you."

"No, thank you. You came to cheer up my night."

"Me?"

"Of course. A man doesn't get to see a woman as elegant as you every day."

She smiled knowingly, premeditatively. It's been a long time since she smiled like that. Since the contact sheets and the flames leaping out the windows of the lighthouse at Fajardo. Since the photos from ambulance chases she had to take in order to buy another good light meter. Maybe she exaggerated. What is certain is that she never smiled like this at *Ultima Hora*.

Virginia drank a beer, she drank two. She had a long conversation with the guy who had approached her to invite her to enjoy the night with him. His name was Juan. He said he worked as a sales rep. He was recently divorced, at least according to him. According to her the guy was a tasty bonbon. And Pepe still hadn't shown up at the bar. She should go. She had come out to spend time with friends from work, not to pick up a salesman who would warm her bed for a night. Her life isn't the same as it used to be. Before, she would have gone wherever, beneath a palm tree, in a car parked by the edge of the sea. But now she couldn't. She had to get up early tomorrow; go to the office to work.

"You work on Saturdays?"

"I work all the time. That's how life is at a newspaper."

"Which one do you work for?"

"*Última Hora*."

"Are you a journalist?"

"No, a photographer."

"Are you the one who designs the front page? The one with the dead bodies?"

"That's me."

"Really?"

"You don't believe me?"

"I just can't imagine you doing that kind of work."

"I keep telling myself the same thing. But . . ."

"You gotta live."

"Yeah, you gotta live. . . . Well, thanks for the beer, and good night."

"I'd better walk you to your car. You know how these streets are."

"I sure do."

They both leave the bar, heading toward the brand-new Montero. Juan asks for her telephone number. She suggests he give her his. She doesn't want complications. She doesn't want calls from guys she barely knows bothering her at home when she arrives tired from work. Instead he opts for anonymity. But a kiss on the way to the neighboring street where she had parked the Montero wouldn't be all bad. Nor would another one of those looks, in which she is observed, entering the field of vision with a hunger, a hunger of the eye that snatches a little light, quickly, in one eight-thousandth of a second. Her, frozen in an instant and unable to move, there, in the street, which had forced her to leave everything, to lead a nun's cloistered life to be hunting for one of its pieces. It wouldn't be bad to be on the other side of some cannibal eyes, even if it's just for an instant. She's not asking for anything more. She's content with certain loosenings of the collar that imprisons her neck and her hunger's neck. Everything is for the Montero and the house, Melusina and Silvestre, her lenses, ah, her lenses with which she gives way to hunger itself, free. More or less free.

Suddenly she feels a hand grab her back. It's Juan. But his hand turns him into another Juan. His hand is a strong fist attacking her kidneys, a sharp pain in her side. She can't breathe. And not from anticipation of a kiss.

Another man appears out of nowhere. In a white shirt, old shoes. This one yanks on her purse. She struggles. But then, the same Juan that bought her the beers ends up throwing her on the ground. "No, leave her, no one would give anything for this one," he says and he grabs the keys from her hand. Her eyes, the lenses, are in the car. And the new camera, the light meter, the strobes, a roll of film with images of a beautiful sunset. She forgot to take them out of the car before she took her shower, before she got ready to drink with her colleagues from the newspaper. And there they are, in the car, with the pictures she had taken. She has to stop them now. The hunger sharpens in her eyes and Virginia shouts, she shouts loudly, as she grabs one of the guys by the shirt. Then comes a stunning punch. "Go, cabrón, go," she hears a choked, guttural voice, as one of her aggressors, Juan, the guy who bought her the beers, opens the door of the Montero. He gets in. The tires screech. There go her high monthly payments, her monthly payments from her steady job.

The punch burns in her ribs. The Montero is lost in a curve and she feels like crying. She's alone on the street and doesn't even know if she should ask someone to call the police. Then she feels something viscous between her fingers. Virginia looks down at her fingers. She sees that they're reflecting light, mirroring a shimmer, and she doesn't know where it comes from. She finds her shirt torn, and her flesh cut, a bloody gash opened. And she thinks, "A dark light that pulsates." She thinks about her lost lenses, but no cry or curse emerges from her mouth, only a soft shout, too soft, ending in a few drops of inverted light that she doesn't understand.

## V.

"*Última Hora* Photographer Stabbed." Virginia reads the newspaper and it says that the photographer's name is Virginia. Virginia Sánchez. She reads her name from her hospital bed. And she reads "*Última Hora* Photographer." And she doesn't understand anything. Maybe she's still under the effects of the anesthesia.

Pepe brought her the newspaper this morning. And some flowers, and a cup of good coffee, not the kind they sell in the hospital, which tastes like shit. Worse, like shit tea.

"*Chica*, what a fucking mess. That night things got complicated in Editorial. I had to stay in the office until late."

"Don't worry, Pepe. I figured that's what had happened."

"If you had paged me a message. If you had told me . . ."

"Pepe, it's not your fault. How could it be your fault that they attacked me?"

"At least they didn't kill you, or kidnap you. At least . . ."

"Yeah, man, at least I'm alive. And that's what matters. You gotta live, Pepe."

"Yeah, you gotta live."

A conversation, a beer, negatives of old photos of the lighthouse at Fajardo, rolls of new photographs of a sunset, a guy with torn sneakers, another one paying for beers and looking at her with the same hunger with which she looks at life, the Montero, a drop of dark light reflecting off her hands, something fleeting. . . .

"The boys put the news with the day's most important stories. And they published the description of the guys that you gave to the police. The paper's gonna give a reward for their capture."

"A nice thought."

"The story was written by Vargas. Read it."

"*Última Hora* Photographer Stabbed," she reads out loud. She looks at Pepe. Pepe smiles. He looks tired. "Around eleven last night, Virginia Sánchez was the victim of a terrible knife attack. The assailants managed to escape in her blue, late-model Montero. . . ." Virginia continues reading aloud. Pepe listens attentively. The story has no accompanying photograph.

*Translated by Stephen A. Lytle*

# Pedro Juan Gutiérrez
## (Cuba, b. 1950)

Pedro Juan Gutiérrez was born in Matanzas, Cuba, and even as a child seemed destined to become a jack-of-all-trades. By age eleven he had already worked as a paperboy and an ice cream vendor. After serving nearly five years in the early sixties as a sapper in the army, he drifted from being swim teacher to kayak instructor to cane cutter to farm worker. Other incarnations included construction worker, drawing teacher, film technician, documentary director, journalist, radio and TV announcer, used-books dealer, university professor, experimental poet, sculptor, radio and television actor, and indefatigable traveler. He has a degree in journalism from the University of Havana.

Gutiérrez is the author of two works of poetry, *La realidad rugiendo* and *Espléndidos peces plateados*, and has taken part in many experimental poetry exhibitions and performances in São Paulo, Mexico City, San Diego, Pisa, and Malaga. His first novel, *Dirty Havana Trilogy* (1998), a riotous exploration of the seamier side of bohemianism and survival in contemporary Havana, was published in Spain, where it won him instantaneous international recognition and justly deserved comparisons to Henry Miller and Charles Bukowski. Two more novels quickly followed, *El rey de la Habana* (1999) and *Animal Tropical* (2000), the latter continuing the adventures of Gutiérrez's alter ego, "Pedro Juan," who narrated the *Trilogy*, and garnering its author the Alfonso García-Ramos Prize in Tenerife. Now published in more than a dozen languages, Gutiérrez continues to live in Havana, where he devotes his time to writing and painting.

# Nothing to Do

At noon I went to see my aunt in Old Havana. She has cancer of the intestines. The doctors have given up hope. They don't want her in the hospital because they don't know what to do for her. Doctors are good diplomats. They never reveal their ignorance or admit it when they make mistakes. At least, their mistakes they cover up, and ignorance can always be disguised. They told me, "Your aunt is in the final stages of her illness now. She should be kept at home. She has two more weeks left at most." The old lady had been at death's door, in excruciating pain, for two years, hemorrhaging and terrified of dying. She was always an evil bitch. But I don't believe God should punish anyone like that. Of course, God leaves no room for argument.

A neighbor woman takes care of her. I pay her a few pesos, and she tries to help, more or less. Now it doesn't even bother me to see my aunt in pain and all skin and bones. A person can get used to anything.

I started out walking slowly. On Saturdays there aren't many buses running in Havana, hardly any at all. It's best not to worry.

So my aunt is dying of cancer, so there's practically no food, so the buses aren't running, so I don't have a job. Best not to worry. Today there was a front-page interview in the paper with an important minister, a show-off. He was fat and he had a big smile on his face, and he was saying, "Cuba is neither paradise nor hell."

My next question would have been, "So what is it, purgatory?" But no. The journalist just smiled contentedly and used the quote as the front-page headline.

I was relaxed, having lots of sex, feeling at peace with myself. Not worried at all. Well, there are always worries. But for now I was able to keep them at a distance. I pushed them a little way into the future. That's a good way to keep them blurry and out of earshot. A woman was living with me. I had gained back a few pounds. And I was alive, though I had nothing to do. Surviving, I think it's called. You let yourself glide along, and you don't expect anything else. It's as easy as that.

Two big, fat, flabby, ugly, white, red, peeling, slow, self-absorbed tourists were walking very slowly past the National Museum. Yes, that's exactly how they looked. The old man had a cane and an enormous heavy suitcase. I couldn't imagine what he was carrying in it. Apparently, they were out for a stroll on a calm, sunny Saturday afternoon. The woman was just as repugnant as the man. The two of them were dressed for fall in an icy fjord city. They were sweating, and they had a stunned look on their faces as they stared all around. They consulted a guidebook with great deliberation and gazed at the historic ship and historic airplanes under the historic trees. Nothing made sense to them. The man looked at me. His mouth was pushed in, as if someone had punched him hard. He was staring at me. Taking advantage of the situation, I brought out my shiny three-peso coins imprinted with Che's head.

"*Good afternoon. How are you? Do you like a coin? Is a commemorative coin with Che Guevara image. Only one dollar every one.*"

"*No, shit, youggrrrhttchchssyyye, out! out!*"

I didn't understand what he was grunting. He threatened to hit me with his cane. Such hateful people should never leave home. Their livers must be rotting away and their breath must stink of putrid flesh.

"Go crawl up your mother's stinking cunt, you old bastard!"

He didn't understand me either, but at least I had the satisfaction of answering back. Ugh, what monstrous people!

Luckily, not everything is shit. I kept walking along Trocadero toward home, and as I passed 162, I saw a young couple with a little girl. They were out for a walk too. The woman was an incredibly beautiful mulatta, with a white skirt and a firm ass, generous and high-set. A mulatta like that throws the landscape off kilter. It's not just her ass. It's all of her. Her warmth, her sensuality, that tight dress showing off her cinnamon skin. She was one of those mulattas with a swing in her step. They know they're in charge, and they carry themselves incredibly well. They move through life turning everything upside down, destruction in their wake. Next to her was her husband, a well-dressed little black man. Between the two of them was the girl, probably three years old. This is why it's so hard for Cubans to live anywhere else. Here you may starve and you may struggle. But the people are out of this world. Like that mulatta. She must have been twenty-three, but when she was forty or fifty, she'd still be just as beautiful. And you always know she's there and that someday you could love her and the two of you could be happy together. While it lasted.

Before going home, I walked to Manrique and Laguna. There was rum. I got in line to buy my monthly bottle. I had my ration book in my pocket, though by now, 1995, it was a joke. The line was moving slowly, and I had some time. I went to my building. On the first floor, one of the decrepit old ladies sold me an empty bottle. I got back in line, and there was Chachareo singing and fooling around, as always. He was a pitiful, ragged old man. He always managed to wheedle a bit of rum out of people, and he'd collect it in a beer can. He sang, told stories. The people in line would ignore him, but he kept shoving himself drunkenly at them. He'd search out your eyes, then caper around, and when you were buying your bottle of rum, he would ask for a little. It was always the same. He only needed a quarter of an inch every half hour to keep himself perennially tipsy.

Then he looked at a boy, part mulatto but mostly Indian, and just as he was about to dance around singing about beer and rum, the kid blew up and shouted, "Cool it. And stay away from me, or I'll put two bullets through your head, you drunken piece of shit. Don't mess with me!"

He pulled up his shirt and showed his pistol. Chachareo felt challenged.

"You're not man enough to draw that pistol!"

A guy behind me said to me, "That little prick is a policeman. And a nasty son of a bitch. Trust me, this is going to get ugly."

The policeman tightened his lips and looked away, putting on a tough-guy face. Chachareo went on, "Today's the day you die! Do you think you can scare a real man that way? If you draw that pistol, today's the day you die! I'm a real man!"

From the line, two women called, "Chachareo, keep singing. Come over here by us and keep singing."

The policeman tightened his lips. His eyes flashed lightning rays, but he didn't draw his pistol. Chachareo went to the end of the line. The women called him over again. From the line, someone shouted in falsetto, "Policeman, oh puleezeman." People laughed, and the policeman turned bright red.

He was at the boiling point. Near the back of the line, Chachareo was saying something about Easterners who come to Havana and act like big shots, and he started to sing a guarachita, rhyming marijuana with Havana.

No blood was shed, thank goodness.

At last it was my turn in front of the barrel. I got my little bottle filled, my ration book marked, and I paid. Then I went straight to my room on the roof. No one was there. The old man next door had killed himself. The old woman developed a horror of the room and of loneliness, and now she was with one of her daughters. Luisa wasn't home either. There was a strong smell of perfume in the air. She had doused herself with half a bottle. She likes those strong perfumes. Everything about her is outrageous. She must have been out on the Malecón, since it was dark now. Probably she was making lots of money. Fridays and Saturdays are good, though lately there's more and more competition.

I poured myself a glass of rum and sat down quietly outside. El Morro was golden and the sea calm. An enormous empty tanker moved out of the port. Three sailors were working in the prow. They picked something up. The machinery purred softly. The boat was so big and it came so close that I could almost feel the steel plates vibrating. It was green and red, and it steamed quickly away, fading into the evening fog. A solitary figure, dressed in white, leaned against the railing on the third deck. He watched the beautiful golden city in the dusk, and I watched the green and red ship lose itself in the fog as it slipped away.

*Translated by Natasha Wimmer*

# Laura Restrepo
## (Colombia, b. 1950)

Laura Restrepo was born in Bogotá, Colombia. As a child with no regular schooling, she traveled throughout Latin America, Europe, and the United States in a Volkswagen camper with her mother, father, and younger sister. At the age of eighteen, while still a university student in Colombia, she began teaching literature to final-year students at a public high school. Older than she was, and in many ways more knowledgeable about life, her students taught her about the tough realities of their working-class neighborhoods. Eventually, she gave up a university professorship in literature to dedicate herself completely to the political opposition.

In 1983 the then-president of Colombia, Belisario Betancur, named her as a member of the commission charged with negotiating peace with the militant forces in the country. Peace was negotiated, several months of truce followed, and in 1984 the process ended in a bloodbath, forcing her to leave Colombia. *Historia de un entusiasmo* (1986) would chronicle this experience. Throughout her five years as a political exile in Mexico and then in Madrid, she maintained ties to the political wing of the Colombian guerrilla group M-19, while trying to create a new forum for negotiation. This was accomplished in 1989, when the M-19 gave up its weapons and converted to a legal opposition party, which allowed her to return to Colombia.

During her exile in Mexico, she had investigated the facts and circumstances of a very strange story from the beginning of the century, about a shipwrecked garrison of soldiers and their families, marooned for a decade on the island of Clipperton, off Acapulco. The result was her first novel, *La isla de la pasión* (1989). Returning to Colombia she dedicated herself to journalism, heading the national politics section of *Semana* magazine and reporting on the drug trade, the subject of her electrifying second novel, *Leopard in the Sun* (1993). A third novel, *The Angel of Galilea* (1995), offered a humorously ambiguous, lyrical tale of a woman reporter's obsession with an autistic angel. It won the Premio Sor Juana Inés de la Cruz (1998) at the Guadalajara Book Fair and the Prix France-Culture (1997) for its French version, thereby establishing her reputation internationally.

In the late 1990s she spent time in the oil-producing region of Colombia, researching the lives of oil riggers and prostitutes for her most famous, bestselling novel to date, *The Dark Bride* (1999). Based on extensive interviews, it tells the story of a young Indian prostitute and her ambiguous relationship to the society of the postwar oil boom. Restrepo's latest work, *La multitude errante* (2001), extracts a gentle story of improbable love from the violent heart of the civil war presently devouring Colombia. Restrepo lives in Bogotá, where she is at work on a new novel.

# The Scent of
# Invisible Roses

I imagine his hands were sweating, which is unusual at our age, and probably hadn't happened since our high school graduation, when we received our diplomas from the Jesuits. And I'd swear that as soon as he hung up the phone he felt a fresh breeze pass across his desk from that Roman spring forty years earlier. Irreverent and revitalizing, it had suddenly returned to scatter his papers and ruffle his gray hair. The commotion must have seemed amusing to him at his advanced age—men like him don't get their hair mussed very often. With a brusque wave of his hand, he stopped a solicitous secretary who was trying to interrupt him for his signature, an unequivocal indication that he didn't want the unexpected flood of memories to be shattered.

The feminine voice with the indeterminate accent he had just heard over long distance had awakened in him a swarm of thoughts from another time, postponing the urgency of daily business matters and inviting him to interrupt the relentless routine of familiar places and calculated gestures that guarantee the daily well-being of people like him.

\*   \*   \*

Luis C. Campos C., called Luicé Campocé since high school. I think he must have served himself a drink. Like any grand *señor*, Luicé had a small refrigerator in his office, with ice, soda, maybe even olives and maraschino cherries, everything needed to serve a drink when the occasion arose. He leaned back in the tattered but imposing leather chair, inherited from his father, don Luis C. Campos C. Turning toward the window, lost in thought, he gazed out at the shimmering mountains on the other side of the glass. Though "lost" is not totally accurate, because he, as opposed to me, is the kind of man who always wins.

Later, he confessed to me that at that moment he had to summon all his powers of concentration to corner the hungry rat that had for some time been gnawing away at the soft cheese of his memory. He wanted to reset the scene in order to place the woman's voice, recapture each instant, each smell, each color of the sky.

He failed, of course. He tried again, this time without such pretension. If he could rescue at least a smell, or just one color, maybe of the sky, or her dress. Or her big green eyes. . . . They were big, and they were green, of that he was sure, although it was possible that they were a little on the amber side. He couldn't remember anything concretely, only abstractly, but luckily it was enough to keep him soaring with the thrilling sensation of vitality that had come to him through the telephone line.

Photographs carefully arranged on his desk—in heavy silver frames, I should add—from which his wife, children and grandchildren smiled at him lovingly, tried to remind him how faraway and lost that spring was, how much life, proper, dignified and rigid, had passed since that very remote Roman sojourn when he was still single. He returned their gaze with infinite love (because he loved his family, of that I am certain) and he asked their forgiveness for the momentary distraction. He couldn't think about them at this inspired moment. He found it necessary to erase all interference.

I couldn't—and I don't imagine he could either—outline clearly the sequence of impulses that had caused him to dial, after forty years, the international access code, the prefix for Switzerland, 31 for Bern and, finally, her telephone number. I have asked myself why he had called her on that particular day, since until then it had never occurred to him to do such a thing. Why had he suddenly needed to feel her close and indispensable, when four decades of a good marriage with another admirable woman had caused him, until now, to remember her only during our lingering chats at the Automático?

When the Café Automático was still in existence, a group of five close friends, already in our thirties, used to gather there laughing at the bittersweet memories of our lost loves, and on those occasions Luicé, when he wanted to shine, told us about her. He said her name was Eloísa, that she belonged to a wealthy family from Chile and that he had met her on a cruise along the Nile. Over time, the group at the Automático became familiar with the details of the love affair. We knew that Luicé saw his *chilena* for the first time in Luxor, leaning against the gunwale and enraptured with the smooth, golden river, just minutes after the ship had weighed anchor. That he sat beside her that evening at the dinner the captain hosted for the first-class passengers, and that from that moment on they were never apart. Everything about her—according to Luicé—exuded confidence and ease, the softness of her short chestnut hair, her impeccable command of Italian and French, the adolescent agility with which she explored the ruins in her Bermuda shorts, hiking boots and black sunglasses. After ten days, in front of the pyramids in Cairo, Luicé kissed her on the neck and confessed his love for her.

"Be precise," interrupted Herrerita at this point in the story. "In front of which pyramid did you kiss her, Cheops, Khefren, or Mycerinus?"

They set off together for Rome, from where he was to fly on to

England to finish his degree at the London School of Economics and she to Geneva, where she was specializing in languages. They intended to say good-bye at the airport, but found themselves unable to and canceled their flights, took a taxi into the city and checked into a hotel near the Trevi Fountain.

"What a delightful melodrama about a couple of rich kids," interrupted Herrerita, and we hushed him with harsh looks.

A month later, when it was absolutely impossible to further postpone departure for the university, they were once again unsuccessful in their attempt to separate, and celebrating destiny, they moved into a cozy *pensione* in Trastevere, where they lived for three more months, engulfed in a happy, unpreoccupied love affair and spent, on trips to Venice and Amalfi, the funds their respective families religiously sent them from Latin America, secure in the faith that they were still dedicated to their studies.

"Now comes the best part," says Herrerita, eagerly preparing for the end.

The adventure's denouement occurred less than twenty-four hours after the arrival of Eloísa's mother, who had somehow found out about the deception, in Rome with her stern older brother. She was determined to rescue her daughter even if it meant calling the police.

Luicé never knew what happened that night when daughter, mother, and uncle met. He only knew that early the next morning, Eloísa appeared in their room at the *pensione*, red-eyed from hours of crying, silently packed her belongings and said good-bye without looking him in the face, while her family waited below in a taxi with its motor running.

He couldn't prevent his family from finding out about the affair either, and his father grew so angry at Luicé's total irresponsibility that he refused to finance any additional foreign studies. So he had to resign himself to returning to Bogotá, where he earned the modest title of economist from the Universidad Javeriana, which at any rate was no obstacle to his working in his father's enormous company, and upon his death, taking the helm of the organization.

Eloísa, the *chilena*—bourgeois, polyglot and avant-garde—went on to become one of the favorites in our gallery of lost loves, competing against Herrerita's tragic and tubercular baker, the Christian Dior model that Bernardo had pursued around the globe, the three prostitute sisters from Mangangué that had initiated Matuk, the Turk, in the ways of love, and a cousin at the university named Gloria Eterna that Ariel dreamed about feverishly every night from age ten to thirteen.

When the Café Automático closed, I stopped seeing Herrerita and the others, but I maintained a close friendship with Luicé that never diminished, though he kept getting richer and I kept getting poorer, and so I was able to closely follow the path his life took. That is how I learned that despite the abrupt culmination of his romance with Eloísa, and the subsequent establishment of independent lives with an ocean between them—he in Colombia and she in Switzerland—they didn't lose contact over the years. They took advantage of various occasions to reciprocally congratulate one another via brief and rather impersonal notes: first his wedding to a girl from Bogotá society, later hers to a Swiss banker, then the birth of their children, his two and her one, and, years later, the arrival of grandchildren.

If personal experiences were included in the curriculum vitae of high-level executives, under the heading, let's say, of "Important Moments Lived," the first part of his relationship with Eloísa could very well appear in Luicé's as: "everything very proper and presentable, a delightful youthful fling nipped in the bud in the nick of time and transformed into a discreet cordiality between adults."

Then destiny intervened to alter the picture when a note written on white paper in the clean handwriting taught at the Colegio Sagrado Corazón arrived in the mail—I won't say perfumed, because I have the highest regard for Eloísa, whom I have always admired without knowing personally. She had written to tell Luicé that her husband had died two years earlier, after a long and difficult illness. Deeply shaken by this unforeseen event, she had remained silent during her mourning period and finally had permitted herself, in four lines, to break the accustomed distance and let through a barely perceptible hint of nostalgia that was, probably, what had motivated him to call her to convey his condolences in his own voice after several failed attempts to produce a letter that wasn't, as his previous ones had been, written by his secretary.

On the day of their telephone conversation, he returned home agitated by a strange disquiet that would not allow him to enjoy the *ossobucco* that Solita, his wife, had prepared for him. She was given to spoiling him with recipes taken from *Il Talismano della Felicitá*, without taking into consideration the diet recommended by his doctor to ease the pain caused by his gout. Nor was he able to yield peacefully to the Albinoni *Adagio* that always floated him through serene waters to the most harmonious zone of his being. In the late evening his son, Juan Emilio, who came by his father's house every day, said some things about his grandson that he knew intuitively were important, but which couldn't hold his attention. Later, in bed, he asked Solita about it.

"Allergic?"

"What?"

"Is that what Juan was saying about Juanito, allergic?"

"Not allergic, pre-asthmatic."

"Oh, that's not good. . . . Allergic to what?"

"Do you want to tell me where your head is tonight?"

"Nowhere," he lied. He was anxious and distracted all week, as if he weren't comfortable in his own skin, and he was beginning to worry about this absurd and insistent mental itch that was hampering his relationship with his family and interfering with his work, when he realized that it could only be alleviated by calling her again. So he did, and then again the next week, and the next, until he noticed that by Monday night he was already anticipating the call to Bern that he'd make from his office every Wednesday precisely at noon.

Eloísa spoke twice as much as he, in quantity and in velocity, but they limited themselves to socially acceptable topics, like his work, the Colombian ambassador's drunken escapades, the wonders of a van Gogh retrospective that she had seen in Amsterdam, the gout that was strangling his big toe. They were silly topics to be sure, but I like to imagine that each time they chatted the fresh Roman breeze passed through Luicé's office, stirring his papers and his memories.

It must have been in August, two or three months after the calls had become regular, when they first mentioned the possibility of getting together. She proposed it in the most innocent manner when she offered him and his wife the use of her house in Switzerland during the December holidays.

"And if your grandchildren would like to learn how to ski," she suggested, "bring them too. I could start making arrangements now to rent a couple of chalets in the mountains."

The potential trip began to occupy more time in the weekly conversation, with varying locations and circumstances. He told her that his wife would love to go back to Paris and they agreed that would be a good place to reunite, but of course spring would be better than winter. Since it was more a pretext to communicate than a concrete plan of action, they casually skipped from one city to another, from one month to the next, without getting into details or specifying logistics. From Paris they changed to Miami, where he had some business associates that he needed to visit; from there to Prague, a city they both had always wanted to explore; from Prague somehow to Rome, and after Rome, of course, they succumbed to the unseen pull of Egypt. At some point along the way they stopped referring to grandchildren, and then, without knowing quite how, from Wednesday to Wednesday Solita's name was less and less frequently mentioned in the comings and goings, though she had never been informed of the numerous vacation plans in which she had really only been included as a third party.

The mere mention of Egypt, with the emotional charge it held for them, remote yet familiar, added an anxious tone to Eloísa's voice, a feminine need for details, for entering into the concrete with airline fares in hand and specific suggestions for dates and hotels, all of which was to him—who had been speaking just to speak, confident that it was an unrealizable project—a complete surprise and caused him a good deal of worry, making him feel he was on shaky ground.

All these months of listening to Eloísa had naturally been a balm for Luicé against the peculiar insults that a man in his condition experiences at the onset of old age: switching from tennis to golf, being forced to quit smoking, extra holes in his belt, stronger eyeglasses. But between that and risking what he had built over his entire life, to take a trip down the Nile with an old girlfriend was an abyss that he wasn't even remotely prepared to cross. That should have been evident to anyone, but not to Eloísa, and not because she entertained any illusions, but because she was a woman accustomed to having her way.

So, on the next call, they became lost in differing levels of involvement that neither could fail to notice. Her excessive enthusiasm receded, cautiously, when met by his evasive responses, and when they hung up both knew that they had reached a dead point that left them no option but to return to their sporadic, diplomatically worded notes.

During the following two months the telephone did not ring on Wednesday at noon in the house in Bern, and I think it fair to presume Luicé had begun to forget the matter with an unpleasant resignation, somewhere between annoyance and relief. Although secretly he would have preferred to limit himself to *café con leche* and toast, he could once again enjoy the Italian recipes that Solita regularly prepared for him and he happily returned to his old, relaxing habit of listening to the Albinoni *Adagio* before going to sleep.

That Sunday morning when he bought issue number five of a booklet series called *The Treasures of the Nile* from the kiosk on the corner, he did it more as a reflex than anything else, knowing beforehand that he would never buy number six. But that's not how it turned out. Not only did he send a messenger to buy it, but he also asked his secretary to locate the first four issues, which were already out of circulation. I don't think he thought about Eloísa as he scanned the pages without stopping to read the text, a little distracted by other matters, sort of like someone glancing at the classifieds without really looking for anything in particular. Nor did he know why he found looking at the large color pictures so intriguing, though it might have been just to quantify the degree to which his memory had softened and which made him unable to recognize, as if they were from another planet, the places he had visited. Abu Simbel? No, maybe he hadn't been there. He remembered a little more about Karnac, but those giant statues with sheeps' heads, all in a row, had he seen them? If he'd saved his photographs he could have checked. Because he had taken pictures of them together at the ruins, in the excavations, on the boat and during that last night—about which Herrerita demanded that he tell them in detail—the costume ball where Eloísa had appeared stunningly dressed as Isis, or was it Osiris? Anyway, it was an Egyptian goddess.

"You have never confessed what you went dressed as," interjected Herrerita.

"*Hombre*, that's because I can't remember."

"As a eunuch, maybe, or an obelisk? An odalisque, a date, a foreign legionnaire? I've got it! A Persian rug, or a camel's hump. . . ."

Luicé had burned the photographs several days before the wedding, together with any others that included the presence of women that, if discovered, could cause his wife to worry. It had been foolish after all, because Solita loved to hear about his old adventures, and on the shelves in the living room she had several albums from her youth where she appeared in bobby socks, long skirts and saddle shoes, laughing and dancing wildly with other men.

The *Treasures of the Nile* had reached number twelve in the series when, one Wednesday around two o'clock in the afternoon, leaving his office for lunch, he was stopped at the door by his secretary.

"You have a long-distance call, *señor*. From Bern. Should I tell them to call back after lunch?"

He rushed to the telephone more hastily than he would have liked his secretary to have seen, and I think I could safely say that he had to breathe deeply so that his wavering voice didn't reveal how hard his heart was beating. Eloísa was brief and to the point, not asking questions or permitting interruptions. Her daughter, a photographer, was having an exposition the following week in New York and she was going to accompany her. Afterward they were going for a few days of sun to Miami, where she would wait for him two weeks from today at six o'clock in the evening, at Gate 27, Concourse G at Miami International Airport. If he took a flight that afternoon on American Airlines he would arrive just in time. He didn't need to worry about reserving a hotel room, because she had already taken care of everything. Since she supposed that after so many years he wouldn't recognize her, she told him that she would be wearing a lavender silk dress.

I wonder what his first reaction to such a proposal was. It must have seemed terribly rash. After discarding other hypotheses, I'll stick with this one, which I'll divide into two. One, he laughed at the strident, executive tone and the unhesitating resolve with which she transmitted the order. And two, he admired the audacity of Eloísa, who, in response to his earlier tactic of defusing the compromising situation with silence and indefinite responses, was now counterattacking with rock-solid proposals. At any rate, Luicé was only able to say one thing before she hung up.

"As you wish, *señora*."

"As you wish, *señora*." What was that supposed to mean? He might as well have said "If it pleases you," "You're the boss," or any other convenient expression to get out of the tight spot without committing to anything and without being so rude as to refuse outright. But the idea was turning round and round in his head.

Checking here and there, I eventually found out that the waiter who served him his consommé with sherry for lunch that afternoon was surprised that the *señor*, usually so serious, laughed to himself. Then the waiter noticed that he kept smiling all through the fish course, and when it was time for dessert he grew tired of asking which the *señor* preferred, as he was much too distracted to hear anything. So he took it upon himself to risk bringing a caramel flan, and he watched as it was ingested by the *señor* in a state of such self-absorption that he was sure that if he had brought duck *a l'orange* or a bunch of parsley he wouldn't have noticed.

Despite the good humor that the telephone call produced, Luicé must have returned to his office determined not to let the afternoon pass without calling Eloísa to dissuade her, but instead of doing that, he asked his secretary to check the status of his U.S. visa.

"Just in case," he said.

The next day he had to go to the dentist to have a tooth removed, and more than by the violence of the extraction, he was hurt by the response he got from the dentist when he asked if he was going to replace the lost tooth with a false one.

"We can't," he said, using the humiliating plural out of pity. "We don't have anything to secure it to. Remember that we've lost the neighboring molars. . . ."

"Are you telling me that you, too, are a toothless old man?" he said in response to this indignation, and returned to his house, in a foul mood, his face swollen.

It is easy to comprehend why, at his borderline age, Luicé had given such an exaggerated importance to the incident, which when added to the gout torturing his toe and his necessary but offensive decision to retire soon, leaving the office in younger hands, seemed to be the cause of the sudden, uncontrollable rebelliousness that possessed him lately, and which his surprised wife called "adolescent." But it was really just an old horse kicking at anything that tried to tighten the cinch. He began closing himself up in his room to stare at the ceiling, smoking in secret, and becoming obsessed with the idea that his grandchildren were being brought up poorly.

"Your father is a wreck," Solita told their sons.

He was even irritable with the one person who inspired his most unconditional adoration, his son Juan Emilio.

"Did you know, Papá, that the *Adagio* that you've been listening to isn't really by Albinoni?" his son had the unfortunate idea of asking him.

"What do you mean?" he barked. "Who is Albinoni's *Adagio* by, if not Albinoni?"

Juan Emilio tried to explain that it was a masterly falsification by Remo Giazotto, Albinoni's biographer, but was able only to further disgust his father.

"That was the last thing I needed," he grumbled. "I've spent three whole years, eight hundred nights straight, listening to something, and now they tell me it's something else entirely."

In addition, he had adopted the habit of chastising his secretaries for silly things, which was falsely interpreted in the office as an intolerance of errors. From what I could gather, what upset him was their extreme youth, their exuberant green apple fragrance that made his own transition to dried prune even more noticeable.

In yet another manifestation of his solitary protest against those around him and especially against himself, he deliberately put off, day after day, that unavoidable telephone call to Bern to excuse himself. Not because he really considered going, but simply to feel the pleasure of being irresponsible. And it's important to remember that the only significant act of irresponsibility in this honorable man's life so far was precisely the one that he had committed with the *chilena*.

He must have spent hours racking his brains trying to find the kindest way of refusing Eloísa, without offending her or seeming oafish, but it only took him two minutes of improvising in front of his wife to come up with the first great lie of his married life.

"What a pain, Miami," he said. "But there's no way around it, I have to close the deal there."

The first thing he did when he got on the airplane, even before fastening his seat belt, was to ask for a double scotch. Perhaps to camouflage the fear of arriving at that enormous, bustling airport? It's understandable; he didn't have a telephone number or an address, or any other reference except an appointment subject to a thousand unforeseen obstacles, set two weeks earlier and never confirmed, all in search of a ghost from his past wrapped in lavender-colored silk.

He landed in Miami a quarter of an hour early, with five scotches under his belt and an unbridled enthusiasm that conveyed him straight to Concourse G. There were about twenty-five people at the specified gate. He studied them one by one and realized worriedly that nobody was dressed in lavender.

Had I been in his place, I'd have spent the time telling myself it was too early to worry, that surely Eloísa's airplane hadn't landed yet. But what if she had already arrived, and he was waiting in the wrong spot? He did the same thing I would have done. He walked back out to the entrance to the gate and looked at the sign to make sure he hadn't made a mistake. He was, however, at Gate 27 in Concourse G. He checked his Omega watch. It was barely 5:45. Except for his nerves, everything was under control.

But, what about the time change? The possibility that it might be an hour later than he thought made his heart freeze. Luckily, just across from him, big and round, was a wall clock with clear Arabic numbers coinciding exactly with the time on his watch; reset, he thought he remembered, during the flight at the captain's suggestion.

Visibly more at ease, he found a spot that afforded the best view of the passengers. He sat down, and although he was able to relax a bit, anxiety pushed him to the edge of his seat. Ten minutes passed, then twenty. As the effects of the whiskey wore off, so did his enthusiasm, leaving him with a cruel doubt. Could Eloísa have changed her mind? Or worse, had she taken as a joke a date that he, naively, had kept?

If I were in his shoes, it would have made me laugh to think that at my age, and by my own will, I had gotten involved in such a ridiculous scenario. But my laughter would have turned into melancholy and I wouldn't have been able to control the urge to go home. Maybe he was already imagining Solita's face as he returned from Miami before midnight the same day he had left, when his attention was drawn to a tall, thin woman at the end of the passageway with a large scarf on her head.

With a graceful, easy stride, the woman advanced to the gate entrance and stopped there. He watched her scan the room, as if looking for someone. She was young and quite beautiful, and she possessed certain exotic yet familiar features that produced a hypnotic effect on Luicé.

He would have liked to remain there, contemplating her without being seen, but her eyes fixed on him, surprising and then disturbing him as he realized that the young woman was smiling at him and had begun to walk toward where he was sitting. As she crossed the twenty yards that separated them, still looking at him and without losing her smile, his eyes were fixed on her billowing white dress. When there were only five yards remaining he could see the sparkle in her amber eyes. At four yards he shuddered when he realized that the large silk scarf she wore wrapped around her head was lavender. With only two yards to go, he was floored by a terrifying realization: the woman was Eloísa.

In a few seconds—the time it took her to walk the last two yards—he retrieved from the murky labyrinth of his memory a sequence of images from that cruise down the Nile. There they were again, laceratingly intact, the god Horus with his falcon profile, the magnificent solitary obelisk that guarded the entrance to the temple of Amon, the lapis lazuli and malachite scarabs, the living procession of biblical figures along the two green riverbanks, the cobras draped around the necks of the merchants in Aswan. And in the middle of it all, there she was, exactly as she was now, forty years later, standing before him at Miami International Airport.

The years had passed through her like a ray of light through a window: they had left her untouched. He felt his long-lost love and an oceanic admiration for her well up in the depths of his chest, proportional only to the disgust that began to form like bubbles around his own body. His bulky middle seemed unpresentable and he tried to straighten his suit, which had become wrinkled during the flight. The bags under his eyes seemed heavier than ever and he knew that the cigarette he had just smoked had left his breath foul. He had never felt so abandoned as at that instant, as if he were the only inhabitant of the inclement country of time, the sole and select victim of the passing hours and days, which had chewed him with their minuscule teeth.

"I am Alejandra, Eloísa's daughter," she said, extending her hand, without ever suspecting from what dark abyss she had rescued him.

"Eloísa's daughter . . ." he breathed. "The apple doesn't fall far from the tree! You look just like your mother," he added, his soul now back in his body. "How did you recognize me?"

"She showed me a picture of you and said, imagine him with gray hair, add some weight and glasses, and you can't miss him."

Alejandra made some confusing explanations about why her

mother had been delayed in New York for a few more hours. Eloísa had sent her ahead to meet him so he wouldn't worry and to keep him company until nine o'clock.

"Eloísa's arriving at nine?"

"That's right. If you'd like, we could go ahead and rent a car, and if you're hungry we could get something to eat."

"You were together in New York?"

"Yes, but she couldn't be here at six, because of the problem that I told you about," said Alejandra, getting caught up again in vague excuses that had something to do with airfares.

He needed her to thoroughly explain the problem that had caused the delay in order to regain some control over the situation, but now Alejandra was introducing him to a pale, rail-thin man, wearing a worn jacket and an indifferent air, whom he had not noticed before.

"This is Nikos, my boyfriend."

Forming a tense, mismatched committee, the three set off to rent an automobile and then to eat something light, mixing embarrassing silences with fragments of a stiff and formal conversation that Nikos neither added to nor helped along with his disagreeable attitude. Luicé struggled to conceal his dislike of Nikos, and if he didn't flee the airport, where he felt as if he were an extra in a strange comedy, it was surely due to resignation to the unavoidable chain of events that stemmed from an erroneous act. He had committed an error when he boarded the airplane, or perhaps months earlier, when he called Eloísa for the first time, and he was too old not to know the rules of reality according to which every path taken requires as many steps to turn back from as it does to advance along.

I know, however, that a certain sweetness soothed his misgivings. It was Alejandra's presence, her honest smile and her warm manner in trying to make this bizarre meeting a marvelous encounter of love for her mother. Life certainly is strange. This precious girl who just before had appeared before his eyes like

Aphrodite incarnate, now awakened in him a more paternal inclination, and I'm sure that when he looked at her he couldn't help
thinking about Juan Emilio, because he spoke to her in a lowered
voice, with a conspiratorial tone, taking advantage of the fact that
the cadaverous Nikos had gone to get some coffee.

"I would love for you to meet my youngest son sometime. His
name is Juan Emilio and he's a terrific guy. Recently separated, too."

A little before nine the couple said good-bye to Luicé, leaving
him alone to wait for Eloísa. Of all the feelings he had experienced recently, only fatigue remained, and he collapsed in the first
seat he found, hoping for a moment of peace. Not two minutes
had passed when Alejandra came running back toward him. She
unwrapped the ethereal lavender silk *écharpe* from around her
head and gave it to him.

"Please give this to my mother. It's part of her dress," she asked
him, giving him a light kiss on the cheek. "I hope you have a very
happy time together."

Then the girl ran off and Luicé found himself alone again,
burdened with his fatigue, the wilted *écharpe* in his hands. A loud-
speaker announced the departure of some flight and after a rapid
flow of people and luggage the gate became silent and empty, and
he was able to stretch out his legs over two neighboring seats. He
let himself slip into a soft, undulating drowsiness, then he settled
into a deep, seamless sleep, uninterrupted by the wave of flowery
perfume that filled his nose, the cascading laughter flooding his
ears, or even the soft touch of a hand on his knee. After some
time, like someone crossing a lake underwater and not coming up
for air until reaching the other shore, his consciousness surfaced,
returning him to the blinding fluorescent light.

He looked around with newborn eyes, still seeing more within
than without, and jumped when he registered the proximity of a
*señora* with red hair who was looking at him.

"Give that back to me, *señor*. It's mine," she said, laughing and taking the *écharpe*, which was the same color and material as the rest of her outfit.

Petrified, he looked at her as if he had awakened to a dream more unreal than the previous one, and he was unable to say or do anything. She tried to smile and then put a nervous hand to her hair, perhaps blaming its appearance for his shock.

"Too red, isn't it?" she asked.

"What's that?"

"My hair . . ."

"A little red, yes."

Aware of each of his gestures, slowly and stiffly like a marionette, he stood up and gave the woman a hug like a bishop's which, instead of conveying the warmth of a reunion, was proof of the enormous distance that separated them. While he was held by arms that seemed not to want to let go, he noted, I'm sure, the difference in volume between this Eloísa and the one from his past, and his hands, resting on her back and waist, felt how, on the other side of the cold silk, her feminine shape fused into a single abundant warmth of cushioned flesh. At least that's how it would have seemed to me.

"So much risk and such a long journey," he must have thought, "just to find another *señora* like the one I left at home."

When he escaped from the embrace and could retreat a few inches, he made an enormous effort to recognize her. But there was nothing. This redheaded woman wrapped in clouds of sweet perfume and lavender silk, who had Eloísa's face, who spoke and laughed like Eloísa, really didn't look like anyone, not like his memory of young Eloísa, or Alejandra, or even what anyone would have supposed that Eloísa would look like at a mature age.

She was in a hurry to explain how that morning when she got up she had discovered in front of the mirror that her gray hair was beginning to show under her dyed hair. In Switzerland she had arranged everything, nails, skin, depilatory, dying her hair, tan-

ning, absolutely everything, and just this morning, as if purposely
growing during the night, there they were again, crafty devils, her
shocking white roots.

"With so much to pack, I made the mistake of leaving it for the
last minute," she continued, unstoppable.

"Leaving what?" he asked, with the hope, I think, of changing
the topic.

What else, but the drama of the gray hair, going to have her
hair dyed again to hide the gray. She went to the beauty parlor on
the way to the airport, with her luggage waiting in the car, sure
that it wouldn't take more than an hour. Alejandra was waiting for
her, leafing through magazine after magazine and glancing impatiently at the clock. And actually, the stylist took exactly one hour.

"So why the delay?"

"The color! They left me looking ridiculous, worse than what
you see now. When I saw it I told Alejandra, go on to Miami, I'm
not leaving here until they turn off this blazing hair."

"And the mix-up with your ticket? Were you able to resolve it?"

"There was no mix-up with my ticket, silly. The hair was the
real reason for my being late."

As they walked side by side down the airport corridors, he
tried earnestly to cut through the curtain of words that she was
building so that he could reach the Eloísa he had once loved. With
his hope set on the possibility of finding something familiar, some
secret sign of reviving the intimacy between them, he noticed her
hands with the painted nails, her diamond ring, the rapid staccato
of her short steps. No, there was no signal that would open the
door. The small Bermuda Triangle that had appeared over this
brutal convergence of past and present devoured all identities: the
*señora* with the red hair wasn't Eloísa, just as he wasn't the *señor*
who was walking in his own shoes, nor was this her voice reaching
him as from a far-off echo, nor the words that came directly from
her tongue, without passing first through her brain.

Eloísa—this apocryphal Eloísa of today—overwhelmed him
with unrequested explanations, without even realizing how irra-
tional, obscure, and independent of her was his real reason for
having come: to find a way to extend his life. I don't think that
even he knew this with any certainty, but that is why he was here,
to rediscover his youth, to make up for lost time, and she was failing him miserably. Eloísa, that sacred and immutable depository
of an idyllic past, instead appeared to him, as if by a curse, as a
faithful mirror of the passing of the years.

"You're lucky. Three hours ago it was much worse. It was as
red as a stoplight," she insisted. "Phosphorescent carrot, something horrible. You can't imagine."

He didn't know when this conversation would end and the
hollow resonations in his brain would stop, but the hair saga was
still going on when he found himself immersed in the problem of
baggage. Standing beside the moving belt, Eloísa pointed one by
one at her belongings and he tried to yank them off, suffering beforehand—like any man of our age—the backache that the
hypochondriac in him presupposed.

"That big one!" she shouted. "The little blue one over there . . .
That canvas bag . . . No, not that one! This box that's coming . . .
It got by you! It doesn't matter. Next time around. Yes, that one
too. . . ."

The rental car papers specified a burgundy Chevrolet Impala
that they were supposed to find among several dozen vehicles
parked in front of them.

"It's this one."

"It can't be. It's not burgundy."

"I think it is burgundy."

"It's cherry. It must be that one over there."

"That one's burgundy, but it's not a Chevrolet."

He must have felt trapped, as if in a womb, by the soft, red up-
holstery of that car full of luggage as she flew down the highway at
ninety miles an hour toward Pompano Beach, where an amorous

interlude fatefully awaited them and about which Luicé had serious doubts, in terms of mood, and more especially, physically, as to how he would be able to respond.

Her voice, which maintained a constant communication, penetrated less and less into the ears of someone who had arrived at a final conclusion about the futility of making an effort to salvage a situation that from the beginning looked waterlogged and which sooner or later was going to sink as disastrously as the *Titanic*.

More for Eloísa than for himself, he had wanted everything to turn out well, for this unholy reunion to live up to the level of care that she had put into planning it. But nothing could be done, except to trust that Eloísa would also end up realizing that it was absurd to force, all of a sudden, such a compromising intimacy between two people with only the memory of a memory in common.

She, nevertheless, seemed to have the opposite idea about how this momentous occasion should be handled, and she set about with admirable tenacity to break the ice. She apologized for the number of suitcases, offered cigarettes, talked about the stupendous apartment she had arranged right on the beach in the middle of a golf course, of Alejandra and her torturous relationship with the indecipherable Nikos, about the directions they were supposed to follow to reach Pompano Beach without getting lost. But he was riposting with an efficient tactic that consisted of a combination of apathetic comments and monosyllabic answers, until she, apparently defeated, decided to keep her mouth shut.

The night surrounded them like an endless cave and the Impala, indifferent, devoured, with its bulky snout, the hundreds of thousands of white lines demarcating the highway. After a number of miles one of them turned the radio on and the torrential voice of the broadcaster flooded the car with sound, artificially dissipating the air of loneliness that was growing thicker by the minute.

The apartment was the perfect manifestation of that comfortable, new, air-conditioned private world that we have made synonymous with paradise, and which seems to have its principal domain in Florida. Alejandra had already been there, leaving everything ready: an enormous vase of white roses at the entrance, a stocked refrigerator, towels in the bathroom and the beds made. He noticed, with immense relief, that two separate rooms had been prepared.

An Eloísa that floated somewhere beyond illusion, who was no longer trying to force things and who had removed her jewelry, her makeup and her shoes, served them fresh orange juice on the terrace. The night, warm and dark, pulsed with the sound of the crickets and with the roar of the nearby but invisible ocean.

He saw how, leaning against the railing, she let her eyes stare off into nothing and let herself be lulled by the sonorous blackness, forgetting about the color of her hair and giving in to the pleasure of the gentle breeze. He saw her standing there without a care, in the ampleness of her lavender dress, accepting the defeat of her large body in place of that of the thin woman she had once been. As he studied her profile, he focused his eyes on a tiny but propitious detail, somehow almost redeeming: in the middle of her face marked by time, safe from human contingency, that upturned nose, capricious and infantile; the same, identical nose that he had seen, forty years earlier, over the waters of the Nile. "Yes, it's her," he must have admitted, moved, but he was too tired to perceive the thread of wind that came off the oxidized walls of Trastevere to blow through this apartment leaving the white furniture, recently purchased at some shopping center, sprinkled with the sand of the centuries.

"Thank you, Eloísa," he called her by name for the first time. "Thank you for all of this."

"Go rest now," she said, kindly, and without the slightest hint of flirtation. "Sleep well and don't worry about anything."

The next morning he was awakened by the most pleasing smell in the world, the smell of freshly made breakfast with toast, coffee and golden bacon, everything set out on a floral tablecloth in the sunny kitchen, where a happy Eloísa, dressed casually, seemed to have erased from her memory the less than pleasant moments of the preceding day. They played golf the whole radiant morning on a course worthy of dreams, and he had to really push himself, and ended up sweating just to keep up with Eloísa, who surprised him with two birdies in the first nine holes.

I don't know for sure where they had lunch, but I like to think that they had salmon and white wine in a restaurant on the beach, discussing business with the settled indifference of those who already have all the money they need and aren't worried about making more. As they were drinking their coffee, he suddenly changed the topic to make a confession.

"When I saw Alejandra I thought she was you, and I felt terribly old."

"And when you saw me?"

"I pledged not to admit that we had both grown old."

After lunch she went shopping and he closed himself in his room, where I can see him as if I had been there: lying on the bed in his underwear, devouring the news on television, checking in with his house and his office, asking Juan Emilio about his grandson's health, covering his head with a pillow and taking a long, peaceful siesta, snoring like a freight train, from which he awoke in a splendid mood when the first stars were already shining in the sky.

That night, in a velvet, smoky nightclub they toasted with Veuve Cliquot served by cocktail waitresses scantily clad in sequins, and by their third glass, halfway through Frank Sinatra's "My Way," he sprinkled the smoldering ashes of their old love with champagne and was amazed to see how they burst into blue flames.

They made up for forty years of separation by sharing an intense, happy and honest week. Childlike and naked, Luicé dove into Eloísa's laugh as if into a bubble bath. He thrived on the wonderful feeling of freedom that, now and always, she radiated. In the enthusiasm of that brief and final passion that life, with gracious acquiescence, gave him as a gift, my friend Luicé burned away the bundle of fears inherent in the ungodly process of growing old. These are things I can guess without obtaining confirmation from him. Our sharing of lost and forgotten loves had its inviolable rules, and it was fair sport as long as we meticulously avoided any mention of weakness in the male soul.

What a lucky guy, Luicé Campocé. I would also have loved a woman like Eloísa—actually, I have loved her just by hearing about her since the days of the Café Automático—and I would have been grateful for a boost like that at the final turn in my life's path.

There are details that I won't go on about because they have more to do with me than with Luicé, like the fact that on the corner where the Automático was they opened an ice cream shop called Sussy's, with insipid tables of yellow Formica and high stools in the same color vinyl. There's not a vestige of the opaque lamps that bathed the afternoons spent with friends in a soft, confidential light, nor of the great chrome coffee machine that gave off vapor like a cauldron and impregnated the block with the inviting aroma of freshly brewed coffee. However, I continue to frequent that corner. I sit on one of the stools at Sussy's next to messengers greased up like John Travolta and secretaries wearing miniskirts and panty hose. I ask for vanilla ice cream in a cup and while I eat it with a plastic spoon I think of her, of Eloísa the *chilena*, the love of my friend Luicé's youth. I also think about the sweet, hidden memory of those other phantasmal girlfriends, theirs and mine, since I had my own, though none named Gloria Eterna, and which I never mentioned during our afternoon gatherings in order to preserve them intact in their secrecy.

But I invoke Eloísa with more feeling, I, who always found the scent of invisible roses more real than roses themselves; I, who don't know how to slay a baker woman with love, or make the whores of Mangangué shout with pleasure; I would have divined in the young Eloísa the splendid woman that she would become over the years, and I would have loved in the mature Eloísa the young woman she had been. So, from the yellow desolation of Sussy's I remember her, so valiant and tenacious in her attempt at resurrection in an apartment in Pompano Beach. Eloísa, the *chilena*, who over the course of a week managed to wriggle away from the sated belly of the past, which changes us and converts us into leftovers with its gastric juices. Eloísa, my favorite, who knew to slip past the overwhelmingness of today, so much more vital and real than Luicé or me, incarnated in all the splendor and silliness of her red-dyed hair and her lavender silk dress.

As for her, we'll never know how she felt retracing her footsteps. But I imagine that she managed to make out all right, after having dealt, in her own way as an independent woman, with an old chapter of her life that had been put on hold by familial interference. This second time the separation wasn't as forced or theatrical as before. It came about on its own terms and with mutual acknowledgment, as with old actors who realize that the principal roles are no longer appropriate for them. What Eloísa and Luicé couldn't promise one another they plotted on the penultimate afternoon of Florida neon, half dreaming, half playing, for their children Alejandra and Juan Emilio, about whom they talked obsessively: imagining ingenious hypothetical situations for introducing them, tricks for getting rid of Nikos, pretexts for Juan Emilio to travel to Switzerland; strategic fantasies to grant their children a future together, something which they themselves would never have.

The last thing they did, intentionally, solemnly, to finalize the farewell that they knew would be forever, was to buy an Italian silk blouse for Luicé to take back as a gift for his wife, Solita. Making fun of his taste and ignoring his suggestions, Eloísa chose, after looking at more than ten, an expensive and discreet pearl-white long-sleeved blouse with subtle, pale white arabesques in a classic style that she had wrapped in tissue paper and placed in a box.

Back at home, Luicé watched as Solita took it out of his suitcase, put it on over her nightgown and looked at herself thoughtfully in the mirror.

"Incredible," he told me she had said. "This is the first time in your life that you have brought me a present from one of your trips that I like, that is appropriate for my age and that fits me well. I would have bought the same thing for myself. If I didn't have blind trust in you, I would swear that another woman chose this blouse."

He smiled under the covers, bundled up in the warmth of an indulgent peace. A little later, before he fell asleep, as his heartbeats matched the deep rhythm of the *Adagio*, he knew that Albinoni was sending him a signal and inviting him to cross, free at last from all reticence and fear, the threshold leading to the gentle fields of old age.

"The *Adagio* is yours, old Albinoni," he must have thought, with clear conviction. "Yours and no one else's."

*Translated by Stephen A. Lytle*

# Carlos Franz
## (Chile, b. 1959)

Carlos Franz was born in Geneva, Switzerland, and studied law at the University of Chile. In 1980, he was invited to participate in a writers workshop by the Chilean novelist José Donoso. He was appointed Professor of Literature at Diego Portales University in Santiago in 1995. Two years later Franz himself cofounded and directed the National Library of Chile's Writers Workshop, which has had an enormous influence on recent trends in Chilean letters. He has spent time abroad in Germany, invited to the city of Berlin as a writer in residence, and in England as a visiting fellow at Cambridge University.

Franz began publishing his short stories in 1984. He has also written two prize-winning novels, *Santiago Cero* (1990), which took First Prize in the Cuarto Concurso Latinoamericano de novela (CICLA) in 1988, and *El lugar donde estuvo el Paraíso* (1998), chosen First Finalist in the 1996 competition for the international Planeta Prize. A haunting novel of multiple betrayals set in the Ecuadorian Amazon, this latter work went on to become a bestseller throughout Latin America, with critics comparing the author to Conrad, Lowry, and Greene. Translated into over half a dozen languages, it has recently been adapted as a feature film.

Franz's stories have appeared internationally in countless literary anthologies. In addition, he has published a first book of literary essays and collaborated regularly with numerous periodicals and magazines, including *Granta* in London, *Quehacer* in Lima, and *Clarín* in Buenos Aires. He currently lives in London.

# Circle

*For Lastenia Oliva,
who managed to tell me this story*

Giving a name to describe what she saw in her grandmother's bedroom would have been arbitrary. She was six years old and had no need for names. Now that an eternity has elapsed, she only remembers that it all seemed to be engulfed in mist. A mist frozen into an aseptic frosty ether, and probes and threatening syringes on the bedside table. Or was it something even finer, something so intangible . . . The fact is that she was only six years old, dressed in crisp organdy and listening to the squeak of her rubber soles on the polished parquet floor when, reaching up, she pulled all her weight on the door handle, and the door opened. Her grandmother's life was suspended from the walls of the room. There was an oil painting of her grandfather in riding garb, just as he was dressed on the day of the accident. Her grandmother also had portraits of each one of her daughters on the day of their first communion; and in their fluffy dresses when presented into society; or floating in tulle, evidently so rosy-cheeked that it even showed in the sepia photos, as they left church on the arms of solemn, heavily mustachioed men. There were also miniatures of her mother, of remote great-grandmothers, of ephemeral children who died of innocuous diseases. But the girl did not recognize anyone. And even more frightening than those faded faces from the past were the hatboxes up high on the tall wardrobes, together with an image from atop the chest of drawers of the Infant Jesus of Prague, whose extended hand was offering her a sphere. Perhaps—and this is as much certainty as she was able to draw from the drowsiness enveloping her childhood—perhaps what frightened her the most when coming close to the cagelike grid of her grandmother's brass bed were the scents of her D'Oriza powder and, after forty years of use, her Flower of Love cologne, redolent of the barely worn silk petticoats stuck in the drawers, layer upon layer. Perhaps what she feared was the musty smell of the cape jasmine petal pressed in her grandmother's missal, the lavender fragrance of her small lace handkerchiefs that emanated from the wardrobes and rose to hide between the curtain folds. Perhaps all these smells, together with the bright bands of sunlight, the shadows of the brass grid on the bed, and the sullen expressions of the portraits, were really what caused the nebulous condition of the bedroom. And perhaps that was what made it feel so deep. Like a time well into which she was falling fast.

Sometimes she does not feel the nape of her neck or the back of her head for quite a long time. Then she imagines, considering that her angle of vision is limited on both sides by rounded white hills, that what is happening is not that she has lost sensibility in this area, but that the big pillow must be so soft that her head sinks softly into its hollow. It means that the white hills she perceives on each side must surely be the same big pillow or others around it. "Now, if I have been able to think this thing out," she concludes, "it means that I am not asleep. I was, a while ago, or maybe I woke up a long time ago. That's difficult to know without a watch." She imagines that if her bed has, as usual, a low railing at her feet, and a headboard that is taller, it would be possible to fix on it a structure like a small metal mast from which to hang a watch, exactly at the center of her field of vision. "And in order for it to hang, the watch must have a chain. A gold chain, like the one Arturo used to wear." Now she could see the watch clearly, and the white hills could easily be sand dunes. And so, in between the sand hills, two gossamer silhouettes, vaguely human, are advancing as if they were weightless shadows. One of them stops, while the other proceeds toward a green patch of sea. The one that stopped has Arturo's watch in his hand. When the small gold lid opens, it produces a metallic sound. "So this must have been Arturo," she says to herself, "unless I have fallen asleep."

Other times, by lowering her eyes as much as possible, she manages to see the upper part of a door. Then, looking up, she can still see the plaster moldings at the corner where the walls meet the ceiling. As far as she can see, the molding is an interminable succession of grapevines loaded with fruit, petrified up there. Upon opening her eyes, this is the very first thing she looks at. This way she can tell whether her body position has been changed while she was asleep. Because, upon waking, she always suffers an anguished vertigo: the moment her eyelids open, she is suddenly falling facedown toward the immense saline plain of the ceiling, over which she has been suspended. But she never experiences this anguish coming back from her memories.

Other times, she well knows what is going on. Though she might forget names, and certain blurred faces might confuse her, she finds herself trembling with affection, or at least, that is the way it feels. That is how affection felt. Even though now perhaps it is just the coldness of those evenings when the sun is suspended in its yellow hour so obliquely that she can barely see it. Then she knows that one season has followed another, and that this one is colder than the previous one. On those afternoons, her attic rack of a body writhes, making her hips ache like in the days when she still was a woman. She trembles. She keeps shivering until someone comes in the morning, and through the nebulous veil of her cataracts she sees a mirror held close, and she is made more comfortable and has her dry tears wiped, tears from an interminable night of sleepless stupor, not knowing who Arturo was.

Other times, she distracts her dead hours with the old vanity of sensing her body. And since she cannot move, she only recalls how it felt to make a fist, or with a little more concentration, she attempts to feel the bedsheets covering her bony knees. After playing this game for a long while, she no longer knows whether she has fallen asleep again, and therefore she dreams that she is really touching the wrinkled net of her dry stomach. Then, halfway in between the salty blank sky of the ceiling and the luminous warmth of her persistent siesta, it all becomes blurred. An enormous tin sign screams out a hotel's name: "Plaza Hotel," and while she believes she is touching her withered navel, that gets mixed up with another image. It must be that of Arturo, who incessantly opens and closes his pocket watch with the accompanying metallic ring of a xylophone note, and he dances with her to this, amid the rustle of flapping coattails, of starched shirts with mother-of-pearl buttons, and of the young ladies' billowy muslin gowns overflowing the marble staircase. Yes, it is Arturo at last, embracing her tightly while the waiters pop champagne corks and someone shouts "New Year," as if saying New century! or New eternity! A new eternity to live again . . . And Arturo hugs her and confuses her. She gets so confused that she no longer knows if her own flaccid breasts—those of an old mother, now unnecessary—are the same ones that surge firmly a century later, or if they belong to the other, the one still remaining in the fugitive region of her memory, whose bosom almost shows in the satin and velvet neckline as she dances and blushes in all shades when Arturo whispers sweet things in her ear, even though she cannot hear what he says because of the insistent starbursts of exploding fireworks. A blast of consecutive flashes brings her back to the knotty ruins of her body, dragged by a cascade of disappointments, while the other, the irretrievable one, keeps on dancing, her breasts up high, in the balcony of the Plaza: like the ballerina on a music box lid, bidding farewell to the old year, to the century, to eternity, dancing to the metallic quavers of Arturo's watch.

Other times she sees, on the salty plain of the ceiling, the reflections of clouds and traceries that come through the windowpanes when someone leaves the shutters partly open. Timid crisscrossings of shadows that announce the hours until all is dark, though her eyes still keep their anguished vigil over her creaking joints and uncontrollable sphincters which have gone slack. And then comes the horrified scream of an unfamiliar nurse: "She did it, she did it again!" And acrid vapors return her to the humiliation of diapers, to the quick alarm of infant diarrhea, to the great shame every morning at the smell of her own body.

Other times, people enter her room. They surround her, propping her up with pillows. An instinctive twitching of her lips reminds her that she should smile. To smile, which is almost as difficult as knowing who those people are, greeting her loudly in her ear, coming up to the static lightwell of her eyes, shaking their heads: "We'll all be getting there." And soon they disappear, leaving her in the same condition as before, without her being able to tell them to fetch from the wardrobe the Indian rosary that belonged to her great-uncle, "who was a bishop," and the silver comb to fix her thinned-out hair, "because it's been such a long time since I brushed it, and I used to give it a hundred strokes a night." They leave before she can ask them: who was Arturo? who are they? who is she herself? before they can give her an answer, a clue, before the night is back again. The night with its brutal puzzles of names, its impossible guessing games: how did it happen, when, where? Was it my son or perhaps my father? A man or a woman? Day or night? Did he exist, or have I only invented him?

Other times she is delirious. Defying the dim certainty of geometry, she finds herself on a bottomless prairie. The stealthy zigzag of a serpent warns her that she is in the realm of her feverishness.

And inside her fever is her husband, Arturo—now she knows it is he—galloping at the head of a stream of riders, just like that winter morning when he died. They are hunting an unreachable fox, lost in the tumult of time, multiplied by the countless visions of foxes in her dreams ever since. The fox gets closer, followed by Arturo, and finally he is coming, out of breath, to take refuge behind the bony wall of her forehead. Arturo and the stream of riders are approaching her, and it's no use warning them that she is there already, seeing them riding across that prairie and toward her eyes, as if she were watching them from above, at the edge of a table. It's no use, because the horses keep coming closer, driven forward by the carnivorous barking of the dogs, and they come galloping into her head, brushing their sweaty flanks against her parietals, exacerbating the humid pumpkin of her brain. Then Arturo's horse stumbles, rolls over him, and crushes him with a creaking of branches, leaving stamped on his temple a brilliant U from one of its hooves. Then silence, silence: there is only the hissing of the serpent.

But there will be another morning, an unrepeatable dawn when she will think she is hearing small shoes squeaking on the polished parquet floor. The little girl will walk around her room looking for a way to look into her knotted body. The little girl will come with anguish in her heart to see her grandmother. She will pull all her weight on the door handle, too high for her, and the door will open by itself. She will walk to the foot of the bed under the threat of the hatboxes and the frowning portraits, and then move closer to the side of the bed on tiptoe, until all of her six years can look into the lightwell of the eyes in the bald head. Her grandmother will finally wake up from the deep and see above her those gray eyes—just like her own had been—observing her with an entranced expression. Then, the plaster mask of her own face upon the pillows will contort, will smile. And for a vertiginous second, she will believe that the past centuries have been an illusion, that the sands of time are flowing back over her, that she sees herself in the girl's small face framed by curls, brought back to the time of seashells and chalky fingers. She will believe she is not the one crumpled on the bed but the one standing by the bedside, six years old, looking curiously at her grandmother. Even though this vision might last only a second, and the little girl who entered the forbidden room might run away frightened, wanting to play and live her life, to her this will be enough for eternity. It will be enough to make her smile by herself behind the lightwell of her eyes.

*Translated by Dolores M. Koch*

# Anna Kazumi Stahl
## (United States, b. 1963)

Anna Kazumi Stahl was born in Shreveport, Louisiana. Her life thus far seems an unparalleled experiment in the mixture of cultures: her Japanese mother had studied American (as well as French) literature in Kyoto, specializing in Southern drama and fiction; and her father, an architect born in the American South but of German extraction, had followed the path of Frank Lloyd Wright and twice visited Japan to study traditional forms of Japanese architecture. Struggling to find a balance between these strikingly different worlds, Kazumi Stahl escaped by reading books about the mysteries of the world: the Bermuda Triangle and other strange phenomena of the fantastic and the supernatural. At thirteen she began writing stories. Her fiction, she acknowledges, has more to do with the uncertainties of the real world, including the ambiguities of a Catholic schooling, "despite the atheism of my father and the Shinto Buddhism of my mother, which soon taught me there isn't always a solution for every conflict of values."

At sixteen, Kazumi Stahl went to live and study in Boston, and later traveled to Germany, a doorway to European culture and languages, "each of which appeared to offer a distinctive mode of living." When she returned to the States, she moved to California, eventually obtaining a doctorate in comparative literature. In 1988, a trip to Argentina occasioned by her studies proved to be a turning point in her life. She fell in love with its capital, its people, and its language. By 1995, she was permanently settled in Buenos Aires, teaching literature and composition at the university. She had also begun to write in Spanish, and within two years had her first collection of short stories, *Catástrofes naturales* (1997), published in Argentina. She is currently at work on a first novel, *La isla de los pinos*, as well as her own English version of *Natural Disasters*, from which the title story has been selected here.

# Natural Disasters

FORMER LIEUTENANT WILLIAM REILLY HELM: 1991

I'm looking at this hurricane here on the TV. We're seeing it wham into the state of Florida like the holy armed forces outta hell. Reminds me of that other one, rammed into us here, must have been thirty-five years ago. Yeah, that's right. It was 1955; turned New Orleans into a mud puddle. You wouldn't remember; you didn't know me yet. Not me and not this place either.

They called her Betsy. That was back in the days when they gave hurricanes ladies' names, which I think is how it ought to be. That one was called Betsy, and she came dancing into the Gulf like it was Circus Day. Came on slow, though, that's true. Let's say she was doing a kind of slow waltz, moving in the general direction of Texas, like the only thing she wanted to do was give it a little kiss. Looked like a regular tropical storm, dime a dozen that time of year, but she turned wicked when we didn't expect it. Gave us no warning. Flew in and ripped the coast right off of Louisiana, from Biloxi to Lake Charles. Like a messenger from the Devil himself, she made things a living hell all through these parts. Oh, Betsy was big and mean, I tell you. And she had a hundred tornados spinning round her, like a Scarlet O'Hara party dress, but with knives instead of lace.

Betsy tricked us. She waited 'til we were at our ease, sitting back thinking we could just relax and watch the rain fall. That was when she about-faced and came at us vicious as a rabid bitch. A full-on attack, 'fore we even had time to blink. Well, I'm exaggerating, of course. We had half a second to blink.

MRS. WILLIAM REILLY HELM: 1991

I've heard this story so many times already, and I still listen. I do it for him. There are certain things in a marriage you just have to go along with. Things that you find yourself participating in without ever really knowing why or what they're about, but you do it. He tells the "Betsy" story like it was so very important. He's told it a hundred times, and every time as if it was the first. I know he's got some reason for that.

THE HELM RESIDENCE, NEW ORLEANS: 1991

She indulges him, listening once again to the story he tells. Perhaps now, this time, she can feel a shade more involved because the television set is showing scenes of the chaos Hurricane Andrew leaves behind as it continues its path of destruction across the state of Florida. Perhaps it is because of the present storm's aggression that, this time, she listens more sincerely to the old story about Betsy. Or perhaps it is because there's a hint of anger in her husband's voice this time. Is there a hint of anger in his voice? Or is it anxiety? His voice sounds different today.

"Oh, goodness," she says, setting aside the needlepoint she had in her hands. She always puts that same phrase in at this point in his story, never questioning how mechanical her repetition of it is, never asking herself if he's ever noticed. After that first phrase, she echoes what he has said: "'Time to blink' and nothing else. Oh, goodness, that must have been so awful."

He shakes his head. His hair is steel-gray, clipped short and neat. The cord of a transistor radio's earphone jumps about erratically when he moves his head. She can't tell if he's making that gesture because of her or because of some storm information they've broadcast on the radio.

"That must have been so awful," she says again, this time lightly touching his arm.

"'Awful'?" he suddenly fires back, looking first at her and then at the television set. The screen shows mute images, live, from Miami. "No natural disaster is 'awful,' Marybeth," he says, "because you see it coming, and you just get yourself ready for it."

## SUE (SUMIKO) HELM: 1955

Dad already had his eye on Betsy from way before it got to the Gulf of Mexico. Seeing disasters happen was something he really liked, something he knew about because of the war. He got a medal for being heroic in the attack on Okinawa. A big five-point star, made out of bronze, with a red, white and blue ribbon on a pin. He said it was the only souvenir he had or wanted from over there. But Momma came from Japan, too. I guess he must have loved her a lot because he brought her all the way back with him.

But the thing that was still with him from those war days, I mean, what *really* mattered to him in the end was loving the noise and rush of an emergency and the fact that you have to keep your head straight under all that pressure. Disasters are big events in the world, and, if you're lucky, you can get a chance to participate. He specially liked *natural* ones, like fires or hurricanes, because they're the most exciting.

One night I heard him call me from the living room. I was in my room working like a slave on my multiplication tables, and I felt happy to get away from them. When I came into the living room, I saw the TV showing a radar screen with a white spot spreading out by the Gulf of Mexico. It was a storm, still out in the Atlantic but closing in on the Gulf. They called it a Tropical Disturbance.

"Look at that, making a mess outta Cuba," Dad said, smiling and picking his teeth with a whittled match. "Now it's slow, but you just wait, it's gonna be one of the big'uns. It's gonna come on into the Gulf and it's gonna be an *event*."

He said it like it was a racehorse or a Formula One car. I felt excitement and big expectations too. I wanted to know about it, real details like longitudes, latitudes, wind speeds, storm categories and all that. But then my momma's voice came from the kitchen—"*Benkyo wa? Owatta ka?*"—and I had to go back to the multiplication tables.

FORMER LIEUTENANT WILLIAM REILLY HELM: 1991
While she was still Tropical Storm Betsy, small potatoes, nobody thought much about her. She was just another one in a series of ten or twelve storms that kick up a little and then die right out. But when she upped her wind speeds and got named Hurricane Betsy—well, then she became a celebrity.

Hurricane season hadn't even officially started yet. It was just the beginning of June, clear skies, blue as a robin's egg. Hurricane Betsy was still twenty-two hundred kilometers out in the Atlantic, but everybody and his uncle was talking about her. On street corners, in the stores, the filling stations, all the small talk was Betsy this and Betsy that. And of course everybody had his little theory about was she going to come into the Gulf or was she going to whip into the Carolinas and what damage was she going to do.

"What damage" meant, to me, "what *fun*." We had everything we needed to protect ourselves. Hell, I even had enough time to spare to let my little girl help me with the preparations. She was about ten back then, and I thought it'd be a good idea for her to learn about these things.

SUE (SUMIKO) HELM: 1955

I wasn't scared of the hurricane coming at us. I was happy. For
one thing, I knew they'd shut the school for a while. But what
really got me happy and fired up was what Dad said. He said,
"We're gonna break that pony and ride her out!" That, to me,
sounded like Christmas and Disneyland all in one.

The rest of the folks in New Orleans, though, they were scared
all right. They wanted to get away running, specially from our
neighborhood. We lived in a "Mushroom Community." They call
them that because they spring up overnight, like mushrooms are
supposed to do. It was kind of far from downtown, out by the
lake, and it always got flooded. Our house was a prefab like the
rest, except ours was built up higher on an extra foundation. I had
to climb those extra stairs up to the porch every day, which I really
didn't like too much. But when a storm brought flooding, I found
out what kind of a lead we had on the other houses. That extra
foundation was my dad's idea. He's smarter than the rest.

FORMER LIEUTENANT WILLIAM REILLY HELM: 1955

There's always people who pack up and leave just as soon as a
hurricane shows up in the Gulf. "Just in case," is what they say.
That, and "It's a necessary precaution." But what they're really after is an extra vacation for free. Schools close down; nobody goes
to work. I-10 gets more tied up than on the Fourth of July. See,
more than being scared, people try to get something out of it for
themselves.

You will make note of the fact, Sue, that the Emergency Evacuation System of the State of Louisiana has *almost never* been
engaged. When was the last time this place was declared an Emergency Zone? I want you to keep one thing in mind: the governor
of this state has not sounded the alarm. We are going to ride her
out!"

SUE (SUMIKO) HELM: 1955

The first thing me and Dad did was to go to the filling station and pick up one of those maps of the Gulf they give out for free. It had an outline of the Gulf of Mexico in the middle and the Southern states and the longitude and latitude numbers printed in the margins.

When we got back to the house, Dad took out the transistor radio and put a new battery in, it didn't matter if the old one was still working or not. He plugged the earphone in and pushed it into his ear. That way he could always be hearing where Betsy was exactly, with the numbers they announced, and not lose any time sitting by the TV all day.

After he got hooked up like that, I wouldn't see him again without that little pink cord hanging from his ear, at least not until it was all over. He wouldn't be paying attention to anybody or anything else. I don't think he'd have let himself be distracted if somebody choked to death in front of him.

But I think my momma must have had a bad feeling about Betsy. In general, she kept to the sidelines of things, and this time she was even more like that than ever. She was walking back and forth, making faces, it seemed to me. She kept throwing looks at the TV and at us. But she didn't say anything; she just stood there, watching us, with her arms crossed.

After a while, Dad noticed it too, and he gave her a talking to. He said: "Yuki! You're just standing around doing nothing! Don't you realize what's going on here?"

She didn't say anything back.

And anyway, he was too fired up to be losing time with family complications.

"Let's go!" he shouted. "It's pre-season and we already got action! It's a surprise attack! But we're ready for it! Now. Yuki. You know what your duties are. Get the survival rations together: food, water. Go, go, go!"

It was all so exciting; the pink cord danced across his chest; he gave the orders and pointed at the living room and the entrance hall, designating areas for our rations. Then he turned to me: "Sue!" I stood up straight. "We're gonna secure this site!" He meant the house; we were gonna get it ready, get it "storm-proofed."

That included clearing the yard, taking down the swing set, covering all the windows with wide packaging tape and then nailing boards over them to protect them good. I was the assistant; I was in charge of the tape and the nails, I matched up the screws and bolts, made trips back to the shed for tools or whatever else we might have needed. Momma didn't participate. We didn't need her to. She would've just been in the way.

Outside, the air was thick and warm. My arms and legs felt heavy, but I didn't say anything and didn't let my dad know about it. He picked out a few tools, passed me a pair of pliers and a monkey wrench, and we got to work on the swing set. It was like a big dinosaur made of long rusty pipes. It creaked and groaned and didn't want to cooperate, but in the end it had to give. We knocked it over and took it apart. My hands got all orangey from the rust. My jeans got it on them too. But I didn't mind; I liked it. You could tell I'd been working for real.

Dad kept the earphone in his ear, and every now and then he pressed on it with a finger and covered his other ear with his free hand. He looked like Don Pardo (a game-show host) from TV. All of a sudden, he yelled out: "She's growing!" Obviously, he was talking about the hurricane. We grinned at each other. We couldn't have been happier.

Dad was keeping tabs on the storm's position with the map of the Gulf, so we were on top of Betsy one hundred percent. Every hour he put a little red dot where the longitude and latitude lines crossed. And every six hours, or every six little red dots, he drew in a little diagram too, like an eye with two little tails coming off the sides: the official symbol for "Hurricane." Later, he started writing in the date and the exact time, plus the wind speed, and so

Betsy was a little eye with just two lashes, and a long list of numbers on the side.

Around mid-morning, we took a break to watch the TV news. Now they had a whole lot to say about Betsy. They even had a map like the one Dad had, and they used it to explain, to all the people who weren't following her like we were, what was happening and where she seemed to be heading. The announcer said she was going to Brownsville, Texas. Then the screen showed a man on a street somewhere. I guess he was in Brownsville. He had a microphone, and he looked worried. He said people had already started evacuating so that nobody would be left in the path of the storm. After that, they showed how Cuba was: wrecked beaches with knocked-down trees all over the place, and one shot of a car turned over against the side of a building.

Later on, at noon, Dad and I came back inside again. We'd finished clearing the yard. We'd tied down the fence and the old oak, too, so they wouldn't fly away. The sky was getting darker, but everything was calm still. In fact, more than calm, it was like everything was turned off or unplugged. We were bushed and hungry, but we decided to eat as fast as we could and get right back out there, to keep working. We still had to tape and seal the windows.

But lunch was not on the table. It was twelve-something, and lunch wasn't ready. My mother, the one thing she could do right, was always get the meals out on time. That was "regulation" in our house.

Dad looked in the kitchen, but she wasn't there. He had to mark Betsy's twelve o'clock position, which meant writing out a bunch of numbers, besides making the little drawing. So he told me: "Go and find your goddamned momma." Then he said: "Tell her to get some sandwiches on this table now, *right now*! We ain't got time for this. Betsy's picking up speed."

"And"—suddenly he was shouting, with his finger pressing on

the radio plug in his ear—"we want to have this house like a safebox by fifteen-hundred hours today, you hear? You hear?"

"Yessir!" I said, stiffening up, and I went to look for Momma.

I found her in her bedroom. She was packing a suitcase. I yelled, "Momma! What do you think you're doing?" and she spun around taken by surprise. Her hair was coming loose, instead of being tied tight against her neck like usual. There were stray hairs floating around her head, like a cloud or like she had static electricity. I said: "Momma, Dad says you better get in the kitchen and put some sandwiches on the table *right now* because we are working real hard and we have to get back to work and there's nothing to eat and it is past twelve o'clock noon already!"

She started walking to the door in a hurry, but I got in her way. "Momma, you can just forget about that suitcase because, in case you didn't understand, we are going to ride Betsy out. That means: we're staying." She looked at me with an empty stare, and I couldn't tell if she understood or not. But it didn't matter anyway. The only thing that did was having lunch fast and getting back to work.

Dad was leaning over the map writing down the wind speed numbers when Momma passed him on her way to the kitchen.

"Where's your head, Yuki?" he asked her, irritated. "You know what time it is? Our priority is preparing for this event, and every one of us has his duty here."

He stood up then to confront her. "We cannot have you making us lose precious time waiting around for the meals." It was a threat. I could feel the command his height put on my mother, who was small. After a second or two, she walked past him silently and went into the kitchen. He got back to the map, touching the earphone a little to hear the transmission better.

"With the latitudes and these easterlies," he said a little softer, talking just for me, "Betsy's going to get to Brownsville all right, no doubt about it. And when she does, damn, it's going to be *big*!"

Then he laughed. I laughed too. And a few minutes later, Momma came in with a tray of ham and cheese sandwiches and two glasses of milk.

SUE (SUMIKO) HELM: 1991

I have a clipping from the *Times Picayune* a few years back. It's about a Japanese woman, Reiko Shimizu Warren, a "war bride," with a forty-five-year marriage to a former United States Army officer and forty-four years in this country. She walked into the Pacific Ocean wearing a kimono and carrying a small empty urn. I guess she meant to drown herself. But someone saw her and pulled her out alive. The newspaper article quotes a Dr. Harlow who says the woman's mental condition was "delicate," perhaps indicative of the early stages of Alzheimer's or a hormonal imbalance due to the onset of menopause. What he means to say is that she was crazy, and he's a doctor, and the reporter is a reporter, and so we're supposed to believe that she really was crazy. But I don't. I'd bet good money that she wasn't. I don't believe in explanations that simple in cases like this.

I put the clipping next to an aquarium I have with mollusks and oysters in it. Sometimes I sit by it and watch them for a while. Sometimes I see one move. They're fast when they move. They look like rocks, but suddenly one of them opens, you see a grayish-pink lip inside, moist, and then it skates sideways, like a strange and alien thing . . . which, actually, it is. After that, everything goes back to the way it was before, absolutely still.

SUE (SUMIKO) HELM: 1955

After lunch, we sealed the windows with tape and then we cut up some boards and nailed them over the frames. Dad shouted his orders to me, but the wind was getting stronger all the time and I almost couldn't hear him anymore. I could *see* him shout. His mouth stretched wide, and his eyes bugged out. His hair was every which way with the gusts; he looked like a cartoon of a guy who was losing his toupee. The pink cord to the earphone was dancing around like crazy.

"Framing hammer!" he shouted, leaning down to get down to my height. "Get—me—the—framing—hammer!"

I gave him the "okay" sign and ran to the shed.

The sky was the color of barbecue coals, ashy and gray, and looked low enough to touch. We worked for a good while, curving our backs against the wind, and later Dad signaled to me that it was time to go back in and mark the new storm position on the map. I followed him, both of us walking hunched over and clumsy, like we were walking underwater against a strong current. Inside again (and able to stand up straight again), Dad looked at the map, listened sharp to the reports on the radio coming into his earphone. After a little while, he put a new dot on the map with the red marker. The red dots were jumping huge distances now. Betsy was churning faster by the minute, doubling, tripling her wind speeds. The governor of Texas ordered out the National Guard. The president declared an Emergency Alert for the Gulf Coast states. On the TV, they showed a map, and I saw that we were included too.

"Look!" I said, "we're in the Emergency Alert."

Dad laughed and shouted at the screen: "Hey!! Thanks for the free publicity!"

Betsy was going for Brownsville, but we knew the lights and the water would be cut off in New Orleans too. Dad shouted for Momma, and she came out of the kitchen. She didn't look right to me; she was acting strange, too slow, not like usual where she was quiet but always doing stuff, cleaning or cooking or neatening up at a good pace. She came in and just stood there, stiff as a statue. Her body was different, like she was bigger or taller. Momma was different, but I was too busy with what was going on to be bothered with Momma or anything else.

"Food rations!" Dad hammered out the words. His voice was

booming, powerful. "Where you got them?" She just let her eyes lead us to the living room. There, like in some big display stand, she'd set up all the food, dozens and dozens of packages: cookies and crackers, cereal, dried fruit and peanuts, cans of tuna fish and sardines, hamburger buns and dinner rolls wrapped in cellophane, and about a ton of candy. She'd taken out all the food we had. It looked like enough to keep us alive for months. She even had water stored in pots and pans, set out neatly on the floor. I was amazed. But Dad, looking it all over, said: "There's no meat here. Where's the meat?"

She murmured: "*Niku ga nai*, but—"

Dad spun around to me, cutting her off. He put his hand on my shoulder and said, "Okay, partner, your mission is the following: take your mother to the grocery store and get meat, as much as you can. Wieners, deviled ham, whatever comes in a can. Got it?"

"Got it," I replied.

He'd forgotten that I hate going to the store with Momma. But it was an emergency, and I knew he needed to count on me. So, of course, I said yes.

Me and Momma went to the Dixie Market. It was two P.M., but it could have been nine at night. The wind was blowing pretty hard, and the clouds had piled up, making the sky look like some kind of gray paste. And the air was thick, sort of sticky. It wasn't raining yet, but it was going to soon enough, and how.

SUE (SUMIKO) HELM: 1991

That's what you feel at the beginning of a hurricane: the air for a whole month compressed into a single hour. And suddenly all that air is pressing on you, all around you. It makes it more difficult to move; it's harder to think. And at the same time, everything you can see is blowing around in the wind.

Also, you feel deaf. That's because the sound waves aren't traveling as well anymore. Right before the storm hits, the world is a completely silent place.

SUE (SUMIKO) HELM: 1955

The supermarket had all its lights on and the doors open, try-ing to say: "We're still in business!" But it was creepy-feeling in-side, like a bomb had gone off and killed all the people but left the other things. The cash registers were sitting there waiting for cus-tomers, the carts in single file waiting to be used, the aisles were lit up bright and the Muzak was on. But there wasn't a soul to be seen. It looked like a scary movie.

Even so, I took command of the situation. "Get a cart!" I told Momma, "top priority here is a cart." I started going up and down the aisles, but the more shelves I passed, I started figuring some-thing out: the store was open, but there wasn't any stuff left! It was emptier than a popped balloon.

The place looked messed with, ransacked by people in panic. The floor was covered with trash: crumbs, broken jars, pieces of glass. It looked like the aftereffects of a raid by starving thugs. Momma said: "*Senso mitai*, looks wartime."

"Don't talk Jap'nese in the store, Ma," I snapped, relieved at least that nobody was around to hear her. "Let's go," I went on, "there's nothing here. Let's go to the Piggly Wiggly."

She leaned down and started to look at the things lying around on the floor. I didn't know what she was doing, but it looked like one of those foreigner things she always did. My mother didn't have any idea of what it means to live in the United States of America. She kept on acting like she was still in Japan. She talked in Japanese, even in public places. She looked surprised when the phone rang. She saved everything, even old paper towels; she laid them out to dry and use again. You'd think that, after eleven years in a place, she'd have at least understood one or two basic things.

"Let's go," I said again, and raised my voice then, to sound more like Dad: "We're leaving *now.*"

But she wasn't listening to me. She was kneeling down in the middle of the aisle; she was stuffing her head under the bottom shelf. I felt an urge all of a sudden to kick her—she was a perfect target—but I didn't want any more weird reactions from her, so I went up to her and yanked at her blouse from behind.

"Momma," I said, gritting my teeth, "we're going to—"

"*Niku yo!*" she answered me back, pulling herself out from under the shelf. She was holding some cans, all covered in dust. Her eyes were shining, and I knew she was in the right, that we had to get meat, that that was our mission. I knew she was right, but I didn't want to let her know and then lose control of the situation.

"Good," I said, "very good. *Now*, can we pay and get out of here?"

She kept on rooting around under the grocery shelves, the whole length of the aisle. I felt my face going red, watching her grubbing around like a dog on that dirty floor. At least she did it fast, and in more or less good time we were on our way to the cash register with ten cans of Spam and a good bunch of littler cans of deviled ham.

In a hurry, I pushed our cart over to the register, somehow noticing that the music wasn't playing anymore, and then I realized my mother wasn't with me.

"Ma!" I shouted, going back with the cart to where she was, stopped in front of a big display stand of different state and regional maps. "What are you doing, Ma?! We have to get back and finish storm-proofing the house!"

She was concentrating, trying to read the labels that said what each map was for, what states were included, what highways. . . . It looked like she was trying to make a choice, but why? Why now? It was ridiculous, and just typical of her.

"Ma!" I yelled at her, really losing my patience at this point, "we do not need any maps. We know all the highways around here, and anyway, Ma, we have to leave the store *now*! Right *now*!"

Then, she turned a look on me that could've frozen the Devil in Hell. She'd never looked at me like that before. She didn't say anything, though. Just went back to examining the maps. So, I left her there, what could I do? I took the cart to the cash register, where Shirley was waiting to ring me up.

Shirley was the clerk who worked the most hours in that store. She was there from early morning to closing time at night, winter and summer, rain or shine. But she wasn't a very respected girl in our neighborhood. Everybody knew the reason she worked so hard like that was because she hadn't finished high school and had a baby but not even the hint of a father for it. An illegitimate child meant sinful behaving, and that kind of thing wasn't accepted in our community. But I had no prejudices.

When I got up to the counter, I said hi to Shirley and she told me hi too, all as usual, and I was hoping that maybe she hadn't noticed my mother groping on the floor back there.

"Bad storm coming," I said, smiling, showing her I wasn't scared of no hurricane.

Shirley looked at me with her eyes sort of squinting down all of a sudden. She thought I wasn't up to such a serious situation, and she said to me with her eyes narrowed and her head way high: "It's a *hurricane*, honey."

"I know, I know," I clipped back, and gave a couple laughs, to sort of lighten up the conversation. But then Momma came up and distracted me with three of those stupid maps, "Louisiana," "The Southeast," and "The Atlantic Seaboard." It didn't make any sense at all to buy those maps, but it was too late to have it out with her over it and make a scene in front of Shirley.

I mumbled, "Okay, okay," and put them with the cans and shoved the whole pile toward the register.

I couldn't wait to get out of there. That is, not until I actually did. The air was dead. No oxygen. Like air in outer space. Momma pulled up short when it hit us. The time was about two-thirty; the air was dense and weighted down. We stuffed the grocery bags in the trunk and got into the car. I had the feeling something was going wrong. Something in the sky, in the air, in that darkness all around.

On the way back home, I noticed that the lights were off in all the houses. There wasn't a single car parked on our street. They'd all gone away. The neighborhood looked like a ghost town. Our house was the only one with lights on; the windows were just barely lit with a bright outline around the boards nailed on the frames. It was a funny, small brightness.

Dad had finished boarding up the last window. He came up to us with a big smile, and yelled (the volume in the earphone was on high): *"How's it look, huh? Great! Right?"*

Momma went right over to put the new rations in place. I looked at the windows. They were sealed and covered with planks, and he'd even put sealant around the edges, just in case. Inside the house, it was like being in a fishbowl, and our voices even sounded different. We had top-notch protection now, but that fishbowl feeling affected me and I felt suffocated, I needed to get out, breathe some fresh air. All of a sudden, I was scared.

I said, "Dad . . . ," but he didn't hear me. His hand pounded me on the back. He was saying: "The only thing left is securing the barbecue pit bricks I got piled outside. And sealing the doors." Then he grinned at me: "And—that's it! *Let Her Rip!!*"

He kept on talking, revved up with the thrill. I couldn't get into it, though. I felt far away and jittery. I made myself follow his voice to try to get back into the gig. He was saying: "When they cut the juice and we don't have the TV, we'll still be tracking her on the map. It's going to be beautiful; her winds are already up to ninety miles an hour. Hoo-ee! She's gonna make mashed potatoes outta Brownsville!" Then he leaned over to talk right into my ear. He told me: "This what you're looking at here is History, kid. You paying attention?"

I murmured, "Yeah, yeah . . ." Then I forced my voice and said it big: *"Yes!"* and finally, when I said it like that, I started to feel my strength come back. "Get the twine, partner," he said, "we have to secure those bricks." I was one hundred percent again and concentrating. I skipped over to the hall closet, where we kept the twine and string and different ribbons and stuff. Dad went out to the patio. His footsteps made an echo in the house. I followed right after—happy to be getting out of the fishbowl—but then, I confronted something even worse: a belly-low sky, ugly, and a funky, whirling wind.

We started tying down the loose bricks with the packaging twine, but the gusts were so strong now that they were knocking me off balance. I was dancing around like the radio cord hanging out of my dad's ear. I saw him saying something to me, but I couldn't hear. I shouted back to tell him, but the wind erased my voice too. I started panicking again. I wanted to go back inside. Dad had put a ball of twine in my hands and was giving me signals to unwind it while he worked. So I stayed out there, leading out twine that was whipping around, crazy in the pitch dark when it was only four o'clock in the afternoon.

The shed was full of wood boards and tools. We had to tie the bricks to the garage railing, which was made of metal. The bricks were orange, and every one of them had three holes in a row down the middle. Dad passed the end of the twine through the holes and then knotted it to the railing. He added a fisherman's knot at the end, every time. After a few, he taught me how to do it, and making the knots gave me some confidence again.

We'd gotten a pretty good rhythm up, 'til we ran out of twine. Dad had already given up on shouting. He pointed at the empty spool and made signals for me to go get more from the house. I ran, but it was like I was floating, spinning around without meaning to. When I came through the door, my lungs filled up with air like it was injected, and I had a coughing fit.

I tried to keep calm and walked slowly over to the closet. Passing the kitchen, I saw Momma leaning over something she'd spread across the table. When I looked closer, I realized it was those maps she'd picked out at the Dixie Market.

"Aha!" I thought and instantly felt angry. "She still thinks we're going to jump ship. We should let her go outside, see how much she likes it out there with Betsy instead of all safe and protected in here."

"Ma!" I broke in loud as I could. She was concentrating, but she did look up. The expression she gave me was blank. I was fixing to really let her have it, but then I heard the back door close with a thud. Dad came charging in full-speed like a Mack truck. He was yelling curse words and pushed me out of the way.

Betsy had switched directions. Now she was heading northwest at faster than 190 miles an hour. She was coming for us. Then it was *our* governor who called out the National Guard. The official statement came on the TV: "We are implementing the Emergency Evacuation System. The immediate evacuation of all residents of the Southern coastal area is hereby declared mandatory." When Dad came running in, the earphone cord fell out of his ear. It was hanging over his shoulder now. The alarm whined out of it: "Eeeeeeeeeee," echoing in the sealed-up house.

Dad's voice echoed too and bounced booming off the walls: "The rations! The rations! Get the rations!" I rushed over to grab crackers, cans and whatever I could carry. Momma stayed by her maps. Wasn't it getting out that she'd wanted in the first place? But she didn't raise a finger, just left us to run back and forth, trying to cope with the new scenario. Then suddenly she walked into the bedroom, came right back out again with a suitcase—the one I'd seen her packing before. Dad didn't like that at all.

"What's that?" he asked her, sounding real ticked off. He tried to take it away from her, but she held on with all her might, and I watched them face off over it: he, big and burly, and she, ahold of the handle with her fists tight and white-knuckled. Finally, Dad turned and gave me a shove toward the door. Then he pushed Momma in the same direction, but when she got past the door, he yanked that suitcase back from behind. She stumbled, tried to get it again, but he had already thrown it behind him, into the front hall, and shut the door. He was fixing to seal it up good with the caulking gun in his hand.

Momma wanted to open the house again and get it back, but Dad wouldn't let her. She started shoving and then scratching at him, like she could make him disappear that way. He had to struggle with her on his back to finish sealing the door. That was when I dropped my bag of rations and ran up the steps to help him. I saw my mother's hand waving around in the darkness, so I grabbed it and pulled. Momma stopped all her fighting and followed right after me like a pet animal. That scared me at first because I thought it was a trick, but it wasn't. She was following me, and I felt her hand, how hot it was, too hot, and moist.

When we got to the car, Dad was already right on our heels. The rain started coming down in big, fat drops that felt heavy. The wind was throwing leaves and twigs around every which way. In the dark, something small and hard hit me, but I couldn't see what it was. Dad pushed me into the car and shut the door. Momma was sitting up front, very still. I could see her head and there were strands of hair sticking up all over the place like a crazy person's. Dad gunned the engine and pressed the gas; we jerked forward a ways, but then the engine died. He started it again, floored it this time, and we pulled out of there like a rocket.

There wasn't another car in sight. I wondered if we were the very last ones to be leaving. I felt like we were people in a movie, the last survivors, at high risk and being heroic. The car bucked against the wind and rain to keep straight. Dad seemed lost; we took a bunch of different streets but seemed to just go in circles. We couldn't find the highway. Then, before we got to I-10, the wind changed. The rain had been falling pretty hard, but now, all of a sudden, it came down in a single mass. The wipers were on maximum, but the windshield looked like boiling water. Dad was cursing nonstop. The car was creeping forward. We couldn't see the road anymore.

Suddenly, there was a knock on the window, on the driver's side. Dad looked, but it was impossible to see past the glass. He rolled down the window a little, and there was a policeman standing there, right next to our car. The rain whooshed inside the cabin. I saw the policeman's yellow raincoat whipping around his legs. He handed my dad a piece of paper, soaked through, and leaned in to shout over the noise of the storm: "Too late! Go back!"

Dad threw the paper to me in the back and put the car in reverse. The engine made an awful noise and we wrenched back a few feet. We inched our way down the highway on-ramp. On the soaked piece of paper, I read off out loud the names and addresses of the Civil Defense Shelter Sites in our area. Dad drove us to the closest one: it was the Carmelite nuns' Catholic high school.

We left the car in a parking garage by the school, then we ran through the pounding rain to the door that had a big yellow-and-black sign on it, the symbol for nuclear bomb shelters. The door was made of wood and looked too small and flimsy to offer any kind of protection from anything. But we went down a set of metal stairs and came to other doors, which the nuns opened for us, huge doors, and heavy because they were lined with lead. And so we went in, and the nuns closed the shelter doors behind us, leaving Betsy and the mayhem on the other side.

SUE (SUMIKO) HELM: 1991

I remember that shelter; it was the basement at a Catholic school. Actually, New Orleans doesn't have any basements, but this was a high-tech addition: specially designed to protect the populace against hurricanes, and then later reinforced to withstand the Bomb.

SUE (SUMIKO) HELM: 1955

When we got inside there, the people from the Red Cross and the nuns had already been handing out blankets for hours. But there were still enough cots left and a ton of cookies and hot drinks. Dad was in a bad mood and grumbling. I got kind of critical too. The whole place smelled like mothballs and mold. The blankets must have been rotting in storage since the last big storm or flood.

And it was dark in there. There was only one light on, over in the farthest away corner, by the bathrooms. In the whole room, which was the size of a gymnasium, I couldn't hardly see anything, just these big bundles grouped together. Later I realized it was the people, lying on their cots.

After a while, I noticed the cots' springs were squeaking; it was almost a kind of music except it didn't have a rhythm or a melody. Nobody was sleeping good that night. There was a chrome counter against the back wall, and it had a little red light on it, one small fixed point in the dark. It was part of a big coffeemaker, the kind they use for school fairs. The red light meant "Ready."

An older nun gave us our cot assignments and our blankets. Her hands were shaking. At the time I thought it was because of being scared, but later I found out she had something called Parkinson's disease. So then I felt glad I didn't touch her myself. She had handed our blankets over to my momma.

Our cots were in a row by the coffee machine. Momma made the beds, and then, without saying a word, not good night, not nothing, she lay down and went to sleep.

Dad stayed up, smoking. I didn't feel sleepy either. I tried to make some conversation, but I guess he was in a real bad mood and that was why he wasn't talking. The transistor radio couldn't pick anything up from inside the shelter. After switching it off, he just sat there on the edge of his cot. From time to time he looked over at Momma, who was just one more bundle among the rest of the shadowy, sleeping shapes.

I knew there was something sort of complicated behind Dad's mood, and I didn't have trouble figuring out it had to do with the way Momma had messed with things and fought him when we were leaving the house. All because of that stupid suitcase. It made me real mad, the way she could turn every little thing into a problem, and, that night in the shelter, I really wished she would go somewhere else, anywhere, back to Japan, or to Canada, or France, I didn't care where, until finally I fell asleep.

When I woke up, the shelter was exactly the same as before, except now the people were moving around. I could make out Dad sitting on the edge of his cot still, his body propped up against the wall. His head was leaning sideways, and I could tell he was so deep asleep that even that weird position didn't bother him. I hurried up to fix him a cup of coffee, just the way he likes it. I brought it to him, put it right under his nose so he could wake up to the good smell. Since he wasn't reacting, I had to say: "Dad, Dad" to get him to open his eyes.

He woke up with a start and sat up so sudden that I almost spilled the coffee all over him. He stretched and then downed the coffee in one shot. That made it look like he was back to normal. He started looking around, and said to me: "Jesus, is it day or night in here? When do we get let out?"

That was what I wanted to know too, and I started looking around for the nuns or the Red Cross people to ask them. That was when Dad looked at the third of our cots. It was all made up neat; it even had the corner of the sheets turned down like they do in hotels. He stared at it for a second, and I watched him do that. Then he swung around all of a sudden and shouted where the hell had the people gone to. I don't know why he didn't just think my mother was in the bathroom or something.

The volunteers from the Red Cross told him to keep his voice down, there were people who were still asleep. One of them came over and whispered to us: "People started leaving at six this morning, sir, when the governor gave the authorization." It was already past nine.

Dad grabbed my arm and dragged me through the lead-lined doors and up the metal stairs. I couldn't go as fast as him, I fell and banged my knee pretty bad, and he acted real mad, like I was dragging him down. When we got outside, I couldn't believe what I saw: the sky was clear, a pretty blue, and the air was light and fresh. Dad yelled at me to get over to the car, and we actually ran the rest of the way to the garage. The car was there, in the same place he'd left it, but he checked it inside and out anyway, even inspected the engine. Everything checked out. I didn't understand what he was doing or why. I started to ask him about it, and also where was Momma, but he cut me off, saying: "Get in."

We drove back to the house. The streets were littered with junk, all kinds and scattered everywhere: kettles, bricks, pieces of books, loose boards, wall clocks, picture frames, pots, window handles, tiles, jars, bicycle pedals, a little plastic soldier. When we got there, Dad sprinted up to the door, taking the steps in one jump. I tripped but followed after him, running too. When I caught up, he was staring at the door. It was closed, but the seal was broke; it had been peeled away from the edges of the door frame, real neat, and was lying in a coil on the porch.

Dad reached out for the handle and turned it. Everything seemed to be happening in slow motion. Even the door, the way it swung open, seemed delayed. We stepped inside. The air in the house had gone bad and smelled plasticky, like an old balloon. The entrance hall was empty.

"It's not here," I heard him say, and then I remembered the suitcase. It wasn't where he'd thrown it when we'd left.

Dad started going through the rooms, inspecting everything piece by piece. I knocked something over, but kept right behind him. I was scared. Not because I didn't know where my momma was, but because I'd never seen my dad act like that. He looked deep and hard at everything, checking the position of all the objects, scrutinizing them, just like he'd done with the car. The last room was their bedroom, and everything in there looked just like normal.

He went to the closet and yanked one of the doors open like he was going to find somebody hiding in there. I happened to be standing right behind him; I saw his suits hanging up, all in a line, and his old uniform next to them, in a clear plastic bag, everything as usual. After his suits, there was the special hanger with his ties on it, and then his one dozen starched white shirts. Underneath the hanging stuff, I saw his shoes lined up, all like usual too, and the shoe-shine kit behind them. From where I was standing I could catch sight of the other end of the closet, too, but it was just a long row of hangers, hanging there empty.

I didn't see Dad's face, but I heard him make a sort of grunting noise. I didn't quite know what that sound really meant, but it set off an instant exhilaration inside me. I suddenly felt lighter than air: I could be free forever—she was gone!

I felt like grabbing hold of my daddy's hands and saying something. I took a couple steps around the side of him, so I could smile in his face, but he just then turned around to leave the room. I went after him, still feeling that big emotion, feeling dizzy and high on my new freedom. I wanted to say to him: "Well hey, Dad, that's it then, right? Now we're on our own! How do you like that?" But the only thing I got out was "Well hey, Dad . . ." and a cramp gnarled up my stomach, the muscles in there did a whirlwind, and I threw up.

FORMER LIEUTENANT WILLIAM REILLY HELM: 1991

I have never seen such bullshit strategic planning. The very idea of sounding the alarm that late in the game, making people head out with the storm on top of them already. That kind of thing, you just do not do.

THE HELM RESIDENCE, NEW ORLEANS: 1991

The former lieutenant falls silent. His wife picks up her needlepoint again and carefully sews in a green dot to start a wreath of holly leaves on pillow covers for next Christmas. She now asks, for the hundredth time, as she threads a lighter green on her needle: "And that was when your first wife went missing then, honey?"

He suddenly looks at her as if he didn't know her. Then he turns back to the TV screen. "Yeah," he answers. "Poor thing. Betsy took her."

Marybeth Helm repeats his phrase, more softly though: "Poor thing," and she knows now, by rote, that it's over with. Until the next time he needs to tell the story.

SUE (SUMIKO) HELM: 1991

Reiko Shimizu Warren was retrieved from the ocean off the Santa Monica coast. The facts are: forty-five years of marriage, forty-four years in the USA. Her life must have been very similar to my mother's. She'd have married young, to an officer of the enemy army, one of those triumphant Americans who occupied Japan after the Unconditional Surrender. She'd have escaped her world that way. A world of hunger and pain, exchanged it for another one, far away and full of victory. She'd never go hungry again. But there'd have been a different hunger, a secret yearning that possessed her, without her being able to name or satisfy it.

Where is my mother? I do not know. It isn't something I can know.

The newspaper clipping is by the steel-gray aquarium my stepmother gave me in 1957, trying to make friends. She thought having fish would be nice, but I picked oysters and mollusks instead. And for all these years I've made sure there were always some alive in there.

They're in the bottom of the tank, opaque, immobile, my colony of stones that contain secrets. Tomorrow I'll change the water and put in the antifungal drops. I like the antifungal solution: it's dark blue, a denser liquid than water, and it makes whorling designs as it sinks. It'll float and fall through the water alongside the article about Reiko Shimizu Warren. It'll fall and whirl, like liquid smoke, like milk in black tea.

I think to myself, this is what I can do; this is what I will care for, storm or no storm. I have a kind of shelter here.

# Federico Andahazi
## (Argentina, b. 1963)

Federico Andahazi was born in Buenos Aires, the son of an artist and a psychologist. As an adolescent he began composing verses and soon developed such a passion for writing that, even after taking a degree in psychology at the University of Buenos Aires, he continued perfecting his craft while pursuing his career as a psychologist. Finally, in 1995, he achieved sudden fame by winning three simultaneous first prizes in Argentina: one from the Concurso Desde la Gente, organized by the Instituto Movilizador de Fondos Cooperativos (for his story "The Sleep of the Just"); and two others—for a single story and for an entire collection—from the Concurso Buenos Artes Joven II, sponsored by the Federación Universitaria de Buenos Aires. Three of these prize-winning stories were eventually collected in *El árbol de las tentaciones* (1998).

In the meantime, fame soon erupted into scandal. In 1996 the jury of the Fortabat Foundation's Joven Literatura Prize, made up of four prestigious Argentinian authors, unanimously awarded Andahazi the prize for his first novel, *The Anatomist*. After reading the manuscript, however, Amalia Lacroze de Fortabat, president of the foundation, rejected her own jury's decision and suspended the award ceremony, refusing to honor a work that, in her words, "does not contribute to exalting the highest values of society." The story of sixteenth-century Italian physician Mateo Colombo and his ill-conceived passion for a Venetian courtesan, the novel became an international sensation when published the following year, and has since been translated into over twenty languages.

In 1998, Andahazi published *The Merciful Women*, a droll, decidedly vampirish tale of Byron's intimate circle, exploring the unfathomable mystery of their creative powers. This was followed two years later by *El príncipe*, a political allegory on the absurdity of all charismatic power, whether democratically achieved or autocratically imposed. Andahazi lives in Argentina, where he continues his professional practice while completing a new novel about the murderous rivalry between two Renaissance masters of the Flemish and Florentine schools of painting: *El secreto de los flamencos*.

# The Sleep of the Just

It was the same year that Confederation troops converted General Eusebio Pontevedra into a rosary in Toba Indian style, braided with the skin they pulled off his back and strung with the yellow beads of his teeth; the same year that the forces of the United Provinces decapitated Colonel Valladares and fought over the trophy of his head—still grimacing—in a game of kick ball. That very same year, on the feast of Saint Simon—the patron saint of commissioned officers—my lieutenant put me in charge of the transfer of a female prisoner from the barracks at Quinta de Medio to a particularly faraway mountain on the other side of the border, where she was to be shot and buried by a servant.

"She's in your charge and she's your responsibility," is how Severino Sosa, my lieutenant, put it to me when he handed me a rifle and a shovel, while a detail of four soldiers led the captive to the barracks' front gate.

The prisoner was an old woman, a tiny speck of humanity made of skin and bones. She had a light red blush on her nose that seemed to be her only vital sign, along with a sharp sense of pride, the same chilly countenance that gringos have. She acted elegantly resigned to the rope tied around her wrists, sitting bareback on one of a group of square-shouldered percherons, which was a lot of beast for so little rider.

Severino Sosa had personally planned and carried out the capture of Mary Jane Spencer, an Englishwoman married to a cabinet member from the other side. The aim of the operation was to negotiate the exchange of prisoners and to force the occupying troops to capitulate. At the same time, my lieutenant hoped by these means to obtain his well-deserved elevation to colonel and to receive the recognition of our commander in chief, Comandante Libardo de Anchorena.

Nevertheless, something had gone wrong. I heard from the mouth of a certain colonel that the captive Mary Jane Spencer wasn't Mary Jane Spencer but as it turned out Miss Sinead O'Hara; that she wasn't an Englishwoman but Irish; that she wasn't the wife of one of the enemy's cabinet ministers but the grandmother of a highly regarded military man; that she hadn't been kidnapped from the minister's house but instead Severino Sosa had mistakenly barged into Comandante Libardo de Anchorena's house, at that time commander in chief of all divisions of our army and by chance the neighbor of the occupation minister.

My lieutenant was in trouble, not just because there were no prisoners whose release we could negotiate, but also because we had no way to force the occupation troops to hoist the white flag; he had kidnapped, plain and simple, the comandante's venerable grandmother; on my mother's life, were I a believer I would have sought the protection of Santa Lucrecia, who protects soldiers from the wrath of their superiors. For a much lesser offense, the comandante had ordered the deceased Sergeant Obregozo flayed alive—may God keep him at his right hand—and so as to kill him a second time, ordered him decapitated.

Severino Sosa passed the hours puffing on his Meerschaum, pacing back and forth like a captive tiger. "What for shit's sake is the point of having a brain if those imbeciles are just going to walk into any house whatsoever and bite at the first thing that crosses their path?" He was bellowing and pointing at us with his rosewood cane. "What the fuck are we going to do with granny now?" Shouting like a hyena, my sorry lieutenant had no idea how to disentangle himself from the heavy weight of his guilt, and more important, how to free himself from the urgency of the matter at hand: the next day, Comandante Libardo de Anchorena—who had sworn he was going to skin the miserable abductors of his precious grandmother alive—was arriving to review troops and personally inspect the barracks.

Around daybreak and without having slept a wink, Severino Sosa called me to his study.

"Get the gringa out of here," he ordered me, without any further instructions.

"And where am I going to take her, Lieutenant?" I remember asking him before his hand gripped his scabbard, and, red as a chili, he chased me from the room at the point of his cutlass.

"Kill her. Take her far away and kill her," he ordered me before he disappeared on the other side of the door.

I set out with the captive before the sun was fully up. We rode in silence. It was beneath the gringa even to take a look at me. I must confess that it broke my heart to see her tied up like a sheep. Before we reached the frontier I dismounted and untied her hands. But the old lady didn't take her eyes off a place beyond the horizon.

"Do you want some water?" I asked her as I held out a pouch that still held some fresh water. But she didn't even have the decorum to turn her face toward me. God alone knows how her indifference tormented me.

Around noontime we stopped near the edge of Laguna del Medio. The old lady showed no signs of fatigue, or hunger, or thirst or tedium, not even fear of the death that would soon be upon her. Her pride was as great as my shame. The little mountain that gave birth to the lake was a good enough place, I told myself. I picked her up in my arms, lowered her from the horse and set her down on the dark sand. The old lady didn't move. I was going to load the rifle but it seemed too much for such a tiny figure. I unsheathed the dagger and without letting her see it, calculated the force of the blow to her heart. If only she had insulted me. If only she had given me the tiniest reason, an excuse. . . . But there was nothing, the old lady was like a defenseless lamb and at the same time so arrogant. No. I couldn't do it. I walked over to the saddle on my horse and gave myself a shot of courage from the wine that I had in another canteen. Only then could I see that the gringa was staring at the thin red stream that fell from the hilltop, her eyes full of an unending anxiety while the sides of her nose dilated as if they had just smelled the sweetest scent in the world. I handed her the drinking pouch like someone granting a last wish. The old lady moved a little closer and with the brute force of a bear taking a swipe with his paw, with the invisible quickness of a frog's tongue, she slapped me; then I watched, dazed, as those twisted and enfeebled fingers pressed the skin of the pouch like two boas pouncing on their prey. In one great gulp the gringa had drained the pouch to the last drop. She let loose with an earthy belch, sat back down, and for the first time, looked at me; she looked at me with the sweetest and most thankful eyes, in a way no one had ever looked at me before. She was utterly smashed, and seeing her as I saw her then, I knew that just so, as drunk as a barrel, this was how she made her sober arrangements with the things of this world; just so, with the material drawn from the heavy fumes buried inside the casks of whiskey, out of that same substance that the Irish spirit was made. Seeing her as I saw her then I knew beyond the shadow of a doubt that I couldn't kill her. The gringa, gently stretched out on her scaffold, sang the sweetest song ever sung; she sang in such a free and faraway language that you would say it wasn't from this world. Just so, with her eyes closed while she was whispering, she carried me to a place between the crucifix which hung between her neck and her breast and just so, beneath the warm wing of her hand resting on my cheek, like that, in the sleep of the just, that's how I slept. I slept for I don't know how long. I slept as if sleeping were something new, something I had never known until then.

We awoke fugitives. Before the sun came out from behind the mountain, we had walked around the lagoon in the direction of the muddy border where Quinta del Medio meets Paso de los Monjes. The gringa led her horse by the muzzle, and it passes understanding how such a pile of flesh gave in so easily to the will of that tiny, stooped woman; I, for my part, had to struggle with my horse, who made life difficult, as he had a fondness for wandering off the path.

Night had fallen when we reached the other side of the frontier; only then did we understand that we didn't know where to go. Stretching them as far as we could, we only had a day's supplies: a little beef jerky, some biscuits, and a drop of wine. We headed, who knows why, to the north. It wasn't fear that drove me, nor the memory of the late colonel Paredes, the deserter who'd been used to send a message, my lieutenant having hanged him with his head below—only in a manner of speaking because the colonel had already been decapitated—so that it was clear what was done to those who took off; no, it wasn't fear that motivated me, but the sweet whisper of the gringa as she sang, her hands that caressed the horse's neck as he followed gently and blindly; I wasn't full of cowardice but the conviction that I would never be separated from that woman, because, and I knew it, between the crucifix and her breast, underneath the warm wing of her hand, no evil could come to me in this world. If I'd had a house, I would have taken her there, but I never had any shelter other than army barracks, no other family than my fellow soldiers, no Federation, no Union, no other country than the saddle on my horse.

By dawn we were already out of beef jerky, biscuits, and wine.

We had to go into Paso de los Monjes. My uniform revealed me as much as any prisoner's garb. The perfume of roast lamb floated out from the settlement and I could see how bright the gringa's eyes got when the cook, standing in front of the golden Christ of the crucified animal, lifted a bottle of grappa to his lips. I had to grab her by the arm. I had too much pride to beg, but not enough courage to go and rob them. Our mouths were watering. I took off my jacket, belt and bandolier; I left my cutlass, my dagger, and my pistol and told the gringa to wait for me. "Wait here," I said to her, "I'll be right back." I crossed myself and came out from the underbrush without my clothes, my heart in my mouth. They were fearful-looking men.

"On your own and down on your paws, my friend?" The cook was wary of me without raising his eyes from the blade of the knife that turned around and around on the spit like a threat.

"As you see, this is it," I said, and I held my pack out toward him.

"Nobody denies food to a Christian," said another man who came out from the hut, "but why don't you stay to eat with us? Do we look like lepers to you, boy?"

"At least he's not traveling alone," broke in a fat man who was picking his teeth with a knife and who came out from behind the other one.

"Who knows," said the man at the spit.

"Who knows," agreed the third man.

Judging by the dissimilar brands on the flanks of the horses grazing in the clearing, the men were horse thieves. I could see they knew something and were trying to draw me out. These guys were capable of selling their mothers. I could see how the other two were whispering among themselves and looking up the hill with their hands shading their eyes. Then it hit me that they knew everything and were searching for the gringa, who clearly had a good price on her head. I turned on my heels and sped off. I felt a fire in my arm—they'd shot me. When I came to, the three were standing over me. "Where did the old lady go, you son of a bitch?" They were shouting and drawing the knife across my throat. "Pull on his tongue until he speaks, brother." They dragged me by the hairs on the back of my head. "Where did the old lady go, you piece of·shit?" I thought I had died when I no longer felt anything. I opened my eyes and could see all three were looking in the same direction, their mouths open. Standing near the clearing, as bent over as a willow tree, as wrinkled as a raisin and defenseless as a lamb, there was the gringa. They dropped me like an old mop. I was about to start running when I saw the old lady take her hands out from behind her back, and, before they could take a step, raising the pistol that she had gotten out of my cartridge box, she shot the fat guy between the eyes. "The old lady is full of shit," the second one was going to say, but he couldn't end the sentence: she'd already hit him in the heart. The gringa had the aim of a marksman. The third took off down the road. Only then did she blow on the mouth of the barrel and lower the pistol, walk over to the table, drink the bottle of grappa in one swallow, tear off a piece from the shirt of the fat man who was floating in a pool of blood, come over to me, wrap my arm in a tourniquet and, making room for me between the crucifix and her breast, kiss me on the forehead.

We ate.

We left Paso de los Monjes at night—horse thieves and fugitives—taking more livestock with us. We continued heading north, who knows why, driven by the same unwavering will that governs compasses. The gringa rode in silence; you could see that with every step, as we crossed the countryside, my prisoner, in the same measure, was stripping away a punishment as old as it was secret, a grief that could be called octogenarian, as vast as the ocean that separated her from her Celtic roots.

In Trinidad de los Arroyos we sold the livestock at a good price. In La Caleta we robbed a warehouse; in Corcovado, we fled from soldiers who were just about to grab us; in El Casado we had a wrangle with highway robbers—a question of jurisdiction—and may God forgive us, no one has seen them since. And that's how it was, absolutely fugitives, and almost without wanting to, in Belen de las Palmas we robbed the Caridad Bank. The gringa aimed and, "Holy shit, look at that shot, pal, the old lady fires like a marksman. Please fill up the bag so we can leave quickly, and don't forget the coins, buddy." There was never a question that Granny would get nervous.

In Maderos we woke up rich and famous. There was nothing else for us to do but move on, keep going, always ahead, always heading north. And so we went; mornings we rode in the fresh air until we arrived at a town and then, "Put everything in the bag and don't play the hero, pal, you could piss the old lady off." And like that we rode until night fell and the gringa made room for me between the crucifix and her breast and so, with sweet whispers and the warm wing of her hand, I slept. I didn't want anything more than that from this life.

It was the feast of San Ramón Nonato—the saint that novices pray to, to have fresh milk and plenty of it. That morning, as she always did, the gringa stopped to read her fortune in the veins of the trunk of a poplar tree. As always, she said nothing. She looked at me and tried to smile. But something gloomy was written there. A calm and patient rain fell.

The gringa didn't take her gaze off the horizon. About noon we heard the hoofs of countless horses. We rode in single file by the side of the mountains. Coming up to the edge of a large brook we could see, on the other side, a formation of no less than twenty soldiers: my comrades. I saw Pereyra and my friend Lauge, the Indian Almada and Cirio Rivera. They were aiming at us. We both spurred our horses at the same moment and took off at a gallop in the opposite direction. We reached a stand of pine trees that happened to be in front of us: on the other side, at the crossroads, twenty other horsemen came out in front of us. At the head of the troop was my lieutenant, waving his cutlass in the air.

Forty rifles fired but it was like a single shot. Stretched out at the foot of the percheron, torn to pieces and bent over like a small willow tree, the gringa seemed to be looking at me. I dismounted and walked over to her, so that I could remain inside the sweet sleep of the just between the crucifix and her breast, beneath the still warm wing of her hand, where nothing, not death—which today awaits me—can do me harm.

*Translated by James Graham*

# Ernesto Mestre-Reed
## (Cuba, b. 1964)

Ernesto Mestre-Reed was born in Guantánamo, Cuba, the second of five sons from a devout middle-class family. His father, a doctor, and his mother, a teacher who turned to raising their children, were "at first very nonchalant about the success of the Revolution," Mestre-Reed recalls. "It was only when certain rights were curbed, especially in relationship to the Catholic Church, that they found need to react against it." His mother said she would never have left Cuba were it not for her children. Mestre-Reed remembers as a child getting little packages from relatives in the States, "full of things such as bubble gum and baseball cards that we thought the glory of America." He also remembers the pleasure of struggling through Juan Ramon Jimenez's *Platero y yo*, the book that first taught him to love stories. All in all, "a classically happy childhood," until he was six, when one of his uncles tried to escape from Cuba through the American naval base and was shot down near the Cerca Peerless, the fence that separates American land from Cuban land. "I remember sitting on the porch steps of my grandmother's house, and being told what had happened. My grandmother poked me twice in the belly and then in the chest as she told me the places that the border guards had shot my uncle." In 1972, when Mestre-Reed was eight, the family took one of the last of the Freedom Flights to Madrid, where they spent eight months before coming to Miami. When he first heard his cousins speaking English, he thought it sounded "like beetles chewing on garbage. Wishy-washy, wishy-washy," my uncle teased me, "someday you'll speak it as well as them." Eventually, he mastered it well enough to graduate from Tulane University with a B.A. in English literature.

In 1999, he published *The Lazarus Rumba*, which had taken him nine years to write, in English. It is, to begin with, an extraordinarily ambitious but breathtakingly realized first novel, following the lives of three generations of Cuban women in the Lucientes family and centering upon the character of Alicia Lucientes (married to a disgraced *revolucionario*), who becomes the most famous dissident on the island. Critics hailed the novel as a virtuoso performance and a stunning literary achievement, with material enough for ten ordinary novels. Mestre-Reed's most stunning achievement, however, was a kind of literary alchemy: through his subtle and sensual crafting of the rhythm, inflection, syntax, and voices in the novel, his readers are made to feel as though they are reading in Spanish . . . in English. Mestre-Reed lives in Brooklyn and teaches at Sarah Lawrence College. He is at work on a second novel.

# After Elián

She made up her mind on the morning that they took Elián away. She said the same thing many Cubans in Miami had said that balmy mid-spring Saturday, after watching countless replays on the special reports of the *puta* marshal carrying the horrified boy away, "I can't live in this country anymore. *Yo me voy.*" Leaving. All leaving this city they had invented, this *güajiro* resort town that they had transformed into a sleek international metropolis in less time than it takes to build a cathedral. *Pero claro*, none of them had really meant it. Leaving? *¿A donde carajo?* Where could they go?

But Única Aveyano knew where to go. That Saturday evening she asked the head nurse, Lucas Duarte, to let her use the computer in the supervisor's office. She thought Lucas looked like Marlon Brando in *On the Waterfront*, young and ruggedly handsome, already a little balding, but not quite as pudgy. She often told him this (though she left out that middle part). When he thanked her, his voice was lispy and girlish, like Brando too. He had won her over almost from the day she had arrived with her husband, Modesto, after the first intense phase of the chemo, looking like a mad gypsy with a motley scarf wrapped around her head. Her daughter-in-law Miriam had decided it would be better if they had daylong professional care. That's how she put it, in a methodical, even voice that sounded as if she were reading directly from one of those dreadfully blithe pamphlets from the Leukemia & Lymphoma Society, or the American Cancer Society, or Jackson Hospital, which after her diagnosis appeared almost daily in all their festive birdlike colors, stuffed into the wrought-iron mailbox like a cluster of Christmas cards.

They arrived in the nursing home a few weeks before the celebration of the new millennium. When they were set up in their room, each with a bed (which was fine with Única; in the last weeks in Miriam's house, after she had come from the hospital, she had mastered the art of dozing in and out of her nights on the very edge of their bed), Lucas told her if there was ever anything she needed to ask, *sin pena ninguna*. And she did ask, for the thing she needed most then. There were four or five thin white hairs growing from her chin, and her husband would not pluck them anymore. Somehow, they had withstood the chemo. Could he do it? Could he pluck them, *por favor*? Modesto let out a little noise, as if he had just dropped something small and fragile; but Lucas nodded and quickly returned with a pair of tweezers, and took her face in one hand, carefully, as if handling a newborn, and plucked her unsightly hairs. And from then on, he did it every third week.

On that night, after they had taken Elián away, Única assured Lucas it would only be a minute. She wanted to order some stuff on the Internet. She reminded him that she had her grandson's credit card, his AOL password. She whispered this in Lucas's ear, using her most practiced vanquished voice. Lucas was clearly of Patricio's type—what happens to all these men, she often wondered, that they forget about the joys of a woman?—so every time she mentioned her grandson's name, his face softened, lost all its boyish tension.

"*O sí, sí*, Patricio," he said, his ears reddening, his serpent green eyes cast away. And he let her into the supervisor's office,

walking her to the wide mahogany desk and sitting her in front of
the computer. He stood guard outside. It took Única less than half
an hour to find what she wanted. The empty late-night hours that
she had spent on her daughter-in-law's computer had paid off.
She found it appropriate that the company that made the inflat-
able raft was called Caribe. Without a motor, it came to $289.95,
plus shipping and handling. She charged it to her grandson's
credit card. It would arrive at Miriam's house in eight to ten days,
which was a little too soon, she thought, but at least it would give
her time to plan, to tell Modesto (if she had to, if he ever talked to
her again: his silence these days menacing and oversized as a
butcher's knife). She would tell Miriam that it was Patricio's birthday present. She would ask her grandson to come visit them for
his birthday, which was in May. She had already convinced
Miriam to let them stay at her house again for a few days, like she
had been promising for weeks now. Once there, it would be easy.
Patricio rarely talked to his mother (though Patricio's silence was
different from his grandfather's; he wore his silence like an athlete
his medals, as something hard fought for, deserved), so he wouldn't
call her before he left Key West and that would give them the time
they needed. She thought all this out before she stepped out of the
supervisor's office, and the only thing that bothered her about her
ingenious plan was that she would have to lie outright to her
grandson. She had never done that. She pulled out one of the forbidden cigarettes from the secret pocket in her robe and smoked
half, till her dentures began to hurt (her palate felt like the soft
rotted roof of a rain-soaked bohío, at any time ready to collapse
from its own weight), and then she put it out on the silver ashtray
and left it there. She leaned on the desk and on the walls and shuffled to the door. She knocked lightly and heard Lucas jangling his
keys before he let her out.

"OK?" he said.

"OK."

"What were you ordering?"

"A birthday present, *para mi nieto.*" She took his forearm.

"What did you get him?"

She dismissed his question with a flick of her hand, "Something." She stumbled.

"Where is your new cane?"

"*¿Quién cojones sabe?*"

"It's not funny." But he laughed, as he always did when she cursed in Spanish. Like so many young Cuban-Americans born in this country, Lucas didn't speak Spanish very well. So she spoke to him mostly in English, which she had forced herself to learn to speak in her old age, mostly by watching American movies that she had first seen during the early years of her marriage, when Modesto acted as if he were still courting her, surprising her with gifts that he would hide in their tiny apartment in Guantánamo and she would find only after he had left for work: in the mop bucket under the kitchen sink, potted violets whose tiny flowers were delicate and unfathomable as their new life; hanging by a meager thread from the lightbulb above her mother's fire-scarred four legged bathtub, a miniature gilded box of coconut truffles, succulent and lingering as grief; taped under the sewing machine that had been a wedding present (the only one) from Modesto's half-sister Rosana, an envelope with love notes written on pressed and dried magnolia leaves. Those first years, he courted his own wife as if he were not sure that the law of man meant anything as far as they were concerned, as if the tragedies that had immediately preceded and followed the day of their wedding had rendered it void, annulled, as if she were not yet, and could never be, his. On Friday nights, he took her to *el teatro* on Calixto García to watch American movies. The badly dubbed voices always reminded Única, as she watched the oblivious yanqui actors, moving their lips and saying nothing, or screaming with their mouths shut, of the possessed man in the Gospel of Luke. And when she watched these movies again, so many years later, to learn English so she could talk to her own grandson, the actors having regained their voices (their very selves it seemed), it was as if in the inter-vening years, the Lord had touched them and cast out all their demons. She had learned to read English a long time ago, as a girl, with the books her stepfather, Dr. Esmeraldo Gloria, snuck out of the library in the yanqui naval base for her to keep, only the best, as he said: the noble doomed language of Thomas Hardy and the voluminous excursions of Charles Dickens and her favorite, the drunken prose of William Faulkner. But speaking English was surprisingly more difficult than following the logic of the torren-tial sludgy sentences of the Mississippian—all those silent letters hidden within syllables, scarring pronunciations like a salty wind. But Única persisted, as she had done with Faulkner, until she was better at it—speaking it, reading it, writing it—than most native English speakers. At first, she had thought it was a shame that so many young Cubans were losing their native language, but such things mattered less and less as time passed. She adapted; and now she spoke so much English that some of her laziest thoughts—about the weather, about the movie they had watched the previ-ous night in the rec room, about her necessities—appeared to her like clouds of mosquitoes in that menacing tongue.

She stopped and pulled out Patricio's credit card from her robe pocket. She pointed to the little photograph on the corner.

"He's a good boy, *coño.*"

"Yes, and very handsome," Lucas said, which should have both-ered her, but it didn't. She nodded and looked into Lucas's star-tling green eyes and then again at the little picture of Patricio, the swarthy complexion he had inherited from his mother, the spilt-ink eyes set against the toothy bright smile that he used to disarm others, and that he wore always, like a favorite wrinkled linen shirt. "*Bueno, así es . . .* maybe . . ." but she couldn't finish her thought, so she took Lucas's forearm again and let him lead her back to the rec room.

"My mouth hurts again."

"You shouldn't have smoked then."

She wasn't surprised that he smelled it on her. "I'd rather smoke cigars," she said, "but no one will get them for me."

He ignored this, as he always did her requests for the things that would kill her, the only kind of request he would ever ignore. He led her to an examining room, put on some gloves and a mask and put his fingers under her chin and examined the week-old wounds in her mouth. "Open." He stuck his finger in one side of her mouth and stretched it out gently. He peered in and she could smell his citrusy breath through the mask. "You're lucky, you could have really hurt yourself."

"I left the butt in there," she said when he let go of her mouth. "Left it right on her ashtray." She nodded once, as if to make a point, but she knew Lucas hadn't been talking about the cigarette anymore.

"I know. I'll clean it up before morning."

"Poor boy."

Lucas didn't respond. She had heard him speaking to some of the other nurses about Elián, how he thought the boy belonged with his father. She wondered if Lucas had had a good father. Then she thought about her own son, who never had much of a chance to be a father.

"Poor boy," she said again, though Lucas couldn't know she wasn't talking about Elián this time.

He tapped her hand. "Anyway, they're due to fit you for new dentures next week, aren't they?"

"I won't need them."

"Please, señora Única, *no se ponga dramática*." He addressed her in the formal mode. His Spanish was good when he tried. He took off his gloves and put out his hand. "Now, give me the cigarettes."

"No," she whispered, as if there were anyone else there to hide her contraband from.

"Give them." He wiggled his fingers. He had long feminine hands for such a well-built boy.

"*Ay niño, por favor*, what good is it not smoking now?" She wished she could pull away from him, leave this room, but she was afraid she would fall before she reached a wall. "Ya, ya, the price is paid. Anyway, if you take them . . . I can get more."

He reluctantly lowered his hand. It always worked, whenever Lucas challenged her, she summoned the specter of her illness.

"I want to see my husband," she said. He nodded consolingly.

Modesto was asleep on the couch in the rec room. His mouth was set in a pout, a dribble down one corner. His glasses had fallen off his nose and lay on his belly, strands of his neatly greased hair had come loose from the top of his head and hung over his forehead, and his long legs were splayed out in front of him like a pair of loyal sleeping hounds, but his hands were neatly folded over his chest (just like when he took his siestas). Lucas led her to the couch and politely asked one of the younger residents, a russet-skinned woman from Alabama, to make room for Única. She took his glasses, folded the arms, and put them back on his belly.

No movie tonight. The television was tuned to the Cuban station, still blaring with news about Elián. A photograph, whose authenticity the newscaster questioned, had just been released. Elián in his father's arms. His famous smile. Única soon found herself translating the news bits for the woman from Alabama, as competently as she translated the old American movies for her husband. At first she agreed with the newscasters, the picture was certainly a fake. She knew what could be done with computers these days. But then she wondered if Elián wasn't the type of boy who could be happy anywhere, with his beautiful cousin, with his *comunista* father. There was an art to it—this living in happiness. One had to be born with it, she supposed, like an ear for music. And develop it, lest it wither.

"Too bad," she said to the woman from Alabama, "we won't see how he turns out."

The woman looked at Única over the rims of her glasses, her

cloudy eyes puzzled, her lips wet and parted, as if she were waiting for a translation, though Única had spoken in perfect English.

Modesto stirred beside her, his hands unfolded and he grabbed
her wrist frantically. She winced. Ever since the chemo, her bones
felt as if they each had been dropped from a great height, shattered, and then hastily pieced together with the incompetence of
a child gluing together a broken vase. Her kidneys were ailing, the
doctors said, but there was hope, the cancer was taking a beating.
They spoke of it like a wounded boxer. She imagined it otherwise.
She imagined it leaking like a juicy rumor from the fatty part of
her bones to every region of her unsuspecting body.

"*Estoy aquí. Aquí estoy.*" And she turned and translated for the
woman from Alabama. "I am here. I am here for him." She
shrugged and the woman smiled. Única pried her husband's fingers off her and made a note to trim his fingernails. If he ever let
her near him again.

When he noticed how his hand had instinctively reached for
her, Modesto quickly let go and grabbed his glasses. He pulled his
heavy legs toward him, took out an old plastic comb from his
pocket and passed it through his greased waxen hair, until it was
all set back in place. He didn't ask her where she had been. It had
been over a week since he had said *anything* to her. He grunted as
the TV showed one more replay of the events of that morning and
then cut to the smoky streets, erupting in riots. Everyone in the
room seemed captivated and disgusted at the same time. Some eagerly looked for a glimpse of their grandkids at the riots, others
cheered the rioters on, and one old man got up and poked the
screen, pointing out someone he knew. Única wished they could
watch a movie as they usually did on Saturday nights, but Lucas
hadn't even bothered to rent a video, knowing the news about
Elián would take precedence. Única had wanted to watch *Bringing Up Baby* again. She liked how Modesto laughed so long and
hard when Cary Grant was forced to wear the lady's nightgown

that she didn't need to translate any of the dialogue. She had heard that Cary Grant too had been like Lucas and her grandson, but at least he had been married, which is what they all should do, and keep their dirty little things on the side. *De todos modos*, all men did it. O God she knew! Their dirty little things. That's how God made them. Of that she was thankful, that God hadn't made her a man, as gawky and as jittery and as foolish as Cary Grant singing about love to the wrong baby, who could cleverly assemble his outsize dinosaur monster but not notice love when it was biting him in the cheeks. She looked up again at the endless reel of Elián being carried away, his boxer shorts slipping from his hips, his little hands like a frightened kitten's paws on the shoulders of the *puta* marshal, and she wondered what lucky girl would one day take his virginity from him, and how happy the young lovers would be that night, and how far away this night of terror would seem.

Única Aveyano had learned to go almost without sleep. She sometimes slipped her painkillers that she had hidden under her tongue into Modesto's daily dosage of pills so that he at least would get some sleep and not worry about her wandering the halls at night, pressed to the walls like a mouse. The other pills she took. Especially the little egg-shaped Marinols, which were supposed to combat nausea, but they made her tittery too, and daring. Later, they were to blame it on them, on the little egg-shaped pills, as if it had been the first time.

The nursing home was a six-story building, two blocks away from the fashionable beach. Storm shutters hung halfway down over the windows at all times like droopy eyelids, so very little light was ever let in. When the windows were left open, she could hear the music from the oceanfront cafes late into the night. Sometimes she asked a night nurse to bring her a chair, and she sat in the hallway, crouched by an open window, and listened to the sounds of life outside. She hadn't been to the beach in ages.

One night, a week before Elián had been taken away, she made up her mind to see the ocean as it is when the moon flirts with its restless surface. When Modesto fell asleep, she took her cane (which she rarely used) and made her way to the end of the hallway. She stood by a window, pretending to listen, and waited for the night nurse to forget her presence and then she lumbered into the stairwell. The two flights did not prove as painful as she imagined. She planted both feet firmly on each step before she proceeded to the next one, one hand on the railing, the other firmly on her cane, each step as precise and deliberate as a musical note. If this were all, she thought; her arthritic knee, her brittle bones. Before the chemo her cane had always stood in one corner of the bedroom that they used in Miriam's house, what had once been Patricio's room. When she made it up to the top floor, she was surprised to see the door to the roof ajar, a breeze passing through it. She had not been outside in weeks, since the last time she was in Jackson Hospital and the treatments had been temporarily stopped, and the night air sneaking into the stairwell felt as precious and as dangerous as something stolen. She wished she had woken Modesto and brought him up. He missed his long afternoon walks to the bodega, strolling patiently on the edge of the roads near Miriam's house. Única had accompanied him once and was surprised to see that most of the way to the bodega had no sidewalks. Nobody walks in this part of town, Modesto explained proudly, as if he were the last practitioner of an art long forgotten. Sometimes Miriam came on weekends and took him out for a stroll on Ocean Drive, but the nurses forbade Única to go unless she used a wheelchair. They said she was still too weak from the treatment. A wheelchair! As if she were an invalid. ¿Y qué? He always came back from his walks more depressed than when he left. He told her in two words he didn't like to be apart from her. Miriam had wanted him to stay in her house, and that's how he had responded, with the same two words, "No puedo." It's true what they said about old age. He was turning into a boy again and he needed her as simply as a child needs its mother. Just to be there. Única gave a good push to the roof door and then climbed the last step and stood in the doorway, loving the way the gentle breeze teased the new naplike growth on her skull. She had not looked at herself in weeks, had hung a hand towel on the mirror over the bathroom sink (which Lucas kindly rehung every morning after Modesto was finished shaving), and now she wondered how much grayer her hair was; the doctors had said that it would probably grow in thicker but grayer, maybe even a little curlier. It was more difficult once she was out on the roof, having only the use of her cane. She wished she had worn something other than her slippers and her ratty night robe (but she wasn't sure if she still owned any shoes, and whatever old dresses hung in her closet always went unused). She had refused also, after the first phase of the chemo, when they were still living with their daughter-in-law, the use of those monstrous contraptions that they called walkers. She'd rather stay in bed all day, she told her daughter-in-law, rather have her bones in a sack.

"You don't listen to anyone," her daughter-in-law had told her the night after Thanksgiving, the day after they had found Elián floating on an inner tube. They had just eaten turkey sandwiches for dinner. "You never have. That's why it's better that you have daylong professional care. Them you'll have to listen to, *coño*. It is for your own good, mamá."

What use living in a country where family can say such things? How dare she call her mamá?

There were a couple of lawn chairs on the roof, a beach towel draped over one of them. Maybe the nurses came up here to sunbathe on their breaks. For a moment, looking at the chairs, Única lost her direction. Which way was the ocean? She shuffled on the sticky tar, leaning on the cane with both arms, to one edge of the roof and grabbed tight to the low concrete parapet. Below, there was only an alleyway and across an abandoned building, its windows shuttered with flimsy plywood. She found it odd that there were any buildings so near the ocean left to sit useless. In one of his rare talkative moments since they arrived here, Modesto had told her what a great job they had done with all the hotels on Ocean Drive, how they had restored them to their old art-deco splendor. Fifteen years before, when they had first moved to their little apartment on Meridian Street and Miami Beach wasn't as fashionable, the hotels were teeming with the old waiting on their porches, their ratty structures crumbling, the wood perforated with termite damage. She was very eager to see how much they had changed, but she did not let Modesto know. The breeze picked up and she heard the irascible rumbling of the ocean, as if it were expelling the elements of a chronic irritation. She stayed close to the parapet and moved toward the sound. When she saw the tall palms that lined Ocean Drive, their fronds swaying lazily as if they heard nothing of the troubled ocean, but only the music from the open-air cafes, she dropped her cane and grasped the edge of the parapet with both hands. She moved along faster, her back foot skittering up to the front one and then the front one sliding forward. The sea continued its rumbling and its constant perturbation inspired Única—this will to never let anything stay as it is. She dismissed the blood pulsing like an alarum on her swollen knee, the hundred needles of fire pricking at her bones, the suspicious feeling that her tongue could easily reach up and lick the seat of her brain. She made it to the corner and she felt the sea's presence before she could cast her eyes on it, its brackish breath assaulting her. She raised her chin.

"*Sí, sí,*" she said, as if she were welcoming Modesto (as she never could anymore) in his still too-frequent attempted incursions into her ruined body, where he would end up doing everything himself, spilling his tepid come on her inner thighs, on her belly, on the fleshy hollow between her collar bones. (No child then.) She could not remember when she stopped loving him. But again, she wished he had come with her, though he would have certainly refused when she offered, called her *una loca*, as he often did these days. At seventy-eight, and though on plenty of preventive medication (twelve pills a day), he had never spent a night in a hospital, and now he was confined to a nursing home because of her. Yet, he had never had the strength to stand up to their daughter-in-law, had lost all vigor on the morning Única was given her diagnosis, had suffered all the doldrums and depression that the doctors had told her were her due. Única was glad, very glad that God hadn't made her a man. If it had been her, her the healthy one, oh the fight she would have put up.

She moved along the front parapet, keeping an eye on the dark sea. No moon tonight, but from the glow of the street lamps she could make out the white of the foam crashing on the sand like spilt sugar. A pair of men wearing only sandals and shorts strolled by holding hands. They too were listening to the embroiled sea. The bounty of that day's sun still stuck like sap to their burnt shoulders. Then a pack of wild pale boys ran by them, screaming obscenities, and for a moment the friends lost hold of each other, and for such virile young men seemed too easily parted, cowering—till the wild boys had passed, quickly and clamorously as an afternoon thunderstorm—and the friends found each other again and made their way toward the darkness of the shore before they held hands again. She thought about Patricio. She wondered if he ever held hands with his friends. Maybe that's why he had moved to Key West. It was safer there. They were less outnumbered.

If she leaned forward enough she would just stumble off the roof to the pavement below. Maybe the two friends would find her on the way back. Maybe the pack of wild boys. She let go of the parapet and found her body surprisingly light, as if she were floating in the warm sea. With her bent fingers she undid her robe, pulling it up to reach the lower buttons. She let it fall off her shoulders, and the sea air draped in around her, it whistled on the catheter above her breast. She had forgotten what a great joy it was to go without clothes. She could not unclasp her bra (the nurses always did that), so she pulled the straps over her arms and slid it down to her waist, twisting it around her till she found the clasp, but still she was not able to undo it, so she left it there and slid her hand under the band of her bloomers and let them drop, and she stepped out of her slippers and slid over, leaving the bundle of clothes aside like a shed skin. She felt feverish. As dangerous and as daring as the young friends holding hands. She laughed as if she were being tickled. She raised her hands in the air and called out to the friends, *"Aquí, aquí, mis vidas!"* But no one heard her, so she moved farther away from her pile of clothes. She wished she could get rid of her bra but it would not go down below her belly button, even though she was, like Miriam said, as thin as a lizard. It hung above her waist like garters, like a dancing girl, so she lifted her feet off the ground, one at a time, trying to keep rhythm to the song rising like a prayer from the street below. How she wished Modesto had come with her! She would relent. She would pretend to love him again. They would do it right here, *coño*, on the roof of the *maldita* nursing home. Why not? She would give in. He would hold her on the ledge of the parapet and fuck her and fuck her until both their bodies crumbled at last. He would fuck her and fuck her till they tumbled over together and they were no more.

Fuck.

She loved that word. It was one of the first English words she had learned to speak, though she rarely got to use it. For some reason the word always made her think of Faulkner, of poor Joe Christmas. She had used it a few times on her daughter-in-law and she was going to use it tonight if anyone tried to stop her.

"Fuck you," she mouthed it, pounding her fist into her palm in mock fury. "Fuck me."

Sometimes English to her was like one of those thin-headed shiny hammers used for precision nailing.

She kept dancing, her bare twisted feet barely lifting off the ground, the sea air like another's breath on the new soft hairs running up the inside of her legs, under her armpits. She would never shave them again. In Key West, she had once met a friend of Patricio, a short stout woman who let hair grow all over her body, except on her skull, which was buzzed like a soldier's. Única wondered how much she looked like this woman now, this woman she had then found loathsome, unnatural. Now, *comadre*. She kept on dancing and giggled provokingly, like someone who is holding back a great secret. And when she laughed, she covered her dry rotted mouth, as if not to infect the guiltless night with all the ills that had befallen her.

Many songs rose from below, ballads whose words she could not quite hear but whose gist she understood by the baleful abandoned voice of the crooner, by the desperate plucking of chords— *así es la vida, señores y señoritas*, only our wounds, our wounds, awaken us, make us compelling—and then the songs stopped and all she could hear were the sighs and the drunken broken laughter of those who had still not gone home, so she danced to the uneven beat of their noise. She had never in her long life been drunk, but this is what it must be like, the poisons transfigured into this windy riotous joy (she raised her empty hand in a toast)—and then the laughter stopped and all she could hear was the waking groans of the ocean, calling to her.

A light, soft and hushed as the steps of a lone ballerina, appeared in the frayed edges of the mantling sky; it should have comforted her, she knew, but she suddenly felt the excoriated folds of her innards, and she became frightened of the gentle light. She grabbed the parapet again and shuffled over to her cane. She took it and left the pile of clothes and made her way to the stairway. Pieces of stone dug at her soles, and just before she reached the doorway, she fell to her knees. The light grew, more suggestive now, as if others—more vigorous, more grounded dancers—had joined the lone airy ballerina. Única was on all fours, the siren pain at her bad knee and the hidden wounds within her and the proud young morning all denouncing her mad little excursion, so she crawled into the shadows of the stairwell, dragging along her

cane. By the time she got up, both hands on the railing, dangerously close to the precipice of the stairway, the light fell on the
roof like the waves of a thunderous symphony that had no use for
dainty ballerinas. There was blood on her knees, which she
touched with her fingers and spread on her breasts and on her
cheeks. She slid along the wall with her hands, smearing it, and
picked up her cane. She was as patient going down the stairway as
she had been coming up, first the cane and then one foot and the
other on each step and then the next step and the next one. She
imagined the notes of Bach's *Goldberg Variations*, played in an im-
possibly slow tempo, each key struck one by one, as if the notes
existed alone, independent of each other—Modesto had listened
to it again and again on the night they had found out about their
son. But the farther she got away from the garish morning light,
the more she felt lost, forgetting which floor she was on (had she
passed one doorway, two, three?) and the colder the concrete
steps became, sending a chill up her legs, up her spine, till she was
unsure of whether she was descending or climbing. She lost hold
of her cane and heard it tumble eagerly away from her, as if it
could be of better use elsewhere. And for a moment, she leaned
forward and she thought she would follow it. But this passed. She
turned and faced the wall and grabbed the railing with both hands
and continued, sideways, unsure as a sleepy crab that has been
dug out of its place, both feet on each step, passing her cane,
which she spitefully kicked aside twice (till it tumbled farther
down the stairway). She passed doorways that looked out to
empty hallways and kicked her cane along when she felt it graze
against her feet, till she reached the bottom door and, ignoring the
warning in bold red letters that this was only a fire exit and that an
alarm would go off, she pushed it open and heard nothing of what
had been warned and felt the morning's warmth again, and she
thought she had just traveled in a loop back up to another roof.
She picked up her cane and made her way out.

It was an alleyway, which she followed to its opening, not ques-

tioning how there could be streets up on a roof, as if a whole deserted city and its nearby beaches could naturally sit atop some
great renovated art-deco building. She stayed close to the walls of
the buildings, hiding in their shadows, her whole body turned
away from the waking world, from the prying sun, as she plodded
up the street toward the sound of the ocean. Someone called to
her from a balcony, and then that someone called to her God,
"*¿Dios mío, Dios mío, qué es esto? Una viejita sin nada.*" She had
to hurry, they would surely send someone after her (even though
she was just what the woman in the balcony had called her, a little
old woman with nothing), so she quickened her pace, pressed
closer to the walls, as if she were blind now, ignoring the honks
from cars and the bleary looks of those who like her had spent the
night sleepless and were in various euphoric stages of undress.
But when she made it to the corner of Collins Avenue, the wide
street seemed as impassable as a rushing river. At the corner of the
last building, she pressed her cheek to the wall and let her
scorched feet rest in the thin strip of its shadow and looked out
over the vast expanse, knowing how close the sea lay beyond it.

"*No puedo.*" Then, "*Sí, coño, ¿cómo que no? Todo se puede.*"
So she went on—admonishing herself on what a fool she was and
with the same breath calling on all the saints that she had not
prayed to in ages not to abandon her in this quest, this way and
that—till she whispered a quick plea to St. Lazarus of the Wounds
and she found the courage to venture away from the wall, at first
holding onto the frame of the wrought-iron fence that surrounded
the building's front garden, at whose center sat a lone majestic almond tree, and then with only her cane as aid, both hands
wrapped around it and the insufferable weight of her years bearing down on it. She did not make it far. Before she had reached
the curb, she fell again, this time unable to break the fall with her
arms so that her chin bounced on the pavement and she bit hard
on her tongue and on her lips. The roof of her mouth rattled in its
place and felt as if it had come loose and settled back in askew.

She pushed her head up and then her torso till she was again on all fours like an animal. Bright drops trickled from her mouth and splattered on the sun-bleached sidewalk, giving a shocking splendor to the drab piece of cement. If she let go now, she could just let it happen here, on this corner, in this sparkling hour before the morning truly came, before anyone save those who had not yet gone to bed were awake to bear witness. Her cane had bounced away from her and she could not see it anywhere. She could not recall where she had been heading, but something, the raw briny primeval odor perhaps, of nakedness, of a thing just killed and laid open, told her she could not be far. Here. Here. What better place? She crawled into the garden, under the shade of the almond tree, and pushed off her arms and sat back on her bottom, her useless legs folded in front of her. (She was going to a place where she would not need them.) Again, she smeared blood on her cheeks and on her breasts. More cars passed by now, but they wholly ignored her unless they were stopped at the light, and then she heard vulgarities about her drooping breasts, about her age, about her tortillera's haircut, about her shriveled sex, and they called her what Modesto would have called her, *loca, loca de remate*. No one stopped to inquire what she was doing at dawn, wearing her bra as a garter belt, seated and bare-assed, a trespasser in the garden. So why not here? Why not on this spot where no one would ask any questions? Here, here there would be no two-faced daughters-in-law, no *marica* nurses, no stone-hearted doctors to get in her way, to tell her of the need for patience, for fortitude, for faith, who talked as if these things were something one put on as easily as smearing blood on one's cheeks, on one's breasts.

It was funny, the way they talked to the condemned.

So on her little spot of private grass, she giggled and then laughed vehemently, but this time did not bother to cover her mouth. Her shoulders shook, her bloodstained breasts jiggled, her breath fouled the salty air, her peals filled the hushed morn-

ing, and now, when cars stopped at the light, the passengers
would cast their eyes from her, and the driver would let the car
dangerously inch up toward the intersection, away from her, and
she was sure that none would ever be brave enough to approach
her.

The boys were still dancing when they approached—the same
wild dance that they had begun when they ambushed the friends
who held hands the night before—dancing still, in a whirlpool,
arms flailing, chanting their own song, as if casting a spell on the
soberness of the new day, summoning back the outlandish night.
There were five, six, seven of them, or more, she could not tell because by the time she noticed them, they had already surrounded
her, some on their knees like supplicants, some rolling on the
ground like fallen creatures, some hanging off the almond tree
like monkeys, and some, she thought, hovering above her on their
tiny wings, were whispering in her ear, blowing kisses on her neck
and passing their soft hands over her bare scalp, and, except for
their threadbare loose shorts, were as naked as she was.

"*¿Qué pasa, Abuelita?*" they whispered. "*¿Qué pasa?*"

One of them undid her bra and passed it to another, who wore
it tied under his chin like a bonnet, and it was as if they had put on
him a crown, for he forthwith became their leader. He tucked his
long dark hair behind his ears and straightened his milky lanky
hairless frame. He barked orders simultaneously at those on the
ground, those on their knees, those in the tree, those in the air, his
reptile eyes boring intently into them, as if their existence depended on his seeing them, waving one hand around like a con-
ductor, keeping one finger of the other hand pointed directly at
her, as if to signal, for those dumb enough, or stoned enough, not
to get it, who his orders were about, and then, in a sugary voice
that was half pitying, half mocking, he spoke to her:

"We're taking you, Abuelita. We're taking you where you were
heading." He reached down and touched the catheter above her

breast, confused by it, and then with his thumb he wiped some blood from her lips and traced a circle on his scrawny chest and smeared his tiny brown nipples. "*Vamos, vamos,*" he yelled, turning from them and raising his bloodstained hand in the air, "take her!"

She felt their hands under her armpits, grabbing at her waist, pushing up on her rump. Others reached into her mouth and took her blood and smeared it on their chests like the leader had done. Her arms flailed as she rose. "My cane, *coño*," she protested, "why can't you find my cane?"

The leader, who was already halfway across Collins Avenue, turned and stared at her. Cars passed him, swerving wildly to one side or the other, as if he were made of some substance that repelled all physical objects. He nodded and moved back toward them, ignoring the screams and the horns blaring at him. He returned to the garden. He surveyed its grounds and hopped up on the almond tree, leaning one way and then the other, passing his hands over the branches, till he found the right one and with one quick turn of his wrist broke off a young branch, as easily as if he were cracking a chicken's neck. He peeled off the leaves and branchlets and handed it to her. "Your cane, Abuelita," he announced. And then he bowed before he was off again; and with her new cane, the others surrounding her nakedness, pressed so close they kept her from stumbling, she followed him, across Collins Avenue, across Ocean Drive, toward the sea, and none dared stop them.

On the beach there was an early-morning jogger who would later tell those in charge at the nursing home and the police investigators that he thought it strange that a bald naked old woman was steadfastly making her way across the wide stretch of sand toward the water, leaning on a long crooked staff, determined as a prophet crossing the desert toward Jerusalem, but that this was a crazy town and that he had seen crazier things before, so he didn't stop her. She seemed deranged, dangerous, caked in dirt, or blood. Maybe she was homeless, going for her morning bath. Maybe she had just murdered someone. At any rate, he had been either not interested enough, or (more likely) frightened too much to do anything but keep on jogging.

And there was no one else on the beach?

No, no one else, just the crazy old woman, and a pair of half-naked gay boys sleeping on the sand, wrapped around each other.

"There was no one. You appeared on the beach by yourself. There were two men sleeping there. They saw you go in the water and, like the jogger, they thought you were *una loca, desnudita como el día así como estabas*, going in for a morning swim."

"Ay Lucas, some people need to be blind. Those little wild angels came to get me, not them, that's why they couldn't see them. You can tell yourself that you saved me when others wouldn't. If it makes you feel better."

So she told Lucas all that happened just before he came and rescued her, all that had happened that the jogger and the two friends sleeping on the sand couldn't possibly tell him about.

Their numbers grew as they approached the water. Some she thought had surfaced from the foamy shore and were coming toward her. These were as naked as she was and thinner and darker than the others, and their skin glistened with droplets of broken light, like shimmering scales, and their hair was strung with seaweed, and their eyes spread wide on their heads, and their sex livid and heavy as ripe plums—these were all the other little ones, Única thought, who had had no band of dolphins to protect them, no mothers prescient enough to give them a bottle of fresh water, who had never made it across the treacherous straits and had grown older with the creatures of the sea—and they seemed ill at ease on the sandy earth, wobbling, their arms thrust out for balance, ungainly as newborn calves. They approached her, carrying handfuls of seashells that they tried to shove into the folds of her body to give it a drowning weight. The other boys joined them—joined her—in their nakedness. They slipped off their threadbare shorts and cast them in the air with a whoop. The boy who was their leader threw off his bra-bonnet and also cast it in the air, and when their shorts and her bra rained down, he was like them and they were all like her. Maybe that's when the others noticed them (if they noticed them at all), the friends who had been holding hands the night before, because they had been sleeping (on that detail the jogger had been right), wrapped around each other, the sand covering their lower halves up to their belly buttons, so that it seemed that they had been struggling up out of the earth and had perished just when they were almost there, had perished without letting go of each other. But at some point the two friends must have awakened (perhaps because of the whooping of the boys) because one of them raised his head and called out to her and that's when the wild boys left her. They seemed astonished that there was anyone else on the beach besides them and her. They crouched. They dropped their handfuls of seashells. They fell to the sand, grabbing at it as if it were a sheet. They looked up at the sky, at the sea, back out to the hotels on the street, their bright eyes wide and darting end to end. The ones that had come from the sea fell from their stagger and crawled on the ground back to the shore and disappeared into the foam. The others, once they had figured out where the voice came from, moved toward the half-buried friends and surrounded them in the same manner that they had surrounded her under the almond tree. Some dug under the sand and crawled beneath them, others lay beside them and tangled their long limbs with theirs and others yet tarried above them like days to come.

She could not tell for sure whether they meant to harm the friends (like the night before) or let them in on some great joy.

Única moved on without them. When she had made it deep enough into the water, with the aid of a rope that floated out to a faraway buoy, she let go of her almond branch. It was dragged back to the shore. The warm sea slapped off the blood from her breasts, from her cheeks, it gurgled in her catheter, it stung in her mouth, it lifted her and dropped her as casually as if she were a windblown scrap. She held on to the rope until her feet could no longer graze the bottom and when she let go, she felt little hands grabbing at her feet, at her thighs, kelplike arms wrapping furiously around her waist, tugging her outward, and it was as if a world of little fishlike saints had grabbed her and with all their diluvian cunning were whisking her to her glory.

# Ángeles Mastretta
## (Mexico, b. 1949)

Ángeles Mastretta was born in Puebla, "a blue city, two thousand meters above sea level, where I passed my happy childhood beneath the light and the enigma of two volcanoes." Her father's death in 1971 left a lasting impression on her: "He liked to write as others liked to dream, and I write to honor the world of chimeras and courage that I could read in his furrowed brow on those Sundays he would sit down to write an article for some thankless local newspaper."

In 1971 Mastretta took a degree in journalism from the Autonomous National University in Mexico City. She worked for many years as a journalist and columnist for such Mexican newspapers and magazines as *Excelsior*, *Ovaciones*, and *La Jornada*, *Siete*, *Nexos*, and *Proceso*. A selection from her column, "Puerto Libre," would eventually be published under the same title in 1993. She has also served as political commentator and talk-show host for Mexican radio and television.

In 1983 and 1984 she wrote her first novel, *Tear This Heart Out*, which, when published in Mexico in 1985, won the Mazatlan Prize in Literature and was immediately recognized as a classic. Told from the bed of a powerful but corrupt aging politician in the postrevolutionary Mexico of the thirties and forties, by his passionately conflicted younger mistress, Catalina, destined to become his wife and then betray him, the novel's seemingly meandering drama of social violence and individual passion builds to a mesmerizing conclusion. Translated into over a dozen languages, it has sold close to a million copies in Mexico alone.

In 1990, Mastretta published her first short-story collection, *Women with Big Eyes*, which confirmed her reputation as an author of the first rank. Her second novel, *Lovesick* (1996), won her the prestigious Rómulo Gallegos Prize for the best novel written in Spanish during 1996 and 1997. Set in the beginning of the twentieth century, it tells the story of a woman torn by her love for two men (a revolutionary and a physician) and the feelings each of them provokes in her, as she comes of age in the dramatic years of the Mexican Revolution. Like Mastretta's first novel, it became an international bestseller, with more than a million copies in print worldwide. Mastretta lives in Mexico City, and has been recently collaborating with the actress Salma Hayek on a film adaptation of *Tear This Heart Out*.

# Aunt Concha Esparza

Near the end of her life she cultivated violets. She had a bright room that she filled with flowers. She learned how to grow the most extravagant strains, and she liked to give them as gifts so that everybody had in their houses the inescapable aroma of Concha Esparza.

She died surrounded by inconsolable relatives, reposing in her brilliant blue silk robe, with painted lips and with an enormous disappointment because life didn't want to grant her more than eighty-five years.

No one knew why she hadn't tired of living; she had worked like a mule driver for almost all of her life. But those earlier generations had something that made them able to withstand more. Like all earlier things, like the cars, the watches, the lamps, the chairs, the plates and pots of yesteryear.

Concepción Esparza had, like all her sisters, thin legs, huge breasts and a hard smile, absolute disbelief in the plaster saints, and blind faith in spirits and their clownish jokes.

She was the daughter of a physician who participated in the

Revolution of Tuxtepec, who was a federal deputy in 1882, and who joined the anti-reelection movement of 1908. A wise and fascinating man who filled life with his taste for music and lost causes.

However, as fate likes to even the score, Concha had more than enough father but less than enough husband. She married a man named Hiniesta whose only defect was that he was so much like his children that she had to treat him just like another one of them. He wasn't much good at earning money, and the idea that men support their families, so common in the thirties, didn't govern his existence. To put food on the table, keep house and buy coverlets for the beds, to pay for the children's schooling, clothe them and take care of other such trifles, was always up to his wife, Concha. He, meanwhile, schemed up big business deals which he never pulled off. To close one of these deals, he had the bright idea of writing a check on insufficient funds for a sum so large that an order was given for his arrest and the police arrived looking for him at his home.

When Concha found out what it was all about, she said the first thing that popped into her mind:

"What's happened is that this man is crazy. Totally nuts, he is."

With this line of reasoning, she accompanied him to his trial, with this line of reasoning she kept him from mounting his own defense, which might have really done him in, and with this line of reasoning she kept him from being thrown in jail. Instead of that horrible fate, with the same argument Concha Esparza arranged for her husband to be put in an insane asylum near the pyramid of Cholula. It was a tranquil place, run by friars, at the foot of the hills.

Grateful for the medical visits of Concha's father, the friars agreed that Mr. Hiniesta could stay there until the incident of the check was forgotten. Of course, Concha had to pay for the monthly maintenance of that sane man within the impregnable walls of the asylum.

For six months she made an effort to pay for his stay. When her

finances could allow no more, she decided to retrieve her husband, after first having herself declared his legal guardian.

One Sunday she went to get him in Cholula. She found him
breakfasting among the friars, entertaining them with a tale about
a sailor who had a mermaid tattooed on his bald spot.

"One wouldn't look bad on you, Father," he was saying to the
friar with the biggest smile.

While Mr. Hiniesta was talking, he watched his wife coming
down the corridor to the refectory. He kept talking and laughing
for the whole time it took Aunt Concha to arrive at the table at
which he and the friars were talking with that childish joy that
men seem to have only when they know they're among themselves.

As if unaware of the rules of a gathering such as this, Concha
Esparza walked around the table in the clickety-clacking high
heels she wore on occasions she considered important. When she
was in front of her husband, she greeted the group with a smile.

"And you, what are you doing here?" Mr. Hiniesta asked her,
more uncomfortable than surprised.

"I came to get you," Aunt Concha told him, speaking as she
did to her children when she met them at school, pretending to
trade them the treasure of their freedom in exchange for a hug.

"Why?" said Hiniesta, annoyed. "I'm safe here. It's not right
for me to leave here. What's more, I'm having a good time.
There's an atmosphere of gardens and peace here that does wonders for my spirit."

"What?" asked Concha Esparza.

"What I'm telling you is that for now I'm fine right where I am.
Don't worry. I have some good friends among those who are sane,
and I don't get along badly with the loonies. Some of them have
moments of exceptional inspiration, others are excellent speakers.
The rest has done me good, because in this place even the scream-
ers make less noise than your kids," he said, as though he'd had
nothing to do with the existence of those children.

"Hiniesta, what am I going to do with you?" Concha Esparza inquired of the empty air. Then she turned and walked toward the exit with its iron grille.

"Please, Father," she said to the friar accompanying her. "You explain to him that his vacations cost money, and I'm not going to pay for one day more."

One can only guess what the father told Mr. Hiniesta, but in fact that Monday morning the latch on Aunt Concha's front door made a slow sound, the same leisurely noise it used to make when her husband pushed it open.

"I came home, Mother," Hiniesta said, with a mourner's sadness.

"That's good, Son," answered his wife without showing any surprise. "Mr. Benítez is waiting to see you."

"To offer me a business deal," he said, and his voice recovered some liveliness. "You'll see. You'll see what a deal, Concha. This time you'll see."

"And that's the way this man was," Aunt commented many years later. "All his life he was like that."

By then Aunt Concha's guesthouse had been a success, and had provided her with earnings that she used to open a restaurant, which she closed some time later to get into real estate, and which even gave her the opportunity to buy some land in Polanco* and some more in Acapulco.

When her children were grown, and after Mr. Hiniesta's death, she learned how to paint the waves at "La Quebrada," and how to communicate with the spirit of her father. Few people have been as happy as she was then.

That is why life really infuriated her, leaving her just when she was beginning to enjoy it.

*Translated by Amy Schildhouse Greenberg*

---

*Polanco: an expensive district in Mexico City.

# Edgardo Vega Yunqué
## (Puerto Rico, b. 1936)

Edgardo Vega Yunqué was born in Ponce, but was raised in the small mountain town of Cidra, the model for Cacimar, the fictional town in the same area where many of his characters originate. His maternal great-grandfather, Cesáreo Martínez, fought during the Lares uprising in 1868 to free Puerto Rico from Spanish rule, and then in 1898 against the United States, when it invaded his homeland. Over the years he himself has observed that "being born in one of the few existing colonies in the world presents unique problems and perspectives for a writer."

Vega Yunqué arrived in the United States when he was thirteen. He has spent nearly half a century "suspended between two languages, two cultures, and two races." He has worked in theater, radio, television and film, as an actor, producer, director, and playwright. He has also taught in the writing and literature programs of such CUNY colleges as City, Hunter, and Hostos, as well as at The New School for Social Research and the Latin American Writers Institute, and reviewed books for any number of periodicals from *Nuestro* to *The Philadelphia Inquirer.* He is, above all, however, a writer of narrative fiction.

*The Comeback*, his highly satirical debut novel about the adventures of a Puerto Rican–Eskimo hockey player, came out in 1985. His short stories have appeared in a variety of anthologies and literary magazines including *Revista Chicano-riqueña*, *Nuestro*, *Maize*, *The American Review*, New York *Latino*, and *Bomb*.

His first collection of stories, *Mendoza's Dreams* (1986), was nominated for the Bay Area Reviewers' Award. A second collection, *Casualty Report*, was published in 1991. The following year he was nominated for a Pushcart Prize. He also has half a dozen novels hiding in his trunk; and, when literary science finally comes up with a cure for the editorial myopia of MRS (magical realist syndrome), some prescient publisher will finally bring out his unpublished masterpiece, a symphonic novel about American jazz and the Vietnam War, entitled: *No Matter How Much You Promise to Cook or Pay the Rent You Blew It Cause Bill Bailey Ain't Never Coming Home Again*. Vega Yunqué lives in Brooklyn.

# Eight Morenos

Driving to Penn Station to pick up his son, Rafael Aguilar kept his eyes carefully on the road. His vision and reflexes were no longer as sharp as they once were and the snow had been falling steadily since noon. Rather than diminishing in strength the storm appeared to have gained intensity as the day progressed, making the highway hazy in the failing winter light. The flakes hit against the windshield like large cotton balls obscuring momentarily Aguilar's view of the traffic. As quickly as they hit, the wipers swept the thick flakes away with their hypnotic motion against the grayish whiteness, before another flock of them spent themselves against the glass. Everyone but Kevin was already at the house and ready for Thanksgiving dinner, the expectation of his arrival making everyone nervous and excited. On the phone Kevin said it would've been no problem to take a cab, but that wouldn't be right. Kevin was bringing his girlfriend and everyone was looking forward to meeting her. She was a beautiful blond girl from Georgia. What kind of first impression would that make on her? What kind of people would she think they were? She and Kevin had known each other about a year and this was her first time meeting the family. Kevin had undergone rigorous training to fly large transport planes. He had ferried troops from Germany to Mogadishu or someplace like that in Africa where *morenos* were starving and killing each other like savages. Kevin's picture in his flight clothes and sunglasses standing by the big airplane increased Aguilar's pride in his son. The photo had been enlarged and was displayed in a matted fourteen-by-twenty-inch glass frame in Aguilar's den, together with other photos of his children. Aguilar couldn't help smiling each time he saw the silver bar, the wings on the jumpsuit and in clear letters the name Aguilar.

Kevin had served for three years and was now talking about getting married, finishing out his four years and applying for work with one of the airlines. Aguilar would advise him to choose TWA or American Airlines. They seemed like the best, although United was good as well. But he should choose whichever one gave him the best benefits so he could retire comfortably when the time came. Aguilar felt as if he'd done well in his own life, but the telephone company did not have the best benefits. He had worked hard and had been a good provider for his family. He and Victoria lived comfortably, the house was paid for, but the neighborhood was no longer the best. Too many bad elements were moving in. Aguilar did not think of himself as a prejudiced man, but in his opinion the people moving in were not the best of their race. He could not bring himself to calling them black even though now that is what they called themselves. It seemed like an extremely disrespectful thing to say about someone. Instead, like most of the Puerto Rican people, he used the term *morenos*. He didn't agree with the way they behaved but he tolerated them. At the telephone company he had known some good ones, but most of them were not very serious, always joking and saying that terrible word. Everything they said had to have the word attached to it.

Whatever Kevin decided he would always do well. Very smart boy, Kevin. Very steady and serious. All of his children were bright.

All of them had graduated from college, but Kevin was different. He was special. Giselle was special too, but she had a very argumentative attitude for a young woman. Of all of them Kevin resembled his mother most. The girls had married young Puerto Rican men, and Rafael Jr. had married a Puerto Rican as well. All of them professionals. Kevin was going to marry an American girl. A blonde. *Una rubita.* Secretly, he felt a greater pride in Kevin's choice although he would not say so. Kevin was now a first lieutenant and probably would be a captain before he finished his four years. Aguilar hoped that Kevin would be wearing his uniform now, as he had when he came home that first time.

As he drove, Aguilar recalled a day like this one when he'd worn the uniform of the United States Air Force. He wasn't an officer but he had served the country. And like today it had been snowing and he was headed for the train station. He didn't like thinking about those times but the memories flooded his mind as if he had little control over them. He wondered whether he was nervous about meeting Kevin's girl. She had a beautiful name. Peggy Buford. A very American name. And she sounded very polite and kind on the telephone. He was certain that everyone would like her. The South had changed so much. It wasn't at all like it had been when he was there. Jimmy Carter had helped change that. And he was from Georgia. It was crazy, but he hoped that the Bufords knew the Carters. He had been a fine president.

Clinton was also from the South but Rafael didn't know what had gone wrong with him. He had voted for him the first time, but he couldn't do so the second time. Maybe it didn't matter what he did in his personal life, but something wasn't right. And that poor woman. Rafael had never let himself dishonor his marriage vows. He wished the station were closer and it wasn't snowing so much. He continued watching the highway and the other cars, making sure he drove carefully, and gave himself up to remembering. He drove steadily now as the snow continued falling. As he turned onto the Williamsburg Bridge, the snow obscuring the Manhattan skyline across the river, the atmosphere had the same feeling as that day so long ago.

Back then he had eaten breakfast and said good-bye to his mother, his sister, and his two younger brothers. All of them, except his mother were smiling. Standing in the doorway his mother looked the same way she had when his father left two years before. His father had said nothing. One day he was there and the next day he was gone, his dark face betraying little.

## Moreno One—The Cabdriver

Aguilar had trudged through the heavy downfall with his duffel bag, his brogans crunching the fresh snow. On the corner of 104th Street and Lexington Avenue, he stopped and waited for an empty cab. When one approached, making its way slowly, the tire chains producing a muffled dull clanking sound, he hailed it and got in.

"Penn Station," he said, confidently.

"Right, man," the driver said, chuckling a little. "Where you heading in all this snow?"

"Keesler Air Force Base," Rafael said, proudly. "Radar school."

"Where's that?"

"Biloxi, Mississippi."

"Uh-whee," the man said. "You better watch yourself down there."

The driver was a Negro man and although Aguilar did not like to think of it, he was reminded of his father. The man was darker but he had the same wide nose, thick lips and bad hair. He was glad once again that he resembled his mother and had her light skin and thin nose. He wasn't sure if his lips were too thick. He often made them thinner by biting down on the bottom one and tucking in the top one.

"What do you mean?" Rafael asked.

"That's a bad place, man. Don't you go messin' around with none of them blue-eyed gals. They don't like that kinda nonsense down there."

Aguilar laughed and asked him why.

"Just take my advice, son. Just don't mess aroun' with them gals."

He paid little attention to the cab driver. He wanted to tell him that he wasn't his son, but kept the feeling of revulsion to himself. Here was an older man joking with him about girls. They had women and he hadn't so he was making fun of him about him being cherry. He knew Puerto Rican girls with blue eyes. Or were they green? No one had said anything about them. He gave the words little thought and went back to thinking about the train ride. In late afternoon he would go to the dining car, order a steak and mashed potatoes. He would read until it got dark and he would then ask one of the workers on the train to prepare his sleeping compartment. He would read until he fell asleep to the clacking sound of the wheels on the tracks. He remembered the trains in Puerto Rico. Most of them carried sugar cane, but once in a while, he had seen one with people when his father had taken him to the coast. His family had left Cacimar before he had a chance to ride on the train.

As he drove carefully through the snow he knew the Puerto Rican trains were gone now, replaced by concrete highways. His daughter Giselle said roads were built to benefit Luis Ferré, who owned cement plants. Ferré had become governor and wanted Puerto Rico to become a state. Giselle believed in Puerto Rican independence. Aguilar felt it should stay the same. However, whenever she started attacking the United States he often smiled, held up his hands and said he didn't want to discuss politics. The United States was the country of her birth. How could she be against it? Why change anything and upset everybody? he'd thought, privately. Maybe Puerto Rico as a state wouldn't be a bad thing, but it definitely should stay the same, a commonwealth. It had a good sound. The Commonwealth of Puerto Rico. *El Estado Libre Asociado*. Giselle was very disrespectful and called it *El Estado Libre Ensuciado*. *Ensuciar* meant to make dirty, but it also meant to go to the bathroom.

The cab had reached Pennsylvania Station. Aguilar paid his fare, gave the Negro driver a tip, and entered the station. Madison Square Garden stood now where the old station had been. He could still recall the immense ceiling and the people bustling about. The trains still ran beneath the arena but it wasn't the same. The grandeur of the columns, the wooden benches, the smooth floor and the large glass windows were all gone. Once in a while Aguilar saw the station in black-and-white films and his heart ached for his youth. What would the first stop be? He walked farther into the station, looked at the train schedule, learned that the first stop would be Newark, and found a bench near the assigned gate. When it came time to board the train he moved quickly, but politely. After all, he was a representative of the United States Air Force and he must conduct himself with courtesy. He allowed women and children to board ahead of him. He saw an elderly man struggling with a suitcase and aided him, carrying the bag and helping him to find a seat. Eventually, he found a window seat and placed his duffel bag in the luggage rack above. It snowed heavily through New Jersey. The landscape was flat and white, the factory towers and smokestacks extending into the snowy sky.

## Moreno Two—The Jazz Musician

In Philadelphia the train stopped for some fifteen minutes. Aguilar recognized a Negro airman from basic training in San Antonio. The young man was saying good-bye to his girlfriend. They kissed and held each other and then he entered the train and the train began moving again. The young Negro came into the car and recognized Aguilar.

"Ralph Aguilar, right?" the young Negro had said. "I remember you. I'm George Fuller," he added and extended his hand, smiling. He was carrying what appeared to be an instrument case. "You probably don't remember me." Fuller was very light skinned even though his features were those of a Negro. He pronounced Rafael's name Agwilar.

Aguilar nodded, and shook Fuller's hand. He liked the sound of it. It sounded American. Ralph Agwilar. But he liked the sound of Spanish. Giselle had said that *aguilar* meant a place for eagles. He'd thought all along that it meant something like that. They were soon talking about the influences of Latin music on jazz.

"Man, you gotta hear this side that Diz did where he uses an all-Latin rhythm section. You ever hear of Chayno Pozzo?"

"Chano," Rafael corrected, recalling that his father had known him. "Chano Poso."

"Is that how you say it?"

"Yeah, man. Chano. Chano Poso."

"You play?"

Rafael had shaken his head and recalled his father, with his own green army duffel bags holding his congas. He was often gone for days and then returned early in the morning with his musician friends. They leaned their instrument cases against the wall and drank beer and rum and played records; hugging and kissing the young, nice-smelling girls that they'd brought; dancing until late into the day and his mother staying in the bedroom. And then he left that one time and never came back. His father was teaching him to play the congas before he left. He'd loved the sounds of the drums from the time he was a little boy. Giselle said that the tradition of playing African drums had been lost in the United States because of slavery, but that it had been retained in Puerto Rico. Aguilar was proud of this. Once his father left, he hated the drums even though he still loved the music. It was part of him, in his blood so that the beat would not let him forget who he was. He was Puerto Rican. He would never forget it. Never.

"Anyway, I play alto," Fuller had said, tapping his case, now leaning upright against the seat. "I'm going to D.C. to be in the air force band. It's great training and I'll be able to learn a lot from the older cats."

"That's hep," Aguilar had said.

"Anyway, you gotta hear this side," Fuller had said, hoisting the case up on the rack and sitting across from Aguilar.

"I'd like to hear it," Rafael said.

And so it went until they reached Washington, and Fuller got off to go to Andrews Air Force Base. Without Aguilar noticing, the snow had stopped falling before they got to Washington. The sky was now cloudless, bright and clear.

## Moreno Three—The Red Cap

Aguilar came off the Williamsburg Bridge and continued west to find Sixth Avenue. As he drove he shook his head. Sides we called them, he thought. The world had gone from 78s to 45s to 33s to tapes to CDs, and now the mini-disks and everything was on Walkmans. Pretty soon you'd go into surgery and they'd put something in your head and you'd just tune in the music. It was crazy.

Back then in 1955 the train did not leave D.C. for another hour. He sat around watching the American girls, their coats buttoned tight against the cold, their faces ruddy and pretty. Everything was so much bigger. It was as if the farther he moved away from home the bigger things got. He hoisted the duffel bag, placed his arm through the strap, slung it over his shoulder and walked over to a newspaper stand. He bought several candy bars, gum, and cigarettes. He opened a Clark bar, bit into it, tasting the inside, crunching it between his teeth and letting the chocolate melt and blend with the peanut butter or whatever the inside was. He set his bag down and studied a book rack, deciding what he should purchase. He loved adventure stories and was undecided between *The Pearl* by John Steinbeck and *Kingsblood Royal* by Sinclair Lewis. In the end he'd bought both books.

Now as he turned onto Houston Street to head west he once again shook his head and peered into his mind to recall everything. Three candy bars (Clark, Peter Paul Mounds, Hershey) fifteen cents, Wrigley Spearmint five cents, a pack of Chesterfields twenty-five cents, two pocket books fifty cents. Total ninety-five cents. Today he would have to place a $20 bill on the counter and hope he got some change back. He had read the books but could only remember the one about the pearl divers. Maybe because there had been a film with Pedro Armendáriz and María Félix, the two great Mexican film stars.

But now, as he turned onto Sixth Avenue he was bothered that he couldn't recall the subject of the other book. *Kingsblood* had to be about knights and olden times but he had no clear recollection of it. He worried that he could be developing Alzheimer's and went through his children's birthdays. Aurea 7/11, Giselle 9/27, Ralph Jr. 12/22, Kevin 9/14. And their mother. He couldn't forget that one. Victoria. His Vicky. His little Puerto Rican beauty. He still loved seeing her when he walked in the house and recalled the times they had lain forever in each other's arms when they first got married. Her skin was so soft and white and her hair so straight, cascading over him when she leaned to kiss him. October 12, of course. She was still so pretty. In a few years she would be sixty years old.

At the other end of the counter his eyes met the eyes of another young airman who seemed as eager to establish contact with someone as himself. They walked toward each other and asked the usual questions. How long had they been in the service? Where had they done basic training and where were they heading? The other boy had been at Lackland in San Antonio as well, but in another squadron. He was from just outside of Washington in Virginia and was headed for Keesler Air Force Base in Biloxi. Aguilar's eyes lit up. They were equally excited. Rafael's new friend was a tall, thin young man with very blond hair, cut very short. His eyes were blue. Aguilar imagined his new friend having a sister. She would be as blond as he was. Aguilar wondered whether it would be okay with his new friend, Bill Gunther, if he spoke with his sister. He was sure it would be okay. He asked him if he had brothers and sisters. Two brothers and two sisters, he said. By the time they were finished talking they found out that they were going to the same school to be radar operators and would be working in towers. They promised to stay in touch no matter where they ended up. If there was such a thing as love at first sight between men, this had to be it. It was like they had been friends forever. Bill Gunther had asked him all sorts of questions about where he lived. Everything Aguilar said was a source of further curiosity. He wanted to know about his name and about Puerto Rico and whether he spoke Spanish at home. He said that they spoke Spanish but he was an American. Bill had nodded and said of course, otherwise they wouldn't be in the air force. Everyone in the air force was American.

They returned to the bench to await the boarding announcement. They talked excitedly about their new assignment and how technical school would be. Would it be difficult? Would there be tests? Was it true that they would learn to watch airplanes and detect their position just from green dots on a black screen? That had to be seen to be believed, Bill said, and they both laughed out loud, their laughter flying from them and climbing to the high ceiling.

They were full of questions. Would they have time to go into town and see girls? Did he have a girlfriend? Yes, Bill had said. Aguilar shook his head. He had no one other than Lillian Morales, to whom he had written from Lackland. She was going to college after she finished high school in June. Hunter College, which was an all-girls college downtown. She was not very pretty but very smart. She had told him she wanted to be a lawyer like Mr. Marcano, who had the storefront on Lexington Avenue across from the Boricua Theater where they showed Mexican films. He had made the mistake of telling Nelson Figueroa and Gabriel Carasquillo and they said she was probably a *cachapera* and liked girls since only men became lawyers. They had smirked and wiggled their tongues. He looked at them, shook his head in disapproval and walked away.

Lillian was nice and she didn't laugh when he talked to her about the books he read. No one knew he was writing letters to her, not even his mother. Bill showed him a picture of his girlfriend. She was a plain-looking girl with black hair, no more attractive than Lillian. Aguilar kept Lillian's picture in his wallet. Maybe he would show it to Bill later when he knew him better. The feeling of being ashamed of Lillian because she was *trigueñita* felt awful. *Trigueña* was the word Puerto Ricans used when someone was dark like Lillian. Giselle said that *trigo* was wheat in Spanish and that it was a way of not admitting that the person was African. He didn't like Giselle talking like that. It was very disrespectful. He remembered that he'd been told that his new base was on the Gulf of Mexico and it was warm and had beaches. He was sure it would be like Puerto Rico.

His daydreams were interrupted by the boarding announcement. The voice was firm and official. He couldn't recall the name of the train but it was something picturesque, exciting, like the one he had traveled on to basic training: The Texas Hummingbird. But this was something equally beautiful. The Carolina Traveler or the Georgia Peach. No, that was Ty Cobb, the baseball player. The destination was New Orleans with stops in places like *Roanoke, Virginia; Raleigh, North Carolina; Charleston, South Carolina; Savannah, Georgia; Atlanta, Georgia; Mobile, Alabama*

*and points West. Destination: New Orleans, Louisiana. All aboard.*
The voice pronounced it Loosiana. He liked the sound of it. He
had heard of *Mardi Gras* and promised himself he would go
and see what the carnival was about. It was probably like the
feast of the patron saint of Cacimar, with rides and games and
fireworks. He and Bill slipped their arms into their duffel bag
straps and headed for the gate. They walked with the rest of the
passengers until they saw them getting on and followed. When
Bill got on Aguilar tried following his friend up the steps and
into the car. A man in a railroad uniform put his hands in front
of him and pointed down the platform to the next car. Aguilar
had explained that he and his new friend were together, that he
had a first-class ticket. The man said he understood but again
pointed to the other car and explained that he'd be more comfortable there.

Aguilar had continued to appeal to the railroad man. Eventually, a Negro Red Cap had come over, smiled at him and pointed
in the same direction as the white man. Aguilar had wondered
why this was, but headed to the next car and got on. Bill Gunther
had stood above him with a puzzled look, wanting to protest but
not having the words to do so.

He got on board and when he got inside he saw that not too
many people were in the car. Perhaps that was it. The other car
had been full. It was too bad because this car was old and un-
painted. On some of the seats the straw weave that covered them
was coming loose. He found a seat in the middle of the car, took
off his overcoat, removed the small bag with his toothbrush and
his other toiletries from the duffel bag, locked the bag once again
and placed it on the luggage rack. He took off his jacket and hat,
placed them on the seat next to him, loosened his tie, and opened
*The Pearl*. Soon after, the train began moving. As the train picked
up speed he watched the buildings and houses, the desolate winter landscape barren in the failing light of the day.

## Moreno Four—The Old Sandwich Man

When the train was into its rhythm, Aguilar tried reading. He soon tired of the book and fell asleep. When he woke up it was completely dark out and the train was moving at top speed. The velocity startled him since he could see nothing out the window except the night. His heart skipped a little and he felt alone. He felt hungry and quickly buttoned his shirt and pulled up on his tie. He stood up, put on his jacket, buttoned it and headed for the bathroom, where he washed his face and combed his hair.

When he was done he went out the door of the car and into the next one. People stared at him intently as he walked through. He didn't find this odd since he was in uniform and people stared at servicemen. When he reached the end of the car he could see the dining room beyond the door. Between the two cars he was met by the same man who had stopped him before. The man was annoyed and impatient as he kept his hand on the handle to the dining car door.

"Where are you heading, boy?"

"I thought I'd get something to eat," Aguilar said, pointing to the dining car. "I'm hungry."

"You can't go in there."

"Why not?"

"It's closed right now. Dinner's over," he said, looking beyond Aguilar, the nervous tic next to his nose moving rapidly. There was a faint scar above his right eyebrow, the white skin smooth and shiny. At that point an elderly white couple came to the dining room door and the man in the uniform held the door open for them.

"Why did they go in?" Aguilar asked when the man in uniform had again closed the door.

"They were in there before," the man said. "The husband forgot his pills. When we get to Raleigh one of your people will be back there with sandwiches and coffee."

The trainman had said this with disguised anger, and Aguilar, for all his questioning of the situation, could not figure out why this should be. He finally thanked the man and returned to his seat. He began reading again but had trouble concentrating on the words. He read the same paragraph several times to the rhythm of the wheels hitting the crack where the rails met. First the front wheels and then the back ones. Clickety-clack. Over and over. He again tried reading but found it difficult to concentrate. An overwhelming loneliness attacked him, enveloping him completely. He placed the book on the seat next to him and closed his eyes. He recalled being chased once by a bull when he was a little boy.

The fear had been like nothing he had ever imagined. Now, riding the train through the night, Aguilar was afraid again. He looked out the window of the train and saw nothing in the darkness. In the distance he heard the horn of an oncoming train, and shuddered once more as he saw the bull in his mind. After a few minutes the memories of the bull receded as his hunger returned. He wondered again why the man had not allowed him to enter the dining room. And why he had been angry with him. He had done nothing wrong. It didn't matter. Soon someone from the air force would be on with food. If the dining room was closed at least the air force was thoughtful enough to send someone to the train.

Aguilar became optimistic again and tried to imagine how life would be at the new base. Basic training was very strict. Technical school must be different. There probably wouldn't be as much marching. There had to be time to study if they were going to school. What would Biloxi be like? He remembered some of the airmen from the South and how they had pronounced the name. They sounded like cowboys in the movies. Keeslah Ah Base, Biloxa, Messesseppa. It was beautiful the way their voices went up and down. Like Spanish—up and down. Like the girls on the block—up and down went their high-pitched voices.

He spent the next twenty or thirty minutes thinking of all the exciting things that would happen to him in the next seven months. He would write to his mother and tell her all about it. Maybe he would write to Lillian Morales as well. The train was slowing down and he broke away from his daydreams. All he could think about was food. He wondered what the air force base in Raleigh was called and considered himself lucky to be getting this kind of attention. The train pulled into the station and some of the people who had been sleeping began stirring. For the first time since boarding the train in Washington, Aguilar began to take notice of the people in the car. He didn't know why, but a feeling of disgust and fear began to grow in him. Before he could think about it further he heard someone announcing "samiches and coffee." Aguilar turned to look and coming down the aisle was an old Negro man with white frizzy hair. He seemed bent over from the weight of the large tin box he carried in front of him.

"Samiches and coffee," he said, his voice tired.

"Sir, what kind of sandwiches do you have?" Aguilar said, being polite to this man who obviously worked for the air force.

"I got ham 'n cheese, and I got egg salad," the old man said.

Aguilar ordered two egg salad, one ham and cheese, a cup of coffee with plenty of milk and two teaspoons of sugar. The old man said he sure must be hungry.

"You're not kidding," Aguilar said. "They closed the dining room and I couldn't get any supper."

The old man chuckled and then couldn't contain his laughter.

"Now that is funny," he said. "Funniest damn thing I ever heard."

"I don't think it's so funny," answered Aguilar, good-naturedly, enjoying the old man's laughter. "How would you like to ride the train without supper?"

The old man had stopped laughing. The mirth had been replaced by sadness.

"Where you from, young fella?" he asked.

"New York," Aguilar said. "Why?"

"You ever been down here before?"

"First time."

"You poor thing," the old man said, shaking his head from side to side. "Poor little lost child."

Aguilar had dismissed the old man's sentiment as old age, thanked him, and began to unwrap one of the sandwiches.

"You owe me ninety cents," the old man said.

"Ninety cents?" Aguilar said, slightly annoyed. "The air force sent you, didn't they? The man on this train told me that some of my people would be coming on at Raleigh with sandwiches and coffee. Why are you charging me?"

"It's all right, son," the old man said, sadly. "Go ahead an' eat." He was shaking his head and then muttered: "Poor lost little lamb, poor lost child."

## Moreno Five—The Nigger Man

Aguilar was perplexed by the old man's words but soon forgot about it and ate his sandwiches and coffee. As he was finishing, the train began moving again. At the same time he noticed someone standing next to him. He looked up and saw a tall Negro dressed in an air force uniform. Aguilar said hello and asked him to sit down.

"You used to be in the barracks next to mine at Lackland, didn't you?" he said, sitting down and taking off his cap.

"I don't know," Aguilar said.

"My name's Bobby Fletcher," the young man said, sticking out his hand. "What flight were you in down at basic?"

"I was in eleven-oh-five."

"That's right. We was eleven-oh-six. What's your name?"

"Rafael Aguilar," he'd said.

"What kind of name is that?"

"Spanish," Aguilar said.

"Oh, yeah?"

"Yeah," Aguilar replied, challenged by the Negro's arrogance.

"Well, how do you like the way they treat us down here? It ain't the same as New York, is it?"

"What do you mean?"

"They got us all bunched up in one railroad car, sleeping on these hard-ass seats all the way to hell. You like that?"

"That's the way the air force wants it, I guess."

"The air force ain't got a damn thing to do with it," the tall Negro replied.

"You're not from New York, are you?" Aguilar asked uncomfortably.

"Nope. From right here in Raleigh. I heard what you said to the old man selling sandwiches. You owe me a dollar, pop."

"I owe you a dollar for what?"

"For three sandwiches and a cup of coffee, which you gobbled up without even taking a breath. Ante up, Mr. Zorro."

"That was somebody from the air force."

"The air force? What are you talking about? Just give me my dollar. I paid for you and I want my money. Look around you. How many people in air force uniforms do you see?" He was gesturing like *morenos* did. "Them two women sitting over there. Do they look like they're in the air force? And that man with the little boy? They look like they're in the air force?"

Aguilar began to feel afraid again. The fear disgusted him. He again began to ask himself why they had placed him in this car instead of with the blond airman he had met in Washington. He looked around and saw nothing but frizzy heads, some with their hair slicked. Not one head had good hair.

"Why did they put me in this car?" he asked. "I thought the other cars were too crowded."

"Too crowded?" Fletcher said, chuckling deep in his chest. "You must be jiving, boy."

"Well, why?"

"You mean you don't really know?" asked Fletcher, truly surprised.

"Know what?"

"It's 'cause you ain't the right color, man. You are black and that ain't the right color down here this year."

"I'm not black," snapped Aguilar, feeling insulted. "I'm not."

"What are you, then? You white?"

"I don't know. What difference does it make? All I know is that I'm not black."

"All right, so you're brown. But that ain't gonna do you no good down here. When they say 'boy' you better know they're talking about you."

Aguilar was stunned. He had never thought the color of a person's skin mattered. He knew he was different because he spoke English and Spanish. And yet he was conscious of good and bad hair, of big lips.

"You mean that they put me in here because they thought I was a Negro?" Aguilar said.

"What do you mean, they thought? Ain't you?"

"No, I'm Spanish. I'm from Puerto Rico."

"Well, then, you ain't Spanish."

"I know. That's what people say in New York."

"Let me tell you, man. You're going to have a hard time convincing people that you're Spanish. This ain't New York, you know."

"Do they really make it hard for you down here?" Aguilar said, suddenly feeling sick. "I thought people would be nice and it'd be like Puerto Rico.".

"I don't know nothing about Puerto Rico, man," Fletcher said. "The people are nice as long as you stay on the right side of town." He laughed and shook his head. "They got special places for folks like us. Separate beach, separate parks, separate places to sit in restaurants, separate water fountains and you get to ride in the back of the bus. How do you like that? They even got places that got signs that say that niggers ain't allowed."

The word hurt Aguilar. It was an ugly word. He had heard the word used and yet had never heard the anger with which Fletcher had said it. He wondered what to do or say if someone called him a nigger. He was not a nigger, he thought. As he thought this the people he'd known he now saw only as being black or white. Whereas once he had fond memories of his father's mother, so kind and gentle, he now saw his grandmother only as a big fat nigger. He remembered how dark she was and was ashamed. He put his head down for fear that Fletcher could read his thoughts. How much he hated himself. Now he hated his parents for not making him completely white. That's what people get for messing around with niggers. More niggers. Spanish-speaking niggers. Black spics, brown spics, white spics. All niggers. All mixed up *morenos*.

Aguilar's mind was beginning to muddle, and he felt tired. A whole new panorama of hate, disgust and fear was opening up to him. The short conversation with the tall Negro airman had left him exhausted.

"Hey, listen," said Aguilar, "I have to get some sleep."

He went into his pocket and gave Fletcher a dollar. He knew it was ninety cents but maybe Fletcher had given the old man a tip.

"You sleep tight, heah," Fletcher said, taking the dollar. "You better pull that shade down. We'll be going through Georgia pine country in the morning and those folks don't even talk English. They talk shotgun. They don't like to see niggers sleeping in the daytime. They're liable to take a shot at your Spanish ass."

Fletcher laughed. Aguilar knew he was making a joke but instinctively pulled on the shade to shutter himself from the night. Fletcher chuckled and got up to leave.

"Don't feel bad," he said. "I've been a nigger for twenty years, man. It ain't all that bad. Maybe you'll even get to dig grits."

"Just leave me alone," Aguilar said, scared now of the Negro.

His head was throbbing, and he thought he would have to vomit. The idea of being a color other than white had shocked him so much that he was now obsessed by it. He kept thinking of all the *morenos* he knew. Every one of them now seemed disgusting to him, unclean, bad. Nothing but dirty niggers. It took Aguilar a long time to fall asleep. The noise of the wheels on the train tracks seemed to be saying *oldblacknigger*, *oldblacknigger*, *oldblacknigger* over and over.

## Moreno Six—The Air Police

His sleep was fitful, the seat uncomfortable and his neck hurt. He woke up several times during the night, drenched in sweat and gasping for breath. When he would fall asleep again, he would dream of the old man selling sandwiches. In another dream he was racing down railroad tracks. He looked behind him and saw the train coming but it made no noise. He tried getting off the tracks but he couldn't. The snow kept falling, blinding him. The train was still behind him but getting no closer. He was finally able to get off the tracks and he came to a house. He was tired and hungry but the house had a sign on it: NO NIGGERS ALLOWED.

Toward morning he'd gone into a calmer sleep. When he woke up he did not remember much of the dreams but enough to again cause him to feel afraid. He went to the bathroom and washed up. When he came out the train had stopped and people were getting off. Some were boarding the train. Aguilar stepped outside. He was not wearing his jacket or hat and his shirt collar was open, his tie pulled down. He looked up and read a sign that said Atlanta. He walked slowly and looked straight ahead, not wanting to think of who was white and who was black. He entered the station. His mouth felt dry and his head ached.

Aguilar had walked over to a water fountain and bent over it.

He drank, rinsed out his mouth, spat and began to drink again when he felt a hand pull roughly on his shoulder.

"Boy, what in the hell do you think you're doing?" the voice said.

He turned around and saw a large red-faced policeman staring down at him. He stared blankly at the policeman and turned around to drink again. The voice spoke once more.

"Boy, I asked you a question," the policeman said. "What do you think you're doing?"

"*Tomando agua,*" Aguilar answered.

"Don't you sass me, boy. You're a pretty smart nigger with that double-talk, ain't you?" The policeman had grabbed his arm and turned him around. "Niggers don't act that way around here. You have your own water fountain. What you doing drinking from white folks' water fountain? Smart-ass Yankee nigger."

The policeman started to raise his hand but at that moment two air police showed up and intervened. One was white and the other one black.

"We'll take it from here, sir," the one AP said, and led Aguilar away.

When they were alone they questioned him. Aguilar explained what happened.

"Nigger, what in the hell got into you?" the Negro air policeman had said. "Are you drunk or crazy?"

The white AP told him that he was out of uniform and that in itself was a serious offense. They escorted him back on the train and helped him find his seat. He wanted to thank the two air policemen but the words wouldn't form in his mouth and he sat down dejectedly, staring out at the station. After a few minutes the train began moving and he fell asleep. He did not wake up until the train arrived at the Biloxi station. His sleep had been restful and he got himself together, straightened out his clothes and got his things into his duffel bag.

As he got on the large blue air force bus he looked around but the place did not look anything like Puerto Rico. Something had changed drastically in him. He no longer felt hopeful about what this new life would bring. The young blond man had approached him on the bus to renew their friendship but Aguilar was hesitant, aloof. The blond boy had persisted but Aguilar had kept him at a distance. During his time at the school he concentrated on his studies. He had gone through radar school, had enjoyed the training and was then assigned to the Azores, where he spent eighteen months before coming back to the United States to be stationed at Andrews Air Force Base. He saw the air force band several times but never looked for the young Negro who played saxophone. In fact, he could not recall what he looked like. All of them, the blacks, the Negroes had blended into one. They were *morenos*.

## Moreno Seven—The Bride

As he parked his car near Pennsylvania Station, Aguilar told himself again that he was not a prejudiced man. He trudged through the snow gingerly, conscious of how unsteady his steps had become as he aged. As he had done so many years ago, he checked the arrivals and departures board and found the gate at which Kevin and Peggy would be arriving. *On time*, the schedule said. He looked at his watch and headed for the gate. Minutes later people began exiting the gate and finally there was Kevin carrying two suitcases. He was not in uniform but Aguilar's heart swelled with pride at seeing his son. Right behind him came Peggy Buford. She was much taller than he had imagined her. Kevin was just under six feet and in her boots she was nearly as tall as him.

Kevin hugged him and kissed his cheek. And then he brought Peggy forward and introduced her.

"Pop, this is Peggy," he said. "Peggy, this is my dad."

"Hello, Mr. Aguilar," she said. "I'm very happy to meet you."

"Welcome to New York," Aguilar said. "I'm sorry the weather is so bad."

She smiled at him, patted his arm and told him not to worry. She was certainly a beauty, he thought, very blond and blue-eyed, but there was something strange about her, something familiar that caused him to feel suspicious. Her hair was straight, although a little wavy. But it was her nose. It was too round, her lips too full, but certainly a beauty in anyone's book. He tried to think of a movie star and only Lana Turner's name came up. He didn't know what to think. Out in the street he asked Kevin to drive and sat in the backseat.

Once they reached the house Kevin introduced Peggy all around. They loved her and she got along with everyone. At dinner he sat back and watched his children and their mates and his grandchildren and felt enormous pride at what everyone had accomplished. Aurea and Giselle had married nice Puerto Rican boys and Ralph Jr. had found a girl just like his mother. And they all spoke Spanish, as did their children. Only Kevin had decided to marry an American girl and that was okay. He knew what he was doing. The conversation at the table had been so bright and varied. Aguilar hardly ever said anything when his children were around, but he loved hearing them and watching their excitement and laughter.

They discussed books and politics, films and TV programs, their jobs, their children's progress in school, philosophy and social issues. And then Giselle, who had studied psychology at City College and had gotten a Master of Social Work at Hunter, began talking about how things had changed very little in recent years in terms of civil rights.

"Well, don't try and tell my grandma that," Peggy Buford said. "She doesn't have to sit in back of the bus anymore."

It was as if someone had suddenly slapped everyone's face simultaneously. As Aguilar looked around the room, the only one who wasn't in shock was Kevin. Although he wasn't smiling, there was a curious conspiratorial look in his eyes. And then Giselle started laughing.

"Girl," she said, turning her head to one side and pointing her finger at Peggy, "you colored folks?"

"What you think, Mama?" Peggy said, her English suddenly sounding like a *morena*.

"Look here, you passing and whatnot?" Giselle said. "Don't play yourself, girl! Don't tell me you one of those Mariah Carey, honky-looking, narrow-butt sisters?"

"Look out!" Peggy said, laughing, shaking her shoulders and closing her eyes in the most vulgar manner.

"Girl, you better chill!" Giselle said. "You got that good hair and blue devil eyes and you trying to get my baby brother lynched? You done did it now!"

And then everyone was laughing and Giselle and Peggy were high-fiving over the pumpkin pie and everybody was talking in that peculiar way that Nuyoricans had, going back and forth from English to Spanish, and when it was English sounding like *morenos*. Aguilar knew that he didn't like them talking that way but they didn't seem to care. Their mother, Victoria, wasn't quite sure what was going on but Aguilar did and it made him too uncomfortable. He smiled and got up from the table. His children paid no attention to him. They were too busy welcoming Peggy again in much too warm a manner for him. Giselle and Peggy had gotten up from the table and were hugging and kissing and pawing each other like they had known each other all their lives. Vicky asked him if he wanted a little coffee. He said he would and that he would be downstairs in the basement. He went down the stairs at the end of the hall to the little apartment he had fixed for guests, mainly his children when they came over. There were two bedrooms, a kitchen, a bath and a small living room with a color television. To the side was Kevin's large photo as he stood beside the transport plane.

After a while Victoria Aguilar came down with his coffee and set it next to him on a table on his right.

"Are you okay, *Papi*?" she asked.

"Sure," he said.

"The girl upset you."

"*Mami*, she's a *morena*."

"I know. Kevin loves her. It doesn't matter."

"She should've said something."

"She did in her own way."

"It wasn't right."

"She's a good girl, Rafi. She's smart, she's beautiful and it's obvious that she loves Kevin. And Kevin is crazy about her. Can't you see how he looks at her? He adores her. *Papi, se quieren mucho*, honey. Like you and me. Don't you see it?"

She knelt in front of Aguilar and put her head on his lap. He kissed her forehead and smoothed her hair, now graying a bit, her skin whiter than any Puerto Rican he'd known. She was his little *jíbara*, born and bred in the Bronx but *blanquita* like the snow falling outside.

"They'll have beautiful children, Rafi," Victoria said, sitting up and looking at him. "You'll see."

"*Morenos*," Aguilar said.

"Yes, and you'll love them like you do all your grandchildren. Look at Petey, Aurea's son. *El es bien grifito y trigueñito*. He's dark and his hair is frizzy. Don't tell me you don't love him."

"He's not a *moreno*," Aguilar said stubbornly. "He's Puerto Rican. He's my flesh and blood."

"Rafi, stop it," Victoria said sweetly. "So will Kevin and Peggy's children be your flesh and blood. You've always said that you're not a prejudiced man. Why start now? Come back upstairs. Everyone's wondering if you're okay."

"I'll be up later," he said. "Tell them not to worry. Tell them I'm resting."

## Moreno Eight—The Fiction

Victoria stood up, kissed his cheek, and went back upstairs. Aguilar sipped his coffee. And then his mind was traveling back to Keesler Air Force Base. In time he got used to the routine of learning radar and making new friends. Some of his friends would invite him to go into town but he remained on the base finding ways to amuse himself. He created a place inside himself that no one could reach. Even the few Puerto Ricans he ran into from New York could not penetrate the wall he had created around himself. In this place he was simply Puerto Rican and color was not supposed to matter. There was a movie theater and a PX where he could purchase things to send his mother. He would write every week as she asked and would go to the chapel each Sunday and pray for everyone. Each night he knelt and prayed as she had asked. He stopped writing to Lillian Morales. In his spare time he read many adventure books.

And then as he took another sip of coffee he recalled vividly *Kingsblood Royal*. He could see the cover of the novel and the name of the author, Sinclair Lewis. The cover was of a white man in a suit. It was a novel about a man who became intrigued with his last name, which was Kingsblood. He thought that perhaps he was related to English royalty. He had red hair and was white and when he began looking into his background he learned that he was descended from Negroes. He lost his job as a scientist and was forced to live like a Negro. He wasn't sure but he thought that the book had taken place in the North, rather than the South. In spite of the way Kingsblood looked he was a *moreno*. He remembered back then feeling great compassion for the man. The years, however, had changed him. It served Kingsblood right for trying to be something he was not, he thought now. He took another sip of the coffee and for the first time since he had known Victoria, her coffee tasted bitter.

# Ignacio Padilla
## (Mexico, b. 1968)

Ignacio Padilla studied communications and literature in Mexico, South Africa, and Scotland. His early fictional works include the short-story collection *Subterráneos* (1989), winner of the Mexican Alfonso Reyes Prize for young writers, and *La catedral de los ahogados* (1994), which garnered the Juan Rulfo Prize for First Novel. That same year his novella, *Imposibilidad de los cuervos*, was published in a collective volume entitled *Tres bosquejos del mal*, which included the novellas of two other young Mexican authors, Eloy Urroz and Jorge Volpi. The three had met in high school, attended writers workshops together, published an ephemeral literary journal, and even tried their hands at a collective and irreverently antirural story entitled "Variations on a Theme by Faulkner." In 1995, together with Pedro Angel Palau and Ricardo Chavez Castaneda, they published their now-famous, quintessentially iconoclastic "Crack" Manifesto. His second novel, *Si volviessen sus Majestades*, appeared the following year.

An author as prolific as he is multifaceted, Padilla has been the recipient of numerous prizes in different genres, from the Juan de la Cabada Prize in Children's Literature for *Las tormentas del mar embotellado* (1994), to the Malcolm Lowry Essay Prize for his book on the "Mexican mirages" of Paul Bowles (1994), to the Gilberto Owen Short Story Prize for his *Antipodes* (1999), from which the present story has been selected.

In 2000, he was awarded yet another prize, the Premio Primavera de Novela, for *Amphitryon*, a Borgesian novel of intrigue involving a fateful game of chess, a diabolical legion of doubles, and the army of the Third Reich. Padilla currently resides in London, where he also serves as cultural attaché to the Mexican consulate.

# The Antipodes
# and the Century

For them, Edinburgh was not so much a name for somewhere else but a secret voice that invoked the blessed city that had been destined for them from the beginning of time. It also meant undergoing forty days and nights in the Ka-Shun desert, lashing camels near to death. One after the other, men and animals would collapse exhausted on the dunes, gasping out a kind of prayer as they gave up the ghost, although no one could make out what language that wandering band had chosen to speak. All of a sudden, their eyes, dry now for so long from the wastes of stone and salt, filled once again with tears, in which Scotland's capital gleamed for a moment, a palace preserved in amber. It was as if someone had intruded into their retinas an elephantine fortress of streets, bridges, and windows which, like alien eyes from another century, would watch their own eyes close in final peace in their tombs of sand. Only then could the survivors leave behind their dead with their minds at ease, certain that both conquerors and conquered would find themselves again in the city that waited for them behind the Great Wall, where they could quench the dry thirst of the journey, to the sound of the bagpipes they had fashioned, out of yak bladders, using old instruments for pipes.

Under the weight of so many deaths and such longings, the wanderers had little time to think of the days they had left behind. A faint remembrance of a delicate rooftop in Beijing, the feel of rice paddies on the knees, or the memory of an unsuspecting foreigner who, involved in preparations for his journey, had come over to ask of them where their caravan was headed. It amused them to recall how one of the guides, tight-lipped or timid, answered that question with a vague shrug, waving a hand toward the western peaks and muttering the arcane name of the city in such an unmistakable Scottish accent that the questioning foreigner was sure he had misheard. "Edinbro" repeated the guide with a vague priestly gesture, before leaving abruptly, as though the mere mention of that name had acted like a spur to his side.

In fact, nobody had any exact idea in which meridian lay the city of such illusions. Not even the men who acted as caravan guides dared to go farther than a narrow pass on the horizon, a stony gash through which it was possible to make out a shimmering haze of towers that could well be a glassy mirage. Those who went past the point disappeared once and for all and, if on some occasion even the guides let themselves be led astray by the travelers, there was no way of knowing in Beijing if the caravan had gone beyond the spur of stone, or if sun, thirst, and the tortures of sand had obliterated them in the journey, as we might brush away a trail of insects. On such occasions, they had to discover all over again the traces of the city, decipher its location from the blind voices of opium smokers, or in the imprecise maps made on feverish nights when a sated nomad let fall to a prostitute more than he should have. Sometimes, however, the dark weight of the secret or the intensity of those who held it could not prevent some loudmouth from waking up in the common stocks, silenced as a warning to any who were dreaming of an opportune moment to set off in search of Edinburgh. They say too that in Mongolia today ghostly stories circulate about a German Jesuit who in his letters to Rome spoke of the existence of a kind of global map in the very heart of the Gobi Desert, a vague though tangible diorama of the cosmos, its center a replica of the Scottish capital. But the voices tell also how that man, with his books and his visions, was gone before anyone had been able to understand what he said. All in all, for the men of the Gobi, their city was neither replica nor reflection of anywhere else: it was the home, real and unique, that a divine messenger had ordered them to build half a century ago, when for them the world was little more than an expanse of dunes, kept alive by two feeble and cretaceous rivers.

They say too that in those days, far in the past by now, that divine messenger bore the name of Donald Campbell. He was the most distinguished member of the Geographical Society and had arrived in China too late to join the legendary expedition of Younghusband. Perhaps it was the vertigo of the desert or perhaps simply his sense of duty that drove Campbell to take to the desert alone, nursing the hope of one day becoming the Briton who retraced the steps of Marco Polo. But Younghusband never managed to meet his Scottish follower, for Campbell had not traveled more than a hundred miles when he was set upon by a patrol of Tibetan guards and left half dead in the dunes in a mess of blood. Nobody knows for how long or how fiercely that man wished for some wind from Scotland while his skin and his brain were broiling under the sun. What is known is that, one fine afternoon, a tribe of Khirgiz nomads saved him from death, set his body astride a camel, and so led him to the beginning or the end of his unfortunate journey.

Certainly it was then that the Scottish engineer lost the blessing of forgetting, to a point where time and the cosmos fused in his hallucinations. Suddenly, everything became for him a plan in which realities, wishful and actual, alternated, and the shiftings of his disturbed memory neither could nor wanted to sustain him in the desert. In his sun-scorched mind, those who saved his life

were not the Khirgiz but a battalion of grenadiers who had discovered his inert body in the sand, an army surgeon who healed
his wounds, and a naval vessel that had taken him and his men to
his beloved Edinburgh. Initially, perhaps, the city in its details and
the faces that greeted him in his family house in the Lawnmarket
seemed hazy to him, as if the spires, their features, and even their
speech were still contaminated by the unpleasant memories of
China that kept troubling his feverish brain; or perhaps some
morning his sickroom seemed to be covered with pelts, while the
waves of the North Sea sparkled for him with a sandy light, which
he put down to the effects of his sojourn in the Gobi Desert.
Campbell, however, was not long in returning to his university
chair in Old College, and if at times the faces of his students startled him with their slanted eyes, he was soon able to convince himself that things would eventually resume their proper course, and
that the desert would stay in his remembering only in the form of
those tricks of memory that would seem trivial to him, however
appealing.

The Khirgiz, meanwhile, gave themselves over with great passion to deciphering the delirious voice of the prophet the desert
had brought to them. With the help of those who knew something
of the world and its peoples who lived on the other side of the
Great Wall, the Khirgiz managed to transcribe his words one by
one. With great care, they transferred them to wooden tablets,
and they pored over them like scholars. Only then did they dare
to question Campbell, but only when they saw that he was distracted, wrapped in the all-embracing smile of those monks who
seem never to wake from their dreaming. With some luck, after a
few months, they were able to follow his instructions and carry
out his wishes, in utter conviction that a blessed deity had chosen
them to receive his designs from the Other Side. Later, when the
divine messenger showed signs of returning strength, they found
for him a cedar board and pieces of black chalk, so that he might
show them the shapes and measurements that previously in his

tent he had traced in the air with the passion of a teacher lost in his fanciful lecture. So, little by little but inevitably, through a mixture of patience and devotion, they learned the exact height that Edinburgh Castle must attain, the precise length of the bridge that connects the High Street with Waverly Station, the correct calculations necessary to establish the perimeter of Canongate Cemetery, or the true distance between the two spires of St. Giles Cathedral.

It was not many years before those drawings in the air began to take form among the rocks of the Gobi. The rumor that a divine voice was present in the desert drew a multitude of men and women who wished to dedicate their lives to building a vast sanctuary for a new religion, with a Templar-like liturgy in the form of measurements, azimuth lines, parabolas, and a whole host of topographical directions that the new inhabitants of Edinburgh had followed without thinking for various decades. Insatiable, devoted, they dug unceasingly in the sand, they shaped the rock as if it were just a question of helping the earth to become finally the place that had been taking shape deep within it for several centuries. Nothing drove them as much as the declining age of their prophet. Long had they waited for their moment of fulfillment, and in consequence their lives were filled with a cathedral-sized joy such as you find only in those races that have spent aeons in contemplating only the landscape. They were sure it would give them no trouble to learn later just how they should live and die in the city they were building. In time they would burn in the same Canongate three women heretics for their traffic with false dogma, they would drink malt beer from large ceramic mugs, and their children, heads full of elves and fairies, would end up detesting the English, although they dressed just like them and ended up speaking their language with a Caledonian cast; and they memorized the verses that Campbell, stirred by dreams of his students in Old College, would read to them for evenings on end, gesticulating in the air with his left hand and reciting the beginnings of the small universe that was taking shape for him in both stone and memory.

For forty years, Campbell had dispensed his knowledge in the halls of Architecture in Old College, fruitful years, no question, attached as he was to Edinburgh with the enthusiasm of someone who knows his words will not go wasted on the air, but will take on substance in the thousands of faces that passed before him in those years. Bit by bit, he gave up his Sunday habits and refused to be apart from his disciples, for he had discovered how much he loved them, how much he needed to speak with them, as a grounding for his mind, a distant mind that kept tricking him with nightmares and fantasies from the unfortunate wanderings of his youth in the deserts of China.

Finally, one morning, his body worn out with crisscrossing in his mind the map of his beginnings, he announced that this day would be the last of his life. Campbell appeared in the halls of Old College and told his students that he wished to say good-bye to the sea. Hundreds of hands bore him reverently to the top of Calton Hill, and from there the old architect wept for joy at the sight of the waves of the North Sea. Meanwhile, his beloved followers were watching in the far distance a mounting pinnacle of whirling sand, the prelude to the storm that would ultimately level the century, burying it under a vast sand dune, mountainous and mute.

*Translated by Alastair Reid*

# Carmen Posadas
## (Uruguay, b. 1953)

Carmen Posadas was born in Montevideo, where she lived until she was twelve. In 1965 the family moved permanently to Madrid, with interludes in Moscow, Buenos Aires, and London, where Posadas's father was ambassador. She began writing fiction in the mid-seventies, and confesses that her early dream was to "conceive a story in the style of Cortázar, but they all seemed to come out with a very Roald Dahlian touch. Not that I pretend to be able to write like Roald Dahl (I wish I could), but from that period on I developed an irresistible weakness for surprise endings." In 1984, the first of the seven novels she would write for young readers, *El señor viento Norte*, was chosen as the best children's book of the year by the Ministry of Culture. She has also published four books of essays, including one on "the Rebecca Syndrome" (1988), and collaborated on numerous scripts for television and film. It is her adult fiction, however, that has brought her international recognition.

In 1989, she published her first collection of stories, entitled *Mi hermano Salvador y otras mentiras*, which she would thoroughly revise and republish eight years later (with four additional stories) as *Nada es lo que parece* (1997). Her first novel, *Cinco moscas azules* (1996), a corrosively comic mystery reflecting the mores of Madrid's "snobbish" transition to democracy, won her high praise from critics and authors alike (including the Spanish novelist Manuel Vázquez Montalbán). Her second literary mystery, *Little Indiscretions* (1998), won the Planeta Prize and went on to sell over a half million copies in Spain alone. Posadas slyly teases the motives for murder out of a handful of dubious characters she has assembled for a night at the summer residence of a wealthy art collector, following the "accidental" death of a pastry chef who is suddenly trapped inside the kitchen locker-freezer. Published in France two years later, it sold another quarter of a million copies. Her latest novel, *La Bella Otero* (2001), is woven around the fictionalized biography of the celebrated Paris courtesan of *la belle époque*. Posadas lives in Madrid.

# The Nubian Lover

## I. I Don't Like Brahms

I don't like Brahms, but he does. I also know he prefers his oysters without lemon, loves beef Stroganoff, and adores homemade desserts. So I'll make him a rice pudding: the details are so important on a first date. . . . ("As if this were our first date, Laura! Come on, don't be silly. But isn't it? Of course it is.")

Everything must be perfect. For background music we'll have Brahms's *Sonata for Piano*, with Rostropovich and Serkin. Then I'll manage—even though I usually pay scant attention to such things—to have the place looking as homey as possible. It won't be difficult. The building has an old-fashioned feeling about it, and those who have been here have found it marvelous. My bedroom, which leads to the terrace, has a double bathroom. The living room is not very large, but the ruins of the shipwreck, that is, whatever was left from a quick divorce, fits nicely.

Lots of flowers. Just the right touch. I already bought them this morning. I'm no good with plants, so the place usually seems a bit cold. But I'll set a bunch of lilacs by the window, yellow roses on the sideboard, a pretty centerpiece on the dining room table, and voilà, the perfect home of the perfect successful woman. It's not good to show a weak side in front of men; they get scared easily if they think one desperately needs them, or is short of money—at least one of which is true in my case. ("But come on, Laura, you've always been great at keeping up appearances.")

And my physical appearance? Oh, I'm not so worried about that: I'm a natural redhead. Not that this, by itself, guarantees beauty, but in my forty-three years I have seen that we redheads emanate something mysterious in the eyes of certain men; it's as if suddenly they needed to be reassured that even when naked we still look like the beautiful pre-Raphaelite women that Dante Gabriel Rossetti immortalized in every imaginable pose. And from then on, I don't know how to explain it, a spell is cast that makes men helplessly dependent—as long as we possess the pre-Raphaelite trait I'm talking about. (And in my case the answer is yes, I am a true redhead, wherever they may look at me.)

It is seven now. I have enough time to finish the most cumbersome chores: to prepare dinner, arrange the flowers, and then, around eight, I'll be able to take care of my favorite task: the personal preparations. Actually, I think I enjoy the preparations more than the dates themselves. Much more than the time I actually spend with a friend, or a possible lover, I love the preliminaries, and I never allow things to be so rushed that I am deprived of this unique moment of private pleasure when I am alone with the anticipation and the idea that everything will be perfect. To dress for a man . . . there is nothing like it, with a lot of time to choose and to try on this dress and the other, with the mirror as an accomplice and solitude as a matchmaker. And solitude is always the best advisor: "No, no, none of that sex-shop underwear," it tells me, "though it's true that men are fascinated by garish reds and whorish blacks. But let's be shrewd, my dear: for a first date it's not good to look like Jean Harlow with her satins, and much less, like Jayne Mansfield with her garter belts. No, no, it's much better to wear something discreetly sexy, as if we had not expected to end up in bed. This way, the secret language of intimate clothes will suggest, 'Oh, how marvelous, darling, I could never have imagined that this would happen.'" Because that is how clothes that are well chosen speak for us. They are both innocent and cunning, how could I say it: they are so Lolita.

Afterward I'll have to think about my dress, because I'll wear a dress, and not pants: this is essential, never to hide your legs on a date like this. Well, Laura, now you have three delicious quarters of an hour to try on one dress, then another, and another . . . and when finally you have come to a decision, you must—and I will—leave it on the bed, next to the lingerie. After I get my clothes ready, I still have another fifty minutes to spend on my makeup, on my hair, and bathing, all exactly in reverse order, thinking, always thinking of the call I received at the office on Thursday, so sudden and unpredictable, who could have imagined it? "Hello . . . Laura? Do you know who I am?"

The water is very hot, but it doesn't matter, I'll take advantage of this modern bathtub, with its alternating cold and warm sprays, to have a really long and leisurely bath. Now it's not so hot anymore, it's very pleasant. This is a good omen, everything will go well now, I'm sure.

My body lets go so completely . . . and that is when I start to think about how the last four years have been for me since I separated from Miguel; hot water tends to play mean tricks, and it is a great lie that bubble baths only evoke moments of pleasure; sometimes they bring back memories of everything we have lost. What a colossal mistake the whole thing was, Laura. Thirty-nine is a very tricky age, at least it was for me. Thirty-*nine*, it sounds like a department-store promotion: *nine ninety-nine* and you fall for it and buy it, you buy what you shouldn't, because it looks like a bargain, and it's pretty, and seems indispensable really. That is how I bought my freedom from Miguel, believing I was carting off a bargain. And how not to be fooled? When you get married at twenty and live for another nineteen years with the same man, suddenly you have vertigo, what some people call a midlife crisis—but this sounds like psychobabble and I don't believe in psychology. However, I do believe in the power of numbers. Thirty-*nine*, just like nine ninety-*nine*: buy it now, don't miss this last opportunity, get it now or you'll be forever sorry. And I took it all, I mean, took my things, left the house, and moved in alone, and it didn't turn out too badly for me, at least professionally. In fact I have been much more successful than in all the time I was married: men never feel a lot of respect for their wives' professional careers. They still think we work in order to realize ourselves, or some such foolishness; they give us no support. That is why, to succeed in a profession, it's better to be alone. Fine, now that I already know this is true, my objection is precisely that it's much too true: once you have succeeded, you realize that you are lonelier than an oyster.

Of course there were many men in my life, and the hot water brings back the memory of all their embraces. I think there was a time when I even collected them, collected guys the way one collects stamps, cataloguing them: some for their aesthetic merits (Jorge, Alberto, Gian Carlo—ah, Gian Carlo!); others for their pecuniary merits (José Luis, Alfonso, and also that fool from the Holding Bank, whose name I can't remember). I even catalogued guys for their rarity, as if they were a stamp from Burundi, or from Papua, New Guinea (here let me not forget to mention Néstor, Hassim, even Sergei).

Enough. The water is hot and, in spite of everything, there are obvious stains in life that can never be lifted, not even with turpentine, let alone water, no matter how hot it is; but enough of that; besides, it's very late, quarter to nine, and I still have to get myself ready.

\*      \*      \*

As I sit on the bed, putting on my hose very carefully, all these
names come back to me. And it isn't fair for them to pester me this
way, since I have never brought any man here. In that, I'm very
old-fashioned: one's own bed is not for love affairs but for *love*.
How could it be otherwise? It's really stupid to contaminate one's
bed with ephemeral passions, with memories of sexual acrobatics
that make you laugh just thinking of them, with huffing and puffing, with faked kisses. Who can sleep with so many pesky ghosts?
My bed is mine, and so is my house; I never bring anybody here.

Shit! The beef Stroganoff. I left it on the fire, I almost forgot. I
hope it hasn't charred to a crisp. I also have to make sure the wine
is at the ideal temperature. . . . And the oysters? The oysters,
thank God (and my fish man) are already open and ready. Nine-
thirty. Just in time. How do I look? Perfect, I couldn't have chosen
a more appropriate dress, black is fantastic for us redheads. . . .
Does my kitchen smell? No, everything is under control; anyway,
I'm going to light one of those scented candles I got for Christmas. (They were from that dummy, Luis Jaime, do you remember,
Laura? The idiot made a big production out of bringing them,
saying that he got them at Floris of London, when here in Madrid
they are sold practically everywhere.) Well, enough of these
idiotic thoughts. What do I still have to take care of? The flowers
are ready. I'll draw the curtains and lower the lights . . . and then
the only thing I need to do is to start the music. Just in time. I hear
the porch bell: within minutes he will be here and at the moment
I open the door, Rostropovich and Serkin will be playing the *allegro affettuoso* or, better still, vigorously attacking the *allegro ap-
passionato*, as if I had been listening to that music for hours: a little
white lie, and so what! I don't like Brahms, but Miguel, my ex,
loves it.

## II. The Good Neighbor

"Egypt," Enrique said, wrinkling his nose. He has the most perfect nose I know, but when he wrinkles it, he spoils his Greek profile. Then he added, "But how conventional . . . and edifying. If you want me to tell you the truth, my precious, it looks like a real bore. When you could skip over, I don't know, say to Aruba or the Virgin Islands. Who would think of a marriage reconciliation trip to the old Nile to look at stones upon stones, monuments, and mummies? Of course, there's always hope you may find a few surprises, like a really stunning Nubian behind some reeds."

I had just told Enrique about my date with Miguel. I described to him in detail how well the Brahms tactic had worked, how little by little we kept cutting down the barriers that we had so carefully constructed during those four years of separation, although I refrained from confessing to him our intimacies on a night of rediscovered caresses with all their disquieting particulars. Enrique has an incredible knack for trivializing everything. (I'll never know whether that is a defect or a cardinal virtue. At times I suspect it's the latter.) And as soon as I told him about our plans for reconciliation, Enrique wrinkled his perfect nose to say flatly: "Egypt . . ."

Enrique is my neighbor and my best girlfriend. I intentionally said "girlfriend" because I've never had a more level-headed confidant; I have many friends of my own sex, but when I feel like talking about really intimate things, I always end up telling them to Enrique: he has the advantage of possessing a tremendous feminine intuition without the inconvenient, inevitable rivalry: after all, he's a guy.

When I moved to this house, it took me a long time to find out that one of the handsomest men in all Madrid lived next door. As often happens, to reinforce the apparent truth of the most common stereotypes, Enrique, with his six-foot-one frame, feline eyes, and a nose that could have been sculpted by Praxiteles, ended up having more feminine hormones than I. We spend afternoons doing laundry together, we lend each other skim milk, olive oil or Clorox. And we also help each other in all kinds of ways. Sometimes it is tactical logistic support, as when we use each other for an alibi. For example, once in a while he asks me: "Laurita, my precious, if you wouldn't mind, when Javi or Eduardo comes over, would you please tell them that I had to leave suddenly for a casting in Ibiza?" And then I ask him: "Henri" (he loves it when I call him Henri), "I'm going to transfer all my calls to your phone line. When that idiot from the Holding Bank calls, you tell him that your name is Ernesto, that you are my new husband, and he should take a hike."

We also support each other emotionally. He tells me all his troubles, which are many, and I tell him mine; we lick each other's wounds, as they say, which is very nice in these times, when it's quite a feat to find a shoulder to cry on. This is why I didn't understand why he took such an extreme position when he learned about my reconciliation with Miguel. After all, that was what I wanted most.

"You don't know what you want, sweetie," he said, and right away I realized that he was in his skeptical (or should I say cynical?) vein. Enrique never says "sweetie" seriously, and always changes his tone to make it sound ridiculous: "You don't know what you want. Have you already forgotten all of your conjugal tedium? How about those card parties with other couples that bored you to tears, making you conclude that if this was life, it was better to slit your wrists? And those endless hours watching football in front of the TV, with Miguel eating sunflower seeds and you biting your fingers to keep from hitting him? And the toenail clippings in the bathtub? And the tube of toothpaste always left open until it dried up? You women forget too soon the marital inconveniences that caused you to separate in the first place. These petty things end up weighing even more than the infidelities, my precious. Infidelities cause pain at least, but tedium makes you numb. It really kills you, I'd say. There's nothing more lethal than boredom."

He told me all this in earnest, while he ironed a light blue dress shirt. It is quite something to watch Enrique ironing. He's such a hunk, in just khaki shorts as if he were the English Patient in the middle of his trip through the desert. Except that we were not in Africa (not at the moment anyway) but in Madrid, with Henri involved in his domestic chores and, at the same time, trying to ruin my newfound happiness: at last meeting with Miguel, after wanting it for so long . . . and our plans for reconciliation. He even dared to make fun of the trip to Egypt that we were planning to take the following week. Who knows? Maybe Henri is right; it might be a stupid romantic idea to seal our getting together again with a kind of honeymoon trip. It's a corny idea befitting Doris Day, but, what would love be without these foolish sentimental touches?

Henri kept ironing his shirt and I wondered what kind of date he was getting ready for. He seldom wore dress clothes—by this I mean a suit and tie—but I did not ask any questions. My friend tends to be very reserved at the start of a new love relationship. It's only later, when everything annoys him, that he tells me about it. There are people who need friends to help them pick up the pieces once the whole thing has irreparably broken up; I am not like that. On the contrary, what I wanted was to share my joy with Henri. But he kept meticulously ironing his shirt, never admitting any of the favorable omens, only the ones that meant trouble.

"And then you have to take into account," he continued lecturing me, "that sequels are never any good. And don't you believe, sweetie, that this is just a worn-out old saying. It's the voice of experience, I'm afraid. You, and all those who realize they have been wrong in a big way, might think that a reconciliation means starting again from the beginning, as if you could suddenly erase four years in a person's life. But you cannot erase those four

years, much less forget them, and men will bill you retroactively
for each minute you have not lived with them. Don't I know."

Henri was talking like a scorned and spiteful old aunt, bent
over the ironing board, and I had to make an effort not to laugh:
neither he nor anyone else was going to ruin one of my happiest
moments in years, no matter how much he lectured me.

"The worst part by far is the jealousy, let me warn you," he
continued as he finished the cuffs. "The truth is, women have no
idea how a guy thinks. So that you'll know, when a woman has
been his, she is his forever, even though she might have spent four
years playing the successful entrepreneur, free and independent.
Now Miguel will say that he doesn't care what you've done with
your life during that time. But I assure you: it all comes out the
moment you're back together, the past loves . . . and the ghosts
that appear at every corner and come to life again as soon as you
look at another guy. Think about it, Laura, over there in Egypt
you won't have your old friend Henri to give you advice, or to
serve as your accomplice or your alibi."

At that point I got up to leave. It's almost not in character for
Henri to get into a Miss Frances mode and launch so suddenly
into unsolicited advice. For a moment I thought there was something more personal in all this. Why was he talking that way? Was
it possible that *he* was jealous of Miguel? Nonsense, he never
cared for women, and me least of all, because I am his "wastebasket," as he says with doubtful elegance: the receptacle in which,
sooner or later, he deposits all his crumpled papers—or dirty
laundry. And, hormones aside, one doesn't fall in love with people
whose most unutterable faults are too familiar. Impossible. Much
more likely was that all his lecturing came from his fear that my
new relationship would deprive him forever of his wastebasket,
his confidante, or what amounts to the same, his neighbor always
ready to come to the rescue, even at the most difficult moments.

He must be just feeling selfish, that's it. Probably I even said so, I don't know, I was pretty mad at him. And I really felt like walking over to his ironing board and wrinkling that stupid shirt he was fussing over. But Henri continued unperturbed, giving the finishing touches to the pale blue front panel, and in order to annoy me, I suppose, he began to sing, softly to himself, one of the great tangos, the one that fits us forty-year-olds so well: "*Volver, con la frente marchita, las nieves del tiempo,*" etc. Yes, to go back with a withered brow, once the sands of time . . . "You rat," I thought, and although I didn't dare wrinkle his shirt, which is what my body demanded, I do remember shouting at him on my way out: "I hope your new lover turns out to be as idiotic as all the others!"

And he smiled, totally unflappable. No, I'm lying. It was even worse: I saw him laugh with those God-given perfect lips. Before I slammed the door after me, I managed to hear his final words.

". . . however, since I am your friend, my precious, and want to prove that I do love you and wish the best for you, let me hope that on your trip you find yourself a Nubian lover."

I wish he had not said that.

## III. The Trip

I don't believe in forebodings, so I saw nothing peculiar in the many little mishaps at the start. Maybe I shouldn't call them "little mishaps" because the trip Miguel and I took to Egypt was accident-riddled from the beginning.

Everything went all right until we got to Paris, where we were supposed to make a connection with flight 714 to Cairo. But after our arrival at Orly, things began to go wrong. I'm not afraid of flying but, like everybody else, I get nervous when there is a bomb threat. We had one, and the tarmac was full of policemen and firemen, and the big question was, What's going on? What are they going to do with us? Useless questions against the proverbial re-

serve of flight attendants and their flight commander. We were finally able to board, just to disembark forty-five minutes later,
more bored than nervous by then, but still retaining the appropriate spirit of tourists headed for Cairo. That is, after a tiresome wait,
all of us—well, most—had on our laps a copy of *Death on the
Nile*. (As anyone who has visited Egypt knows, Agatha Christie's
old novel occupies as indispensable a place in any tourist's luggage
as antidiarrheal chewable tablets or SPF 15 sunblock.)

We were almost ready for takeoff when one of those soothing
voices with a nasal twang announced from the pilot's cabin: "We
are sorry to inform you that, for security reasons, this craft will be
vacated. We expect to resume flight procedures within an hour
and a half at most (what a euphemistic schedule), and we hope
that you will forgive . . ."

Six hours later, around five! in the morning, an exhausted group
of French and Spanish tourists, some of whom were wearing
Egyptian outfits before departure (they brought their kaffiyeh and
matching *igal* from home instead of buying them in the country's
markets), finally took off toward Cairo without any more incidents.

At least, not until we got there.

Cairo is one of the most intimidating cities I know. It is fascinating, moving like a great serpent that coils and uncoils on itself. Its
traffic jams are notorious, but even more so is the incessant din of
the thousands of cars crossing it at all hours, day and night, without the slightest regard for traffic laws and, I would dare add,
even for the law of gravity. To this imposing procession of teeming, honking, overwhelming, pestiferous vehicles, there is also,
blended in, a surprising parade of countless Egyptian film ads
(some with sound): gigantic posters of smiling fake blondes and
their mustachioed cavaliers imitating Clark Gable. But there is
still more: for how can I leave out the calls to prayer from the
ubiquitous mosques. And the shouts and swearing in the streets.
And the beggars' litanies. The whole place vibrates in such a way

that the traveler is helplessly enveloped in this unique Cairo din that accompanies him or her until the very moment of boarding the plane to go back home.

But we have barely arrived and I still haven't gotten to the brief story of another incident (not a particularly bad omen) that we lived through that day. It's a matter of logic that on a "honeymoon" a couple would prefer the most pleasant surroundings. Miguel had made a reservation at the Mena House Oberoi, an old hotel in Cairo, perhaps not the best, but surely the most charming, with magnificent vistas of the pyramids, located in a somewhat run-down Islamic building where it would not be overly surprising to suddenly encounter Somerset Maugham's double reading *The Times* on the veranda.

However, due to one of those unfathomable misunderstandings among tour operators, we landed in another hotel of inferior rank (and in Egypt "inferior" means frightful). It had to be reached by going through a patisserie named Le Bec Sucré, and then a sordid hallway. In fact, the only thing that was sweet about the place was this little cake shop, because the rest of the lodging, with its plastic flowers and its questionably clean blankets, left much to be desired, at least for us, being basically—very basically—a brand-new couple.

It's interesting to observe how love reconciliations develop under two different psychologies that coexist and overlap. In the first place (and now I am talking not in the abstract but concretely, about Miguel and me), both lovers are trying hard to respect the distances and niceties of living with a novice lover, making every possible effort to avoid any anticlimax that could spoil their love. During the first days that Miguel and I spent in Egypt, I was surprised to find myself laughing at our behavior. Because we were being so tentative with each other that the whole situation reminded me of Albert Cohen's novel *Belle du Seigneur*. Above all, it brought to mind, and this made me blush, the hilarious episode in which the lovers, Solal and Ariane, with the eagerness of neurotic criminals, attempt to erase all the usual unpleasant traces left by humans living together, and which become so unforgivable when both are trying to keep a love relationship in the antiseptic realm. Like them, in silent agreement Miguel and I took turns getting up from bed, for instance, in order to avoid any kind of confrontation regarding the use of the shared bathroom. Sometimes Miguel got up really early, and emulating Solal, tried to save me from the preliminary thunder, and then from the disastrous clamor of flushing the toilet. At other times, just like any Ariane would do, coiffed, bathed, and in a white déshabillé, I ran to open the bathroom window in order to freshen the air. Both attitudes were so charmingly Versaillesque as to deserve a medal for their hopeful, romantic efforts.

The curious counterpoint to this consummate behavior was our lovemaking.

The most surprising fact of such reunions is that, crossing the barriers of time, the body is capable of reestablishing a unique and personal relationship so easily, as if in the meantime there had not been other bodies, other kisses. Four years of estrangement represent, when one is getting closer to being half a century old, some inevitable physical changes. Miguel's baldness was a little more noticeable, and he had gained some weight. Perhaps his eyes, which were always his most interesting feature, did not shine as before; but in a dark embrace one is blinded to all these transformations. In contradiction to this blindness, other body parts, including hands, lips, and also the tongue, keep their faculties in prime condition, so that each one, with great celerity, finds its path to the most recondite nooks. In amazement, the lover undertakes in this way the same old excursions with wise fingers that haven't changed but now enjoy the priceless advantage of being able to raise pleasure to a level attainable only when passion has not yet become a routine.

"Have you realized how easy this has been?" Miguel asked me one night. We were not in bed, nor in view of the pyramids, nor of any of those colossal monuments, so often encountered in Egypt, that make us realize how small our petty worries are, and how silly our disaffections seem. We were simply sipping a Coke at the bar of the unsavory hotel with its bunches of plastic flowers and its smell of tablecloths washed in cheap soap. Then I took his hand. I have a lot of trouble explaining what I feel when it is something deep and important, but Miguel already knows well my "silent answers," as he used to call them in the old times. Silent answers which at once I usually tried—and I still try—to translate into kisses, because that's what they really are and mean. Kisses that say "I love you" and "I need you" and also, as on this occasion, kisses that shout: "Don't you ever leave me, let's get old, you and I together until death do us part, yes, only death, and nobody else."

Sweet words of love are commonplace, and they are also corny or else become hollow from overuse, but kisses that act as mediators speak with an eloquence no poet will ever achieve. That's why, that evening at the hotel bar, I kissed Miguel's hands meaning all those words, witnessed by some yellowing plastic magnolias that will never guess from what depths this silent verbiage was coming.

"And tomorrow we'll fly to Karnak," Miguel said, because men get a bit upset (actually a lot!) at declarations of love when they were not the ones who planned the when and the where.

"The boat that will take us downriver is the *Sobk*," he added. "I think *Sobk* refers to a serpent goddess or a crocodile goddess, I don't know, something like that. But in any case she's considered the queen of the Nile," he insisted. "That's a good omen, don't you think, dear?"

## IV. The Crocodile God Makes His Appearance

The *Sobk*, a boat of the Queen of the Nile line, turned out to be the sixth in a series of closely docked vessels so identical in appearance that I soon had to learn to distinguish it by the details of its interior decoration. The number of vessels cruising the Nile with thousands of tourists of all nationalities is such that it would be impossible to dock them except with gunwales touching, and so they form a strange and undulating tunnel. In order to reach the *Sobk* (which, by the way, does not refer to a goddess but to a crocodile god), each of us had to go—loaded with luggage, several cameras, and last-minute souvenirs—through five other ships that were as much queens of the Nile as ours. The first one was decorated in Chinese style; the second, in its turn, honored the Taj Mahal, plaster elephant and all. Farther on was the peacock vessel with details reminiscent of Persia; then came one decorated with Andalusian doodads where one could hear, of course, "Ay, Macarena"; and finally we reached the *Sobk*, which fortunately was pretty restrained and not very cosmopolitan.

Our group of around twenty (half were Spanish and the other half French and looking terribly intellectual) began dispersing slowly toward the staterooms, under strict orders to be on deck at three sharp, ready for our first Nile visit: the magic enclave of Karnak.

I suppose I should dedicate a few lines here to describe the people that chance had assembled for our tour. As I said before, it was a combination of Spaniards, mostly Catalans, and a French group which, considering the unfailing attention they were paying to our guide, probably had to pass a test on advanced Egyptology on their return home. They all went around carrying various books, looking at maps, and jotting things down in their waterproof notebooks. I have never seen such frenzied interest. On the other hand, we Spaniards, with our more relaxed cultural spirit, let's say, were having more fun. Miguel and I soon befriended a young couple from Tarrasa. We began by sharing a table in the dining room, and we became inseparable after that. It is always pleasant to have someone with whom to comment on the events of the day, and, with the instant complicity that being in a foreign country produces, we quickly found ourselves gossiping about the other passengers, and also combining our newfound friendship with whatever information and help we could exchange about the photographic equipment that each of us had brought along. In addition, we acted as each other's paparazzi, and in this way Álvaro and Merce would sometimes take our picture next to an imposing column. At other times, the four of us had to run (once Miguel's Nikon was set) perhaps in order to pose by the lonely obelisk at the entrance to Luxor, while deploring Egyptologist Champollion's daring feat of having carted the twin obelisk off to Paris, to adorn the Place de la Concorde, no less.

Out of the French group that always moved like a compact herd, I was interested only in a woman about thirty-something, traveling with her husband or lover of about the same age, but who had a much duller presence. Unlike the others, they kept apart from their group, whispering into each other's ears and embracing behind each rock. What caught my attention, however, was not their infatuation, which frequently happens on tourist trips, after all, but rather her physical resemblance to me.

I found it strange that nobody else noticed this resemblance, not even Miguel mentioned it, but we redheads (and she was, too) know how to find certain shared traits that perhaps are not obvious to other people. I'm referring to little habitual movements like the particular way of lowering one shoulder, or moving the fingers in a soft cadence: characteristic gestures that in her case, however, were obliterated in the presence of other more conspicuous attributes. Sirrine, that was her name, was one of those women for whom it is impossible to go unnoticed. She was small but voluptuous, a fact that she showed off by wearing tight T-shirts that did not take into account her thoracic perimeter, and jeans two sizes too small for her curving behind. "Just a vulgar redhead," I thought, without being able to avoid the critical, comparative reflection. I have always considered that I belong to the group of sophisticated redheads, but even so, we had something strong in common. How lucky I was, I told myself with some relief, that the resemblance is only obvious to me.

Another character worthy of comment was our tourist guide. Her name was Françoise Durand du Selle and she adored her work. Only that can explain her constant readiness to climb the steepest crags or to descend with adolescent enthusiasm dozens of feet underground, just to show us by the light of her small flashlight, who knows, maybe a tiny goddess Maat, for instance, identical to hundreds of other tiny images of Maat that we had already seen in hundreds of hieroglyphic murals, also identical.

Moreover, Françoise was perfectly bilingual and she explained the marvels before our eyes in precise Spanish, after having said the same thing in French, and always ending her comments with the words "*bien entendu.*"

With a smile and a soft cadence, she would unfold her descriptions until she ended up with "*blah-blah-blah et voici la déesse Isis qui protège la momie. Elle est aussi l'épouse d'Osiris, bien entendu.*"

Her last phrase became a kind of alarm clock for me. Perhaps this comparison is not a very felicitous one, but the truth is that it served me as an infallible call to attention: I knew that after those two words I had to prick up my ears because very soon another interesting explanation would follow in Spanish, about the mysteries of old Egypt.

It was not until the third day of our tour that I could finally decipher another mystery, not precisely millenary, but rather modernly bureaucratic. From the moment we left Cairo, next to Françoise there was always a silent character who would be replaced every two or three days. A shadow that never failed to accompany our guide.

First she was joined by a woman wearing flowing garments and a kerchief over her head, tied under her chin. Judging by her looks, she could have been one of the many housewives one meets around the markets, but her eyes revealed a sharp intelligence, and, at the same time, *something* that I would dare call a predatory, silent cruelty; I don't know how to explain it any better. However, one day she vanished, but was soon replaced by a man wearing a gray djellaba who looked quite harmless. He only moved among us making use of a pretty fly whisk with an ivory handle.

"They are official Egyptian guides," Merce whispered to me one day when we stopped at a stand to buy water for our canteens. Merce always whispered when she had a bit of information, even if there was no one remotely within earshot and the information totally lacked any relevance.

"Look, I found out all about it," she explained in the expeditious tone adopted by those devoted to investigating minor details as well as big secrets.

"Here in Egypt it's the law that local guides must accompany foreign ones everywhere they go. This is *absolutely* obligatory, though they might not even have to say a word. We are assigned one for each zone we visit. Can you imagine? Madame Vulture Eyes accompanied us in Luxor and Karnak; the Lord of the Flies escorts us today and also tomorrow for the visit to the Kom Ombo temple. Two very forgettable characters. I wonder who will be assigned to us for our visit to Aswan. I hope that one is nicer than these two, for we'll have to live together on board for three days." Merce continued talking. It was a delight to have her as a traveling companion, with her efficient news reports saving me the nuisance of having to read the program for the day.

"Listen, after the visit to Abu Simbel we still have to stay in Aswan for two days to see other things up the Nile. And by the way," she added suddenly with that Catalan accent that I find so charming, "do you have any idea at what time we are leaving for tomorrow's excursion? At three in the morning!"

"*Osti tu,*" I felt like saying to Merce in Catalan, because for any tourist in Egypt there is really nothing worse than the punishing schedules. It was indeed a punishment to join the caravan of tourist buses on the way to Abu Simbel at such an inauspicious hour, supposedly in order to avoid the heat (an unnecessary precaution at that time of the year). But even so, what's the use of complaining: everything on an escorted tour operates with a logic that has nothing to do with common sense. You learn that on the first day, and from that moment on, you have to let yourself be led by the good shepherd (bubbly Françoise, in our case). The good shepherd calms her herd and allows no possibility for straying, except at most for a two-minute delay, by some daring sheep, in getting on or off the bus.

I decided to sleep on the way there, nested against Miguel's compassionate shoulder. The bus kept jolting us for hours, and there were tactical delays that nobody cared to explain, hours that did not exist for me, dreaming in my husband's arms. That is why it was such a big surprise when I opened my eyes and realized that the tourist bus had already stopped. I was completely alone in the bus. Through the window I could see Françoise and the French group walking away toward the entrance to the temple. A little closer, and having fun aiming their cameras at my dazed, sleepy face, Miguel and Álvaro were taking turns, click, click, immortalizing my embarrassing situation.

"Please allow me to help you, madame," said a voice to my left in almost perfect Spanish. "I could carry your backpack for you, if you wish. My name is Kalim. I will be your guide in the land of the Nubians."

The man smiled, revealing the whitest and most handsome teeth I had ever seen.

## V. Do, Re, Mi, Fa, Sol . . .

Daylight was barely breaking and I was not really awake yet. Getting off the bus, I thanked the man for his kindness, and ran to join my group.

Then I could take a better look at him. The Nubian guide, the one who would accompany Françoise during our visit to Aswan, possessed an impressive physique. He was very tall, at least six foot three, and was dressed in Western clothes, with a pair of jeans too short for him and a white T-shirt. He smiled, he always smiled, more with his eyes than with his mouth. His eyes were like those in Renaissance portraits that, no matter from what angle you look at them, always seem to be looking at you. This makes it very difficult to take your eyes off such a persistent gaze.

But Françoise had just pronounced the password and I instinctively turned my head. *Bien entendu.* Now that her French explanation was over she would turn to the Spanish group to delve into the mysteries of one of the most extraordinary places on earth. Concentrate, Laura, this is Abu Simbel, you cannot miss a single word now, I thought. And I was right.

"Abu Simbel," Françoise explained, "is two hundred eighty kilometers away from Aswan. From the old colonial village only two temples carved out of the heart of a mountain remain today. Their location had to be changed due to the construction of the Aswan High Dam, and now we are almost two hundred feet above the original site. It was a big enterprise, worthy of the Egyptian colossi," Françoise added with admiration. "Stone by stone, the temple was moved here," she continued, "first, the small one to your right, which Ramses II ordered built for his favorite wife, Nefertari, and then this one to your left. Take a look at it," Françoise exclaimed, filled with her usual enthusiasm (more than justified on this occasion). "This is the great temple dedicated to Amun, and also to Ra-Horakhty and to the pharaoh himself, Ramses II the Great. Look at the facade guarded by four giant effigies of the pharaoh. Two of them were damaged during an earthquake, but that does not detract at all from their magnificence. To give you an idea of the proportions of these colossi, suffice it to say that the nose of each Ramses is the size of a grown man."

Did Ramses belong to the Nubian race by any chance? I don't

like to interrupt a guide with questions, but those perfect features, those almond eyes and thick lips . . . Heavens. Someone had told me that the southern pharaohs had dark skin like the present inhabitants, beautifully black like the man at the bus who had addressed me in correct Spanish barely half an hour before. And I wondered: So is this what is considered the legendary Nubian beauty? All the romance novels and even the serious ones set in Africa speak with admiration of this unique race, and all the romantic topics rushed into my head at once. Come on, this is simply a touristic curiosity, nothing more, I thought, but so many questions popped into my mind. Why not ask him? He spoke Spanish even better than Françoise. What did he say his name was? Kalim, that's it, and wasn't it surprising that I remembered his name even though I was half asleep when we met. I glanced around looking for him.

But Kalim had disappeared.

Whether Françoise explained in detail the magnificent facade of that temple, I will never know. By the time my mind returned from its wanderings in an ethereal ramble devoted to thinking of *another* tourist guide, Françoise's voice had already started a new explanation for the French group.

"Come, let's take advantage of the cultural reprieve to pose for a picture next to Nefertari's statues," Miguel said then, dragging us all, including Merce and Álvaro, who did not miss the opportunity to comment that Nefertari was the best-endowed woman in all of ancient Egypt. (Is there any male tourist on the Nile who can refrain from eventually making the same remark?) Merce then joked, "Well, the temple that Ramses built for her looks like a doghouse next to his, but at least he remembered her, while most other pharaohs didn't even know where their wife was buried."

"*Blah-blah-blah et bien entendu,*" we heard Françoise conclude from far away, and we had to run not to miss her next explanation. In the life of a tourist, there is no respite.

Françoise had another favorite word, "amigos," when starting her commentaries in Spanish: "Let's see, amigos." It's a ubiquitous word in American films when a Mexican or a Latin American speaks, but I have never heard a Spaniard use it. Foreigners love it.

"Let's see, amigos," she announced, and then launched enthusiastically into an interesting anecdote.

"You should know that the great pharaoh Ramses II was a Nubian (ah, here's the answer to my question, I couldn't help but appreciate with a special pleasure). He was born precisely in this region of Egypt, the one closest to the Sudan, but his hair was *red*. That was quite unusual, especially among Nubians. When you visit the Cairo museum, if you go to the hall of the mummies, you will see for yourselves that the famous member of the Ramsesside Nineteenth Dynasty and one of the most famous pharaohs in history, besides being very tall and perfectly proportioned as Nubians are, was also a redhead. And now, I'll tell you something that is not strictly historical," Françoise added, just like someone who is about to reveal a scandalous bit of gossip about a neighbor or relative. "Do you remember that I told you (I did not remember anything, perhaps I was thinking about something else when she told us) that during his reign Ramses fostered the worship of Seth, already established by his father. Seth is a mean god and a lord of the desert, in a word, an untamed force," Françoise whispered, her tone getting more confidential. "His father had ratified the cult of Seth, but it was Ramses II who really institutionalized this god. Now, could it be that, considering himself different because of his hair color, he felt the need to be surrounded by this ambivalent spirit? *Ah, mystère!*" intoned Françoise, this being *another* of her most resounding pet phrases. "Anyway, to get to the truth after three thousand years is impossible," she continued. "In my opinion, the most logical explanation is that Ramses introduced this perverse god all over his realm because the southern tribes worshiped it. That is, because it was a Nubian like him. And by the way, do you know that nobody has been able to decipher what this god's face represents? Is it a dog? Or a pig, perhaps? Or is it a donkey? In any case, the truth is, amigos," Françoise concluded with a very French shrug of her shoulders, "that it's a very strange deity of a very red-haired pharaoh."

I had to turn my head. Sometimes it seems as if one had eyes in the back of the head. I felt sure that someone was looking at me from behind. And there was Kalim, with his all-embracing gaze that might have been focusing on me, on Merce, or on any of the other tourists as well, even on the French redhead who wore those tight T-shirts. He was not smiling, and he was toying with his belt, the style of which seemed to me much less Western than his jeans or the rest of his clothes. It was just a plain black leather strip, hanging from which there were four or five flat metal figurines, each one about the size of a small cigarette lighter. When he noticed that I was looking at him, he put his arms behind his back, like a well-behaved child, and smiled. I thought he was rocking himself back and forth from the tips of his shoes to the heels, but I couldn't really tell, since his face made it difficult to focus on other parts of his body: Such perfect teeth, I thought, and when I turned my attention back to Françoise, our bilingual guide was already addressing the French group.

This time I did not make use of the pause to joke with Miguel or Merce, or to increase the already large number of photographs, videos, and so on, that we had accumulated in the course of the morning. I chose to remain where I was, next to Françoise and listening to her explanation, which I only half understood. But I did not care. At her side, always like a silent shadow, the Nubian guide toyed with the metal figurines on his belt. And he would make them tinkle, one by one, as if they were tiny bells: do . . . re . . . mi . . . fa . . . sol . . . , a musical note for each of the five identical effigies.

*       *       *

My French is not very good, but I wanted to hear, in a preview version, the information about another famous phenomenon found inside the Ramses temple.

"But Laura," Miguel insisted behind me, "why are you being so stubborn, if a minute from now she will tell us, in plain Spanish, what you're trying to—"

Yet Françoise's explanation was easy to understand. Besides, Kalim was there.

"Twice a year," our guide began in her native French, "on February nineteenth and on October twenty-first, the sun comes in through the door of the big temple and illuminates in succession only three of the statues inside, which, except on those two dates, remain in utter darkness. One of the statues represents Amun, the second is Ra-Horakhty, and the third one, Ramses. The fourth statue, next to these, remains in the dark all the time: it represents Ptah, the supreme artist of the gods."

Little by little I had separated from the group to delve deeper into the interior of the temple. The four gods, so dark and silent, were scarcely visible in their niche, though the sun outside was shining gloriously on Abu Simbel. I took a look at the statues, which resembled the ones that we had seen in other temples and, of course, were much less impressive than the eight colossi, sixty-five feet tall, that watch over the entrance to the temple like silent, majestic soldiers.

Do . . . re . . . mi . . . fa . . . sol . . .

This time I did not need to turn my head to know that the Nubian guide had followed me there. A very soft ray of light reflected on the ceiling from the metal figurines hanging from his belt, with which he so often toyed. And again that tinkling sound reverberated through the millenary walls. Do re mi fa sol. . . .

"Lauraaa!" It was Miguel's voice, calling me from outside.

"Shit, Laura, I've been calling you for the last half hour: Can you tell me what the fuck you were doing inside there?"

## VI. A Costume Party

Three days and three nights. Three days sailing up the Nile. Once our visit to Abu Simbel was over, we boarded the *Sobk* again, which was waiting for us at the port of Aswan to take us to Elephantine Island, the Aga Khan's house, and to Lord Kitchener's botanical garden, all of this on the first day. On the second day, we would see the temple of Edfu, and, on the third, the marvelous temple of Hathor.

It is fortunate that we had cameras and video cameras, because thanks to them I am able to write today just as well as if so much splendor had been imprinted in my memory instead of only being recorded on photographic paper and magnetic tape. I know, for instance, that we saw the house of Aga Khan because I have proof: a photo with Merce and me riding on a camel. "Come on, girls, get a little closer, don't be afraid, no one is going to bite you. Yes . . . that's better." (Fragmented memories that come back to me when I see the albums again.) It is also easy for me to reconstruct the tour thanks to some almost professional snapshots that Álvaro took: Miguel and I holding hands, wondering at the thousands of botanical specimens that Lord Kitchener had ordered to be planted when he was in this region. And then, forever present in my photo album, the temple of Edfu, seen now admirably intact after being dug out of the desert sands that for centuries had preserved it from plunderers and from the spoliation of time. And finally in our home video, there is the tour to Dendera, the temple with the brightest colors of all those we saw. There is a pretty original take of its famed vestibule, twenty-four images of the goddess Hathor, aligned in groups of six. Besides, on that same video, there is Miguel, besieged by a swarm of beggars and peddlers, some wearing turbans, others with mysterious archeological pieces wrapped in newspapers: "*Compra, siñor, compra, please buy me, achetez, achetez . . .*" And then Miguel, now irritated as we can see in the video, is buying me one of those long white pieces of cloth to wrap around my head as a turban. I protest then, annoyed but smiling, "No, no, please, don't do that, let me be."

Yes, all of this appears in the video and in the photos, and that's why I know that it happened.

In my true memory, on the other hand, there is only one thing I remember, and it is not touristic at all.

They say that passion—or should I write the madness of love?— is turbulent. That it attacks suddenly, blurring reality to such an extent that, as we bestow all sorts of virtues on the beloved, we end up converting them into perfect beings. But nobody warns us about the obstinate attachment that our body acquires for this perfect being. How to explain then that we cannot draw our eyes away from the beloved's gaze, no matter how much we try? And if he is close enough, what an enormous effort it takes to stop us from a caress? "Holy Heaven! my hand, that unruly finger . . . ," and finally, overcome, we resign ourselves to merely touching his clothes furtively. Then, there are the sounds we love dearly, those we learn to distinguish among a thousand others: his breathing, the ground beat of his steps: "He's coming, it's him," and we tremble with anticipation, "he'll be close to me, I'll be able to perceive the scent of his body, and watch the tensing of his muscles under his dark skin. . . ."

Because of all this, of the three excursions I just spoke about, there is no trace in my memory of the blue headdress of the goddess Maat, but of the undefinable gray of a Nubian shirt. The same thing happens with sounds: the desert wind among the ruins never existed for me, I did not hear it sing through the temple openings, as all tourists will swear it does. The only sounds I remember are those sandal steps behind me (and God Almighty, I detest men wearing sandals; love *is* truly blind): "Kalim is here" was my only thought. He was always near me, without ever saying a word or smiling. In fact, he had not said anything besides a "good morning" since we met inside the temple of Ramses. What a mess; now I knew what torture is, and love and anxiety and fear, fear above all, that someone, Miguel precisely, would surely notice the madness, since I was convinced that it was written all over my face.

"Well, I am going to wear a mask," Merce told me on the third day. "I don't give a hoot, you know, if Cleopatra didn't wear one. With all these zits from the Egyptian sun, you cannot expect me to appear at the party showing my face."

"You could wear a veil; I'm not sure Cleopatra did, but it will suit you better," I replied.

On the evening before our last night on board, there was going to be a costume party, and Merce and I were very eager to put together the right costumes for us. Finally, we took the easiest way out. Merce bought for herself a kind of red tunic and a matching veil with small golden coins hanging on her forehead, while I chose the same model but in black, nothing very original, but who cared about the party; I could think of nothing else but Kalim. I anguished at the thought that he might not be invited, even though it would be the logical thing. All these ships hold noisy dance parties where people mix, talk, and sometimes dance, I thought to myself, like a schoolgirl anxiously waiting for her prom, expecting (and wishing) that thanks to the alcohol and the euphoria, or the alibi provided by the costumes, she would be able to talk to that boy with whom she had only had shy exchanges during the whole term.

"Anything wrong?" Miguel asked me when we were both dressed up, I with my black tunic and he in his Hercule Poirot disguise—though he's not fat or bald enough, and also lacks the absurd black mustache.

"What do you think? Surely nobody thought of being a character from *Death on the Nile*. How do I look?" he asked as if trying, on purpose, to change the topic.

"Perfect, very funny," I answered automatically, but in fact he looked ridiculous, and it was worse still when he stuck on his up-per lip a bristly fake mustache. And that false mustache bent down to kiss my red hair, which I had decided to let down, think-ing of Kalim. Then my husband, forgetting his first question, and as if his new incarnation as a detective allowed him to read frag-ments of people's thoughts, pronounced the name *Kalim* (he must have become an intuitive detective, though not a very shrewd one) and then casually made some comments.

"Guess what Kalim told me yesterday?" Miguel had stuffed a pillow inside his pants to simulate the girth of Agatha Christie's detective, and was now struggling to zip them up.

"Who are you talking about?"

"Kalim, Kalim," he said, repeating it twice, "you know exactly who I'm talking about, the oh-so-handsome Nubian guide. Help me with this," he added, and I just prayed he wouldn't notice ei-ther my trembling hands or the quaver in my voice.

"What, what did this K-Kalim tell you?"

"Oh, a funny thing: he asked me if I could help him find a job in Europe as an interpreter, insisting that it would not be difficult because he speaks Spanish and French fluently. Just imagine, who could be interested in hiring a Nubian interpreter? Anyway, I'm sorry for him, he seems to be a quite capable guy, don't you think?" and he looked at me with those Hercule Poirot beady eyes he had just acquired with the addition of the mustache.

"Quite capable," I repeated, finally succeeding in zipping up his pants with the clumsiest fingers ever seen on this side of the Nile. Then Miguel kissed me and said, "I love you, Laura."

Kisses from amateur detectives are irritating.

The great hall in the *Sobk* kept its lights very low during dinner. Dim light is a state of grace that doesn't promote general conver-sation. It seems instead to elicit rather personal confessions, and most everybody turns to the next person and whispers something. Next to me was Álvaro. He was wearing the relatively interesting

costume of a nomad camel driver, but it was spoiled by the taci-
turn, sullen air that overcomes many people when they are, reluctantly, supposed to be having fun. I gazed casually around the
dining room (where is he, please, I can't believe he's not here),
and while my yearning searched for him, my eyes uselessly met
with three other Hercule Poirots (one of them a Japanese); several
Cleopatras, all wearing veils, including Merce, who had finally decided to wear a wig and an asp curled around her arm, instead of
a mask. There were several pharaohs; a Lawrence of Arabia, and
countless belly dancers, among whom the most notorious was Sirrine, the French redhead, who was dressed in orange, a highly
risky choice for our hair color.

"Did you see how vulgar she looks?" Merce blurted out. "Ever
since Françoise told us that the great Ramses II was red-haired,
that hussy flips her hair around differently; perhaps she thinks
that will help her lure some desert god, or some Nubian lover,"
she added in a tone I did not really appreciate. I smiled then, because it's better to let some comments pass without getting caught
up in them.

That was how dinner went, until dessert arrived accompanied
by the very spectacular entrance of a group of Nubian dancers
and singers (oh, my God, where is he?). And tambourines. And
kettledrums with bells. And a pleasant, rousing music made its
way to the dance floor to bring fire into people's eyes, and a more
than a little tremor throughout my body: Kalim was there.

He was not among the dancers with long white tunics and colored turbans. Nor was he going from table to table greeting the
guests, as Françoise kept doing whenever the very long trail of her
Selkit (the snake goddess) costume allowed. Kalim simply stood
behind a column, looking at me as on that first day when we met
at Abu Simbel. He was dressed all in white, and his undefinable
eyes did not miss any of what was going on. I managed to see
through the semidarkness the candlelight reflection on the five
metal figurines, now around his neck.

I turned toward Miguel. My Hercule Poirot must have imbibed several glasses of Egyptian champagne because he was joking a lot with a French Cleopatra with whom we had not spoken a word during the whole tour. I looked at him again. "*Adieu, mon cher* Poirot," I shouted at him in silence, because even in the most tragic moments of my life, I can't resist the temptation of making a theatrical exit, and I went to meet Kalim.

He extended both hands toward me.

## VII. If You Call Me, I'll Follow You Anywhere

On the chair, a carnation still on the lapel of the jacket with the matching white pants, lay the remains of the Hercule Poirot costume. A shirt of a light salmon color and a Panama hat carefully were hung on the chair's back. The whole outfit seemed to be watching the sleeping figure of my husband, Miguel.

I was also watching him; I had been awake for so long that I had gotten used to the dark, like an old, dry-eyed owl. One does not cry in such circumstances, it's too soon, because the events of the previous hours are still stumbling against one another, and moments of torment and of ecstasy fuse together in such a way that in trying to give shape to the experience, one manages only to evoke one huge jumble that a sick mind would produce.

I could not even justify myself with the excuse that alcohol precipitated the whole thing. I barely drank a glass of Egyptian champagne before leaving the dance floor. It was another kind of drunkenness that dragged me to Kalim's cabin, and once there, I was trapped by an even baser force, one familiar only to those who can find beauty in sordidness. It is difficult to explain to a person who has not experienced it how one suddenly falls in love with a filthy place and a poorly ventilated cabin, where even the scattered clothes serve only to exacerbate our desire, because the body that our body has desired so much from afar is right there.

And we also know better than anyone else that there is no greater aphrodisiac in the world than a deliberate distance; it is like giving another turn to the string pegs on an invisible and exquisitely tuned guitar until it plays the purest of notes.

Whether Kalim intended or not to have his recent aloofness tune the strings of my passion to their limit, it no longer mattered to me. In fact, nothing else mattered: neither the dirty socks lying on the floor, nor the cockroaches I presumed were our witnesses in between the fissures of the bunk. Only one thing mattered: the body next to my own.

"Why are you wearing these figurines around your neck?" I must have asked him this question in one brief respite from making love, one of those moments in which a couple play at stroking each other's skin—very lightly—with their lips; and mine met with the five golden images Kalim always wore.

That was the only moment in which I saw a gleam in his eyes that was alien to what united us, and he gave me a vague answer having something to do with his religion. It also seemed to me that he was betting against himself, that those were Seth gods, and I had already guessed what that meant (I avoided saying he was wrong; with all the undigested Egyptological information one receives on these tours, I could not even be sure of who Osiris was). "He who follows Seth will get to become like Ramses," Kalim proclaimed, but a sweet glimmer returned to his gaze as he caressed my hair, kissing it many times while moving the figurines around to the back of his head. In this way he managed to dispel any of my suspicions about Egyptian gods the moment those golden effigies were out of sight.

Now, in the darkness of our cabin and with Miguel asleep so trustingly next to me, I was not concerned, however, with Kalim's necklace or the way my body had behaved. After all, the excesses of the body are more forgivable than those of the spirit. Instead I

was tormented by what I had *said* to the young guide during those
hours. What did I swear to him? What had I promised while his
black hands, with such pale fingernails, were searching for hidden
recesses never explored by other hands? Mad words, eternal
pacts. He said that he wanted to follow me to Spain, that he spoke
both Spanish and French well, that everything would be all right,
that this could only be the beginning of something wonderful.
And his kisses made it all seem plausible, because in those moments one believes that love is almighty and that love is merciful.

Laura, you're mad, *mad*, and also unfair. I have always detested
men who promise all kinds of things in bed and forget them a few
hours later; all those lies that can be rolled up into one: "If you call
me, I'll follow you anywhere," as if life were a romantic bolero.
The worst part is that I know now that people *believe* this when
they say it; everything is as completely true in bed as it is false once
you're back in the real world. The same thing was happening to
me and that young man. Did I ever stop to think how old he was?
At most, twenty-two, half my age. He was a man from another culture, from another race, probably full of illusions of prosperity,
with the idea that I can help him find a job in Spain, as I had
promised, along with a lot of other nonsense. Love above all, love
the all-powerful. Who could have invented these big lies that half
of humanity blindly believes?

My owly eyes occasionally managed to close their lids, dry eyes
that perhaps could have been able to drive these images away, but
nothing would make the memory of those words disappear. And
they were many, because my words, in total confusion, had
merged with those of Henri, my neighbor in Madrid, who, like a
Gagman Cricket (its advice coming too late), seemed to be repeating, "the worst part, my precious, is the jealousy, men bill you
retroactively for the time you did not live with them, I assure you.
Miguel will now say that he doesn't care about whatever you did
during those years, but it will all come back to count the moment

you two get back together . . . and the ghosts come alive again at every corner, you'll see: as soon as you look at a man, you have spoiled everything. Think about it, Laura, you won't have your old friend Henri over there in Egypt to give you advice, or to serve as your alibi. . . ."

Oh, love, I thought, how many stupidities are committed in your name! My birthright for a pottage, my newly recovered marital bliss in exchange for a mad passion. And do I love Kalim? Of course I do; I *want* him in the most basic sense, but that is not enough. Love has never been enough to make people happy, that is another precept one does not learn from the soap operas, but that's the way it is.

Miguel turned in his sleep, with his trusting face now toward me. Henri had been wrong at least in one thing: Miss Frances's caustic advice had attributed to my husband a certain defect he doesn't have at all. Miguel is not mean, nor distrustful. At no point has he billed me for anything that happened during the four years we were separated, and even more to his credit, he also hasn't done so for what was now going on. If he noticed my attraction to Kalim (and how could he not, if it was written all over my face), he chose to pretend he didn't see it, which is a very subtle, intelligent way of going about it: he knows me as well as I know him; not for nothing did we spend twenty years together. Now everything was crystal clear: that furtive kiss with the ridiculous Hercule Poirot mustache, his very veiled allusions to Kalim; only a dazed fool like me could believe that he didn't know what I was going through. But he chose not to say anything: to wait, tolerate, keep silent. A permissive husband, that is something that Henri and most people can't understand, and therefore despise. People think that anyone in love who is tolerant of these matters is just weak, but much can be said otherwise. I'm old enough to know that. Actually, it demands a lot of courage—and intelligence—to pretend to be blind to circumstance, but it always wins in the end.

The fact that the Poirot costume was so carefully arranged on the chair was evidence that Miguel had quietly gone to bed in spite of my absence, that he had not been anxiously waiting for my return. I even seemed to see in his face a little mocking smile. "Fuck!" I thought, and like a fool repeated to myself a very obvious truth: yes, and they always win in the end, pretending not to notice: to love and consent, what a smart move. That's how those cunning bastards make us—the sinners (how does that sound?)—become our own watchdogs, and be the judges of our own worst stupidities. And there are no judges more merciless than we are to ourselves.

I got up from bed to take a shower. When I came in around three, I'd enough energy to throw myself on the bed. And now I was awake for hours with insomnia. Morning would break soon and I wanted to erase from my body even the last vestige of the night. Smells are treacherous, and scents of the love embrace are not the best ally when one is trying to think clearly.

Cold water did the rest. It was six-thirty, and soon another tourist jaunt would begin: the last one accompanied by Kalim. Françoise's voice would be out there describing one temple and the next, and then another in her enthusiastic commentary. And her *bien entendu*. And her "Let's see, amigos," with her shadow, Kalim, always beside her. How was I going to react? What would my body's reaction be? Oh, my God! What I would have given to have someone to talk to about all of this. A friendly but severe hand to hold me back (like Henri's, for example), someone I could ask: "If you see that I can't help but look at him; if any gesture renews my desire to touch his body, you slap me twice, Henri, I beg you, and you slap me a couple of good ones." That's what I needed.

That and a few minutes alone with the young man, so I could apologize to him: I had to say something to him, and the sooner, the better. There was no point in delaying the inevitable. But how terrible to be seeing him once more, and feeling his eyes on me again. . . . Barely past twenty, Laura, he could almost be your son, such innocent eyes. It was still early, but the sole idea that time was rushing me into that unavoidable moment made me feel an absurd warmth in my thighs. The manifestations of anxiety are always contradictory. Finally, I opted for another solution: I would write him a letter, as cowards do. Dear Kalim, I could say, let me beg your forgiveness, it has all been a mistake, don't you ever think it's easy for me to write these lines, just as it won't be easy for me to forget you. I want you to know that I have really loved you, that everything I said to you was true, but things are the way they are, and not the way we would like them to be. It's very nice to say, "If you call me, I'll follow you anywhere," but, love, my love, life is not a bolero.

And how the hell is Kalim going to know what a bolero is? Let me start again, I thought to myself for a moment. This letter is the most vile thing I have ever done in my life. But I must write it, I owe it to a man who has made me feel alive. Come on, Laura, no more cheap shots; begin again and tell that poor fellow that everything you swore to him last night is no longer true today. Do it in the most dignified way, the least painful way, that is the least he deserves, he who has fallen head over heels for this silly, deluded redhead.


## VIII. Do . . . Re . . . Mi . . . Fa . . . Sol . . . La

"Hatshepsut," Françoise began as soon as we had all gathered around her. She was the mother hen, and we, her obedient little chicks who followed her everywhere. "The great Hatshepsut, in spite of being buried here in the Valley of the Kings and of possessing all the attributes of a pharaoh, was a woman. We must see all the things she did in order to hold on to the throne! Let me tell you her story. Let's see, amigos—"

The Valley of the Kings, that is, the site where most of the

pharaohs of ancient Egypt are buried, is one of the highlights of
the tour. One can perfectly imagine how those tombs were before
being robbed by thieves: imposing sarcophagi overlaid in gold,
war chariots, jewelry, treasure, pieces of furniture; everything the
soul of the pharaoh might need in the other world. All the mak-
ings of an incredible funeral spectacle that one can easily imagine
while visiting the halls, in the Cairo museum, dedicated to Tut-
ankhamen, whose tomb is the only one that was discovered intact
in all its splendor just as it has been prepared for a young king,
barely nineteen years old.

My awkward words in that letter were still going around in my
head. (Should I have taken out that hopeful "my love"? And the
reference to the bolero? How would a poor Nubian boy know anything about Latin music? He will not understand that allusion,
that's for sure.) I followed Françoise from tomb to tomb like an
automaton, and without paying much attention to the comments
made either by my friends Merce and Álvaro or by Miguel.

And Miguel? How was our waking-up time after my Nubian
night? Two or three times during breakfast I caught myself trying
to read *something* in his face, some indication even though it
might be a reproach, and better still if it was: one can find justifi-
cation for oneself or get infuriated in the face of recriminations,
but there is nothing one can do against the most impenetrable
blank expression.

"Are you taking your sunburn cream?" was the only thing he
asked me. "Today the sun is going to hit us full force." And I, like
all transgressors, began to look for a thousand hidden meanings in
that phrase. Fortunately, Merce, who was having breakfast next to
us, managed to dissipate any suspiciousness with her banal commentaries, and she took me by the arm while suggesting we sit together on the bus for the tour to the Valley of the Kings.

"Let Álvaro and Miguel have their fun with the things that fascinate them, like video cameras and such, right? Say yes," she said, "and in the meantime you and I could immerse ourselves in what we're going to see today. Do you know that three dynasties of pharaohs, from the eighteenth to the twentieth, are sleeping under the stones in this valley of death, where one tomb is more spectacular than the next? Dammit! You know that we've spent a lot of days here in Egypt, and for the life of me I can't understand this eagerness to embellish death. Let them tell me more about this world, and as for the other, I don't give a hoot. Hey, *somiar truites*!"

We got on the bus. Kalim was sitting four rows ahead of us. He was not wearing a cap, and I looked with infinite tenderness at his beautiful head and short hair. Inside it were so many crazy projects, to follow me to Spain, to work on anything . . . and I felt truly miserable sensing in my left pants pocket the letter I had written to him a few hours earlier. I had to look for a moment alone with him in order to hand it to him personally. To the infamy of not apologizing directly to him, I did not wish to add the cowardice of sending a furtive note to his cabin. I had to show him, at least, the minimum feminine courage that men usually deny us when they break a love relationship: to be able to look into his eyes and tell him, something like: "Read this, and I hope you'll understand." A few words, said face-to-face, was the least that such a beautiful being deserved.

The bus kept jolting us on the way to the Valley of the Kings and Kalim's head showed once in a while among the rows of seats, as did that of Sirrine, the French redhead. Yes, it was her. Just before the bus stopped, while we were going around a sharp curve, a hand with long red nails reached for support on Kalim's seat, as if Sirrine feared falling down.

"*Attention, madame* Pernod!" warned Françoise, who from her seat in the front row must have watched the whole scene in the rearview mirror, and she laughed. "*On arrivera dans cinq minutes.*" And we did. A few minutes later the whole crowd was following

Françoise's commentaries about the Valley of the Kings, while I was looking for the right moment to find Kalim alone, and to go up to him with my cowardly missive.

Meanwhile we visited several tombs, some of them pretty claustrophobic and not propitious for confidential exchanges. Françoise kept gabbing away. And, as always, in between rigorous explanation and unalloyed admiration she mixed in some archeological gossip, delivered with eyes wide open and an intimate tone, as if she were being terribly indiscreet.

"Have you heard today's gossip?" Merce warned me, elbowing me to pay attention to our guide's words. "It seems that today's story is about foxes."

"The desert fox," Françoise was explaining when I decided to tune in, "is totally unknown in Egyptian iconography. But look, take a look here," she whispered as if she were about to show us an erotic or pornographic fresco, as she pointed to a dark corner inside the tomb that once belonged to Queen Hatshepsut. "Many years before Seth was exalted by Ramses II, Hatshepsut's craftsmen engraved this cartouche. And what does the god Seth look like here? Tell me, tell me," and as we were not saying anything, Françoise declared triumphantly: "A fox! Amigos, here we have the discovery of a new sacred animal. And mind you, this is not my opinion, the discoverer was Billy Kuoto, a Japanese from Pennsylvania," Françoise added, pronouncing the name Kuoooto with an admirable Nipponese accent. "This is something quite rev-o-luuu-tio-nary. Take a look at this drawing," she said with an enthusiasm worthy of a better cause. "Seth was a fox! Isn't that incredible?"

"As for me, he could have been a goose," hissed Merce. "Who cares? After all, hey, what's a fox? It's only an overrated animal in all cultures. The only thing it actually does is steal people's hens. And the old ones too," she added with finality.

"Well, it seems very suggestive to me," I countered. In fact, I had been trying for a long while to involve myself in the archeo-

logical explanations, and there was something about the story of
the fox that caught my attention. On the other hand, for Merce it
all seemed an erudite delusion without any practical importance.

"Bah, I don't understand what she's trying to tell us; after ten
days in Egypt, my little noodle can't take in any more symbolism.
What is the connection between a lady pharaoh, dead for four
thousand years, and Ramses, such an egomaniac, and now this
business of the foxes? I'm beginning to get tired of all this dubious
speculation. No one knows anything. And now, a fox!" she repeated as if this were totally boring to her. And with a definite boycotting intent, she concluded, "I'm getting out of here, I'm sick of
looking at figures, all reps, hey, mass-produced, don't you think?"

"Symbols mean nothing in themselves; they only have value for
those who can apply them to something in their personal life," I
said, because that's the only symbolism that makes sense to me.
But Merce did not give a hoot for my philosophical explanation
either. She walked toward the tomb entrance, and waited outside
for us, drinking a diet cola.

It was not until the afternoon that I was able to get near Kalim. I
had been waiting the whole day for an opportunity. We were visiting the polychrome tombs of some nobles when, suddenly, I saw
that Kalim was separating from the group to go into an empty
room. It was the same maneuver he had used at Abu Simbel when
he followed me into the temple. And the situation was so similar
that instinctively I looked up: in fact, just like before, I could see
on the ceiling (which in this case was full of lapis and golden figures, of ducks and gazelles) the changeable reflection of Kalim's
necklace. Do re mi fa sol la. There was something magical in all of
this, as when someone repeats an incantation: do re mi fa sol *la*.
But was it really *identical*?

"This can only be the beginning of something marvelous, of
something really important." It was Kalim's voice, his same words
from last night, which now I only half understood. French is not

my forte. Then I heard the echo of a kiss, followed by the ringing of *something* I knew very well: do re mi fa sol *la*.

A woman's red hair at times showed behind the silhouette of Kalim, who was totally concentrated on her, with his back to me. I pressed the letter I was carrying in my pocket against my flesh; I was burning and trembling at the same time.

"I could go with you to France," he was telling her. "What a beautiful name you have, Sirrine," and that black hand, the same one that had caressed my skin, my hair, the night before, was now following the same route on Sirrine's body. "What a beautiful name."

Do re mi fa sol *la si*.

*La* for Laura . . . *Si*, the next note in the French musical scale, for Sirrine. . . . It all seemed like a bad joke. But the reflection of the figurines in his necklace, dancing on the ceiling, confirmed everything. How many figurines were there yesterday? Five, I was sure. I had counted them, kiss by kiss, in bed with the man who was now caressing that red hair, just like mine. And today there are six. Like the notches on a revolver. Like the cold statistics of summer flings in the diary entries of a cheap seducer.

"I'll follow you to Paris," Kalim lied, "I'll love you forever, Sirrine. How wonderful is your hair, red like that of the great Ramses II. And now, do you want me to tell you a secret?" he said suddenly, in a different tone: "My family descends directly from the Ramses line. We have behind us thirty-four hundred years in a lineage of pharaohs."

A tone of immense superiority was undeniable in the voice of that collectionist of redheads. And while I tore the crumpled letter I had in my pocket into a thousand pieces, I could only manage to ask myself why, choosing between two old hens, the fox had chosen one, and not the other—that is, Sirrine and not me—to reveal to her the deepest secret of his Nubian pride.

*Translated by Dolores M. Koch*

# Edgard Telles Ribeiro
## (Brazil, b. 1944)

The son of a diplomat, Telles Ribeiro spent his childhood in France, Switzerland, Greece and Turkey (where his father was variously posted), as well as in Brazil. In the late sixties and early seventies he published a number of articles on literature and film. He went on to study film at the University of California, Los Angeles, and made several short documentaries, including *Vietnam, Voyage in Time*, which was screened at the Director's Fortnight of the Cannes Film Festival in 1980. Thereafter he joined the Brazilian Foreign Service, and published his only work of nonfiction in 1989, *Cultural Diplomacy: Its Role in Brazilian Foreign Policy*. Diplomatic service has brought him to places as diverse as Ecuador, New Zealand, Guatemala, and the United States. As a result, most of his literary output reflects universal themes, although the flavor and nuance of his fiction remain uniquely Brazilian.

In 1991, Telles Ribeiro's first novel, *O criado mudo*, was quietly published in Brazil. Despite praise from Brazil's most discerning critics, who have rightly placed Ribeiro in that impeccably urbane tradition running from Machado de Assis to Paulo Emilio Salles Gomes, the novel failed to bring the author national recognition. Its publication in an English translation three years later, however, as *I Would Have Loved Him if I Had Not Killed Him* (1994), finally brought him a much wider audience, not just internationally (with Dutch and German editions) but in his native Brazil, where his publishers quickly brought out a short-story collection,

*O livro das pequenas infidelidades* (1994), and a new edition of the novel.

He has since published a novella, a second novel, and a new collection of stories, *No coração da floresta* (2000), from which the present story is taken. Telles Ribeiro lives in Wellington, where he is serving as Brazil's ambassador to New Zealand. He is currently at work on a new novel and is soon to have a third collection of his stories published in Brazil.

# The Turn in the River

No one could trace the secret roots of Skinny Pedro's devotion to
the world of machines. Yet nobody doubted the young man's
earnestness as he read and reread old instruction manuals that
kept arriving in the camp on a fairly steady basis, despite the ex-
asperating sluggishness of the banana boats which wound their
way upriver to connect that forgotten part of the jungle to the rest
of the world.

Some thought the mystery bore a direct relation to the green
tangle that tightly encircled the two dozen shacks balanced pre-
cariously between the rainforest and the yellowish waters. Indeed,
the diverse lush tones joined forces with the suffocating heat of
the jungle to disguise an essential monotony whose primary function was to drive crazy anyone who might be inclined to formulate
an original thought. Skinny Pedro's obsession might thus be related to some form of insanity.

Others were sure the enigma could be explained in a much
simpler, more prosaic way: it was merely due to the river silt—
from which no one had extracted gold or any kind of stones for

months, but whose sticky texture bespoke a desire to reclaim the immense resources stolen from nature. Skinny Pedro must certainly have fallen victim to some kind of sorcery. Whatever the reason, the fact was the young man felt called to a purpose, which he repeated aloud to whoever would listen: he wouldn't give up until he had built and piloted his own airplane.

An outrageous ambition, given that he was stuck in an outpost whose end had been decreed a few months earlier by its own creators. The act of extinction, formalized during the course of a tense meeting, involved opposing factions in the company responsible for the destiny of Skinny Pedro and his companions.

"We can't just leave those people out there, can we?" pondered the employee on whom the future of that handful of men depended.

"For the last six months they've been a dead loss to us. Let them come back on their own if they can!" retorted the manager, brandishing his report, as if the river's refusal to produce any more gold was due to the prospectors' incompetence.

When, many years later, Skinny Pedro happened to learn the details of this scene, he wasn't surprised. The forest had taught him that men, remote from its confines, can be regulated by cruel and rather unpredictable codes.

Not to mention unjust. God knew how hard they had all worked to fill the quotas fixed by the company, churning through mud that had become the source of a collective hysteria. The prospectors liked to compare the warm, unctuous caress of the silt on their legs and thighs to the kisses of ten thousand feminine lips, rather than imagine that the river had nothing to offer them—except mud.

It had all been in vain. The gold, modest in quantity even in the early days, had simply disappeared. The geological maps had proved useless. And the wrong people had been bribed. The camp was simply crossed off the map. The breeze would spread the sweetish odor of death through the forest and the animals would take care of the rest.

Except for Skinny Pedro, none of the men doubted the company's good intentions. Not even those who, inspired by occasional bouts with yellow fever, had sure access to fleeting moments of lucidity. They all believed that in some large city (the exact location of which remained unknown to them), company managers were actually dedicating their best energies to relocating a labor force that, besides being cheap, had never given them the slightest cause for complaint. Throughout the history of gold panning, workers had never been abandoned in remote or forgotten areas of the jungle. It didn't occur to anyone that it might be expensive to bring back what had cost so little in the first place.

In the beginning, everything went on almost as usual. The jungle quickly swallowed the little landing strip used by the small planes on their weekly visits—but the banana boats continued to resupply the almost sixty men for some time. And even if it had been months since the last boat had disappeared downriver, with much waving on both sides, there was no reason to worry: thanks to Skinny Pedro, they wouldn't starve.

For he had been given the task of coordinating the fishermen in charge of feeding the prospectors. A job he had accepted happily, as from his boyhood he had loved to fish—and furthermore, it was no good questioning the foreman's commands. A violent type who never separated himself from the camp's only available gun, the foreman was feared by everyone because of his strength and the nonchalance with which he seemed ready to dispose of other men's lives.

But Skinny Pedro had accepted the task for another, more important reason. The long hours spent fishing were also good for meditating and reinforced his belief in the destiny marked out for him. He was convinced that the sum of knowledge he had acquired in his boyhood, simple but rich in wisdom, made him a chosen man. A man, above all, in tune with the drama unfolding around him. From long analysis of the intricate diagrams in his manuals—and developing, thanks to this exercise, a reasoning process of almost alarming clarity—he came to realize that the camp had been abandoned to survive on its own. Since it was unlikely that the banana boats would come back to visit that particular section of the river, which in any case had never been part of their habitual routes, he further reasoned that it wouldn't take long for collective despair and violence to fall on the outpost. And that more than a few innocent men would die due to the foreman's ways.

Being entrusted with such a secret conferred a special power on Skinny Pedro. He felt protected by the same serenity that from time immemorial has illuminated the souls of warriors and martyrs. Thus, instead of contaminating his fellows' certainties with doubts, he read and reread his manuals. Under the noonday sun, or stealing light from the moon, the point of his pencil traced the imaginary movements of the washers, threads, coil springs, cylinders, bolts, and screws which had long enriched the operation of his mind, like stars endowed with a life of their own. Enthusiastically, he took apart and reassembled the only generator that could still be made to work—in the unlikely event that a special ball bearing, ordered six months back, materialized among the bananas.

Poking and puttering in this oily domain helped keep his fingers in shape. He had no reason to doubt the invisible links uniting machines of all kinds in a brotherhood accessible to men of his caliber. The lesson learned in his childhood concerning the fluid relationship among fish, plants, birds, and animals must certainly have its equivalent in the no less animated world of his motors.

Pedro had no surname, and his nickname came from his days at the orphanage. Short in stature, he had long frizzy hair, bright eyes, and hard muscles. Part Indian, part black, his dark skin defied the sun; when night came, it let him melt discreetly into the shadows. Then his eyes shone like lamps among the trees. Where he came from, he didn't know; he had simply *arrived*, in a boat, as a very small child, like so many others before him. But he had been raised in Acajatuba, a small village on the banks of the Rio Negro.

Adopted son of the forest, he had grown up playing soccer with the natives and the missionaries of a sect for which he still felt affection, thanks to the prevailing tolerance of its members. He had learned to read and write from these men in their white robes, who spent most of their time cataloguing leaves, roots, and seeds, the latter planted lovingly in little labeled pots that, twice a month, were placed in the backseat of a pickup truck and taken to the airport to disappear into the skies over the Amazon.

They didn't do a lot of praying, those monks; perhaps for that reason they were esteemed by the natives. They were particularly interested in the health of the indigenous people and recorded in great detail the answers that, between chuckles and puffs on their pipes, the less bashful members of the surrounding tribes gave to their patiently formulated questions. Zealously they transcribed their own observations on the relationship between certain plants and diseases into notebooks, which they then locked up in a small cupboard.

These missionaries revealed another world to Skinny Pedro on the day they allowed him to watch a strange surgery being performed on the mission's pickup truck. Perhaps this episode was most ostensibly responsible for the obsession that, from that time on, he had harbored for machines. Ostensibly; because from his indigenous friends, he had learned another lesson: one's eyes register the details of a scene only when that image fuses with its twin, submerged in the viewer's memory. Thus he believed that in some moment of unfathomable origin, an equivalent scene, involving machines or motors, had taken place in his past. And this mirror, uniting like events experienced at different times, was to constitute the basis from which his pilot's dreams would someday take flight.

                              *     *     *

The young man was barely twenty when he found himself abandoned in the middle of the jungle by the men from the city. It
would take him another twenty years to build and pilot his own
airplane. I had the honor of being his first passenger—news that
froze me in my seat as we flew over jungle as thick and remote as
that which he had managed to conquer as an adolescent.

"Today I'm flying officially for the first time," he shouted with
pride from his seat, tipping the wings of the tiny plane over the
green immensity. I couldn't find the strength to offer him my con-
gratulations. We flew on in silence for another half hour, until a
fork of lightning flashed close by, followed suddenly by a thun-
derclap exploding almost on top of us. Visibility went quickly
down to zero.

"That's flying in the Amazon for you," he commented. We
were barely two yards apart, he in the tiny, doorless cockpit, I in
the only available passenger seat, the others having been removed
to make room for the cargo.

At one point, the fear that squeezed my stomach tighter and
tighter gave way to stupefaction: a hard jerk of the plane had loosened from a hook in the fuselage what seemed to be a bundle of
cotton. At my feet, the pale folds of cloth gradually untied to reveal two half-open eyes, surrounded by curly hair which, tossed in
the wind, looked strangely alive. I was looking at the small cadaver of a little girl, which rolled from one side to the other at the
mercy of the storm tossing the aircraft. That small body swathed
like a mummy, our blind flight over the treetops, the prospect of
disappearing in the middle of the jungle without a trace—all this
converged to focus a singular sense of intensity on the moment.

"Who is it?" I yelled, not recognizing the hoarse voice coming
from my own throat.

"The girl?" he screamed back, after a quick glance behind
him, as if the rest of the cargo might hide other surprises. He was

afraid too, I realized from the tone of his voice. The clouds around us grew denser.

He started talking about the girl almost compulsively. He told me the child's left leg had been chewed off below the knee by an alligator, and it had been impossible to staunch the bleeding. He also told me that, delirious, the little girl continued to see the alligator working its way up her thigh, its cold eyes fixed on hers. Her last wish was to be buried on solid ground. A luxury for someone who lived on the river, he added by way of explanation. As he was a friend of her parents, he was doing them this favor, making sure the child was buried in a Christian cemetery.

Without transition, he spoke to me of his boyhood spent fishing on the Amazonian mudbanks, and how this experience had served him well when he started working for the tourists, from whom he received five dollars per alligator captured alive, diving at night under reflector lights in the dark waters of the Rio Negro.

Thus, as the plane bumped and tossed its way through the tempest, he told me of his life; jumping from one tributary of the river, one forest, clearing, or swamp, to another; traveling along the meandering course of his past with the same velocity as our little plane hurtling through the clouds.

Believing in his stories actually saved me, so intently did I concentrate on his words. If we didn't crash into the jungle that afternoon, it must have been due to my sheer faith in his narrative talent. At one point, taking advantage of a brief moment of calm, he threw me a plastic folder with a half-dozen faded photos in which he appeared, fifteen years old, true to his nickname, among fat tourists from whose hands dangled small alligators and piranhas. He had worked together with a Paraguayan guide who claimed to have left his country and made his way up the continent jumping from river to river until reaching the Amazon.

Then he told me of Jeff, an American from Florida, who had taken a month's vacation in the Amazon. If it hadn't been for Jeff, he never would have found the determination to carry out his dream—of building and flying his own airplane. The same airplane which now seemed destined to disintegrate in midair.

Fishing had brought them together, as both were expert anglers. In his small canoe, Skinny Pedro had taught Jeff to use a net and taken him far beyond Lake Ubim, where no tourist had ever been. They spent entire afternoons fishing. The American, who in the photos looked like an English explorer of the nineteenth century on a visit to Africa, was a man of few words. But exactly three months after he left, the promise he made to the young guide was honored: through a fellow tourist to whom he had recommended the hotel, he had sent Pedro a model airplane kit.

The arrival of the small glider had probably represented the most important single event in Skinny Pedro's youth, since it gave a concrete form to his passion. For the first time, he looked at the sky with a feeling of possession and intimacy.

Pedro had assembled his little plane, made entirely of pieces of fine, smooth wood—the lightest and most delicate wood he had ever seen—with the affection of a newlywed husband who, in the silence of the dawn, leans over his sleeping bride to hear her breathing. He used the glue sparingly, for he knew it would be difficult to obtain more. Assisted by his Paraguayan friend, he read and reread each paragraph of the instructions before carrying out their commands with a religious fervor.

But he had forgotten the monkeys. And when, at daybreak on January 15, 1972 (a date forever engraved in his memory), he had climbed the highest of the three towers built by the hotel, he failed (unlikely as it may seem) to recall the warning every guide repeated to the tourists: an inspired monkey is capable of causing as much havoc as an elephant. And five monkeys had been present at the silent launching of the fragile glider, which should have stayed in the air for some minutes, borne on the bosom of the wind, and landed sweetly in a treetop, from which it would then

be retrieved for another flight. Two of the monkeys had applauded the event with hopping and grunts—but the other three
had shot like arrows into the trees, chasing after the peculiar bird
that had remained indifferent to their antics.

So Skinny Pedro had experienced the pain of seeing his dream
realized—and shattered. Each monkey had kept a piece of the little glider. And no one at the hotel ever mentioned the incident
again, out of respect for the alligator-hunter's feelings.

But he didn't give up. Quite the opposite. He dove into the
black waters with redoubled energy, accumulating ever more generous tips—for he was the tourists' favorite—and didn't rest until
he obtained from the hotel management the promise that their
agent in Florida would send along another model plane with the
first willing tourist—equipped this time with a cable and a motor.

"The problem then was the macaws." Not really a problem,
more of a false alarm. The macaws only wanted to inspect the in-
truder; they didn't seem to feel their territory was threatened. Two
of them flew slightly above the small airplane and its cable. Pedro
had painted the model in bright colors: red, blue, and yellow, and
the circular ballet of the trio against the green jungle didn't feel
out of place; rather, the birds seemed to enjoy the celebration.

After some time (a time enchanted by Pedro's innumerable stories
and having little or nothing to do with the duration of our flight,
encapsulated as we were in their magic realm), the clouds around
our airplane began to dissolve, as the rain beat less forcefully on
the windshield. In a corner of the cabin, the dead girl finally
rested under her curls. Then a clearing and a tiny landing strip became visible in front of us. A few more minutes and we landed.

When the little plane stopped moving, we remained silent and
motionless in our seats, exhausted but full of a precious energy
bursting with relief. There was nobody to meet us; the jeep that
had been scheduled to pick us up had gotten stuck about ten

miles away and would take another two hours to arrive. Outside, fine rain continued to fall. Skinny Pedro unfastened his seat belt and turned his seat around to face me.

"Things got ugly when they found out the flour had spoiled," he then said. And added, as if it were necessary, "In the camp I was telling you about." The story that had been circling in his memory for years now seemed ready to alight.

The rain, or the rats, had made holes in all the flour sacks. With the high humidity, the entire stock had rotted in a few days. The foreman dragged the fellow responsible for this disaster by the hair to a corner of the encampment and, deaf to his pleas, put two bullets in his head. The prospectors, grouped on a little promontory, shuddered as they heard the shots. For the first time, they regarded the turn in the river with fear.

Pedro sensed the collective dread. His aloofness came from the certainty that he would escape, and from a hope that he could save his companions. But this gap between certainty and hope troubled him. That was where the foreman ruled. To protect himself from the violence he knew was coming, Pedro needed to introduce a new element or they would all be lost.

There were other people maybe fifty miles away. But where? The skipper of one of the boats had told them something they hadn't realized, having traveled at night when they first arrived. The skipper said that just around the familiar turn, the river divided into dozens of branches, which forked and joined again and again, forming a maze so complicated that even he, with more than forty years' experience in the region, had gotten lost more than once, despite his compass and radio. Truth? Lies? Two prospectors who had once flown over the area confirmed that from above, the rivers looked like a handful of gold worms twisting through the green.

Based on these statements, the men had concluded it was better to obey the foreman's orders and wait for the next boat. On it, representatives could be sent to the big city to negotiate the group's destiny. Leaving the camp at that point would only mean aggravating everyone's problems.

Pedro scratched his chin, with his eye on the *other* turn in the river, the one a mile and a half upstream to the right of the camp. They said that if you went that way you could get to Peru. Or Equador. But how to navigate against the current? And for how many days? He looked at the turn of the river, then at the generator. And he then looked at the foreman.

Two weeks went by in this fashion, the prospectors locked into a routine that became a sort of umbilical cord linking them to their past. Although they were convinced there was nothing to be found in those waters, they continued panning. They didn't even bother to spread within the area marked out by the company. Keeping together in groups, they mulled their doubts over in the ooze, their silence pierced only by the screams of birds.

Meanwhile, Pedro fished. He would take the canoe to the middle of the river and throw his net in, pulling it out almost at once with a strong jerk. When he wasn't fishing, he read. Until, one afternoon, he stopped in front of the generator and examined it at length. Then, one last time, he began to dismantle it. But this time his movements were slow and measured, as if he were rediscovering the weight and structure of each of its parts and seeing them from a new and secret angle.

When the men came back at nightfall, they found the components of the generator spread out on a canvas by order of size, gleaming as if they were on exhibit or possibly for sale. The men stared in silence. Fatigue, hunger, and heat kept them from articulating any thoughts.

The foreman came over to the group and asked rudely what was going on. Pedro explained his ideas. He began by pointing to the stars. Ever since he was small, he said, he had known how to find directions by looking at the night sky. For the other prospectors, who came mostly from the northeast, the stars were a mystery, but for him they held no secrets. And since going downstream didn't seem feasible, the best thing was to go upstream. They would stop during the day, when the waters forked, and proceed at night, with the help of the stars. Who knew what they might find nearby?

"Go upstream? Against the current?" exclaimed the foreman while a hundred eyes glittered around him like fireflies. "How?"

Pedro pointed to the parts spread out on the canvas. "By making an engine. For the canoe." In a lower voice he added, "You can come with me, if you trust me."

The foreman laughed. He put both hands on his hips and laughed long and loud at the full moon, his head thrown back. His whole body shook, intimidating everyone. It had been months since anyone had laughed in the camp. Suddenly, with the agility of a wild animal, he grabbed Skinny Pedro by the collar of his dirty shirt and whispered in his ear, "If the son of a bitch works I'll go with you. If it doesn't, I'll kill you."

It would work, Pedro assured him, and got busy on it that very night. For over two weeks he struggled, without neglecting his fishing. On the contrary, he spent long hours throwing his nets into the river and pulling them back with hard, quick tugs. Watching him, they had the impression that he was pulling inspiration for his masterpiece directly out of the water. Every night, they all squatted around the contraption, which to everyone's surprise, snorted and purred, sending out puffs of smoke with all the earnestness of an engine.

The fateful day arrived. They all stopped working to watch the little canoe rocking under the foreman's weight. Skinny Pedro instructed him to sit on the middle bench, facing the turn in the river, steadying between his feet the gallon cans of gasoline with which they would refuel the tank. Four men, wading up to their waists in the river, held the prow fast while another four helped Skinny Pedro fasten the engine to the stern with a single hook. It was heavy, that machine of his! At a command from Pedro, the canoe was launched with a slow push toward the middle of the stream.

Standing, his hand resting on the silent engine, the first machine for which he felt truly responsible, Skinny Pedro wore a fishnet over one shoulder. It fanned outward over the bottom of the canoe, giving him the singular appearance of a gladiator. The foreman sat in the middle of the canoe, both hands on the bench. He studied the muddy waters in front of them as he waited for the morning silence to be filled by the roar of the motor.

Quickly the miracle occurred—and the engine amply fulfilled the collective dream of the men gathered on the bank. With a lightning-fast motion, Pedro tossed a cord around the foreman's neck. With another, he threw the fishnet over him. The motor, freed from its hook by a hard, precise kick, sank into the river, pulling the cord tight and dragging the foreman underwater. The canoe turned over; Pedro disappeared. For a few seconds the foreman struggled, strangled under the fishnet, making a few hoarse, stifled gurgling noises from below the surface—but soon he disappeared too. And Skinny Pedro resurfaced from under the upside-down canoe.

Absolute silence descended on the scene. Men and birds watched Skinny Pedro swimming after the oars, as if his slow arm strokes could help them decipher the mystery they had just witnessed. His movements through the mild current were tranquil, as if he were the author, not only of the sequence of events, but of the very landscape around them.

Once he recovered both oars, he righted the canoe and climbed into it again. Standing up, he shook his frizzy hair back into the wind and turned to look at the prospectors. One of them, fist raised to the sky, let out a long yell, the hoarse shout of a gold-panner. Then they all shouted, jumping up and down in the mud, throwing their shovels into the river. Many hugged and kissed each other.

Skinny Pedro had conquered for each man in the camp the sacred right to choose how to confront his own death. Staying or leaving. Struggling through the jungle or building a raft. And since he had been unable to share the secret with any of them before, he now savored these screams with the joy of one who bends fate to his own will.

When the rain stopped, I felt a need to take a few steps on solid ground. The same solid ground Pedro had mentioned when talking of the little dead girl. To commemorate this luxury of sorts, I accepted the straw cigarette he offered me. Smoking in the dripping jungle, I learned, by way of an epilogue, how half the prospectors had followed him down the river—and how they had been saved, after wandering through the green labyrinth for weeks on end. As for the other half, nobody ever knew what became of them.

*Translated by Margaret Abigail Neves and the author*

# Laura Esquivel
## (Mexico, b. 1950)

Laura Esquivel was born in Mexico City. Before she gained an unprecedented international reputation with her first novel, she
worked as a primary school teacher, founded a children's drama
and fiction workshop, and worked as a scriptwriter. Then, in 1989
she published the Spanish version of *Like Water for Chocolate: A
Novel in Monthly Installments with Recipes, Romances and Home
Remedies*, which eventually went on to sell over four and a half
million copies worldwide in thirty-five languages. When published subsequently in English, it remained a *New York Times*
bestseller for over a year in hardcover alone and, to date, has sold
some two million copies. The film based on the book, with a
screenplay by Esquivel, swept the Ariel Awards of the Mexican
Academy of Motion Pictures, winning eleven in all, and went on
to become the largest grossing foreign film ever released in the
United States. In 1994, the novel also won the prestigious ABBY
Award, given annually by the American Booksellers Association
to the book the members of the organization most enjoyed hand-
selling.

In 1995, she published her second bestseller, *The Law of Love*,
an innovative multimedia novel that includes illustrations and
music provided on an accompanying CD. A futuristic farce of
mistaken identities and reincarnated lovers, the novel has sold
more than a million copies worldwide in thirteen languages. A
volume of shorter texts, *Between Two Fires: Intimate Writings on*

*Life, Love, Food and Flavor*, followed three years later. Esquivel has also written a children's story, *Estrellita marinera* (1999), and an essay on the subject of emotions: *El libro de las emociones: son de la razón sin corazón* (2000).

She recently completed the screen adaptation of Louis de Bernières *Señor Vivo and the Coca Lord*. Her latest novel, *Swift as Desire* (2001), tells the bittersweet story of a daughter's attempt to understand the mystery of her parents' failed marriage, while caring for her dying father. Esquivel has received numerous additional awards and prizes, including Mexico's Woman of the Year in 1993, and in 1995 the "Casita María" for most outstanding Latin Artist in the USA. She lives in Mexico.

# Blessed Reality

Thank God for virtual reality! And the person who invented it! Thanks to virtual reality I have regained my sanity and my joy for life. Before I found it I felt lost and abandoned. Why? Because of my husband. Or rather, what my husband did. Well, no, to be precise, the consequences of what he did. I guess I'd better explain.

It all began after our first year of marriage. I used to blame my husband's friend Juan for everything, but not anymore. Rogelio got smashed during their domino games because he chose to; no one forced him. He drank because he liked it or because it made him feel better or whatever. The point is he drank all night. At first I didn't worry about it because Rogelio was very high-strung and always searching for ways to relax. But how could he not expect his nervous system to be altered if he drank twenty-four cups of coffee and smoked three packs of cigarettes a day?! Well, I really didn't think I should be too alarmed since, after all, he only got drunk once a week.

The real problems started when he decided that drinking on Friday nights wasn't enough and he began partying during the week. Then he wanted more than just alcohol and added cocaine. My life with him was pure hell. He came home if and when he chose. Sometimes he didn't come home at all. He threw up in the living room. He urinated in our bed. He stank to high heaven. He woke the children. He insulted me. He spent all our savings. I cried all the time, worrying that he would fall asleep in the gutter. I was tormented by the thought that he was sleeping with whores and was afraid he would infect me with AIDS. How could I go on living? I didn't have a life anymore and had no idea how to improve my situation. I prayed Rogelio would see the pain he was causing me and change his behavior. I hoped each drunken spree would be his last, that it would make him bottom out and force him to clean up. But the bastard was too strong. In moments of desperation I wished he would just die in an alley and stop torturing me. I wanted him to die so I could be happy again. It never occurred to me that I could alleviate my suffering by leaving him. I don't think I was ready for that, and the mere idea of being alone made me shiver.

Fortunately, one day I decided to visit my friend Lupe and tell her my problems. When I described the nightmare that my life had become and how difficult it was for me to believe that it was real, my friend simply said, "Like virtual reality?" I didn't know what she was talking about, so she explained in detail the wonders of this new invention and that's how I learned that one can put on some glasses and then see, touch and hear things as if they were real. I was so intrigued I stopped crying. I felt immediately that this was the solution I had been seeking. If my husband were going to drug himself to avoid his problems, I would escape my reality in a healthier way. So with the same desperation with which an alcoholic reaches for a bottle to cure a hangover, I dedicated myself to finding and purchasing the glasses.

I can't begin to describe my first experience. I knew the house I was walking through didn't exist, but it seemed so real to me! I could touch the walls, sit in chairs in the living room, breathe tranquilly in the smog-free garden—everything was clean, pretty. It didn't smell like rancid *pulque*, there were no vomit stains on the rug, in short, Rogelio's drunken mess was no longer in my house. I was the owner of the peaceful, harmonious home I had always dreamed of. Of course, I became addicted to the magical glasses. As soon as Rogelio opened the front door I would run to put them on and, blessed mercy, life was beautiful again. When Rogelio saw I was happy he immediately assumed I was fooling around on him. I assured him I wasn't, but everyone knows how foolish drunks can be. So, what I first thought might be an incentive for him to stop drinking soon became the ideal pretext for him to drink and take drugs even more voraciously than before. He said that since I didn't love him and I was cheating on him, he was going to leave me. And he was really going. He wasn't going to come back after a month or two. And I sat there calmly, waiting for it to happen.

When he wasn't around, my need to wear the glasses disappeared. Without him, the house was perfect. I slept better and could do whatever I wanted. But something was missing. You may think I'm hot-blooded, well, maybe I am. I missed the embrace and caresses of a real man and I really could not think of a solution to my problem. Why? Because of my stupid fears and guilty feelings. How would my children take it? Would it traumatize them? Would everyone think I was a whore? If my husband found out, he would surely kill me, etc., etc., etc. But you know what? I know it seems made up, but I promise you it happened like this: I found a pornographic virtual reality program. Well, I wouldn't exactly call it porno, because there were no naked men doing nasty things or anything like that. No, with this program I could make my own movie—and how do you like this—with the most handsome men who have ever existed! There were men for every taste and every age. From Tyrone Power to Brad Pitt, Marlon Brando to Robert Redford or Paul Newman. A woman could choose the one she wanted to spend a delightful night of love

with. What do you think about that? Yes, that's what I think too.
The glories of heaven are nothing compared to this experience.
Modesty prevents me from describing it further. I can only tell
you that my life since then has been beautiful. You have no idea
what it is like to spend an entire night in the arms of a real man—
it doesn't matter whether he's virtual or not. A man who doesn't
have foul breath or fart. Who isn't always sniffing cocaine or
smoking marijuana. Who isn't racist or fascist or reactionary or a
misogynist. A man who, instead of insulting, is sweet and tender.
Since I began to experience virtual sex I get out of bed in the
morning filled with enthusiasm. I am happy to go to my office.
When I come home in the evening I have the time and desire to
listen to my children, laugh with them and help them with their
problems. I fixed up the house. I changed the carpeting and put
vases filled with flowers around the house without fearing that Rogelio will throw them at me. My house smells of happiness. Like I
said earlier, I have regained my sanity and have come to the conclusion that I don't need Rogelio at all. And I can still say this despite the fact that my virtual reality glasses stopped working a
month ago.

*Translated by Stephen A. Lytle*

# Jaime Manrique
## (Colombia, b. 1949)

Jaime Manrique was born in Barranquilla, Colombia. His first book of poems received his country's Eduardo Cote Lamus National Poetry Award. He wrote his early fiction in Spanish, including a short novel and a collection of stories. After settling in New York City, however, he began translating his prose, and then finally composing it directly in English, while continuing to write his poetry almost exclusively in Spanish.

His first novel to be published in English was *Colombian Gold* (1983), a diabolical story of patricide and corruption that won him praise from William Burroughs and Manuel Puig. A second novel, *Latin Moon in Manhattan* (1992), is a delightful tale of the comically precarious existence led by a homosexual court interpreter who lives with his aging cat above a bar in Hell's Kitchen, trying to escape the surrealistic kitsch of his family in "Little Colombia," Queens. Written in English, it secured Manrique's reputation with critics as "the most accomplished gay Latino writer of his generation." A third novel, *Twilight at the Equator*, eventually followed in 1997.

In the meantime, he had published a volume of poems, *My Night with Federico García Lorca* (1995), and cotranslated with Joan Larkin *Sor Juana's Love Poems*. He has also taught in the MFA program at Columbia University and at The New School for Social Research. In 1998, he published *Eminent Maricones*, a memoir about Reinaldo Arenas, Manuel Puig, and Federico García Lorca. He has also been the recipient of various grants and fellowships, including from the Foundation for Contemporary Performance Arts (1999), from the New York Foundation for the Arts in Fiction (2000), and from the John Simon Guggenheim Foundation (2001). A new book of poems, *Tarzan*, appeared just last year. Manrique also reviews for Salon.com and for *The Washington Post Book World*. He lives in New York City and is currently finishing a new novel.

# The Documentary Artist

I met Sebastian when he enrolled in one of my film-directing classes at the university where I teach. Soon after the semester started, he distinguished himself from the other students because he was very vocal about his love of horror movies. Our special intimacy started one afternoon when he burst into my office, took a seat before I invited him to do so, and began telling me in excruciating detail about a movie called *The Evil Mommy*, which he had seen in one of those Forty-second Street theaters he frequented. "And at the end of the movie," he said, "as the boy is praying in the chapel to the statue of this bleeding Christ on the cross, Christ turns into the evil mommy and she jumps off the cross and removes the butcher knife stuck between her breasts and goes for the boy's neck. She chases the screaming boy all over the church, until she gets him." He paused, to check my reaction. "After she cuts off his head," he went on, almost with relish, "she places his head on the altar." As he narrated these events, the whites of Sebastian's eyes distended frighteningly, his fluttering hands drew arabesques in front of his face, and guttural, gross croaks erupted from the back of his throat.

I was both amused and unsettled by his wild, manic performance. Although I'm no great fan of B horror movies, I was impressed by his love of film. Also I appreciated the fact that he wasn't colorless or lethargic as were so many of my students; I found his drollness, and the aura of weirdness he cultivated, enchanting. Even so, right that minute I decided I would do my best to keep him at a distance. It wasn't so much that I was attracted to him (which is always dangerous for a teacher), but that I found his energy a bit unnerving.

Sebastian started showing up at least once a week during my office hours. He never made an appointment, and he seldom discussed his work with me. There's a couch across from my chair but he always sat on the bench that abuts the door, as if he were afraid to come any closer. He'd talk about the new horror movies he'd seen, and sometimes he'd drop a casual invitation to see a movie together. It soon became clear to me that, because of his dirty clothes, disheveled hair, and loudness, and because of his love of the bizarre and gothic, he was a loner.

One day I was having a sandwich in the cafeteria when he came over and joined me.

"You've heard of Foucault?" he asked me.

"Sure. Why?"

"Well, last night I had a dream in which Foucault talked to me and told me to explore my secondary discourse. In the dream there was a door with a sign that said *Leather* and *Pain*. Foucault ordered me to open it. When I did, I heard a voice that told me to come and see you today."

I stopped munching my sandwich and sipped my coffee.

"This morning I had my nipple pierced," Sebastian continued, touching the spot on his T-shirt. "The guy who did it told me about a guy who pierced his dick, and then made two dicks out of his penis so he could double the pleasure."

My mouth fell open. I sat there speechless. Sebastian stood up. "See you in class," he said as he left the table.

I lost my appetite. I considered mentioning the conversation to the department chairman. Dealing with students' crushes was not new to me; in my time I, too, had had crushes on some of my teachers. I decided it was all harmless, and that as long as I kept at a distance and didn't encourage him, there was no reason to be alarmed. As I reviewed my own feelings, I told myself that I was not attracted to him, so I wasn't in danger of playing into his game.

Then Sebastian turned in his first movie, an absurdist zany farce shot in one room and in which he played all the roles and murdered all the characters in very gruesome ways. The boundless energy of this work excited me.

One afternoon, late that fall, he came to see me, looking upset. His father had had a heart attack, and Sebastian was going home to New Hampshire to see him in the hospital. I had already approved his proposal for his final project that semester, an adaptation of Kafka's *The Hunger Artist.* I reassured him that even if he had to be absent for a couple of weeks, it would not affect his final grade.

"Oh, that's nice," he said, lowering his head. "But, you know, I'm upset about going home because I'm gay."

"Have you come out to them?" I asked.

"Are you kidding?" His eyes filled with rage. "My parents would shit cookies if they knew."

"You never know," I said. "Parents can be very forgiving when it comes to their children."

"Not my parents," he snorted. Sebastian then told me his story. "When I was in my teens I took one of those I.Q. tests and it said I was a mathematical genius or something. That's how I ended up at M.I.T., at fifteen, with a full scholarship. You know, I was just kind of a loner. All I wanted was to make my parents happy. So I studied hard, and made straight A's, but I hated that shit and those people. My classmates and my teachers were as . . ." he paused, and there was anger and sadness in his voice. "They were as abstract and dry as those numbers and theories they pumped in my head. One day I thought, if I stay here, I'm going to be a basket case before I graduate. I had always wanted to make horror films. Movies are the only thing I care about. That's when I announced to my parents my decision to quit M.I.T. and to come to New York to pursue my studies in film directing."

His parents, as Sebastian put it, "freaked." They were blue-collar people who had pinned all their hopes on him and his brother, an engineer. There was a terrible row. Sebastian went to a friend's house, where he got drunk. That night, driving back home, he lost control of his car and crashed it against a tree. For forty-five days he was in a coma. When he came out of it, nothing could shake his decision to study filmmaking. He received a partial scholarship at the school where I teach, and he supported himself by doing catering jobs and working as an extra in movies. He told me about how brutal his father was to the entire family; about the man's bitterness. So now, a year after he had left M.I.T., going back home to see his father in the hospital was hard. Sebastian wasn't sure he should go, but he wanted to be there in case his father died.

When Sebastian didn't return to school in two weeks, I called his number in the city but got a machine. I left messages on a couple of occasions but got no reply. Next I called his parents. His mother informed me that his father was out of danger and that Sebastian had returned to New York. At the end of the semester I gave him an "incomplete."

In the summer I started a documentary of street life in New York. I spent a great deal of my time in the streets with my video camera, shooting whatever struck me as odd or representative of street life. In the fall, Sebastian did not show up and I thought about him less and less.

One gray, drizzly afternoon in November I had just finished shooting in the neighborhood of Washington Square Park. In the gathering darkness, the park was bustling with people getting out of work, students going to evening classes, and the new batch of junkies, who came out only after sunset.

I had shot footage of so many homeless people in the last few months that I wouldn't have paused to notice this man if it weren't for the fact that it was beginning to sprinkle harder and he was on his knees, with a cardboard sign that said HELP ME, I AM HUNGRY around his neck, his hands in prayer position, and his face—eyes shut—pointed toward the inhospitable sky. He was bearded, with long, ash-blond hair, and as emaciated and broken as one of Gauguin's Christs. I stopped to get my camera ready, and, as I moved closer, I saw that the man looked familiar—it was Sebastian.

I wouldn't call myself a very compassionate guy. I mean, I give money to beggars once in a while, depending on my mood, especially if they do not look like crackheads. But I'm not like some of my friends who work in soup kitchens or, in the winter, take sandwiches and blankets to the people sleeping in dark alleys or train stations.

Yet I couldn't ignore Sebastian, and not because he had been one of my students and I was fond of him, but because I was so sure of his talent.

I stood there, waiting for Sebastian to open his eyes. I was getting drenched, and it looked like he was lost in his thoughts, so I said, "Sebastian, it's me, Santiago, your film teacher."

He smiled, though now his teeth were brown and cracked. His eyes lit up, too—not with recognition but with the nirvana of dementia.

I took his grimy hand in both of mine and pressed it warmly even though I was repelled by his filth. At that moment I became aware of the cold rain, the passersby, the hubbub of the city traffic, the throng of the New York City dusk on fall evenings, when New Yorkers rush around in excitement, on their way to places, to bright futures and unreasonable hopes, to their loved ones and home. I locked my hands around his, as if to save him, as if to save myself from the thunderbolt of pain that had lodged in my chest.

"Hi, prof," Sebastian said finally.

"You have to get out of this rain or you'll get sick," I said, yanking at his hand, coaxing him to get off the sidewalk.

"OK, OK," he acquiesced apologetically as he got up.

Sebastian stood with shoulders hunched, his head leaning to one side, looking downward. There was a strange, utterly disconnected smile on his lips—the insane, stifled giggle of a child who's been caught doing something naughty; a boy who feels both sorry about and amused at his antics. The smile of someone who has a sense of humor, but doesn't believe he has a right to smile. Sebastian had become passive, broken, and frightened like a battered dog. Fear darted in his eyes.

"Would you like to come to my place for a cup of coffee?" I said.

"Thanks," he said, avoiding my eyes.

Gently, so as not to scare him, I removed the cardboard sign from around his neck. I hailed a cab. On my way home we were silent. I rolled down the window because Sebastian's stench was unbearable. A part of me wished I had given him a few bucks and gone on with my business.

Inside the apartment, I said, "You'd better get out of those wet clothes before you catch pneumonia." I asked him to undress in my bedroom, gave him a bathrobe, and told him to take a shower. He left his dirty clothes on the floor, and, while he was showering, I went through the pockets of his clothes, looking for a clue to his current condition.

There were a few coins in his pockets, some keys, and a glass pipe, the kind crackheads use to smoke in doorways. The pipe felt more repugnant than a rotting rodent in my hand; it was like an evil entity that threatened to destroy everything living and healthy. I dropped it on the bed and went to the kitchen, where I washed my hands with detergent and scalding water. I was aware that I was behaving irrationally, but I couldn't control myself. I returned to my bedroom, where I piled up his filthy rags, made a bundle, put them in a trash bag, and dumped them in the garbage.

Sebastian and I were almost the same height, although he was so wasted that he'd swim in my clothes. But at least he'd look clean, I thought, as I pulled out of my closet thermal underwear, socks, a pair of jeans, a flannel shirt, and an olive army jacket I hadn't worn in years. I wanted to get rid of his torn, smelly sneakers, but his shoe size was larger than mine. I laid out all these clothes on the bed and went to the kitchen to make coffee and sandwiches. When I finished, I collapsed on the living-room couch and turned on the TV.

Sebastian remained in my bedroom for a long time. Beginning to worry, I opened the door. He was sitting on my bed, wearing the clean clothes, and staring at his image in the full-length mirror of the closet. His beard and hair were still wet and unkempt, but he looked presentable.

"Nice shirt," he whispered, patting the flannel at his shoulder.

"It looks good on you," I said. Now that he was clean and dressed in clean clothes, with his blond hair and green eyes, he was a good-looking boy.

We sat around the table. Sebastian grabbed a sandwich and started eating slowly, taking small bites and chewing with difficulty, as if his gums hurt. I wanted to confront him about the crack, but I didn't know how to do it without alienating him. Sebastian ate, holding the sandwich close to his nose, staring at his lap all the time. He ate parsimoniously and he drank his coffee in little sips, making strange slurping noises, such as I imagined a thirsty animal would make.

When he finished eating, our eyes met. He stood up. "Thanks. I'm going, OK?"

"Where are you going?" I asked, getting frantic. "It's raining. Do your parents know how to reach you?"

"My parents don't care," he said without animosity.

"Sebastian, I'm sure they care. You're their child and they love you." I saw he was becoming upset, so I decided not to press the point. "You can sleep here tonight. The couch is very comfortable."

Staring at his sneakers, he shook his head. "That's cool. Thanks, anyway. I'll see you around." He took a couple of steps toward the door.

"Wait," I said and rushed to the bedroom for the jacket. I gave it to him, and an umbrella, too.

Sebastian placed the rest of his sandwich in a side pocket and put on the jacket. He grabbed the umbrella at both ends and studied it, as if he had forgotten what it was used for.

I scribbled both my home and office numbers on a piece of paper. "You can call me anytime you need me," I said, also handing him a $10 bill, which I gave him with some apprehension because I was almost sure he'd use it to buy crack. Sebastian took the number but returned the money.

"It's yours," I said. "Please take it."

"It's too much," he said, surprising me. "Just give me enough for coffee."

I fished for a bunch of coins in my pocket and gave them to him.

Hunching his shoulders and giving me his weird smile, Sebastian accepted them. Suddenly I knew what the smile reminded me of. It was Charlie Chaplin's smile as the tramp in *City Lights*. Sebastian opened the door and took the stairs instead of waiting for the elevator.

The following day, I went back to the corner where I had found him the day before, but Sebastian wasn't around. I started filming in that neighborhood exclusively. I became obsessed with finding Sebastian again. I had dreams in which I'd see him with dozens of other junkies tweaking in the murky alleys of New York. Sometimes I'd spot a young man begging who, from the distance, would look like Sebastian. This, I know, is what happens to people when their loved ones die.

That Christmas, I took to the streets again, ostensibly to shoot more footage, but secretly hoping to find Sebastian. It was around that time that the homeless stopped being for me anonymous human roaches of the urban squalor. Now they were people with features, with faces, with stories, with loved ones desperately looking for them, trying to save them. No longer moral lepers to be shunned, the young among them especially fascinated me. I wondered how many of them were intelligent, gifted, even geniuses who, because of crack or other drugs, or rejection, or hurt, or lack of love, had taken to the streets, choosing to drop out in the worst way.

The documentary and my search for Sebastian became one. This search took me to places I had never been before. I started to ride the subway late at night, filming the homeless who slept in the cars, seeking warmth, traveling all night long. Most of them were black, and many were young, and a great number of them seemed insane. I became adept at distinguishing the different shades of street people. The ones around Forty-second Street looked vicious, murderous, possessed by the virulent devils of the drugs. The ones who slept on the subways—or at Port Authority, Grand Central, and Penn Station—were poorer, did not deal in drugs or prostitution. Many of them were cripples, or retarded, and their eyes didn't flash the message KILLKILLKILLKILL. I began to hang out outside the city shelters where they passed the nights. I looked for Sebastian in those places, in the parks, along the waterfronts of Manhattan, under the bridges, anywhere these people congregate. Sebastian's smile—the smile he had given me as he left my apartment—hurt me like an ice pick slamming at my heart.

One Saturday afternoon late in April, I was on my way to see Blake, a guy I had met recently in a soup kitchen where I had started doing volunteer work. Since I was half an hour early and the evening was pleasant, the air warm and inviting, I went into Union Square Park to admire the flowers.

I was sitting on a bench facing east when Sebastian passed by me and sat on the next bench. Although it was too warm for it, he was still wearing the jacket I had given him in the winter. He was carrying a knapsack, and in one hand he held what looked like a can of beer wrapped in a paper bag. He kept his free hand on the knapsack as if to guard it from thieves; and with the other hand, he took sips from his beer, all the while staring at his rotting sneakers.

Seeing him wearing that jacket was very strange. It was as though he were wearing a part of me, as if he had borrowed one of my limbs. I debated whether to approach him, or just to get up and walk away. For the last couple of months—actually since I had met Blake—my obsession with finding Sebastian had lifted. I got up.

My heart began to beat so fast I was sure people could hear it. I breathed in deeply; I looked straight ahead at the tender new leaves dressing the trees, the beautifully arranged and colorful beds of flowers, the denuded sky, which wore a coat of enameled topaz, streaked with pink, and breathed in the air, which was un-usually light, and then I walked up to where Sebastian sat.

Anxiously, I said, "Sebastian, how are you?" Without surprise, he looked up. I was relieved to see the mad grin was gone.

"Hi," he greeted me.

I sat next to him. His jacket was badly soiled, and a pungent, putrid smell emanated from him. His face was bruised, his lips chapped and inflamed, but he didn't seem withdrawn.

"Are you getting enough to eat? Do you have a place to sleep?" I asked.

"How're you doing?" he said evasively.

"I'm OK. I've been worried about you. I looked for you all winter." My voice trailed off; I was beginning to feel agitated.

"Thanks. But believe me, this is all I can handle right now," he said carefully, with frightening lucidity. "I'm not crazy. I know where to go for help if I want it. I want you to understand that I'm homeless because I chose to be homeless; I choose not to integrate," he said with vehemence. Forcefully, with seriousness, he added, "This is where I feel OK for now."

The lights of the buildings had begun to go on, like fireflies in the darkening sky. A chill ran through me. I reached in my pocket for a few bills and pressed them in his swollen, raw hands.

"I'm listed in the book. If you ever need me, call me, OK? I'll always be happy to hear from you."

"Thanks. I appreciate it."

I placed a hand on his shoulder and squeezed hard. I got up, turned around, and loped out of Union Square.

Several months went by. I won't say I forgot about Sebastian completely in the interval, but life intervened. I finished my documentary that summer. In the fall, it was shown by some public television stations to generally good reviews but low ratings.

One night, a month ago, I decided to go see a movie everybody was talking about. Because it was rather late, the theater was almost empty. A couple of young people on a date sat in the row in front of me, and there were other patrons scattered throughout the big house.

The movie, set in Brooklyn, was gloomy and arty, but the performers and the cinematography held my interest and I didn't feel like going back home yet, so I stayed. Toward the end of the movie there is a scene in which the main character barges into a bar, riding his motorcycle. Except for the bartender and a sailor sitting at the counter, the bar is empty. The camera pans slowly from left to right, and there, wearing a sailor suit, is Sebastian. He slowly turns around and stares into the camera and consequently into the audience. The moment lasts two, maybe three seconds, and I was so surprised, I gasped. Seeing Sebastian unexpectedly rattled me so much I had trouble remaining in my seat until the movie ended.

I called Sebastian's parents early the next morning. This time, his mother answered. I introduced myself, and, to my surprise, she remembered me. I told her about what had happened the night before and how it made me realize I hadn't seen or heard from their son in quite some time.

"Actually, I'm very glad you called," she said softly, in a voice that was girlish but vibrant with emotions. "Sebastian passed away six weeks ago. We have one of his movie tapes that I thought of sending you since your encouragement meant so much to him."

Then she told me the details of Sebastian's death: he had been found on a bench in Central Park and had apparently died of pneumonia and acute anemia. Fortunately, he still carried some ID with him, so the police were able to track down his parents. In his knapsack, they had found a movie tape labeled *The Hunger Artist*.

I asked her if she had seen it.

"I tried to, but it was too painful," she sighed.

"I'd be honored to receive it; I assure you I'll always treasure it," I said.

We chatted for a short while and then, after I gave her my address, we said good-bye. A few days later, on my way to school, I found the tape in my mailbox. I carried it with me all day long, and decided to wait until I got home that night to watch it.

After dinner, I sat down to watch Sebastian's last film. On a piece of cardboard, scrawled in a childish, gothic calligraphy and in big characters, appeared THE HUNGER ARTIST BY SEBASTIAN X. INSPIRED BY THE STORY OF MR. FRANZ KAFKA.

The film opened with an extreme close-up of Sebastian. I realized he must have started shooting when he was still in school because he looked healthy, his complexion was good, and his eyes were limpid. Millimetrically, the camera studies his features: the right eye, the left one; pursed lips, followed by a wide-open smile that flashes two rows of teeth in good condition. Next we see Sebastian's ears, and, finally, in a characteristic Sebastian touch, the camera looks into his nostrils. One of the nostrils is full of snot. I stopped the film. I was shaking. I have films and tapes of relatives and friends who are dead, and when I look at them, I experience a deep ocean of bittersweetness. After they've been dead for a while, the feelings we have are stirring but resolved; there's no torment in them. However, seeing Sebastian's face on the screen staring at me, I experienced the feeling I've always had for old actors I love, passionately, even though they died before I was born. It was, for example, like the perfection of the love I'd felt for Leslie Howard in *Pygmalion*, although I didn't see that movie until I was grown up. I could not deny anymore that I had been in love with Sebastian; that I had stifled my passion for him because I knew I could never fulfill it. That's why I had denied the nature of my concern for him. I pressed the play button, and the film continued. Anything was better than what I was feeling.

Now the camera pulls back, and we see him sitting in a lotus position, wearing shorts. On the wall behind him, there is a sign that reads, THE ARTIST HAS GONE TWO HOURS WITHOUT EATING. WORLD RECORD! There is a cut to the audience. A woman with long green hair, lots of mascara, and purple eye shadow, her lips painted in a grotesque way, chews gum, blows it like a baseball player, and sips a Diet Coke. She nods approvingly all the time. The camera cuts to Sebastian staring at her impassively. Repeating this pattern, we see a man in a three-piece suit—an executive type watching the artist and taking notes. He's followed by a buxom blonde bedecked with huge costume jewelry; she is pecking at a large box of popcorn dripping with butter, and drinking a beer. She wears white silk gloves. We see at least half a dozen people, each one individually—Sebastian plays them all. This sequence ends with hands clapping. As the spectators exit the room, they leave money in a dirty ashtray. The gloved hand leaves a card that says, IF YOU EVER GET REALLY HUNGRY, CALL ME! This part of the film, shot in garish, neon colors, has, however, the feel of an early film; it is silent.

The camera cuts to the face of Peter Jennings, who is doing the evening news. We cannot hear what he says. Cut again to Sebast-

ian in a lotus position. Cut to the headline: ARTIST BREAKS HUNGER
RECORD: 24 HOURS WITHOUT EATING.

The next time we see the fasting artist, he's in the streets and
the photography is in black and white. For soundtrack we hear
sirens blaring, fire trucks screeching, buses idling, huge trucks
braking, cars speeding, honking and crashing, cranes demolishing
gigantic structures. This part of the film must have been shot
when Sebastian was already homeless. He must have carried his
camera in his knapsack, or he must have rented one, but it's clear
that whatever money he collected panhandling, he used to complete the film. In this portion he uses a handheld camera to stress
the documentary feeling. I can only imagine that he used street
people to operate the camera for him. Sebastian's deterioration
speeds up: his clothes become more soiled and tattered; his dis-
guises at this point are less convincing—it must be nearly impossible for a starving person to impersonate someone else. His
cheeks are sunken, his pupils shine like the eyes of a feral animal
in the dark. The headlines read: 54 DAYS WITHOUT EATING . . . 102
DAYS . . . 111 DAYS. Instead of clapping hands, we see a single
hand in motion; it makes a gesture as if it were shooing the artist
away.

Sebastian disappears from the film. We have footage of people
in soup lines and the homeless scavenging in garbage cans. An interview with a homeless person ends the film. We don't see the
face of the person conducting the interview, but the voice is Sebastian's. He reads passages from Kafka's story to a homeless
woman and asks her to comment. She replies with a soundless
laughter that exposes her diseased gums.

I pressed the rewind button and sat in my chair in a stupor. I
felt shattered by the realization that what I don't know about what
lies in my own heart is much greater than anything else I do know
about it. I was so stunned and drained that I hardly had the energy
to get up and walk to the VCR to remove the tape.

Later that night, still upset, I decided to go for a walk. It was one of those cold, blustery nights of late autumn, but its gloominess suited my mood. A glacial wind howled, skittering up and down the deserted streets of Gotham. I trudged around until the tip of my nose was an icicle. As I kept walking in a southerly direction, getting closer and closer to the southernmost point of the island, I was aware of the late hour and of how the "normal" citizens of New York were, for the most part, at home, warmed by their fires, seeking escape in a book or their TV sets, or finding solace in the arms of their loved one, or in the caresses of strangers.

I kept walking on and on, passing along the way the homeless who on a night like this chose to stay outside or couldn't find room in a shelter. As I passed them in the dark streets, I did so without my usual fear or repugnance. I kept pressing forward, into the narrowing alleys, going toward the phantasmagorical lament of the arctic wind sweeping over the Hudson, powerless over the mammoth steel structures of this city.

# Julia Alvarez
## (Dominican Republic, b. 1950)

A poet, essayist and fiction writer, Julia Alvarez was born in New York City but grew up in the Dominican Republic, the homeland of her parents. She emigrated to this country and language at the age of ten, a watershed experience that she says made her into a writer. After completing her master's in creative writing at Syracuse University, Alvarez traveled across America as a "migrant poet," teaching writing workshops in schools, nursing homes, prisons, bilingual programs, and church basements from Kentucky to California. She kept body and soul together with these writing jobs as well as grants from various foundations and the unflagging support of friends and *compañeras*, some of whom still have her books and papers in their attics and garages.

In 1991, she published *How the Garcia Girls Lost Their Accents*, a novel in stories (including the one that follows), which won a PEN Oakland Award for works that present a multicultural viewpoint, and was selected as a Notable Book by *The New York Times*, as well as an American Library Notable Book the following year. Her second novel, *In the Time of the Butterflies*, was a finalist for the National Book Critics' Award for fiction in 1995. She has also published two books of poems, *The Other Side/El otro lado* and *Homecoming: New and Collected Poems*. Her poetry was selected by the New York Public Library for its 100th Anniversary exhibit in 1996, "The Hand of the Poet: Original Manuscripts by 100 Masters, From John Donne to Julia Alvarez." A third novel, *Yo*, was published in 1997, and was followed two years later by a collection of essays, *Something to Declare*. Her latest novel, *In the Name of Salomé* (2000), along with *Yo*, has been translated into Spanish for U.S. publication by Dolores Prida. She also writes fiction for children and young adults. Alvarez now divides her time between Vermont and the Dominican Republic, where she and her husband run an organic coffee farm.

# The Blood of the Conquistadores

## Mami, Papi, the Four Girls

Carlos is in the pantry, getting himself a glass of water from the filtered spout when he sees the two men walking up the driveway. They are dressed in starched khaki. Each wears reflector sunglasses, and the gleam off the frames matches the gleam off the buckles on their holsters. Except for the guns, they could be foremen coming to collect on a bill or to supervise a job that other men will sweat over. But the guns give them away.

Beside him, the old cook Chucha is fussing with a coaster for his glass. The gesture of his head toward the window alerts her. She looks up and sees the two men. Very slowly, so that in their approach they will not catch a movement at the window, Carlos lifts his finger to his lips. Chucha nods. Step by careful step, he backs out of the room, and once he is in the hall where there are no windows to the driveway, he makes a mad dash toward the bedroom. He passes the patio, where the four girls are playing Statues with their cousins.

They are too intent on their game to notice the blur of his body running by. But Yoyo, just frozen in a spin, happens to look up and see him.

Again, he puts his finger to his lips. Yoyo cocks her head, intrigued.

"Yoyo!" one of the cousin cries. "Yoyo moved!"

The argument erupts just as he reaches the bedroom door. He hopes Yoyo will keep her mouth shut. Surely the men will question her when they go through the house. Children and servants are two groups they always interrogate.

In the bedroom, he opens the large walk-in closet and the inside light comes on. When he shuts the door, it goes off. He reaches for the flashlight and beams it on. Far off, he hears the children arguing, then the chiming of the doorbell. His heart is going so fast that he feels as if something, not his heart, is trapped inside. Easy now, easy.

He pushes to the back of the closet behind a row of Laura's dresses. He is comforted by the talc smell of her housedresses mixed with the sunbaked smell of her skin, the perfumy smell of her party dresses. He makes sure he does not disturb the arrangement of her shoes on the floor, but steps over them and disengages the back panel. Inside is a cubicle with a vent that opens out above the shower in the bathroom. Air and a little light. A couple of towels, a throw pillow, a sheet, a chamber pot, a container of filter water, aspirin, sleeping pills, even a San Judas, patron of impossible causes, that Laura has tacked to the inside wall. The small revolver Vic has smuggled in for him—just in case—is wrapped snugly in an extra shirt, a dark colored shirt, and a dark colored pair of pants for escaping at night. He steps inside, sets the flashlight on the floor, and snaps the panel back, closing himself in.

When she sees her father dash by, Yoyo thinks he is playing one of his games that nobody likes, and that Mami says are in poor taste.

Like when he says, "You want to hear God speak?" and you have
to press his nose, and he farts. Or when he asks over and over even
after you say *white*, "What color was Napoleon's white horse?"
Or when he gives you the test of whether or not you inherited the
blood of the Conquistadores, and he holds you upside down by
your feet until all the blood goes to your head, and he keeps asking, "Do you have the blood of the Conquistadores?" Yoyo always
says no, until she can't stand it anymore because her head feels as
if it's going to crack open, and she says yes. Then he puts her right-
side up and laughs a great big Conquistador laugh that comes all
the way from the green, motherland hills of Spain.

But Papi is not playing a game now because soon after he runs
by in hide-and-seek, the doorbell rings, and Chucha lets in those
two creepy-looking men. They are coffee-with-milk color and the
khaki they wear is the same color as their skin, so they look all
beige, which no one would ever pick as a favorite color. They wear
dark mirror glasses. What catches Yoyo's eye are their holster
belts and the shiny black bulge of their guns poking through.

Now she knows guns are illegal. Only *guardias* in uniform can
carry them, so either these men are criminals or some kind of secret police in plain clothes Mami has told her about who could be
anywhere at any time like guardian angels, except they don't keep
you from doing bad but wait to catch you doing it. Mami has
joked with Yoyo that she better behave because if these secret police see her doing something wrong, they will to take her away to
a prison for children where the menu is a list of everything Yoyo
doesn't like to eat.

Chucha talks very loud and repeats what the men say as if she
were deaf. She must be wanting Papi to hear from wherever he is
hiding. This must be serious like the time Yoyo told their neighbor, the old general, a made-up story about Papi having a gun, a
story which turned out to be true because Papi did really have a
hidden gun for some reason. The nursemaid Milagros told on
Yoyo telling the general that story, and her parents hit her very

hard with a belt in the bathroom, with the shower on so no one could hear her screams. Then Mami had to meet Tío Vic in the middle of the night with the gun hidden under her raincoat so it wouldn't be on the premises in case the police came. That was very serious. That was the time Mami still talks about when "you almost got your father killed, Yoyo."

Once the men are seated in the living room off the inside patio, they try to lure the children into conversation. Yoyo does not say a word. She is sure these men have come on account of that gun story she told when she was only five and before anyone told her guns were illegal.

The taller man with the gold tooth asks Mundín, the only boy here, where his father is. Mundín explains his father is probably still at the office, and so the man asks him where his mother is, and Mundín says he thinks she is home.

"The maid said she was not at home," the short one with a broad face says in a testy voice. It is delicious to watch him realize a moment later that he is in the wrong when Mundín says, "You mean Tía Laura. But see, I live next door."

"Ahhh," the short one says, stretching the word out, his mouth round like the barrel of the revolver he has emptied and is passing around so the children can all hold it. Yoyo takes it in her hand and looks straight into the barrel hole, shuddering. Maybe it is loaded, maybe if she shot her head off, everyone would forgive her for having made up the story of the gun.

"So which of you girls live here?" the tall one asks. Carla raises her hand as if she were at school. Sandi also raises her hand like a copycat and tells Yoyo and Fifi to raise their hands too.

"Four girls," the fat one says, rolling his eyes. "No boys?" They shake their heads. "Your father better get good locks on the door."

A worried look flashes across Fifi's face. A few days ago she turned the small rod on her bedroom doorknob by mistake and then couldn't figure out how to pop it back and unlock the door. A workman from Papito's factory had to come and take out the

whole lock, making a hole in the door, and letting the hysterical
Fifi out. "Why locks?" she asks, her bottom lip quivering.

"Why?!" The chubby one laughs. The roll of fat around his
waist jiggles. "Why?!" he keeps repeating and breaking out in fresh
chuckles. "Come here, *cielito lindo*, and let me show you why your
Papi has to put locks on the door." He beckons to Fifi with his index finger crooked. Fifi shakes her head no, and begins to cry.

Yoyo wants to cry, too, but she is sure if she does, the men will
get suspicious and take her father away and maybe the whole family. Yoyo imagines herself in a jail cell. It would be like Felicidad,
Mamita's little canary, in her birdcage. The guards would poke in
rifles the way Yoyo sometimes pokes Felicidad with sticks when
no one in the big house is looking. She gets herself so scared that
she is on the brink of tears when she hears the car in the drive, and
knows it must be, it must be. "Mami's here!" she cries out, hoping
this good news will stop her little sister's tears.

The two men exchange a look and put their revolvers back into
their holsters.

Chucha, grim-faced as always, comes in and announces loudly,
"Doña Laura is home." As she exits, she lets drop a fine powder.
Her lips move the whole time as if she were doing her usual sullen,
under-her-breath grumbling, but Yoyo knows she is casting a spell
that will leave the men powerless, becalmed.

As Laura nears her driveway, she honks the horn twice to alert the
guard to open the gate, but surprisingly, it is already open. Chino
is standing outside the little gatehouse talking to a man in khaki.
Up ahead, Laura sees the black V.W., and her heart plummets
right down to her toes. Next to her in the passenger seat it has
taken her months to convince the young country girl to ride in,
Imaculada says, *"Doña, hay visita."*

Laura plays along, controlling the tremor of her voice. "Yes,
company." She stops and motions for Chino to come to the car.
*"¿Qué hay, Chino?"*

"They are looking for Don Carlos," Chino says tensely. He lowers his voice and looks over at Imaculada, who looks down at her hands, "They have been here for a while. There are two more waiting in the house."

"I'll talk to them," Laura says to Chino, whose slightly slanted eyes have earned him his nickname. "And you go over to Doña Carmen's and tell her to call Don Victor and tell him to come right over and pick up his tennis shoes. Tennis shoes, you hear?" Chino nods. He can be trusted to put two and two together. Chino has been with the family forever—well, only a little less than Chucha, who came when Laura's mother was pregnant with Laura. Chino calls to the man in khaki, who flicks his cigarette onto the lawn behind him, and approaches the car. As Laura greets him, she sees Chino cutting across the lawn toward Don Mundo's house.

"Doña, excuse our dropping in on you," the man is saying with false politeness that seems as if it is being wastefully squeezed from a tube. "We need to ask Doctor García a few questions, and at the *clínica*, they told us he was home. Your boy"—Boy! Chino is over fifty—"he says *el doctor* is not home yet, so we will wait until he shows up. Surely, he is on his way—" The guard looks up at the sky, shielding his eyes: the sun is dead center above him, noon, time for dinner, time for every man to sit down at his table and break bread and say grace to God and Trujillo for the plenty the country is enjoying.

"By all means, wait for him, but please not under this hot sun." Laura switches into her grand manner. The grand manner will usually disarm these poor lackeys from the countryside, who have joined the SIM, most of them, in order to put money in their pockets, food and rum in their stomachs, and guns at their hips. But deep down, they are still boys in rags bringing down coconuts for *el patrón* when he visits his *fincas* with his family on Sundays.

"You must come in and have something cold to drink."

The man bows his head, grateful. But no, he must stay put, orders. Laura promises to send him down a cold beer and drives up to the house. She wonders if Carmen has been able to get hold of Victor. At the first sign of trouble, Victor said, get in touch, code phrase is *tennis shoes*. He is good for his word. It wasn't his fault the State Department chickened out of the plot they had him organize. And he has promised to get the men out safely. All but Fernando, of course. *Pobrecito* ending up the way he did, hanging himself by his belt in his cell to keep from giving out the others' names under the tortures Trujillo's henchmen were administering. Fernando, a month in his grave, San Judas protect us all.

At the door she directs Imaculada to unload the groceries and be sure to take the man down at the gate a Presidente, the common beer they all like. Then she crosses herself and enters the house. In the living room, the two men rise to greet her; Fifi runs to her in tears; Yoyo is right behind, all eyes, looking frightened. Laura is raising her girls American style, reading all the new literature, so she knows she shouldn't have beaten Yoyo that time the girl gave them such a scare. But you lose your head in this crazy hellhole, you do, and different rules apply. Now, for instance, she is thinking of doing something wild and mad, sinking down in a swoon the way women used to in old movies when they wanted to distract attention from some trouble spot, unbuttoning her blouse and offering the men pleasure if they'll let her husband and babies escape.

"Gentlemen, please," Laura says, urging them to sit down, and then she eyeballs the kids to leave the room. They all do, except Yoyo and Fifi, who hold on to either side of her, not saying a word.

"Is there some problem?" Laura begins.

"We just have a few questions to ask Don Carlos. Are you expecting him for the noon meal?"

At this moment, a way to delay these men comes to her. Vic is on his way, she hopes, and he'll know how to handle this mess.

"My husband had a tennis game today with Victor Hubbard." She says the name slowly so that it will register. "The game probably ran a little late. Make yourselves at home, please. My house,

your house," she says, reciting the traditional Dominican welcome.

She excuses herself a moment to prepare a tray of little snacks
they urge her not to trouble herself to prepare. In the pantry,
Chucha is alone since Imaculada has gone off to serve the guard
his beer. The old black woman and the young mistress exchange
looks. "Don Carlos," Chucha mouths, "in the bedroom." Laura
nods. She knows now where he is, and although it spooks her that
he is within a few feet of these men, sealed in the secret compartment, she is also grateful that he is so close by she could almost
reach out and touch him.

Back in the living room, she serves the men a tray of fried plantain chips and peanuts and *casabe* and pours each one a Presidente in the cheap glasses she keeps for servants. Seeing the men
eye the plates, she remembers the story that Trujillo forces his
cooks to taste his food before he eats. Laura breaks off a piece
of *casabe* for Fifi on one side of her, and another for Yoyo. Then
she herself takes a handful of peanuts and puts them, like a schoolgirl, one by one in her mouth. The men reach out their hands and
eat.

When the phone rings at Doña Tatica's, she feels the sound deep
inside her sore belly. Bad news, she thinks. Candelario, be at my
side. She picks the phone up as if it had claws, and announces in a
small voice, so unlike hers, *"Buenos días, El Paraíso, para servirle."*

The voice on the other end is the American's secretary, a no-
nonsense, too-much-schooling-in-her-voice woman who does not
return Tatica's *buenos días.* Embassy business, the voice snaps,
"Please call Don Vic to the phone." Tatica echoes the secretary's
snippiness: "I cannot disturb him." But the voice gloats back,
*"Urgente,"* and Tatica must obey.

She heads across the courtyard towards *casita* #6. Large
enough already inside her broad, caramel-colored body, Tatica
renders herself dramatically larger by always dressing in red, a

*promesa* she has made to her *santo*, Candelario, so he will cure her of the horrible burning in her gut. The doctor went in and cut out some of her stomach and all of her woman machinery, but Candelario stayed, filling that empty space with spirit. Now whenever trouble is coming, Tatica feels a glimmer of the old burning in the centipede trail on her belly. Something pretty bad is on its way because with each step Tatica takes, the pain roils in her gut, trouble coming to full term.

Under the *amapola* tree, the yardboy is lounging with the American's chauffeur. When he sees her, quick he busies himself clipping a sorry-looking hedge. The chauffeur calls out, *Buenos días, Doña Tatica*, and tips his cap at Tatica, who lifts her head high above his riffraff. *Casita* #6, Don Victor's regular cabin, is straight ahead. The air conditioner is going. Tatica will have to pound hard with strength she does not have so her knock will be heard.

At the door she pauses. Candelario, she pleads as she lifts her hand to knock, for the burning has spread. *"Urgente,"* she calls out, meaning her own condition now, for her whole body feels bathed in a burning pain as if her flame-colored dress were itself on fire.


A goddamn bang comes at the goddamn door. *"Teléfono, urgente, señor Hubbard."* Vic does not lose a beat, but calls out, *"Un minuto,"* and finishes first. He shakes his head at the sweet giggling thing and says, *"Excusez, por favor."* Half the time he doesn't know whether he's using his CIA crash course in Spanish or his prep school Latin or his college French. But dicks and dollars are what talk in El Paraíso anyway.

When he first got to this little hot spot, Vic didn't know how hot it would be. Immediately, he looked up his old classmate Mundo, who comes from one of those old wealthy families who send their kids to the States to prep school, and the boys on to college. Old buddy introduced him around till he knew every fire-brand among the upper-class fellas the State Department wanted him to groom for revolution. Fellas got him fixed up with Tatica, who has kept him in the little girls he likes, hot little numbers, dark and sweet like the little cups of *cafecito* so full of goddamn caffeine and Island sugar you're shaking half the day.

Vic dresses quickly, and as soon as his clothes are on, he is all business. *"Hasta luego,"* he says, waving to the little girl sitting up and pouting prettily. "Behave yourself," he jokes. Naughtily, she lifts her little chin. Really, they are so cute.

He opens the door unto a crumbling Tatica, two hundred pounds going limp in his arms. He looks up and sees over her shoulder his chauffeur and the yardboy rushing to his aid. Behind him, above the air conditioner's roar, he can hear the little girl shout Doña Tatica's name, and as if summoned back from the hellhole of her pain, Tatica's eyes roll up, her mouth parts. *"Teléfono, urgente, Embajada,"* she whispers to Don Vic, and he takes off, leaving her to collapse into the arms of her own riffraff.

Vic goes first to Mundo's house, since the call came from Carmen, and finds her in the patio with endless kiddies having their noon meal at the big table. Carmen rushes toward him. *"Gracias a Dios, Vic,"* she says for hello. A sweetheart, this little lady, not bad legs either. Unfortunately, the nuns got to her young, and Vic has nodded himself silly several times to catechism lessons disguised as dinner conversations. He wonders if it shows all over him where he's been, and grins, thinking back on the sweet little number not much older than some of the little sirens sitting around the table now. "Tío Vic, Tío Vic," they call out. Honestly, lash me to a lamppost, he thinks.

Quick look around the table. No sign of Mundo. Maybe he's had to take refuge in the temporary holding closet Vic advised him and the others to construct? He smiles comfortingly at Carmen, whose smile back is a grimace of fear. "In the study," she directs him.

The kids keep calling for Tío Vic to come over to the lunch table they are not allowed to leave. He waves at them and says, "Carry on, troops," as he goes by. Over his shoulder, he hears Carmen call after him, "Have you eaten, Victor?" These Latin women, even when the bullets are flying and the bombs are falling, they want to make sure you have a full stomach, your shirt is ironed, your handkerchief is fresh. It's what makes the nice girls from polite society great hostesses, and the girls at Tatica's such obliging lovers.

He taps on the door, says his name, waits, says it again, a little louder this time since the air conditioner is going. The door opens eerily as if by itself since no one admits him. He enters, the door closes behind him, a gun's safety clicks off. "Whoa, fellas," he calls out, lifting his hands to show he's their unarmed, honest-to-god buddy. The jalousies have all been closed, and the men are spread around the room as if assuming lookout posts. Mundo comes out from behind the door, and Fidelio, the nervous one, stands by the bookshelves, pulling books in and out as if they were levers that might work their safe escape out of this frightening moment. Mateo squats, as if lighting a fire. Standing by different windows are the rest of the guys. Jesus, they look like a bunch of scared rabbits.

"Thought you might be SIM," Mundo says, explaining his withdrawn gun. He pulls a chair out for his buddy. The chairs in his study bear the logo from their alma mater, Yale, which Vic notes the family mispronounces as *jail*.

"What's up?" Vic asks in his heavily accented Spanish.

"Trouble," says Mundo. "With a capital T."

Vic nods. "We're on," he says to the group. *"Operación Zapatos Tenis."* Then he does what he has always done ever since back in Indiana as a boy the shit first began hitting the fan: he cracks his knuckles and grins.

*     *     *

Carla and Sandi are having their lunch at Tía Carmen's house, which is not breaking the rules because, number one, Mami told them to SCRAM with her widened eyes, and number two, the rule is that unless you're grounded, you can eat at any aunt's house if you let Mami know first, which goes back to number one, that Mami told them to SCRAM, and it is already almost an hour since they should have eaten back home.

Something is fishy, like when Mami walks in on them and they quick hide what they don't want her to see, and she clips her nose together with her fingers and says, "I smell a rat." Fishy is Tío Mundo arriving for lunch, then not even sitting down but going straight to his study, and then *all* the uncles coming like there's going to be a party or a big family decision about Mamita's drinking or about Papito's businesses while he's away. Tía Carmen jumps up each time the doorbell rings, and when she returns, she asks them the same question she's just asked them—"So you were playing Statues and the two men came?" Mundín is jabbering away about the gun he got to hold. Every time he mentions it, Carla can see a shiver go through Tía's body like when there's a draft up at the house in the mountains and all the aunts wear pretty shawls. Today, though, it's so hot, the kids got to go in the pool in the morning right before Statues, and Tía says if they're very good, they might be able to go in again after their digestion is completed. Twice in the pool in one day and Tía has the shivers in this heat. Something very fishy is going on.

Tía rings the little silver bell, and Adela comes out and clears all the plates, and brings dessert, which always includes the Russell Stover box with the painted-on bow. When the box goes around, you have to figure out by eyesight alone which one you think will have the nut inside or caramel or coconut, hoping that you won't be surprised when you bite in by some squishy center you want to spit out.

The Russell Stover box is pretty low because no one has been to the United States lately to buy chocolates. Papito and Mamita left right after Christmas as usual but haven't come back. And it's August already. Mami says that's because of Mamita's health, and having to see specialists, but Carla has heard whispers that Papito has resigned his United Nations post and so is not very well liked by the government right now. Every once in a while *guardias* roar in on their jeeps, jump out, and surround Papito's house, and then Chino always comes running and tells Mami, who calls Tío Vic to tell him to come pick up his tennis shoes. Carla has never seen Tío Vic bring any kind of shoes to the house but the pockmarked ones he wears. He always comes in one of those limousines Carla's only seen at weddings and when Trujillo goes by in a motorcade. Tío Vic talks to the head *guardia* and gives him some money, and they all climb back in their jeeps and roar away. It's really kind of neat, like a movie. But Mami says they're not to tell their friends about it. "No flies fly into a closed mouth," she explains when Carla asks, "Why can't we tell?"

The Russell Stover box has gone all the way around back to Tía, who takes out one of the little papery molds, and sighs when the kids argue about who will get it. Tío Vic comes out, grinning, and ruffles Mundín's hair, puts his hand on Tía's shoulder and asks the whole table, "So who wants to go to New York? Who wants to see the Empire State Building?" Tío Vic always talks to them in English so that they get practice. "How about the Statue of Liberty?"

At first, the cousins look around at each other, not wanting to embarrass themselves by calling, out, "Me! Me!" and then having Tío Vic cry, "April Fool!" But tentatively Carla, and then Sandi, and then Lucinda raise their hands. Like a chain reaction, hand after hand goes up, some still holding Russell Stover chocolates. "Me, me, I want to go, I want to go!" Tío Vic lifts up his hands, palms out, to keep their voices down. When they are all quiet, waiting for him to pick the winners, he looks down at Tía Carmen beside him and says, "How about it, Carmen? Wanna go?" And the kids all chant, "Yes, Tía, yes!" Carla, too, until she notes that her aunt's hands are shaking as she fits the lid on the empty Russell Stover box.

Laura is terrified she is going to say something she mustn't. These two thugs have been quizzing her for half an hour. Thank God for Yoyo and Fifi hanging on her, whining. She makes a big deal of asking them what they want, of getting them to recite for the company, and trying to get sullen little Fifi to smile for the obnoxious fat man.

Finally—what a relief! There's Vic crossing the lawn with Carla and Sandi on each hand. The two men turn and, almost reflexively, their hands travel to their holsters. Their gesture reminds her of a man fondling his genitals. It might be this vague sexuality behind the violence around her that has turned Laura off lovemaking all these months.

"Victor!" she calls out, and then in a quieter voice she cues the men as if she does not want them to embarrass themselves by not knowing who this important personage is. "Victor Hubbard, consul at the Embajada Americana. Excuse me, señores." She comes down the patio and gives Vic a little peck on the cheek, whispering as she does, "I've told them he's been playing tennis with you." Vic gives her the slightest nod, all the while grinning as if his teeth were on review.

Effusively, Laura greets Carla and Sandi. "My darlings, my sweet Cuquitas, have you eaten?" They nod, watching her closely, and she sees with a twinge of pain that they are quickly picking up the national language of a police state: every word, every gesture, a possible mine field, watch what you say, look where you go.

With the men, Victor is jovial and back-patting, asking twice for their names, as if he means to pass on a compliment or a complaint. The men shift hams, nervous for the first time, Laura notes gleefully. "The doctor, we have come to ask him a few questions, but he seems to have disappeared."

"Not at all," Vic corrects them. "We were just playing tennis. He'll be home any minute." The men sit up, alert. Vic goes on to say that if there is some problem, perhaps he can straighten things out. After all, the doctor is a personal friend. Laura watches their reactions as Vic tells them news that is news to her. The doctor has been granted a fellowship at a hospital in the United States, and he, Victor, has just heard the family's papers have received clearance from the head of Immigration. So, why would the good doctor get into any trouble?

So, Laura thinks. So the papers have cleared and we are leaving. Now everything she sees sharpens as if through the lens of loss—the orchids in their hanging straw baskets, the row of apothecary jars Carlos has found for her in old druggists' throughout the countryside, the rich light shafts swarming with a golden pollen. She will miss this glorious light warming the inside of her skin and jeweling the trees, the grass, the lily pond beyond the hedge. She thinks of her ancestors, those fair-skinned Conquistadores arriving in this new world, not knowing that the gold they sought was this blazing light. And look at what they started, Laura thinks, looking up and seeing gold flash in the mouth of one of the *guardias* as it spreads open in a scared smile.

This morning when the fag at the corner sold them their *lotería* tickets, he said, "Watch yourselves, the flames of your *santos* burn just above your heads. The hand of God descends and some are lifted up, but some"—he looked from Pupo to Checo—"some are cast away." Pupo took heed and crossed himself, but Checo twisted the fag's arm behind his back and threatened to give his manhood the hand of God. It scares Pupo the meanness that comes out of Checo's mouth, as if they weren't both *campesino* cousins, ear-twisted to church on Sundays by mothers who raised them on faith and whatever grew in their little plot of dirt.

But the fag *lotería* guy was right. The day began to surprise them. First, Don Fabio calls them in. Special assignment: they are to report on this García doctor's comings and goings. Next thing Pupo knows Checo is driving the jeep right up to the García house and doing this whole search number that is not following orders. Point is, though, that if something comes out of the search, their enterprise will be praised and they will be decorated and promoted. If nothing turns up and the family has connections, then back they go to the prison beat, cleaning interrogation rooms and watering down the cells the poor, scared bastards dirty with their loss of self-control.

From the minute they enter the house Pupo can tell by the way the old Haitian woman acts that this is a stronghold of something, call it arms, call it spirits, call it money. When the woman arrives, she is nervous and grasshoppery, smiling falsely, dropping names like a trail of crumbs to the powerful. Mostly, she mentions the red-haired gringo at the embassy. At first Pupo thinks she's just bluffing and he's already congratulating Checo and himself for uncovering something hot. But then, sure enough, the red-haired gringo appears before them, two more doll-girls in either hand.

"Who is your supervisor?" The gringo's voice has an edge. When Checo informs him, the American throws back his head, "Oh, Fabio, of course!" Pupo sees Checo's mouth stretch in a rubber-band smile that seems as if it may snap. They have detained a lady from an important family. They have maybe barked up the wrong tree. All Pupo knows is Don Fabio is going to have a heyday on their already scarred backs.

"I'll tell you what," the American consul offers them. "Why don't I just give old Fabio a call right now." Pupo lifts his shoulders and ducks his head as if just the mention of his superior's name could cause his head to roll. Checo nods, *"A sus órdenes."*

The American calls from the phone in the hall where Pupo can hear him talking his marbles-in-his-mouth Spanish. There is a silence in which he must be waiting to be connected, but then his voice warms up. "Fabio, about this little misunderstanding. Tell you what, I'll talk to Immigration myself, and I'll have the doctor out of the country in forty-eight hours." On the other end Don Fabio must have made a joke because the American breaks out in laughter, then calls Checo to the phone so his supervisor can speak with him. Pupo hears his comrade's rare apologetic tone. *"Sí, sí, cómo no, Don Fabio, inmediatamente."*

Pupo sits among these strange white people, ashamed and cornered. Already he is feeling the whip coming down like judgment on his bared back. They are all strangely quiet, listening to Checo's voice full of disclaimer, and when he falls silent, only to their own breathing as the hand of God draws closer. Whether it will pick up the saved or cast out the lost is unclear yet to Pupo, who picks up his empty glass and, for comfort, tinkles the ice.

While the men were saying their good-byes at the door, Sandi stayed on the couch sitting on her hands. Fifi and Yoyo clustered around Mami, balling up her skirt with holding on, Fifi wailing every time the big fat guard bent down for a good-bye kiss from her. Carla, knowing better as the oldest, gave her hand to the men and curtsied the way they'd been taught to do for guests. Then, everyone came back to the living room, and Mami rolled her eyes at Tío Vic the way she did when she was on the phone with someone she didn't want to talk to. Soon, she had everyone in motion: the girls were to go to their bedrooms and make a stack of their best clothes and pick one toy they wanted to take on this trip to the United States. Nivea and Milagros and Mami would later pack it for them. Then, Mami disappeared with Tío Vic into her bedroom.

Sandi followed her sisters into their side-by-side bedrooms. They stood in a scared little huddle, feeling strangely careful with each other. Yoyo turned to her. "What are you taking?" Fifi had already decided on her baby doll and Carla was going through her private box of jewelry and mementos. Yoyo fondled her revolver.

It was strange how when held up to the absolute phrase—*the one toy I really want*—nothing quite filled the hole that was open-

ing wide inside Sandi. Not the doll whose long hair you could roll
and comb into hairdos, not the loom for making pot holders that
Mami was so thankful for, not the glass dome that you turned over
and pretty flakes fell on a little red house in the woods. Nothing
would quite fill that need, even years after, not the pretty woman
she would surprise herself by becoming, not the prizes for her
schoolwork and scholarships to study now this and now that she
couldn't decide to stay with, not the men that held her close and
almost convinced her when their mouths came down hard on her
lips that this, this was what Sandi had been missing.

From the dark of the closet Carlos has heard tones, not content;
known presences, not personalities. He wonders if this might be
what he felt as a small child before the impressions and tones and
presences were overlaid by memories, memories which are mostly
others' stories about his past. He is the youngest of his father's
thirty-five children, twenty-five legitimate, fifteen from his own
mother, the second wife; he has no past of his own. It is not just a
legacy, a future, you don't get as the youngest. Primogeniture is
also the clean slate of the oldest making the past out of nothing
but faint whispers, presences, and tones. Those tenuous, tentative
first life-impressions have scattered like reflections in a pond under the swirling hand of an older brother or sister saying, I remember the day you ate the rat poison, Carlos, or, I remember the
day you fell down the stairs. . . .

   He has heard Laura in the living room speaking with two men,
one of them with a ripply, tricky voice, the other with a coarser
voice, a thicker laugh, a big man, no doubt. Fifi is there and Yoyo
as well. The two other girls disappeared in a jabber of cousins earlier. Fifi whines periodically, and Yoyo has recited something for
the men, he can tell from the singsong in her voice. Laura's voice
is tense and bright like a newly sharpened knife that every time
she speaks cuts a little sliver from her self-control. Carlos thinks,
She will break, she will break, San Judas, let her not break.

Then, in that suffocating darkness, having to go but not daring to pee in the chamber pot for fear the men might hear a drip in the walls—though God knows, he and Mundo soundproofed this room enough so that there is no ventilation at all in that claustrophobia, he hears her say distinctly, "Victor!" Sure enough, momentarily the monotone, garbled voice of the American consul nears the living room. By now, of course, they all know his consulship is only a front—Vic is, in fact, a CIA agent whose orders changed midstream from *organize the underground and get that SOB out* to *hold your horses, let's take a second look around to see what's best for us.*

When he hears the bedroom door open, Carlos puts his ear up against the front panel. Steps go into the bathroom, the shower is turned on, and then the fan to block out any noise of talk. The immediate effect is that fresh air begins to circulate in the tiny compartment. The closet door opens, and then Carlos hears her breathing close by on the other side of the wall.

## II.

I'm the one who doesn't remember anything from that last day on the Island because I'm the youngest and so the other three are always telling me what happened that last day. They say I almost got Papi killed on account of I was so mean to one of the secret police who came looking for him. Some weirdo who was going to sit me on his hard-on and pretend we were playing Ride the Cock Horse to Banbury Cross. But then whenever we start talking last-day-on-the-Island memories, and someone says, "Fifi, you almost got Papi killed for being so rude to that gestapo guy," Yoyo starts in on how it was she who almost got Papi killed when she told that story about the gun years before our last day on the Island. Like we're all competing, right? for the most haunted past.

I can tell you one thing I do remember from right before we

left. There was this old lady, Chucha, who had worked in Mami's family forever and who had this face like someone had wrung it out after washing it to try to get some of the black out. I mean, Chucha was super wrinkled and Haitian blue-black, not Dominican *café-con-leche* black. She was real Haitian too and that's why she couldn't say certain words like the word for parsley or anyone's name that had a *j* in it, which meant the family was like camp, everyone with nicknames Chucha could pronounce. She was always in a bad mood—not exactly a bad mood, but you couldn't get her to crack a smile or cry or anything. It was like all her emotions were spent, on account of everything she went through in her young years. Way back before Mami was even born, Chucha had just appeared at my grandfather's doorstep one night, begging to be taken in. Turns out it was the night of the massacre when Trujillo had decreed that all black Haitians on our side of the island would be executed by dawn. There's a river the bodies were finally thrown into that supposedly still runs red to this day, fifty years later. Chucha had escaped from some cane-pickers' camp and was asking for asylum. Papito took her in, poor skinny little thing, and I guess Mamita taught her to cook and iron and clean. Chucha was like a nun who had joined the convent of the de la Torre clan. She never married or went anywhere even on her days off. Instead, she'd close herself up in her room and pray for any de la Torre souls stuck up in purgatory.

Anyhow, that last day on the Island, we were in our side-by-side bedrooms, the four girls, setting out our clothes for going to the United States. The two creepy spies had left, and Mami and Tío Vic were in the bedroom. They were telling Papi, who was hidden in this secret closet, about how we would all be leaving in Tío Vic's limo for the airport for a flight he was going to get us. I know, I know, it sounds like something you saw on *Miami Vice*, but all I'm doing is repeating what I've heard from the family.

But here's what I do remember of *my* last day on the Island. Chucha came into our bedrooms with this bundle in her hands, and Nivea, who was helping us pack, said to her in a gruff voice, "What do you want, old woman?" None of the maids liked Chucha because they all thought she was kind of below them, being so black and Haitian and all. Chucha, though, just gave Nivea one of her spelling looks, and all of a sudden, Nivea remembered that she had to iron our outfits for wearing on the airplane.

Chucha started to unravel her bundle, and we all guessed she was about to do a little farewell voodoo on us. Chucha always had a voodoo job going, some spell she was casting or spirit she was courting or enemy she was punishing. I mean, you'd open a closet door, and there, in the corner behind your shoes, would sit a jar of something wicked that you weren't supposed to touch. Or you'd find a candle burning in her room right in front of someone's picture and a little dish with a cigar on it and red and white crepe streamers on certain days crisscrossing her room. Mami finally had to give her a room to herself because none of the other maids wanted to sleep with her. I can see why they were afraid. The maids said she got mounted by spirits. They said she cast spells on them. And besides, she slept in her coffin. No kidding. We were forbidden to go into her room to see it, but we were always sneaking back there to take a peek. She had her mosquito net rigged up over it, so it didn't look that strange like a real uncovered coffin with a dead person inside.

At first, Mami wouldn't let her do it, sleep in her coffin, I mean. She told Chucha civilized people had to sleep on beds, coffins were for corpses. But Chucha said she wanted to prepare herself for dying and couldn't one of the carpenters at Papito's factory measure her and build her a wooden box that would serve as her bed for now and her coffin later. Mami kept saying, Nonsense, Chucha, don't get tragic.

The thing was, you couldn't stand in Chucha's way even if you were Mami. Soon there were jars in Mami's closet, and her picture from when she was a baby being held by Chucha was out on Chucha's altar with mints on a little tin dish, and a constant votary

candle going. Inside of a week, Mami relented. She said poor
Chucha never asked for a blessed thing from the family, and had
always been so loyal and good, and so, heavens to Betsy, if sleeping in her coffin would make the old woman happy, Mami would
have a nice box built for her, and she did. It was plain pine, like
Chucha wanted it, but inside, Mami had it lined in purple cush-
iony fabric, which was Chucha's favorite color, and bordered with
white eyelet.

So here's the part I remember about that last day. Once Nivea
left the room, Chucha stood us all up in front of her. "Chachas—"
she always called us that, from *muchachas*, girls, which is how
come we had ended up nicknaming her a play echo of her name
for us, Chucha.

"You are going to a strange land." Something like that, I mean,
I don't remember the exact words. But I do remember the piercing look she gave me as if she were actually going inside my head.
"When I was a girl, I left my country too and never went back.
Never saw father or mother or sisters or brothers. I brought only
this along." She held the bundle up and finished unwrapping it
from its white sheet. It was a statue carved out of wood like the
kind I saw years later in the anthro textbooks I used to pore over,
as if staring at those little talismanic wooden carvings would
somehow be my madeleine, bringing back my past to me like they
say tasting that cookie did for Proust. But the textbook gods never
triggered any four-volume memory in my head. Just this little moment I'm recalling here.

Chucha stood this brown figure up on Carla's vanity. He had a
grimacing expression on his face, deep grooves by his eyes and his
nose and lips, as if he were trying to go but was real constipated.
On top of his head was a little platform, and on it, Chucha placed
a small cup of water. Soon, on account of the heat, I guess, that
water started evaporating and drops ran down the grooves carved
in that wooden face so that the statue looked as if it were crying.
Chucha held each of our heads in her hands and wailed a prayer

over us. We were used to some of this strange stuff from daily contact with her, but maybe it was because today we could feel an ending in the air, anyhow, we all started to cry as if Chucha had finally released her own tears in each of us.

They are gone, left in cars that came for them, driven by pale Americans in white uniforms with gold braids on their shoulders and on their caps. Too pale to be the living. The color of zombies, a nation of zombies. I worry about them, the girls, Doña Laura, moving among men the color of the living dead.

The girls all cried, especially the little one, clutching onto my skirts, Doña Laura weeping so hard into her handkerchief that I insisted on going back to her bureau and getting her a fresh one. I did not want her to enter her new country with a spent handkerchief because I know, I know what tears await her there. But let her be spared the knowledge that will come in time. That one's nerves have never been strong.

They have left—and only the silence remains, the deep and empty silence in which I can hear the voices of my *santos* settling into the rooms, of my *loa* telling me stories of what is to come.

After the girls and Doña Laura left with the American zombie whites, I heard a door click in the master bedroom, and I went out to the corridor to check for intruders. All in black, I saw the *loa* of Don Carlos putting his finger to his lips in mockery of the last gesture I had seen him make to me that morning, I answered with a sign and fell to my knees and watched him leave through the back door out through the guava orchard. Soon afterward, I heard a car start up. And then the deep and empty silence of the deserted house.

I am to close up the house, and help over at Doña Carmen's until they go too, and then at Don Arturo's, who also is to go. Mostly, I am to tend to this house. Dust, give the rooms an airing. The others except for Chino have been dismissed, and I have been entrusted with the keys. From time to time, Don Victor, when he can get away from his young girls, will stop by to see to things and give me my monthly wages.

Now I hear the voices telling me how the grass will grow tall on the unkempt lawns, how Doña Laura's hanging orchids will burst their wire baskets, their frail blossoms eaten by bugs, how the birdcages will stand empty, the poor having poached the *tórtolas* and *guineas* that Don Carlos took so much trouble to raise; how the swimming pools will fill with trash and leaves and dead things. Chino and I will be left behind in these decaying houses until that day I can see now—when I shut my eyes—that day the place will be overrun by *guardias*, smashing windows and carting off the silver and plates, the pictures and the mirror with the winged babies shooting arrows, and the chairs with medallions painted on back, the box that makes music, and the magic one that gives pictures. They will strip the girls' shelves of the toys their grandmother brought them back from that place they were always telling me about with the talcum powder flowers falling out of the clouds and the buildings that touch Damballah's sky, a bewitched and unsafe place where they must now make their lives.

I have said prayers to all the *santos*, to the *loa*, and to the Gran Poder de Dios, visiting each room, swinging the can of cleaning smoke, driving away the bad spirits that filled the house this day, and fixing in my head the different objects and where they belong so that if any workman sneaks in and steals something I will know what is gone. In the girls' rooms I member each one as a certain heaviness, now in my heart, now in my shoulders, now in my head or feet; I feel their losses pile up like dirt thrown on a box after it has been lowered into the earth. I see their future, the troublesome life ahead. They will be haunted by what they do and don't remember. But they have spirit in them. They will invent what they need to survive.

They have left, and the house is closed and the air is blessed. I lock the back door and pass the maid's room, where I see Imaculada and Nivea and Milagros packing to leave at dawn. They do not need my good-byes. I go in my own room, the one Doña Laura had special made for me so I could be with my *santos* at peace and not have to bear the insolence and annoyance of young girls with no faith in the spirits. I clean the air with incense and light the six candles—one for each of the girls, and one for Doña Laura, whose diapers I changed, and one for Don Carlos. And then, I do what I always do after a hard day, I wash my face and arms in *agua florida.* I throw out the water, saying the prayer to the *loa* of the night who watch with bright eyes from the darkened sky. I part the mosquito netting and climb into my box, arranging myself so that I am facing up, my hands folded on my waist.

Before sleep, for a few minutes, I try to accustom my flesh to the burial that is coming. I reach up for the lid and I pull it down, closing myself in. In that hot and tight darkness before I lift the lid back up for air, I shut my eyes and lie so still that the blood I hear pounding and the heart I hear knocking could be something that I have forgotten to turn off in the deserted house.

# Mayra Montero
## (Cuba, b. 1952)

Mayra Montero was born and raised in Havana, where she completed her secondary schooling. In 1972, she left Cuba, pursuing her university studies first at the Autonomous National University of Mexico in Mexico City and then at the University of Puerto Rico in San Juan. She eventually completed her graduate studies at the University of Besançon in France, and began a career in journalism with a sports column for the San Juan newspaper *El Nuevo Día*. In 1979, she took a job as editor at *El Mundo*, at the time the oldest surviving newspaper in Puerto Rico, with the largest circulation.

Subsequently, she traveled widely as a correspondent for Central America and the Caribbean, while publishing her column "What the Cable Didn't Say," which was five times selected as Best Column by the Overseas Press Club of Puerto Rico. In the meantime she was also awarded the Eddie López Prize for Journalistic Excellence (1984), the most prestigious award for journalism in Puerto Rico.

Throughout the seventies and eighties, Montero was also gaining recognition as a formidable talent in fiction, winning several prizes in Puerto Rico and abroad for her short stories, including first prizes from the Ateneo Puertorriqueño (1977) and from *Sin Nombre* (1978), the most important literary review in Puerto Rico, and as a finalist for the Juan Rulfo Prize (1986), given in France. With her novel *La trenza de la hermosa luna*, she also became a finalist for the Herralde Prize (1987), awarded by Anagrama publishers in Barcelona. When her next novel, *The Last Night I Spent With You*, became a finalist for the Premio La Sonrisa Vertical (1990) in erotic literature, it brought her international recognition and was immediately translated into French, German, and Italian, and eventually into English. Other novels include *The Red of His Shadow* (1992) and *In the Palm of Darkness* (1995), both set in Haiti, and *The Messenger* (1998), a passionate tale of Enrico Caruso's doomed affair with a Cuban-Chinese mulatta, set in the Havana of the twenties. In the meantime, after the demise of *El Mundo*, Montero began contributing a weekly column to *El Nuevo Día* called "Scattered Showers," a selection of which was published in 1996. Her latest novel, *Purpura profunda* (2000), was published by Tusquets publishers in the same erotic collection *La Sonrisa Vertical* as *The Last Night I Spent With You*. Montero lives in Puerto Rico.

# That Man, Pollack

Today I saw my father's house. I saw it just the way it used to be, with its circular terrace and stone facade. It was in a book on architecture, a birthday present given to me by Sara, my wife's best friend. She said to me: "Look, Esteban, the houses of Havana," and I had a premonition. I don't know why I imagined I would find it there. Or rather, I think I do know why: the house was fairly well known in its day; it had what people insisted on calling a "Roman bath," which was nothing more than an indoor pool, and in that ironic chamber, that space conceived for who knows what acts of madness, I attained indifference and rancor. At the age of ten, I put an end to my life.

I placed my hand on one of the photographs. There were the lookout tower and tiled roof, and next to them another image: the central courtyard and arcade, each column made of a different marble, just as Papá wanted. Occupying an entire page of the book was the "Roman bath," the furniture and bougainvillea around the pool, and the semicircle with the statue of Aphrodite. The statue wasn't the American architect's idea—Pollack was not a man given to excess—but his Cuban collaborator's, a boy with a degree from Columbia University; his name was Mendoza and my parents gave him a free hand.

I've heard that many people die on their birthdays; today I thought it would happen to me. When I saw the photographs, I felt a tightening in my chest; one of my hands, the left, began to tremble, and I was about to call my wife, but I heard her talking to Sara and I made a final gesture of resignation: it would be better if she didn't see me die, if she found out later when she came in to offer me a drink or to have a look at the houses of Havana. At first she would think I was asleep, but then she would notice my clenched hand and touch my forehead to feel my skin, just the skin is definitive proof. And when she saw the book and the page it was opened to, and read at the bottom of the photo, "Roman bath in the Vilardell house," she would understand the reasons for my sudden death. She was the only one to whom I could tell part of what had happened, a long time after we married, when our own son was a boy of ten. She cried a little, put her arms around me, and whispered, "I'm so sorry, Esteban."

Gradually I began to calm down, my hand stopped trembling, and I looked at the book again. "Papi," I heard myself say. How many years was it since I had recalled my father's face? And my mother's? For how many years had I been trying to retrieve her voice, a voice that shut off one night and was denied to me from that moment on and forever after?

I returned to the photograph of the "Roman bath." I looked at the lattices that filled the spaces between the columns, remembered the scent of fine wood, and thought again about the light, the light that came in through the ceiling, as it did in a Pompeian impluvium, and the delicately patterned, buttery light filtering in through the windows. Mamá spent part of her life there, surrounded by beauty, bathed in that light. I saw her only once with that man, the architect Pollack. I came home early from school, and as I passed by I heard murmurs and stopped to look: my mother, sitting next to the pool, was speaking gently, and that man, Pollack, standing at the far end of the room, simply looked at the floor. Ever since that day his face has been etched in my mind: narrow eyes, hooked nose, mouth tight with filthy talk and rage. Or perhaps not, perhaps that mouth was perfect and amiable, and the rage and filthy talk had to be in me. I remember I went into the "Roman bath" that afternoon and positioned myself between them: I hugged my mother and she asked me if I wasn't going to have a snack. I looked at her and felt that something in her was betraying me. It was not her treatment of Pollack but just the opposite: in the way she ignored him, in the distance she placed between the two of them, I could sense an abhorrent closeness, a complicity with claws, like an animal howling in pain.

There's a text in the book that mentions the architects and discusses the owner of the house; my father's name is there; he worked in the tobacco business but basically he was an artist: he painted the ceiling panels, he painted portraits of Mamá and of me. He stopped painting me when I was ten, there was a break then, a frontier I was pushed across. The book confirms what friends already had told me: the house stands empty, in shambles; the organ in the living room disappeared years ago, and the statue of Aphrodite was stolen; the semicircle fell into ruins. I wonder what kind of stagnant water now fills my mother's pool.

Our chauffeur's name was Pacífico. He died one night in the month of August. He had come into the house looking for my father and collapsed in the gallery that led to the courtyard. He was a heavy man, and when he fell his head split open like a fruit. Almost everything was bleeding: his nose, his mouth, his ears. Mamá came running from her room; Papá, who was in his studio, brought in a bottle of sal ammoniac, but there was nothing to be done. The two maids crouched down and held his head, and Papá placed two fingers on Pacífico's neck. "He's dead," he said, and the maids burst into tears. My mother signaled to me and said: "Go to your room, Esteban."

She didn't have to say it twice: I wanted to get away from there, too. I ran out, but instead of going to my room, I went to hers. I opened the door and threw myself on her bed, which was softer than mine; I kicked the sheets with my shoes, I tossed back and forth in a frenzy, feeling a sudden pain as silent as the death I had left outside. Then I got up and went to her desk; in her hurry she had left it open, and I suffered an attack of temporary insanity; I can't explain it any other way. I pulled out papers, letters, cards; I threw down the photographs of her friends and her friends' children. I crumpled almost everything in my hands, and what I couldn't crumple I ground into the rug with my feet. Then I looked at the papers on her desk. One was a rough draft, with some lines crossed out; the other was the clean copy of the letter my mother had been writing when they called her because of what had happened to Pacífico. I read all of it, but after so many years this is the only sentence I still remember: "It is the intimate aspect of our relationship that causes this immense feeling of guilt in me." The intimate aspect meant Mamá's breasts, her belly, I saw that once; the merciless illusion of her buttocks, I had seen them, too. I didn't need to think it over: my bitter, vengeful heart filled with a desperate euphoria. I left the room holding those papers in my hand, walked slowly through the gallery, passed the "Roman bath," and saw a faint glow coming in through the skylight, the light of deep night. When I crossed the courtyard I heard the leaves of the plantain trees brushing against one another, and I stopped in bewilderment because the marble of one of the columns reminded me of Pacífico's blood. I continued walking until I reached my father. Nobody was bending over the chauffeur now; he had been covered with a sheet, and one of the maids was washing away the blood that had run along the floor. I raised my hand and showed the papers to my father. He looked at me, uncomprehending; I suppose he thought they were drawings. But then he heard Mamá's cry, she recognized the papers and shouted at me: "What are you doing with them?" She ran toward us and tried to recover her letters, but it was too late. My father sidestepped her and went on reading. When he finished, or when he had read enough, he came over to me, put his hands on my shoulders, and shook me; then he slapped me so hard I fell across Pacífico's corpse. I was smeared with blood and began to scream. My mother disappeared and one of the maids helped me to my feet.

The next day the entire house was filled with silence. That's all I remember: the quiet and the sadness. The place where the chauffeur had fallen was clean, and Mamá did not show herself all day. The only thing my father said when we sat down at the table was "enjoy the meal"; Mamá ate alone in her room; I should add that she never ate with me again. Eight years later I enrolled at Columbia University; I became an architect like that man, Pollack, and rarely returned to Havana.

My mother closed the house. My father had already died when she decided to leave it all behind. She moved to Bermuda; I never knew why she went there, or with whom. When she died, someone forwarded a note she had left for me: "If you ever go back to Havana, please tear down the house." I planned to, I intended to, until my friends began to tell me it was all in ruins. I've confirmed it today in this book. Here is my father's house, the arcade with its columns and the "Roman bath" with its evil portent: the statue of Aphrodite that we never liked, not that man, Pollack, and not me.

*Translated by Edith Grossman*

# Javier Valdés
## (Mexico, b. 1953)

Not much is known about the personal and professional life of Javier Valdés, who was born (according to the laconic jacket copy of one of his books) in "the most populous, surrealistic city in the world," presumably Mexico City. For many years he worked as a dentist. During the fifteen or so minutes of waiting for the anesthesia to take effect on each of his patients, he began writing stories to pass the time. Eventually one of his patients from the publishing world stumbled upon the overflowing box of his manuscripts, and, after reading several stories, insisted Valdés put together a selection. Given the clinical turn of his mind, the author quite naturally organized the collection by function, as so much reading for the bathroom. Hence, the title: *Cuentos para baño* (1997). They are dark funny tales, irreverent readings of Simenon, Highsmith, and Stephen King, and they often make the reader wonder whether a character is about to make him die of laughter or push him down the stairs. Yet, Valdés doesn't consider himself an author, but rather someone who simply jots down his own stories in order not to drive his friends to distraction by telling them out loud.

Although this first collection, while critically well received, did not make him enough money to quit dentistry, he did so anyway, deciding that the pain of his patients had finally proved too stressful for him. He briefly contemplated a second collection, to be organized as "Tales for Smokers." Yet, while testing out the idea on

a random sampling of readers, he found they became so obsessed
by the stories that they forgot their burning cigarettes that were
scattered around the room. Afraid he might cause a fire, he destroyed the manuscript. Instead, he published a novel, *Asesino en
serio* (1999), about a serial killer in Mexico City whose female vic-
tims all perish, without a mark on their bodies, in a state of absolute ecstasy. Valdés recently confessed to a journalist, "It seems
to me that black humor is the only possible approach to a sordid
theme, particularly when dealing with the underworld of prostitution and crime, because any other way would be unbearable for
the reader." Valdés lives in Mexico City, where he is collaborating
on a film adaptation of "Serious Killer" and working on a new
novel.

# People Like Us

*Gold is cash and love is a worthless check*

Ana Laura and I decided to spend part of the winter in the mountains. After weighing all the possibilities, we were leaning toward renting a house. Although we wouldn't have the conveniences of a hotel, we wouldn't have the inconveniences either, and it would cost about a third as much.

Besides, we would have the peace and quiet we both needed to be able to work. Ana Laura had to correct six texts that her editor was to publish in February and I had to finish more than twelve stories, which I had started some time ago and which would serve to pay a good portion of my not-unsubstantial debts.

So that's what we ended up doing. We loaded my tiny car with food and equipment for our pending work and then set off for our temporary paradise on earth.

The route to the mountains was rife with splendid aromas and scenes. The birds were singing as if it were the last day of their lives and the painting that nature was unfolding impressed us beyond measure.

We stopped at a scenic overlook along the highway to better appreciate the countryside.

Although many of the trees were leafless, others still glowed a stunning dark green. The ground was carpeted with leaves, forming a mosaic in several shades of brown. In the distance, the tallest peaks were enveloped in snow and clouds that seemed to kiss them.

The air was cold, but pleasant.

We smoked a cigarette in silence as we contemplated the landscape.

"Which way is the house?" asked Ana Laura.

I thought a moment and then pointed to a spot between two low mountains. "Over there," I replied.

Her gaze followed my finger to the horizon.

"Okay then, let's go. This is beautiful, but I wouldn't want to spend the night here."

We got back in the Volkswagen, which soon began to show signs of fatigue as we began the steepest part of the ascent, but German technology ultimately prevailed and the small car successfully scaled the slopes.

We finally arrived at the house around six o'clock and by then it was much colder.

The house was a real icebox and felt even colder than outside, but the fireplace was stacked with dry wood and it didn't take us long to get a good fire going.

We huddled in front of the flames until our bones warmed up again. Then we made several trips to the car to get our bags, Ana Laura's laptop, and my word processor.

Once this was done, we set about inspecting the house.

It was a small structure, fairly old, but immaculately maintained. There was a pleasant living room, a dining room, a big kitchen—which seemed overly large for the tiny house—and a very cozy bedroom with another fireplace, which Ana Laura immediately lit.

We poured ourselves drinks and ate cheese and pâté. After eating, we unpacked, stoked the fireplaces and went to bed. The drive had been tiring, not just for the Volkswagen, but for us too, and the cold made us burrow under the heavy down comforter.

The next day we each began our respective work. The mountain air made me feel wonderful and I finished a story that I'd been stuck on for six months. Ana Laura, on the other hand, worked for a few hours and then started poking around the house. By five o'clock she had already drunk more than half a bottle of vodka. At eight I had to carry her to bed, because she had fallen asleep in front of the fire.

Several days passed in similar fashion. Since she wasn't drunk all the time, Ana Laura soon realized that it had been a mistake for us to cloister ourselves in such a remote part of the world. The poor woman couldn't work and went out for long walks in the forest. She took the car to town several times to buy groceries— and vodka. Meanwhile, I quickly finished one story after another. I felt like a freshly uncorked bottle of sparkling wine and sentence after sentence bubbled out with an ease I had never known before.

Ana Laura's laptop remained solitary and inactive, as if it were nothing more than a prop.

I knew very well that Ana Laura was dying to go back to the city or someplace more lively, but she didn't say a word. She wore her boredom stoically.

One afternoon, at the height of her boredom, she discovered a door to the attic. It had been sealed, but no seal can withstand feminine curiosity and Ana Laura launched an exploration of the space, with the aid of a flashlight she brought in from the car.

At dinnertime she showed me something interesting that she had found earlier that afternoon. It was an old notebook with drawings of the house we were occupying and it showed in precise sequence how it had been built, from the empty lot to the com-

pleted structure. There were details on the foundation, the construction of the walls, even the roof.

Each drawing carried a date at the bottom of the page. The
house had been completed almost a century ago.

"What do you think?" Ana Laura asked as she closed the notebook.

"Excellent artist."

We didn't talk about it anymore that night.

From that point on, my girlfriend's boredom completely disappeared. She spent the days studying the drawings in the old notebook. She seemed hypnotized by them and spent hours poring
over each one, as if it were from a collection of old Flemish masters. Ana Laura stopped drinking vodka and walking in the woods
and hardly ate anything. It was almost as if she were under a spell
of some kind.

The third day after her find in the attic, she interrupted my
work. "Look at this!"

She indicated a particular portion of a drawing. I had no idea
what she was trying to show me. "What is it?"

"It looks like some sort of cellar."

Sure enough, the drawing indicated a large opening right beneath the kitchen floor. "It's probably just a cistern," I said, trying
to get back to work.

"I don't think so," she insisted. "There's plenty of water
around here. And besides, there's a well a few yards from the
house. Why build a cistern? There's something else," she added,
slightly raising one of her beautiful eyebrows, "I already examined
the kitchen floor and there's no opening."

"So?" I asked disinterestedly as I lit a cigarette.

"It could be a secret hiding place. Maybe there's treasure inside. Can you imagine?"

By now my rhythm had been totally broken, so I began to pay
closer attention to what my beautiful companion was suggesting.

"You said there's no opening in the kitchen floor?"

"Look for yourself."

I went into the kitchen with the open notebook in my hands and stood over where I figured the hole should be.

There was nothing. But I did notice the stone floor covering the kitchen floor was not the same as in the drawing of the half-completed house.

This stuff looked newer.

"It's not the same floor," I said, looking distractedly at the tips of my boots.

Ana Laura seemed disappointed when she saw what I meant.

Just to make my lady happy, I tapped all over the kitchen floor with the heels of my boots. It was as solid as a rock.

"Look, Ana Laura, it must have been some sort of storage cellar. There was probably no need for it anymore and when they changed the kitchen floor, the new owners simply filled in the hole."

"I guess you're right, but it was an interesting idea, wasn't it?" She had the look of a little girl who had been scolded.

The next morning, I found Ana Laura lying on the kitchen floor, inspecting it inch by inch.

I had other things to do, so I didn't pay any attention. If she wanted to spend the day searching for clues to a nonexistent treasure, that was her choice. I was going to get my work done.

Next time I looked, I saw she'd given up her scrutiny of the kitchen floor and gone back up to the attic.

A few hours later she came down covered with dust and carrying a roll of very old paper.

Without saying a word she unrolled it in front of me, covering my word processor.

It was a well-designed construction project. Drawn in sepia ink, it appeared to be the original plan for the house. There was no doubt that it was the work of a consummate artist.

And there it was again—the cellar beneath the kitchen, clearly delineated with a dotted line which indicated that it was underground.

Now I had to take Ana Laura seriously.

If it were some sort of storage space and had been sealed, we wouldn't lose anything by looking around a little, if only to please Ana Laura.

The next day we went into town. There was no office for the regulation or registration of private construction projects, but we were told that we could find information on local buildings at the public library.

The matronly woman who attended us in the library was colder than the morning and it took several minutes to convince her we weren't planning to rob the place. Finally, after glaring at us fixedly, she led us to the reading room, ordering us to sit down and indicating that we were to remain silent by putting a finger to her lips. Neither Ana Laura nor I had said a word, but the ugly harpy seemed to enjoy treating us like a couple of school kids.

She disappeared for what seemed like an eternity and then reappeared carrying a very large book and two other smaller volumes, all quite old.

She opened the large book on one of the tables and wordlessly signaled that it contained what she thought we were looking for. Then, speaking in a very low voice—which was ridiculous, because there was no one else in the room—she told us that we would find additional information in the two smaller books. She warned us to be careful with the material, since it was very valuable. She returned after a few minutes to stare at us again, and finally disappeared in the direction of her desk.

Laughing, Ana Laura turned to look at me and whispered, "You better behave yourself if you don't want the teacher to expel you from school."

I had to control myself to keep from laughing out loud. Not that the joke was so funny, but the tension in that place made it seem hilarious.

Stifling our laughter, we began looking through the large volume. It had no title but contained copies of sketches from various construction projects, both in town and in the outlying areas. The drawings were accompanied by brief descriptions of the projects and a set of plans.

We found our house on one of the center pages. The drawing was identical to the one Ana Laura had found in the attic. It looked like a photocopy.

The description of the house didn't give any new information but merely provided technical details.

We looked at several similar projects and none had a cellar.

Ana Laura interrupted my musing. "If it's an ordinary building, why is it included in the town's book?"

Without waiting for a response, which would have consisted of an impotent shrugging of my shoulders, she began leafing through one of the smaller tomes. I did the same with the other one.

The book I was looking at described several homes in the area along with their histories.

The house that we were occupying had the unique characteristic of having been designed and drawn by a prodigal son of the region, who had been an exquisite and impeccable artist.

"Look at this!" shouted Ana Laura.

I barely had a chance to look at the book when a chilling voice sounded, causing the hair on my neck to stand on end.

"If you don't intend to keep quiet, you'd better leave."

It was the librarian. She was visibly upset and threatened us with a long, crooked index finger.

"Please excuse us," said Ana Laura, in a very low, sweet voice.

"That's the last warning. Next time, we will be forced to suspend your privileges."

The old witch spoke in the plural, as if we were in the main branch of the New York Public Library and not in a little hole in some remote corner of the mountains.

Fortunately she returned to her desk and Ana Laura pointed

with a manicured finger to the section of the book that she had been reading.

It described the construction of the foundation of our house, focusing principally on its design. It seemed that the owner of the house had hired the best architect in the area to design a hiding place. Not a simple basement, rather a carefully planned refuge in which the owner could protect himself in case of war.

So that was what made the house special and why it was listed in the books.

Ana Laura politely asked the librarian if we could make photocopies of the plans and drawings, but the witch vehemently refused, arguing that the copying machine was for the exclusive use of the library and not for "rowdy tourists."

"Could you lend us the book then to make copies somewhere else?" she asked.

"Certainly not!" she exclaimed loftily. She would never place the village's treasures in the hands of people like us!

"What do you suggest then?" I asked, amused, recalling my high school days.

"I suggest that you leave. You are not welcome here."

Saying this, she grabbed the three books and proceeded to put them back on the shelves, effectively ending the conversation.

Once in the street, the cold air hit us with such force that we sought refuge in a cafe.

A string of bells rang as we opened the door and the scent of fresh-baked bread and coffee comfortingly enveloped us. A cozy fire burned in a fireplace along one wall.

An obese old man, wearing a large white apron and with a kind face, approached to take our order. His face—especially his nose—showed signs of a long useless battle against alcohol abuse, but he was very attentive and agreeable.

We ordered coffee and a couple of brandies—to warm up.

Only two other tables were occupied and a solitary man smoked a pipe at the bar in front of a steaming cup of coffee.

The fat man brought over what we had ordered. "Tourists?" he asked with a scratchy voice.

After the experience we had suffered in the library I hesitated to respond.

"We rented a house outside of town. We're actually here to work. We're writers." Ana Laura had spoken and was now flashing one of her adorable smiles.

The man smiled back warmly, exposing a large black space where there had once been teeth.

"Welcome!" he exclaimed. Without another word he went back behind the bar and began polishing an interminable supply of glasses and cups.

Like the sugar in our coffee, his behavior rapidly dissipated the bitterness caused by the librarian. After a few minutes, we ordered more brandy. The coffee was very strong, but delicious.

The smiling man served us again. "These are on the house," he said, helping himself to a glass too.

Ana Laura invited him to sit with us and he eagerly accepted.

His name was Guillermo.

"Which house is it that you rented?" he asked after a few minutes of chatting.

We described the house.

"Ah! The Bernabeu house."

"Do you know it?" asked Ana Laura, with a childlike smile of surprise.

"Everyone in town knows it. My father used to say that the owner was a half-crazy Frenchman. He spent his life worrying about wars and invasions. . . ."

He took a sip of his brandy and, after wiping his lips on the back of his hand, continued. "They say he was obsessed with war. He hired one of our best boys to make him a house with a hiding place. He said they weren't going to get him so easily."

Just then, one of the townspeople called out to the barman, demanding to be served.

"I'll be right back," he said, flooding the air with the dense smell of alcohol.

A few minutes later he returned to our table, but didn't sit down. Instead, he crossed his arms and asked, "What were we talking about?"

"You were saying that Bernabeu was obsessed with war," replied Ana Laura, interestedly.

"Ah! Yes! And invasions! It seems that his grandfather had served in Napoleon's army and must have told the poor boy too many awful stories about the war when he was a child."

"But, if everyone knew that he had a hiding place, that didn't give him any advantage, did it?" asked Ana Laura.

Guillermo put his index finger to his temple and made a few circling motions, indicating craziness.

"What happened to him?" I asked.

"To Bernabeu? No one knows for sure. I think after he finished the house he got married and left town."

"Has anyone been in the hiding place?" demanded Laura.

"No one. After the Frenchman left and before the town took over the abandoned house, a lot of curious folks tried to figure out how to get into the cellar. I guess they thought there was something of value down there. But it seems that Bernabeu did a good job. No one has been able to find a way in."

The man went back behind the bar and resumed his polishing.

We remained silent for a few minutes.

"We have to get into that cellar. There must be something there," said Ana Laura.

"Take it easy, my dear. Before we destroy the house, we should look for an entrance to the hiding place. There must be one," I said, hardly convinced.

We paid our bill and went out into the cold street again.

Once in the car, we headed back to the house in silence. The tale of the paranoid Bernabeu stayed on my mind and I thought I might be able to write a good story about it. Or better still, if we were somehow able to get into the cellar, a story wouldn't be enough. More likely a novel, no matter what we actually found there. What else is a writer's imagination for?

Maybe there wasn't anything of value buried there, but, if I could write an interesting novel, that might turn out to be a small treasure in itself.

The house was very cold when we arrived and Ana Laura stoked the fires in both fireplaces.

Although it was still early, the brandy had made us quite warm and so we had several glasses of vodka before sprawling out on the sofa in front of the fireplace in the living room. We watched the flames devour the dry wood for a long time.

"What do you think we should do?" Ana Laura said after a while.

"We could look for some kind of access to the cellar, if it still exists."

She rewarded me with the best smile in her repertoire and replied, "Let's get to work."

Finishing off the rest of the vodka in our glasses, we divided up the labor.

I was to explore the kitchen, the bathroom, and the bedroom; Ana Laura, the living room, the dining room and, just in case, the attic.

We spent hours searching every corner, every nook. If someone had been watching us, he would have thought that we were completely insane, or else that we were rehearsing an Ionesco play.

We crawled on the floor like cockroaches. We took pictures and mirrors off the walls. We felt every orifice and every panel of wood looking for buttons and trick levers.

Nothing.

By seven o'clock we were completely exhausted and starving. We hadn't discovered anything more substantial than a few spiderwebs and a lot of dust.

The air was filled with a sense of failure and disillusion.

We ate a dinner of cold turkey and drank a bottle of white wine. We stoked the fires again and went to bed.

We weren't in a mood conducive to sexual activity and were both soon profoundly asleep.

*. . . I was in Bernabeu's hiding place. It was a small but well-organized room. I saw several large cushions, some blankets and cans of food piled on the floor. Two small containers, about five gallons each, held water. Farther back there were several boxes containing dried meats, crackers, jars of conserved fruits and a burlap bag filled with walnuts, another filled with hazelnuts, and another filled with pinenuts.*

*I walked around the room and, although it was completely dark, I could see everything clearly. The place was very tidy, as if someone had just cleaned it. On top of a wooden box of dried fish there was a sepia photograph. I took it in my hands. It was very old and showed a newly married couple posing soberly for the camera. When I looked more carefully, I couldn't help being alarmed. It was a photograph of Ana Laura and me! . . .*

I awakened drenched with sweat. It took two minutes to convince myself that it had just been a dream—a nightmare—produced by the obsessive search we had carried out the previous afternoon.

I went to the kitchen, turned on the light, and lit a cigarette. The bottle of vodka was within reach so I helped myself to a drink.

Ana Laura and I were obsessing, that was all. If there was a cellar, it had simply been sealed off long ago. Period. I had no reason to keep following my beautiful companion's quest. The subject was closed.

The next day I would clear it up with Ana Laura and get back to work. Back to what would feed me and pay for my share of this house. Bernabeu and his damned paranoia could just go to hell.

I didn't need any more nightmares like that one. . . .

Suddenly I heard a noise. I froze. Not only could I hear, but I could feel footsteps approaching.

For a moment I ceased breathing and my heart stopped. The glass of vodka in my hand fused with my fingers as if it were a part of my body. For a stupid second I gazed at the transparent liquid. As still as a frozen pool.

Now what? Bernabeu's ghost? Some soul in anguish?

I closed my eyes, expecting the worst. When I opened them again I jumped with fright, letting go of the glass, which shattered in slow motion on the stone floor.

A blonde ghost dressed in white was standing in front of me.

"Will you pour me one?" said Ana Laura, her face screwed up. "I've had a terrible nightmare."

Feigning interest, I served her a little vodka in a glass. I cleared my throat, like a chicken in the slaughterhouse, and, trying to sound calm, I asked what she had dreamed.

Ana Laura described her dream down to the last detail.

I felt as if someone had run a piece of ice down my spine.

Ana Laura's dream was identical to mine.

"It must be exhaustion," I said, trying to sound like I believed myself.

She swallowed her drink in one gulp and, giving me a kiss on the cheek, said, "Of course!" Then she went off to bed.

I drank several more glasses of vodka before I found sufficient courage to return to bed, and the unsettling dreamworld.

The next day I awoke with an unbearable headache, feeling as if a sword had been stuck from my forehead all the way down through my neck. I looked at my watch. It was past one-thirty in the afternoon.

Holding my head with both hands to prevent unnecessary pain, I went to the kitchen and took four aspirin.

Ana Laura was nowhere in sight. I went into the bathroom and took a steaming shower, gradually lowering the temperature until

I could no longer stand the freezing water. Then I ran back to the bedroom.

The sword had disappeared, but had left behind a dull hammering in my skull. I got dressed, but didn't have enough strength to do anything, so I lay down on the bed and closed my eyes, wishing I hadn't drunk so much vodka the night before.

*. . . I was in the cellar in front of a large metal door. I tried to open it, but I couldn't.*

*I frantically kicked it with all my strength. It wouldn't budge. A gripping panic overcame me. I wasn't going to be able to get out of the damned hiding place.*

*I began to hear faint shouts calling my name, over and over.*

*It was Ana Laura. I couldn't tell where her voice was coming from, but I could hear it clearly now. . . .*

It was already dark outside when I opened my eyes. Only a light pain remained in my temples from my earlier hangover. The house was dark, so I turned on the lights as I called for Ana Laura.

She didn't answer. I looked all over the house.

There was no sign of her. There weren't even dirty dishes or glasses in the kitchen.

Everything was just as I had left it earlier that afternoon.

I went outside to see if she had taken the car.

The Volkswagen was still where we had parked the night before. It was freezing outside, so I went back into the house and tried to calm myself. She had to be somewhere nearby.

But where? Was she out walking in the woods in the dark? Maybe she had walked into town? Not likely—it was almost two miles away.

Soon I began to feel a tremendous emptiness in the pit of my stomach and my cheeks were burning.

Just as in my dream, I was being overcome by an unbearable panic attack.

Though I knew better, I poured myself a drink, this time choosing scotch. The memory of the hellish vodka hangover was still fresh in my mind.

What should I do now? Go look for her in town?

Had she seen that I was sleeping so long and decided to run some errands? Without the car? Without leaving a note?

I emptied the glass of scotch in one gulp and immediately poured myself another. I was trying to control myself . . . unsuccessfully.

I emptied that glass too. Then I put on a jacket and went out to the car. I was going to go into town to look for her. She had to be there.

Just before I got into the car, I heard—just like in my dream—a voice calling my name in the distance.

Was I hallucinating?

Where was the voice coming from?

I looked in the glove compartment for the flashlight, but it wasn't there. Then I remembered that Ana Laura had used it to search the attic.

The shouts were further apart now, but I could hear them more clearly. They were coming from behind the house.

I turned on the car's headlights. They didn't help much, but it was better than nothing.

I lumbered up the small hill behind the house to where the shouts seemed to be originating.

By now I was sure I wasn't hallucinating. Ana Laura must be in danger!

It had snowed the night before and the ground was very slippery. I was wearing city shoes so every two steps I had to perform acrobatics so as not to fall on my face. That, and my girlfriend's shouting, made me think that maybe I was having another nightmare. But when I slipped and fell, smashing my face against a rock, I knew I wasn't dreaming.

I actually saw stars and my right cheek burned with pain.

There is no worse injury than one sustained in freezing tempera-
tures. I got up as best I could and tried to reorient myself.

The Volkswagen's headlights were by now only dim, and since
I was directly behind the house it blocked their light. The curtains
in the kitchen windows, which looked out at where I was, were
closed and only gave off a faint light around the edges.

I could hear only the howling of the wind as it whispered
through the trees in the dark forest.

Was that all it had been?

A trick of nature?

Then suddenly, from a few yards ahead of me, I clearly heard
Ana Laura's voice, followed by a sharp echo.

I felt my way toward the source of the sounds.

Now her voice was only two or three yards away, but it
sounded heavy and distorted, as if she had placed a cardboard
tube in front of her mouth before shouting.

My eyes had adjusted somewhat to the darkness at this point
and I could make out a shadow in the distance with an arch above
it. . . . It was the well!

Sweating heavily, and with my face still numb from the fall, I
grabbed the edge of the well and again clearly heard Ana Laura's
voice, calling for help from inside the well.

"Ana Laura?"

"Here . . . down here . . ." she said wearily.

"What happened? Are you OK?"

"I feel like shit and I'm freezing to death. Get me out of here!"

"OK. Calm down! Let me get the flashlight."

"I have the flashlight down here, but the batteries have run
out."

Ana Laura's voice sounded hollow.

"How deep is it?"

"About nine feet. Hurry up! I'm standing in freezing water
and it's ridiculously cold down here."

I tried to see the bottom, but couldn't.

"Hang on just a little longer," I told her while I took off my jacket and threw it inside. "Here's this. Don't worry. I'm going to the house to find something to get you out with."

"Hurry up!"

My eyes were fully adjusted to the darkness now and I cautiously returned to the house. I was not eager to fall again. I went to the kitchen door, which was the nearest entrance to the house. It wouldn't open. Then I remembered that the door had been locked from the inside.

I made my way around the corner of the house to the car and the degree of safety that the headlights afforded.

Finally I reached the front door. The first thing I did was open the kitchen curtains.

They didn't provide much light, but it was something.

Then I looked around for something I could use to get Ana Laura out of this mess she'd gotten herself into.

Even if there had been a good rope—which there wasn't—and I could somehow secure it to the arch above the well, it wouldn't be easy for her to grip the rope with her frozen fingers and scale the walls; that only happens in movies.

Suddenly, I thought of something. I went to the door that led to the attic and lowered the wooden ladder leading up to it. I tried to pull it off the door where it was attached.

Impossible.

I went to look for a hatchet I had seen near the car and had used to cut firewood.

After several chops with the hatchet the ladder gave way.

It wasn't very long, only a few yards, but it would help.

I took the ladder and carried it out the kitchen door.

"Here I am, my love," I said, feeling incredibly stupid.

"We can talk later. Just get me out of here," she yelled, then more quietly, "idiot."

"I'm going to hand a ladder down, be careful, I don't want to hit your head."

"That's all I need. Go ahead, lower it down!"

I eased the ladder down with its rough ends first, thinking they'd offer some resistance against the slippery floor.

I leaned way over the edge of the well but still couldn't feel the ladder coming into contact with anything.

"Try to grip it, Annie, but carefully, because—"

"Owww!"

"—it has splinters on the end."

I felt her grab the ladder, and then after some huffing and foul language, her head appeared out of the darkness at the rim of the well.

Without speaking, I helped her out and we went quickly back to the house.

I took her into the bedroom, covered her with the down comforter, and poured her a large glass of brandy. Ana Laura was shivering uncontrollably and her lips were a color somewhere between purple and blue. I made her drink all the brandy.

My first thought had been to put her in a steaming shower, but that might have killed her or at the least ruptured a bunch of blood vessels. The risk of pneumonia seemed the lesser of two evils.

When she finished the brandy, she breathed deeply and started coughing. Good, I thought. That would help her warm up.

I built up the fire in the bedroom until it roared, then went into the bathroom and wet a towel with hot water. I squeezed out the excess water, went back to Ana Laura and removed her clothing. Her skin was covered with goosebumps and her teeth chattered noisily. I rubbed her body roughly with the hot towel. I went back to heat up the towel again and repeated the process several times. She was starting to look better, thanks to the fireplace, which by now had warmed up the room quite nicely.

Soon she stopped trembling and shivering and seemed to relax a little.

I poured her more brandy and she drank it eagerly.

I got out some flannel pajamas and put them as close to the fire as I dared. When they were hot, I helped Ana Laura put them on. She was feeling better by the minute.

When she finished her third glass of brandy, the color had returned to her face and her cheeks were rosy again.

I left her alone for a few minutes to go make some coffee.

It was very hot, so she had to drink it in tiny sips. By the time she finished her coffee, she was a new person.

I was dying of curiosity, but didn't want to grill her yet about how she'd ended up at the bottom of the well. After I'd covered her with the blankets and put more wood on the fire, I asked her if she wanted anything else. She said no.

I gave her a light kiss on the lips and left the room, closing the door behind me. I barely made out a weak "thank you" from behind the door.

Since I had spent the whole day sleeping, the last thing I wanted to do was go back to bed, so I tried to write a little. The words on the screen looked like ants crawling on a wall. There were hundreds of them, but they didn't mean anything.

After a half hour of writing I erased everything I'd written and started pacing around the room.

The day's events had made me nervous and edgy, but at the same time they had pulled me from the stupor I'd been in. There was no doubt that the experience had been completely different from anything I had ever gone through.

I had never rescued a beautiful princess before.

I woke up in front of a dying fire in the living room. All the wood had burned, leaving only bright embers and glowing coals.

I stood up and my shoulder painfully chastised me for the position in which I had fallen asleep. I went to the bedroom to check on Ana Laura.

The bedroom was warm and cozy. She was breathing evenly, and when I touched her forehead, I was relieved to find that she didn't have a fever. It was five A.M. so I got undressed, threw a couple large logs on the fire and got into bed. . . .

*. . . I got to the bottom of the well, but Ana Laura wasn't there. The floor was dry clay and the heat inside was unbearable.*

*I tried to climb back out, but I couldn't. Every time I climbed up a step, the ladder sank farther and farther.*

*Finally, it stopped sinking and I ascended, but when I got to the top of the ladder, even stretching my arms as far as I could reach, I was still more than three feet from the rim of the well.*

*I looked right in front of me and saw a perfect rectangle cut into the side of the well. It looked like the entrance to a passageway.*

*I tried to push it but it wouldn't budge, so I took out my Swiss army knife and stuck it in the crack. It was definitely a separate piece of stone from the rest of the wall, about two feet square. I was certain that it was the entrance to the cellar.*

*Excitedly, I called Ana Laura several times, but she didn't answer my calls. I kept calling. "Ana Lauraaaa . . . ! Ana Lauraaaaa . . . !"*

When I opened my eyes, Ana Laura was very close to my face, shaking me and softly saying, "Wake up. You're dreaming. Wake up."

I focused my eyes. It was already light outside and she was wearing jeans and a camel hair sweater. She was beautiful.

"Is it over?" she asked maternally.

"Yes, I think so."

"What were you dreaming about?"

As I described my dream, her mouth opened in surprise. "The entrance exists," she said excitedly. "Exactly as you described it. That's what I was doing yesterday, when I lost my balance and fell into the well."

We decided to go into town and buy the things we would need to explore what we both thought would be the entrance to the cellar.

On the way I confessed to Ana Laura that I, too, had had the same nightmare she had two nights ago.

She was quiet for a few minutes and finally spoke. "That means that there is something down there waiting for us. The dreams we've been having are only a vibration. A signal."

There wasn't a real hardware store in town, but we found a large old-fashioned general store where you could pick up anything from caramels to the latest model gasoline generator.

We bought three high-powered flashlights and a lot of batteries, a twelve-foot aluminum ladder, a pick, a blowtorch, a shovel, a maul, a hammer, two stone chisels and a pair of snowboots for both Ana Laura and myself.

Ana Laura paid for everything on her credit card. I promised to reimburse her when the stories I was working on were published, but she made a gesture indicating that it didn't matter. It seemed that she was completely convinced that we would find more than enough in the cellar to cover the expense.

We loaded the car and tied the ladder on top as best we could. Then we drove back to the house.

"How do you feel?" I asked Ana Laura in the car.

"I have butterflies in my stomach."

She didn't have to elaborate. I felt the same.

After we put on our new snowboots, the first thing we did was take a look at the well.

From above, even in the light of day, you couldn't clearly see the cut-out section in the wall. You had to look very carefully even to imagine it. The old ladder from the attic looked like something dead inside the well.

We carried the aluminum ladder and the rest of the equipment over to the well and started working.

We heated the rungs of the ladder to a glowing red with the blowtorch and lowered it. There was a hissing and a thin column of steam when it came into contact with the frozen water at the bottom of the well. We pressed it down and it sank a little farther.

It seemed secure, so I descended and lifted up the wooden ladder from the night before. Ana Laura lifted up the top as it emerged and we removed it from the well. We loaded up with the rest of the equipment and Ana Laura followed me down into the well. The sun was at its zenith, so we figured we wouldn't have to use artificial light for the first two hours.

Just as in my dream, I descended the ladder to about three feet below the rim and found myself even with the opening. I used my knife to see whether there really was a separation between the concave rectangle and the rest of the wall, which was covered with a thin layer of clay.

"What do you see? Can you move it?"

"No, not yet. Hand me the maul."

I gave it a couple of sharp whacks, but it didn't move, only made a hollow sound.

"Let me try," Ana Laura commanded impatiently.

I stepped aside and lit a cigarette while she climbed quickly to the level of the opening with the maul in her hand and started swinging wildly at the rectangle.

Fifteen minutes later and soaked with sweat, she climbed down to where I stood, disillusioned.

"We could try chipping the stone," I suggested.

"With one hand? That pick must weigh at least twenty pounds."

I climbed up again, this time with no tool. If it really was an entrance, there must be some way to open it. Bernabeu wouldn't have gone to so much trouble for no reason.

"Give me the hammer."

I hit all the surrounding stones one by one.

Nothing.

I climbed down and Ana Laura took my place on the ladder, pressing stone after stone over and over, with no result.

Half an hour later, exhausted and depressed, we climbed out of the well.

Back inside the house, we took a couple of beers out of the refrigerator. Ana Laura paced in front of the fireplace with a can of
Heineken, her eyes glued to the floor. I was happy just to watch
her. She was a goddess, there was no doubt.

She stopped suddenly. "Let's be logical. If you were Bernabeu,
where would you put the button, lever, or whatever it is that
opened the door?"

I made a gesture of impotence with my hands. "I don't know,"
I replied stupidly.

"Think!" she ordered.

She finished her beer and crushed the can with her hands. "If
it's the entrance to his hiding place"—I noticed that Ana Laura
spoke about it with doubt for the first time—"then the release
mechanism has to be somewhere easy to reach but not noticeable
to others." She paused. "We've been wasting our time miserably,"
she said.

"Why do you say that?" I asked, not knowing what else to say.

"Can you imagine Bernabeu inside the well with a hammer?
He would have wanted immediate access to his hiding place. Let's
go to the well!"

And with that, she ran out of the house and I followed along
behind her.

Out at the well again, Ana Laura felt delicately around the
edge, then searched the stone arch. She had run her fingers
around nearly half of the arch, then stepped down and moved to
the other side to continue her exploration. Suddenly, her face lit
up. "There's something here!" she shouted.

I moved closer to see what she had found. Near the bottom of
the arch there was a separation between two stones. It wasn't very
large—Ana Laura's fingers barely fit.

She poked around for a few seconds in the hole and we heard
a sharp *click*, followed by the grinding sound of rocks rubbing together.

We lowered ourselves into the well where the rectangular

stone was slowly moving. There it was, the dark but clearly out-lined entrance to a tunnel.

Ana Laura was so excited she almost lost her balance on the ladder.

"We did it! We did it! See? I told you we'd do it. What do you think?"

"Let's see," I said cautiously.

I looked into the opening. It really was a tunnel, darker than a bear's cave and equally disturbing, but there it was.

"What is it?"

"A tunnel."

"Let me see," she said, climbing down the ladder and pushing me farther down.

"Hand me the flashlight."

I passed her the flashlight and the next thing I knew this beau-tiful woman already had half of her body inside the opening. Then I heard her voice, echoing, "Follow me."

If I had had sufficient time to speak rationally with her, I would have discussed the possibility of how best to enter the tunnel properly equipped. After all, it was a nasty hole and we would probably find the things one usually finds in holes: rats, spiders, maybe a snake. But Ana Laura's attitude demanded action, so a few minutes later I found myself crawling along the tight passage-way, illuminating Ana Laura's rear end, as she charged on fear-lessly.

It occurred to me that Bernabeu might not have left the en-trance to his hiding place so easily within reach—anyone's reach. There could be an endless array of devices meant to prevent the advance of the enemy inside the narrow tunnel.

Suddenly I was overcome with paranoia and tried to commu-nicate it to my partner, but she didn't even stop to listen to me.

"Shut up and keep following me," she said sharply.

So I did.

After about thirty feet, the tunnel ended. We found ourselves in a space that was larger than the passageway, about five feet square. The only possible way to continue was through a wooden panel on the far wall, more or less the diameter of the tunnel through which we had just come.

There was a bar across the panel and Ana Laura tried to remove it, but it was too heavy. I took the bar, pulling with all my strength, and the panel opened with a loud cracking sound.

Ana Laura shone her flashlight into the opening and immediately commenced her descent.

"Ana Laura!" I shouted. "Wait! You don't know what you're going to find down there."

She didn't bother to answer me and continued her descent.

I stayed, cowardly, at the entrance to this new tunnel, not daring to follow her. "What's down there?" I ventured.

"Another tunnel."

I followed Ana Laura—as usual—and we advanced along the new passageway. This one was only about ten feet long. We came to another open space, this one much larger than the previous one and ending at a door about five and a half feet tall. The door was metal, just like the one in my dream.

Ana Laura moved aside so I could try to open the door. I pounded it fiercely with the maul. The sound echoed against the tunnel walls, but the damned door wouldn't budge. I pressed the weight of my body against it several times in vain; I was going to have to break it, which would be impossible with just the maul. We agreed to climb back up to the surface—the clean surface—to decide what to do next.

Something had seemed strange inside the tunnels, but I couldn't quite put my finger on it. However, once outside, I knew exactly what it was. We hadn't found any spiderwebs along the way, much less mice or rats, which indicated that the stone we had opened in the wall of the well had completely sealed off the air supply to the tunnels.

It was too late to go into town for tools we could use to break down the door, so we got undressed and spent the rest of the afternoon making love all over the house.

We were both in a wonderful mood, since we had made such an intriguing discovery. The next day, one way or another, we were going to get past that door and uncover Bernabeu's secrets—and hopefully, his treasure.

The next morning we left the house at ten o'clock to go into town. We were very nervous and excited, like Oscar nominees feel on the night of the awards.

The store was almost deserted.

The shopkeeper greeted us without enthusiasm, even though we were probably his first customers of the day.

"We need an electric saw, a hundred-yard extension cord, an electric drill and metal drill bits, and some saw blades."

The guy looked at us for a couple of seconds, as if we had ordered a pizza with anchovies, instead of merchandise that he handled every day.

He moved about the store until he had gathered everything we had asked for.

Ana Laura used her American Express card again. I have never seen her as happy as she was when she signed the charge slip. That was an indication of her emotional state—of our emotional state.

Neither of us spoke on the way back to the house.

When we arrived, we unloaded the car and went into the house for a few minutes to warm up and to steel ourselves for the task ahead.

Ana Laura lit a cigarette and breathed in the smoke deeply, then stood up and went into the kitchen. When she returned she had the bottle of Finvodka and two glasses. She sat on the sofa. "Get ready," she said. "We're about to begin the most extraordinary adventure of our lives."

She poured two glasses and we toasted solemnly.

After finishing our drinks, we connected one end of the extension cord to an outlet in the kitchen and went out into the cold to meet our destiny.

Then we lowered ourselves into the well and, holding the flashlights in one hand, sort of crawled through the tunnel. As we advanced, unrolling the extension cord, I imagined all sorts of things awaiting us, from an enormous treasure in gold and silver coins to the appearance of a giant rat weighing fifty pounds, or a vicious spider. The place didn't lend itself to much else.

I was tempted to suggest that we should forget about the whole thing and get out of there, but I didn't want to sound like a chicken.

When we reached the metal door—the one that had been in my dream—at the end of the second tunnel, I switched on the drill and easily perforated the metal. When I removed the drill bit from the hole, I felt something very disconcerting. A tiny current of air was sucked into the space on the other side of the door. It reminded me of what happens when a vacuum-packed can of preserves is opened. I made a few more holes while Ana Laura shone her flashlight on the work area.

When there was a large enough opening in the door to insert the saw blade, the tunnel began to fill with a nauseating odor.

"It smells like death," declared Ana Laura.

In different circumstances the comment would have been nothing more than a simple assemblage of words. But, echoed several yards underground, it made every hair on my body stand on end and sent an ugly chill through my bones.

I vacillated for a minute, but Ana Laura urged me on.

"Hurry up, I don't want to spend all day down here."

I introduced the saw blade into the holes I had drilled in the metal door and turned on the saw.

If the drill had produced an unsettling noise, it was nothing compared to this. The metal yielded easily, but the vibration and the noise were unbearable. When I had cut about thirty inches, I stopped. My hands were sweating profusely and trembling uncontrollably.

Ana Laura took my place and grabbed the saw. "Shine the light on the saw!" she ordered.

And I did, trying to control my shaking hands.

The beautiful girl had a better disposition, but not the strength for a job like that, so after ten or fifteen inches, she, too, was sweating and turned off the saw.

The air had gotten very thin from a lack of oxygen. I suggested that we climb back out for some fresh air, but she refused. "Let's finish, there's not much left," she said, handing me the saw.

We were trying to cut a rectangle and more than half of the work remained undone, so I continued.

Soon the smell of death had completely invaded the tunnel and my stomach churned with intermittent nausea. And my head was splitting from the noise.

Finally—just as I thought I was about to vomit—the door yielded with a loud creaking noise.

With a sharp kick I pushed it in.

Although we both had wanted to reach that moment for several days, we stood there paralyzed.

Neither one of us made a move to enter the newly opened space for several seconds. Finally, Ana Laura took the initiative and shone her light inside.

"You're not going to believe it," she said, clearly surprised.

"What's in there?"

"Come on, you're just not going to believe your eyes." Having said this, she stepped through the opening in the door.

What I saw when I followed her left me with my mouth open.

We were in a cellar exactly like the one in each of our nightmares during that night before we started our search.

But that wasn't the only surprise of the day.

The air inside the hiding place was wretched. It was as if we had opened a tomb. And, without realizing it, that's exactly what we had done.

It didn't take us long to realize that we had made a truly macabre discovery.

The cellar felt very familiar because of our dream. The burlap bags of almonds and pinenuts were there, as were the boxes of dried fish, the crackers, and the jars of preserves.

But something that hadn't appeared in the dream and was indeed present here was a pair of cadavers, sort of mummified, one beside the other on the floor.

We stood there hypnotized, looking at the human remains.

Despite the fetid odor, the lack of air, and the horrible scene, Ana Laura maintained an enviable composure.

"What do we do now?" I asked, trying to breathe as little as possible.

Ana Laura cupped a hand over her nose and mouth.

When she answered my question, her voice sounded appropriate to the situation. It seemed almost like a voice from the other side of the grave. "Let's get out of here."

We exited the tunnels as if the two cadavers were pursuing us.

I had never been so thankful to see the light of day as I was at that moment.

Once outside, we breathed deeply for a few minutes before speaking.

"Let's get in the house!" Ana Laura finally said.

The first thing we did was to take a shower in an attempt at disinfection. The second, of course, was to sit with a few glasses of vodka in front of the fireplace in the living room.

"What do we do now?" I asked, breaking the silence.

Ana Laura ruminated for a few minutes before replying.

"Basically, we have two options. If we call the police, the rental agency could accuse us of damaging their property. The contract clearly states that we can't make any modifications to the house without prior authorization—in writing—by the agency. Besides, anything of value that we find would automatically belong to them. All our trouble would have been for nothing, and even worse, we would have to pay for the damage.

"The other option is to look for anything of value, get it out of there, close up the passageway, and leave as if nothing had ever happened here."

The idea of going back down into the improvised tomb put an ugly knot in my stomach. But there was something else. I had never imagined that Ana Laura would be so ambitious as to dare something like returning to that eerie cellar.

She seemed to guess my thoughts. "The bodies down there must be Bernabeu and his wife," she said. "And they must have been there for more than a century. I don't think it will bother them if we look for a little compensation for our efforts. Do you?"

"No, I don't suppose so. But I don't think I can stand that smell for very long."

"Here's what we'll do. Tomorrow we'll go into town and buy a couple of those masks that painters and carpenters use. That'll make it a little more bearable. You'll see!"

She stood up and took me by the hand. "Meanwhile, let's make sure the time slips by in the most pleasant way possible," she said happily as she guided me to the bedroom.

Ana Laura undressed and got into bed, making a coquettish signal for me to join her.

Thanks to the exhaustion induced by breaking into the hiding place and our passionate sexual activity, we slept peacefully.

Never before had I enjoyed her body and her caresses as much. It was as if she were a condemned woman enjoying her last pleasure.

The next morning, we got up early and went to town to buy the masks. Again, the shopkeeper looked at us suspiciously. He seemed to be imagining what we could be doing at Bernabeu's house. I didn't like the guy at all.

We quickly returned to the house and got to work.

The putrid air in the cellar had dissipated a bit and there was now only a peculiar smell like that of dead rats.

Wearing the masks, we worked in stages. First we looked around for a while, then we left again to breathe fresh air. Of course, we didn't know exactly what we were looking for. Since the cadavers were near the door and were in the way, I decided to move them, barely overcoming the feeling of nausea.

The body we supposed was Bernabeu's disintegrated as if it were made of cardboard and I ended up with a large bone in my hand.

Using a stick, I moved his companion's body, which also pulverized upon contact. I piled the remains of both in a corner and covered them with a blanket.

Then I went out to breathe fresh air. Ana Laura followed me.

It was a particularly cold day, but the temperature in the cellar was pleasant.

After the third trip through the odious tunnels, Ana Laura made a discovery.

She had accidently torn the bag containing the pinenuts, and discovered that it was nearly half full of gold coins. Ana Laura immediately tore the other two bags and found they too contained gold coins. It was a fortune! My beautiful companion began to laugh and shout hysterically, the sound reverberating eerily against the walls of the hiding place, even through the masks. We put a few coins in our pockets and went back out through the tunnels.

We went into the house since it was already late afternoon and we needed time to plan the easiest way to remove our treasure.

After taking a long, steamy bath, we settled in front of the fire with sandwiches and a bottle of white wine.

Ana Laura was euphoric and couldn't stop talking. "I told you. I told you. Didn't I? Do you know how many coins there are down there? There must be a few thousand and they're enormous," she said as she admired the large coin she held in her hand.

She sighed with happiness.

"We have to get them out of there and leave this place as soon as possible."

I agreed.

Though the discovery of the treasure had put me in a terrific mood, I was not at all pleased to have to be constantly returning to the cellar. Somehow I felt as if we were robbing a grave.

The temperature had plummeted and we were spent, so we went right to bed.

Just before falling asleep, I heard my beloved's happy voice, "I told you. Wow! I told you. . . ."

*It had snowed all night and the next day we had great difficulty in reaching the well. At the bottom there was a black stain. It was a dead bird. A crow. Ana Laura paid it no attention and we began our work, only this time the tunnels were even more slippery and inhospitable than ever. After the third trip, just as we were about to finish the job, I felt a presence behind me. It couldn't have been Ana Laura, because she was on the other side of the room. Frightened, I turned around and nearly jumped out of my skin when I saw Bernabeu standing in the doorway to the hiding place.*

*I barely managed a terrified shout.*

*"Ana Laura!!! . . ."*

I woke up shaking and sweating. Ana Laura was looking at me as if I were crazy. There was concern in her face.

"What happened?" she asked in a shaky voice.

"Nothing. I had a nightmare. That's all."

She left the bedroom and returned with a couple of glasses and the bottle of vodka.

She filled both glasses to the rim and drank half of hers in one gulp. I did the same.

"What was your dream about?" she asked.

"It was stupid," I assured her, now that I was fully awake and felt sure of myself.

"What was your dream about?" she insisted.

I described my nightmare and she emptied the rest of her glass in one swallow. Then she took a deep breath.

"It's not possible. I just had the same dream. You woke me up when you called my name. I was just turning around in my dream to look at the door to the hiding place."

Since I couldn't think of anything sensible to say, I, too, emptied the contents of my glass.

It was almost dawn, so we didn't even bother going back to sleep.

A lot of ideas were bouncing around inside my head, and undoubtedly in Ana Laura's. Up to that point, our dreams had been closely linked to real events. The cellar was exactly as we had dreamed and so was the access to it through the well.

Ana Laura hadn't spoken since we got out of bed and was now preparing our breakfast.

"What do you think about the dream?" I asked.

"Telepathy. We've been together for a long time and lately we've been isolated from the rest of the world. I'm not surprised that we can communicate telepathically."

"I agree," I said, "but so far our dreams seem to have a lot in common with reality."

"Javier, please! Bernabeu must be dead over a hundred years now. You don't think he's coming back to claim his money, do you?"

"It could be a premonition."

"Premonition or not," declared my beautiful Ana Laura, "we're going to get all of those damned coins out of there. So let's hurry up and get it over with as soon as possible."

After breakfast, we returned to the well. It was a pretty cold day, but I was relieved when we discovered that it hadn't snowed during the night.

We got to work filling two small suitcases. The first trips to the cellar were relatively simple, but as we repeated the operation, our fatigue mounted since the tunnels were becoming humid with our breath, making the way increasingly treacherous. By noon we had only managed to empty one of the bags and we were completely exhausted. Not even the thought of all that gold could motivate us to keep going, so we loaded the coins in the trunk of the Volkswagen. We struggled to finish in the slippery snow. Finally we finished and went inside. We took a long bath and then lay in front of the fireplace devouring mouthfuls of smoked turkey. We didn't speak much, partly because we were so tired, and partly because somehow the business in the cellar had distanced us from each other.

Ana Laura didn't say so, but I felt that she considered me less of a man than before. And I, at the same time, had discovered that the carefree, bohemian girl I once knew had become ambitious and was capable of doing anything to get what she wanted.

"What are you thinking about?" she asked.

"About us. It seems like all this has damaged the great relationship we had."

She was quiet for a few minutes before she spoke.

"I don't see how one thing has anything to do with the other. Relationships change and ours is no exception."

Then she took my hand and led me to the bedroom, where we made love furiously.

Fortunately, there were no dreams that night.

We woke up well into the morning and repeated the work of the previous day. Our lovemaking the night before not only didn't help bring us closer together, but in a certain way had distanced us even more.

At one point I had imagined that Ana Laura was only trying to please me sexually, without caring about me as she had before. It was almost as if sex were only a way of keeping us together until we finished the job.

In my eyes this made her nothing more than a whore. A very

beautiful one, but a whore just the same. And, even worse, when we found ourselves at the peak of our lovemaking, I was more turned on thinking of her in that way.

How could a couple change so much in such a short amount of time?

We stopped working at five that afternoon, put the coins in the Volkswagen with the rest, and went into the house. After a steaming bath and dinner we caressed one another in front of the fire in a preamble to the night of sex awaiting us. We were both terribly excited.

Once in bed, upon contemplating Ana Laura's lithe body, I fantasized about her being a beautiful prostitute.

We made love savagely. I possessed her roughly, as if I had paid for her body, and I was surprised when she responded enthusiastically. It was sex without love. Animalistic sex.

A few minutes after we finished, Ana Laura was fast asleep. I couldn't sleep. I felt at odds with myself. I couldn't understand how a few gold coins could destroy my real treasure, which was this woman.

I went to the kitchen and poured myself a glass of vodka and then another and another.

I turned the thought over and over in my head. Maybe Ana Laura had changed so much that she would leave me once we returned to the city. Or worse, her ambition could go further. Why divide between two? Once the coins were loaded in the Volkswagen, what would prevent her from getting rid of me?

Was she capable of something like that? Was that what our latest dream had meant? Was it a premonition?

I returned to the bedroom and still had difficulty falling asleep.

The sky was dark when we woke up the next morning. I went to the kitchen to make coffee and saw through the window that it had snowed during the night.

Getting to the well was even more difficult than before, and when I looked down at the bottom, my blood froze. There was a

black stain in the snow. I hurriedly climbed down the ladder behind Ana Laura and shivered violently when I saw that it was what
I had feared: a dead crow.

She was already halfway inside the tunnel when I shouted.

"Wait a minute."

"What?"

"What do you mean 'what?' Don't you see? It snowed all
night, like in the dream. A dead crow in the bottom of the well!"

"So what? You're not afraid of ghosts, are you?"

"No, but . . ."

"If you don't want to come down, don't. Wait for me in the
house. I'm tired of your cowardice."

She turned around and headed deeper into the tunnel.

I went back into the house and found a sharp knife, which I
hid in my clothing. Premonition or not, whatever happened, I
wasn't going to be surprised without a weapon.

The tunnels seemed more slippery than ever and somehow the
smell of death had become accentuated, penetrating the masks.

We made several trips in silence. When we were finished collecting the coins, my hand went instinctively to the knife. As we
turned to leave, there he was, just like in the dream.

Only it wasn't a ghost. It was the man from the store in town
where we had bought all our equipment.

He had a powerful flashlight in one hand and a large pistol in
the other.

"You finally finished? City rats are different from country rats,
as far as I can see. OK, let's see what you found."

"What we found doesn't concern you," said Ana Laura haugh-
tily.

The man discharged his weapon into the roof of the cellar. The
shot sounded like a cannon firing inside the tiny space.

Ana Laura and I quickly opened the suitcase we had just filled
with coins.

The beam from his flashlight illuminated the golden contents.

"My God!" he exclaimed, "that damn Bernabeu had some money, didn't he?"

"Yes, he did." Ana Laura spoke gently. "But there's enough for everyone. You take this suitcase and we'll take the other one and we'll call it even."

"City rats are definitely different. Why should I have to share anything with you when I can take it all myself?"

"Then take it and leave us in peace."

"I will leave you in peace, that's for sure. I have no option. You understand that I can't leave you alive. It wouldn't allow me to enjoy my fortune."

Then the bastard pointed his weapon at my head.

"Wait!" shouted Ana Laura. "This isn't all the gold."

"Oh really?"

The man aimed his flashlight at Ana Laura's face. Then, suddenly, I pulled out the knife and in a surge of anger, cleanly slashed the aggressor's throat.

More dead than alive, he managed to shoot into the air a couple of times, but he didn't hit anything. Then he fell forward, his flashlight making a macabre play of light on the walls and ceiling of the cellar.

He was still quivering when Ana Laura leaned over him.

"He's dead," she said coldly. "Let's get out of here!" she said, grabbing a suitcase full of gold coins.

It was too much for me to take in. I had just committed homicide and my companion was acting as if we had just killed a spider. However, as if hypnotized, I took the other suitcase and followed her through the tunnels.

Outside it had started snowing again, and we made our last trip to the car.

Once inside the house, I felt completely numb—and not just from the cold. Ana Laura poured a couple glasses of brandy, which we drank in silence.

Finally, she spoke.

"How do you feel?"

Curiously, I felt as if everything had taken place on stage. Everything seemed completely unreal, as if it were just one long nightmare, from which I would wake up any minute.

I refrained from answering her and instead asked, "What are we going to do now?"

"Simple, we'll close up the entrance to the cellar and leave everything just as we found it."

"We're not going to call the police?"

"Of course not! No one knows about that hiding place, so no one will come looking for that man out there. We'll wait a few days so they don't connect us with his disappearance and then we'll go."

This was definitely not the sensitive and humane woman that had arrived with me at this damned house only a few weeks ago. Ana Laura had changed.

But when I really thought about it, the man had earned his punishment. He had threatened us and had even pointed his gun at me, surely ready to shoot.

If we notified the police, I would be accused of murder and Ana Laura of being an accomplice. We would lose the money and our freedom. In a small town like this, we were sure to be condemned. It was enough just thinking about a jury of people like the hateful librarian to know what the verdict would be.

Ana Laura was right. There was no other choice. It was best to let a few days pass, then hit the road.

Suddenly, I had a paranoid thought. Was the man really dead?

Gathering up my courage, I decided to go back and see.

"Where are you going?"

"To the cellar. I want to make sure he's really dead."

"That's not necessary. I . . ."

Without letting her finish, I left the house and walked toward the well.

This time the tunnels held the smell of fresh death. When I arrived at the hiding place I confirmed with relief that my victim was indeed dead. A large pool of blood had formed around his head.

I was about to leave when the photograph of Bernabeu and his wife caught my attention. For some reason, I took it with me.

When I exited the first tunnel, I put the wooden panel back in place, and once I reached the well, I closed the opening in the stone wall. Lastly, I removed the aluminum ladder and carried it to the house.

I spent the rest of the afternoon and part of the night getting drunk, trying to forget the ghastly sensation of cutting a man's throat.

The next morning we went straight to the store in town. An elderly man was behind the counter. We bought what we needed to repair the attic ladder and reattach it.

Everything in town was as it had been before, except for the absence of the shopkeeper.

Ana Laura paid for our purchases and we returned to the house.

The Volkswagen was noticeably heavier, but we still managed to climb the steep hills.

As the days passed, the image of the killing was gradually erased from my memory. But I had become obsessed with the fact that Bernabeu and his wife had died inside their refuge. So, as Ana Laura had done earlier, I spent hours studying the notebook of drawings, trying to find the answer.

Curiously, Ana Laura began to finish the work she had been neglecting. Our roles had been reversed.

I remembered clearly feeling a vacuum when I perforated the metal door, which led me to believe that Bernabeu and his wife had died of asphyxiation, having breathed all the air in the small space. This led me to two questions: first, why hadn't he been able to open the door to the hiding place and, second, if the cellar had been designed to hide people for prolonged periods, why didn't it have adequate ventilation?

After turning it over and over in my mind I arrived at the conclusion that the entrance from the well wasn't the main entrance to the hiding place; there must have been another entrance. Logically, it would be much more accessible than the well.

In addition to the drawings, I studied at length Bernabeu's wedding picture, as if it held a clue. I became so obsessed that the homicide and the gold lost their importance. My relationship with Ana Laura had dissolved completely. One day, while we ate dinner, she asked, "What are you planning to do with your half of the money?"

The idea had never crossed my mind. Until that moment I had thought of us in terms of a couple, not individuals.

"I don't know," I replied, and then asked, "How about you?"

"The first thing I'll do is take a long vacation. The beaches in the south, I think."

"Alone?"

She noted the disappointment in my voice and quickly continued.

"Look, Javier, all relationships need to breathe to get stronger."

I knew that it was all over. This relationship didn't need to breathe, because it couldn't breathe anymore. It was dead.

Two weeks after the incident, the homicide, we decided to leave. We packed up the Volkswagen. Fortunately, the return trip would be mostly downhill; otherwise, the tiny car wouldn't have been able to make it.

I put out the fires in both fireplaces and we were about to leave when a thought occurred to me. The only place we hadn't looked for access to the cellar had been the fireplaces.

I thoroughly cleaned the floor of the fireplace in the living room with a brush, and found what I had suspected. Looking carefully one could see a thin line separating the block of bricks in the center from those on the periphery.

Surely Bernabeu had descended to his refuge with his wife,

confident that everything would function well. Somehow, the entrance had sealed hermetically. It didn't matter because there was the entrance from the well. But Bernabeu hadn't taken into consideration the fact that the house would settle with time, so that when he tried to open the metal door leading to the tunnels, he couldn't.

The man had died in a terrible way, in the very refuge he had built to escape death.

I took the photograph, the notebook of drawings, and the architectural plans for the house with me. I was sure no one would miss them since they had lain abandoned so long in the attic.

In order not to give the impression that we were fleeing, we stopped in the town and went to Guillermo's cafe.

The bartender recognized us immediately and sat with us, bringing his glass of brandy with him.

"How's the work going?" he asked in an agreeable tone.

"We've finished," replied Ana Laura, "in fact, we came in to say good-bye."

"Good, I hope you have a nice trip home and that you come back soon."

He drank his brandy in one gulp and returned to his place behind the bar.

When we left he accompanied us to the car.

Ana Laura gave the old man a kiss on the cheek and climbed into the vehicle. As I was about to get in, Guillermo took me gently by the arm and asked me in a low voice, "Was it worth it?"

"I beg your pardon?"

Guillermo smiled genially and winked.

Needless to say, we never went back there.

The coins ended up being worth much more than Ana Laura had calculated, since besides being solid gold, they were very old. A man from Thailand bought the whole lot, no questions asked.

Ana Laura took off as soon as she had her share of the money and I haven't heard from her since.

The plans for Bernabeu's house are now beautifully framed and hang prominently on the wall in my studio. The wedding photograph is on my desk.

I anonymously sent the notebook of drawings—much later—to the town library.

After all, the town's treasures couldn't be trusted in the hands of "people like us."

*Translated by Stephen A. Lytle*

# Edmundo Paz-Soldán
## (Bolivia, b. 1967)

Edmundo Paz-Soldán was born in Cochabamba, Bolivia, where he attended Don Bosco, a private Catholic school that would eventually become the setting for his third novel, *Río Fugitivo* (1998). As a teenager he played soccer, read a lot (especially Dumas and detective fiction), and wrote stories for his schoolmates by plagiarizing the works of Agatha Christie and Conan Doyle. At eighteen, he won a soccer scholarship to the United States, where he obtained a B.A. in political science from the University of Alabama in 1991. He went on to pursue doctoral studies in Latin American literature at Berkeley while continuing to write and publish fiction.

In 1992, Paz-Soldán won the Erich Guttentag Prize for a first novel, *Días de papel*, and in 1997 his story "Dochera" (translated here by the author) was awarded the international Juan Rulfo Prize, sponsored by Radio France in Paris. The following year it appeared in a collection of his short stories entitled *Amores imperfectos*. In 1997, he also published *Alrededor de la torre*, a thriller about the paramilitary attempt on the life of a native Indian presidential candidate. Then 1998 marked the publication of Paz-Soldán's third novel, the first to be devoted to that ambiguously imagined urban landscape resembling the city of his birth: the Rio Fugitivo of its title. In 2000, he published the second of the Rio Fugitivo books, *Sueños digitales*, which deftly mixes a magazine editor's personal disintegration and the digital reconfiguration of a dictator's photographic past to create a nightmarishly virtual tale of contemporary Latin American reality. Along with the Chilean writer Alberto Fuguet, he recently coedited *Se habla español*, an anthology of Latino authors living in the United States. Like the protagonist of his latest novel, *La materia del deseo* (2001), Paz-Soldán currently shuttles back and forth between his native Bolivia and the States, where he teaches Latin American literature at Cornell University.

# Dochera

*for Piero Ghezzi*

Every afternoon Inaco's daughter is called Io, Aar is a river of Switzerland, and Somerset Maugham wrote *The Moon and Six-pence*. Gold's chemical symbol is Au, Ravel composed *Bolero*, and there are dots and lines that, thanks to Morse, can be letters. Insipid is "bland," the initials of Lincoln's assassin are J.W.B., the country houses of the Russian elite are *dachas*, Puskas is a great Hungarian soccer player, Veronica Lake is a famous femme fatale, and *Citizen Kane*'s key word is Rosebud. Every afternoon Benjamin Laredo consults dictionaries, encyclopedias, and past works in order to create the crossword to be published the next day in the *Piedras Blancas Herald*. It's a routine that has been going on for twenty-four years: after lunch Laredo puts on a black suit that is too tight for him, a white silk shirt, a red bow tie, and patent leather shoes that shine like street puddles on a rainy night. He shaves, applies cologne and hair gel, and then locks himself in his study with a bottle of red wine and plays Mendelssohn's violin concerto. Using fine point Staedtler pencils, Laredo crosses words in horizontal and vertical lines, together with black-and-white photographs of politicians, artists, and famous buildings. A phrase wriggles across the width and length of the box, Wilde's being the most used: *I can resist everything except temptation*. One by Borges is his current favorite: *I have committed the worst sin: I have not been happy*. Diaphanous beauty of that which is being created in front of our eyes that never tire of being surprised! Wonder of the novelty in the repetition! Astonishment over the act that is always the same and always new!

Sitting on the walnut chair that has caused him chronic back pain, gnawing at a pencil's splintered end, Laredo faces the rectangle of Bond paper with urgency, as if in it he would find, hidden in its vast clarity, the ciphered message of his destiny. There are moments when a chemical fact does not want to combine with the synonym of *imperturbable*. Laredo drinks his wine and looks up at the walls. Those who can help him are there, in yellowish photographs worn out by so much gazing, one polished silver frame after another crowding the four sides of the study and leaving room only for one more frame: Wilhelm Kundt, the German with the broken nose (people who are into crosswords are very passionate), the Nazi fugitive who in less than two years in Piedras Blancas invented for himself a past as a celebrated crossword maker, thanks to his exuberant command of Spanish (they said he was so thin because for breakfast he would only eat pages of etymology dictionaries, for lunch synonyms and antonyms, and for dinner gallicisms and neologisms); and then there is Federico Carrasco, a Fred Astaire look-alike whose descent into madness was due to his belief that he was the reincarnation of Joyce and had to attempt, in each of his crosswords, an abridged version of *Finnegans Wake*; and then there is Luisa Laredo, Benjamin's alcoholic mother, who used the pseudonym of Benjamin Laredo in order for her crosswords—full of slighted fauna and flora and forgotten women artists—to be accepted and gain prestige in Piedras Blancas. Benjamin's mother, who raised him alone (finding out that she was pregnant, her sixteen-year-old boyfriend took the next train to Chile and nothing else was ever heard of him), and who, when discovering that at five he already knew that a whole seed of cereal was a *kernel*, had forbidden him to solve her crosswords because she was afraid he would follow in her footsteps. "It is tiring to be poor. You'll be an engineer." But she had left him when he turned ten, unable to resist a delirium tremens in which words became alive and followed her around like unbridled mastiffs.

Every day Laredo looks at the crossword in its chrysalis shape, and then at the photos on the walls. Whom would he invoke today? Did he need Kundt's precision? *Carved stone used for arches and vaults*, six letters. Carrasco's arcane and esoteric facts? *John Ford's cinematographer* in The Fugitive, eight letters. His mother's diligence for giving a place to that which was left out? *Adviser of her Catholic majesty, Queen Isabel, author of commentaries to Aristotle's work*, seven letters. Somebody always comes to direct his carbon-stained hands to the right dictionary and encyclopedia (his favorites being María Moliner's, with its scribbled edges, and the Britannica, outdated but still capable of telling him about poisonous plants and card games of the High Middle Ages), and then a verbal alchemy occurs and those words incongruously lying side by side—Cuban dictator of the fifties, Mohawk deity, poison that killed Socrates—all of a sudden acquire meaning and seem to have been created in order to lie side by side.

Afterward Laredo walks the seven blocks that separate his house from the *Herald*'s building, gives his crossword to the editor's secretary in a sealed envelope that cannot be opened until minutes before the layout of page A14. The secretary, a fortyish woman with flowery shirts and immense black glasses like a pair of sleepy tarantulas, tells him every time she has a chance that his works are "diamonds to be preserved in the jewelry box of memory," and that she prepares a chicken fettuccine that "would make you lick your fingers," and that he should consider "taking a break in your admirable labor." Laredo mumbles an excuse and looks at the floor.

Ever since his first and only woman left him at eighteen because she had met a *poète maudit*—or, as he preferred to call him, a *maudit poète*—Laredo has spent his life looking at the floor whenever a woman is around him. When she left, his natural shyness became more pronounced, and he withdrew into a solitary life dedicated to archaeology (third-year dropout) and to the crosswords' intellectual labyrinth. During the last decade he could have taken advantage of his fame on some occasions, but he did not do it because he was, first and foremost, an ethical man.

Before leaving the *Herald*, Laredo stops by the editor's office and, in between warm pats on the back, collects his check. It is his only demand: Each crossword must be paid upon delivery, except those of Saturday and Sunday, which must be paid on Monday. Laredo takes a close look at his check and is surprised by the amount, although he knows it by heart. His mother would be very proud of him if she knew he could live on his art. *You should have trusted me more, Mom.* Laredo returns home with slow steps, chewing over possible definitions for the next day. Extinct bird, one of Babylonia's first kings, ancient civilization on the north coast of Peru, country attacked by Pedro Camacho in *Aunt Julia and the Scriptwriter*, Verdi's aria, ninth month of the Muslim year, tumor produced by the inflammation of the lymphatic vessels, capital of Ivory Coast, blunt instrument, rebel without a cause.

That evening, returning home, everything seemed radiant to Laredo, even the beggar sitting on the curb with a dislocated *waist bone between the back and the inferior extremities* (six letters), and the adolescent—who nearly knocked him over on the street corner—with a grotesque *protruding shape in the neck produced by the thyroid gland* (two words, ten letters). Maybe it was the Italian wine he drank that day in honor of the quality of his last four crosswords. Monday's, devoted to film noir—with Fritz Lang's photograph in the upper left corner and the author of *Double Indemnity* to his right—motivated an immense pile of congratulatory letters. "Dear Mister Laredo: I only write these lines to tell you that I admire your work, and that I am thinking about quitting my studies in Industrial Engineering in order to follow in your footsteps. My Esteemed Benjamin: I wish you would continue with thematic crosswords. Have you thought about one with references to Pynchon's work? What about one with diverse forms of torture invented by South American military forces in the twentieth century?" Laredo touched the letters in his right pocket and quoted them as if reading them in Braille. Was he already of Kundt's stature? Had he acquired Carrasco's immortality? Was he now superior to his mother, so he could recover his name? Almost. Very little was missing. Very little. There should be a Nobel Prize for artists like him. Making a crossword puzzle was as complex and transcendent as writing a poem. With the subtlety and precision of a sonnet, words were interlaced from top to bottom and left to right to create a harmonic and elegant unity. He could not complain. His fame was such in Piedras Blancas that the mayor was thinking about naming a street after him. Nobody read poems anymore, but practically everybody in the city, from veterans to delicate Lolitas—*Humbert Humbert's obsession, Nabokov's character, Sue Lyon on the big screen*—spent at least one hour each day solving his crosswords. Better to have the people's recognition in an undervalued art than a multitude of awards in a field taken into account only by pretentious aesthetes, incapable of feeling the air of the times.

On the corner, one block from his house, a woman in a black furry coat waited for a cab. The streetlights on, their orange glow vain in the pale afternoon light. Laredo walked right by the woman; she turned and looked at him. Her face was of an undefined age—she could be seventeen or thirty-five. She had a white lock falling over her forehead and covering her right eye. Laredo continued walking. He stopped. That face . . .

An old Ford Falcon was approaching the curb. He turned around and said, "Excuse me. It is not my intention to bother you, but—"

"But you're bothering me."

"I just wanted to know your name. You remind me of somebody."

"Dochera."

"Dochera?"

"I'm sorry. Good night."

The cab stopped. She entered it and did not give him time to continue the conversation. Laredo waited until the Ford Falcon disappeared. That face . . . of whom did it remind him?

He was awake until dawn, tossing and turning in bed with the lamplight on, ransacking his memory in search of an image that would somehow correspond to the aquiline nose, the dark skin, and the prominent jaw, the apprehensive expression. A face he had seen in childhood, in the waiting room of a decaying hospital while holding Grandpa's hand and waiting for word of his mother's return from her alcoholic stupor? In the entrance hall of the neighborhood movie theater, eating popcorn, while the girls with shiny miniskirts walked by smelling of lavender and with a brother or boyfriend at their side? There was the image of Jayne Mansfield and her unreal breasts, which he cut out from a newspaper and glued on a page of his math notebook—the first time he tried to create a crossword, the day after his mother's funeral. There were the brunettes whose hair smelled of apples, the blondes beautiful thanks to nature or the tricks of makeup, the women with vulgar faces and with the charm or dissatisfaction of the ordinary.

Sunlight filtered shyly through the blinds of the room when the mature woman with a white lock over her forehead appeared. The owner of the Palace of the Sleeping Princesses, the store in the neighborhood where Laredo, as an adolescent, used to buy the magazines from which he would cut out the photographs of celebrities for his crosswords. The woman who approached him, a hand full of silver rings, when she saw him clumsily hiding, in a corner of the place that smelled of humid newspapers, an issue of *Life* between the folds of his brown leather jacket.

"Your name?"

She would catch him and call the police. A scandal. In his bed Laredo relived the vertigo of instants forgotten during so many years. He had to run away.

"I've seen you around. You like to read?"

"I like to make crosswords."

"Solve them?"

"Make them."

It was the first time he had said it with such strong conviction. One should not be afraid of anything. The woman drew a smile of complicity, her cheeks crumpled like letter paper.

"I know who you are. Benjamin. Like your mom, may God have mercy on her. I hope you don't like to do silly things like her."

The woman pinched him gently on his right cheek. Benjamin pressed the magazine against his chest.

"Now leave, before my husband shows up."

Laredo ran away, his heart beating as fast as it was beating now, saying over and over that nothing compared to making crosswords. Nothing. Since then he had not returned to the Palace of Sleeping Princesses out of a mixture of shame and pride. He had even made detours in order to avoid crossing the corner and running into the woman. He wondered what had happened to her. Maybe she was an old woman behind the counter of the store. Maybe she was playing with worms in a cemetery. Laredo, his body fragmented into parallel lines by daylight, said, "Nothing compares to . . . Nothing." He should turn the page, send the woman back to the oblivion where he had imprisoned her for so many years. She did not have anything to do with his present. The only resemblance to Dochera was the white lock of hair.

"Dochera," he whispered, his eyes fluttering about the naked walls. *Do-che-ra.* It was an odd name.

Where could he see her again? If she took a cab so close to his home, maybe she lived around the corner. He trembled at the thought of such hypothetical vicinity; he bit his already bitten nails. It was more probable that she was returning home after visiting a friend. Or relatives. A lover? *Dochera.* It was a very odd name.

The following day Laredo included this definition in the crossword: *Woman who waits for a cab at dusk, and who turns solitary and inconsolable men into lovesick beasts.* Seven letters, second vertical row. He had transgressed his principles of fair play, his responsibility to his followers. If the lies that filled the newspapers in the declarations of politicians and government officials extended to the holy bastion of the crossword—so stable in its offering of truths easy to prove with the help of a good encyclopedia—what possibilities did the common citizen have of escaping the general corruption? Laredo suspended those moral dilemmas. The only thing that mattered was to send a message to Dochera, to let her know he was thinking about her. It was a small city, she would have recognized him. He imagined that the next day she would do the crossword in the office where she worked, and she would find that message of love that would make her smile. *Dochera*, she would slowly write, savoring the moment, and then she would call the newspaper to say she had received the message, they could go for coffee any afternoon.

That call never came. Instead there were calls from many people who vainly tried to solve the crossword and asked for help or complained. When the solution was published, people looked at one another in disbelief. Dochera? Who had heard of Dochera? Nobody dared to confront Laredo: If he said it, he had his reasons. Not for nothing was he known as the Maker, and the Maker knew things that nobody else knew.

Laredo tried again with: *Disturbing and nocturnal apparition who has turned a lonely heart into a wild and contradictory sum of hope and disquiet.* And: *At night all the cabs are gray, and they take away the woman of my life, and with it the principal organ of circulation of my blood.* And: *One block away from Solitude, at dusk, there was the awakening of a world.* The crosswords kept their habitual quality, but now they carried with them, like a scar that could not heal, a definition that incorporated the name of seven letters. He should have stopped. He could not. There was some criticism; he did not care (author of *El criticón*, seven letters). Laredo's followers got used to it, and began to see its positive side: At least they could start to solve the crossword knowing that they had one correct answer. Also, were not geniuses eccentric? The only difference was that Laredo had taken twenty-four years to find his eccentric side. Piedras Blancas's Beethoven could be allowed outlandish actions.

There were fifty-seven crosswords with no answer. Had the woman disappeared? Was Laredo's method wrong? Should he lurk around the corner of his encounter until meeting her again? He tried that for three nights, with his Lord Cheseline gel shining brightly in his black hair as if he were an angel in a failed mortal incarnation. He felt ridiculous and vulgar stalking her like a robber. He also visited, with no luck, the two cab companies in the city, trying to find a list of the drivers who had been working that Wednesday (the companies did not keep the lists, he would talk to the *Herald*'s editor, somebody should write about it). To put a one-page ad in the newspaper describing Dochera, offering a reward to whoever could tell him about her whereabouts? Very few women would have a white lock, or such a name. He would not do it. There was no greater ad than his crosswords. Now everybody in the city, even those soulless people who were not into crosswords, knew that he was in love with a woman named Dochera. For a pathologically shy individual, Laredo had done more than enough (whenever people would ask him who she was, he would look at the floor, then mumble something about a priceless out-of-print encyclopedia of the Hittites that he had just found in a used bookstore).

What if the woman had given him a false name? That was the cruelest possibility.

One morning Laredo decided to visit the neighborhood of his youth, in the northwestern part of town, full of weeping willows. The juxtaposition of styles through the years had created an area of motley temporalities: mansions with big patios coexisted with modern residences; the Colonel's kiosk, with its dusty window displaying old pharmacy jars with *confections made with sugar and often with flavoring and filling* (seven letters) stood beside a hair-dresser's shop offering *manicure for both sexes*. Laredo reached the corner where the magazine store was located. The sign, with its elegant gothic letters hanging over a metal door, had been re-placed by a coarse beer ad under which read, in small letters, THE PALACE OF PRINCESSES RESTAURANT. Laredo took a look inside. A barefoot man was washing the mosaic floor. The place smelled of lemon detergent.

"Good morning."

The man stopped mopping.

"Sorry to interrupt. . . . There used to be a magazine store here."

"I don't have a clue. I'm only an employee."

"The owner had a white lock."

The man scratched his head.

"If she's the one I'm thinking about, she died a long time ago. She was the original owner of the restaurant. She was hit by a Corona beer truck the day the restaurant opened."

"I'm sorry."

"I don't have anything to do with it. I'm only an employee."

"Someone in the family took over?"

"Her nephew. She was a widow, no kids. But the nephew sold the restaurant a few months later, to some Argentinians."

"For someone who doesn't have a clue, you know a lot."

"Excuse me?"

"Nothing. Good day."

"Wait a minute . . . aren't you . . . ?"

Laredo left hurriedly.

That afternoon, when Laredo was working on crossword number fifty-eight A.D., he had an idea. He was in his study with a black suit that looked like it was made by a blind tailor (the uneven sides, a diagonal cut in the sleeves), a red bow tie, and a white shirt stained by drops of red wine (Merlot, Les Jamelles). There were thirty-seven reference books on both the floor and the desk; Mendelssohn's violins were caressing their spines and wrinkled covers. It was so cold that even Kundt, Carrasco, and Laredo's mother seemed to be shivering on the walls. With a Staedtler in his mouth Laredo thought that he had demonstrated his love in a repetitive, insufficient way. Maybe Dochera wanted something more. Anybody could have done what he had done; in order to distinguish himself from the rest, he had to go beyond himself. Using the word *Dochera* as the foundation stone, he had to create a world. Ganges tributary, four letters: *Mard*. Author of *Doctor Zhivago*, eight letters: *Manterza*. Capital of the United States, five letters: *Deleu*. Romeo and . . . six letters: *Senera*. To go somewhere, three letters: *lei*. He put the five definitions in the crossword. He had to do it little by little.

Adolescents in the schools, employees in their offices, and old men in the squares asked themselves if this was a typographical error. The next day they discovered that it was not. Laredo had gone way beyond the limits, some thought, irate for having in their hands a crossword of impossible solution. Some applauded the changes and thought they made things more interesting. *Only the difficult was stimulating* (two words, ten letters). After so many years it was time for Laredo to renew himself, everybody already knew by heart all the tricks in his verbal juggler's repertoire. The *Herald* started publishing a normal crossword for the dissatisfied. After eleven days it was discontinued.

The nominalist fury of Piedras Blancas's Beethoven increased as the days went by and there was no news from Dochera. Sitting in his walnut chair afternoon after afternoon, Laredo destroyed his back and built a world, superimposing it on the one already existing, the one to which it had contributed since the origin of time so many civilizations and centuries—all now converging in a disordered study in Piedras Blancas. Diaphanous beauty of that which is being created in front of our eyes, never tired of being surprised! Wonder of the novelty in the novelty! Astonishment with the act that is always new and always new! Laredo saw himself dancing with his mother in the Maker's Heaven—where Crossword Makers occupied the top floor, with a privileged view of the Garden of Paradise—while Kundt and Carrasco looked him up and down. He saw himself letting go of his mother's hand, becoming an ethereal figure and ascending toward a blinding source of light.

Laredo's work gained detail and precision while his provisions of Bond paper and Staedtlers ran out faster than usual. Venezuela's capital, for example, was called Senzal. Then the country of which Senzal was the capital became Zardo. The heroes who fought in the Independence wars were rebaptized, as was the orography and hydrography of the five continents, and the names of presidents, chess players, actors, singers, insects, paintings, intellectuals, mammals, planets, and constellations. Piedras Blancas was Delora. Author of *The Merchant of Venice* was Eprinip Eldat. Famous crossword maker was Bichse. Nineteenth-century vest was *frantzen*, and object of cloth that one wears on the chest as a sign of piety became *vardelt*. It was an infinite labor, and Laredo enjoyed the challenge. A delicate bird feather sustained a universe.

On day 203 A.D., Laredo returned home after turning in his crossword. He whistled *La cavalleria rusticana* out of tune. He gave some coins to the beggar of the dislocated *doluth*. He smiled at an old lady running after an ugly Pekingese (Pekingese? *zen-*

*dala!*). The sodium streetlights flickered like enormous glow-worms (*erewhons!*). There was a mint smell flowing from a garden in which a bald and melancholic man watered the plants. *In a few years nobody will remember the real names of those geraniums and peonies*, Laredo thought.

On a corner five blocks from his house a woman in a black furry coat waited for a cab. Laredo walked right by the woman; she turned and looked at him. She was young, of an undefined age. She had a white lock falling over her forehead and covering her left eye. The aquiline nose, the dark skin and the prominent jaw, the apprehensive expression.

Laredo stopped. That face . . .

A Ford Falcon was approaching the curb. He turned around and said,

"You are Dochera."

"And you are Benjamin Laredo."

The cab stopped. The woman opened the back door and, with a hand full of silver rings, made a gesture to Laredo, inviting him to enter.

Laredo closed his eyes. He saw himself stealing issues of *Life* in the Palace of Sleeping Beauties. He saw himself cutting out pictures of Jayne Mansfield and crossing horizontal and vertical definitions in order to write a crossword. *I can resist everything except temptation.* He saw the woman of the black coat waiting for a cab that faraway afternoon. He saw himself on his walnut chair, deciding that the Ganges tributary was a four-letter word. He saw the phantasmagoric course of his life: a pure, amazing, translucent straight line.

*Dochera? Mukhtir!*

He turned around. He started walking, first with slow steps, then with little jumps. He ran the last two blocks that separated him from the study in which, on the walls crowded with photographs, there was a space waiting for him.

# Rafael Franco Steeves
## (Puerto Rico, b. 1969)

One of the new generation of Puerto Rican writers to emerge in the 1990s, Rafael Franco Steeves studied anthropology with David Carrasco at the University of Colorado, Boulder campus, and the University of Puerto Rico at Río Piedras. After living in Colorado, Alaska, and New York, he returned to the island in 1996 and began writing as a journalist for *The San Juan Star*, where he worked as a reporter for over three years. Since 1998 he has reported on island issues as special correspondent for New York *Newsday*, and his island dispatches have been posted on the Web by Latino.com.

His first short stories appeared in the UPR monthly magazine *Diálogo* and in the literary magazine *Huevo Crudo*, which he helped found in 1992 and redesigned and coedited in 2001. He has adapted his short stories to comics and his poetry has appeared in island newspapers and underground magazines, like *Grillo*. His short fiction can also be found in the anthologies *Mal(h)ab(l)ar*, edited by Mayra Santos-Febres, and the upcoming *El rostro y la máscara*, second edition, by Isla Negra, as well as on Web sites such as Trixel.com. Along with Santos-Febres, Franco Steeves translated the work of Nuyorican poet Willie Perdomo. The Spanish publisher Grupo Santillana also included his story "Hongos" in their *Language and Communication* series of textbooks. Among his works are *La pareja y el extraño*, a collection of stories (from which the title story is taken here in the author's translation), and *Este presente sucio*, his first novel.

Franco Steeves belongs to a new batch of writers characterized by their departure from the sociopolitical approach of earlier generations. His fiction offers unusual insight into the alienating effect of addiction and often explores the themes of violence and loss. He recently collaborated as photographer with performance artist Jesús Gómez, and is in the process of preparing another issue of *Huevo Crudo*. He lives in Puerto Rico.

# The Couple and the Stranger

## I.  The Homer Spit

*Puffins ashore are always watching one another or poking*
*a beak into another bird's business.*
—NATIONAL GEOGRAPHIC

Even before Mac and Cappi walked in drunk to the Salty
Dawg Saloon a little past nine in the afternoon—kicking up the
sawdust, which in that dead-end hole could've been a carpet or an
ashtray, or both—my days were no doubt already numbered. Not
only in that strip of sand, which I had nicknamed Homer's
Tongue with the affection it deserved, but in the entire Alaskan
peninsula as well. The three fishermen who had each lost a game
against me were from Seward, Soldotna, and the third originally
from Portage. The fourth one, who now had five solid balls on the
table, while I had only one, was the second fisherman's cousin but
was really from Kenai. Between the four of them they had the entire peninsula covered. If things turned ugly, and all the telltale
signs were there, (scowls, excited phone calls at the end of the bar,
their unblinking eyes fixed point-blank on mine, dollar bills crumpled and thrown carelessly on the faded green felt), my only hope
was to sneak into the Seldovia-bound ferry without anybody

noticing, maybe leaving false clues as to my whereabouts, fool them into looking for me along the Sterling Highway, perhaps. Uma would've definitely come up with a suitable scheme to throw them off. . . .

If only it had just been the two of them, that would've been the plan, but that asshole Cappi came in with that statuesque woman better known as Raven by the spit rats living in the tent city improvised along the whole northwest tip of the tongue (or the "fucking Homer's Phlegm," as Leña, the sole other *boricua*, called the spit, a sandy finger poking into Kachemak Bay from the town of Homer, on whose beaches itinerant fishermen camped along with the remaining drifters washed ashore).

Raven. The first time I saw her was from afar as I was setting up my movable home on the beach. With a cat's stealth she was quietly making her way through the mess of tents and bonfires, her loose auburn hair flowing from her head like watered-down blood. Who among the hundreds of males living on the spit, after seeing her carelessly cross the tent city, pretending not to prowl, had not longed for her wildly so as to keep the piercing cold at bay even though it still cut through the tent's fabric in the middle of summer?

"That kind you have to be real careful with, you gotta fear them." Leña used to say stuff like that when we were sitting on that driftwood log watching the rocky sentinels on the other side of the bay.

"I don't have to," I would lie, "a little abuse is enough to take care of that."

Leña smiled sarcastically and always went for the binoculars. "That calls for yet another alias: Sex Ed. I still think my favorite is Continuing Ed, or even better Zalapaster Ed. Couldn't decide."

Raven, hanging from the arm of big ol' Cappi, who was not fat but plain old big. According to the gossip going around he had earned another name in recent years—Busta Cappi—right after he popped Yoni's left kneecap with a .38 Special while on the high seas for reasons, and under circumstances, that were never cleared up by the pertinent authorities. Not one of the seven fishermen who were signed on with the *Crabmeister*, not counting Yoni, said they saw anything. Without corroborating witnesses, Yoni chose not to take the stand in a courthouse that was for all intents and purposes a throwback to the previous century, and thus refrained from pressing charges against the big old guy. He had to settle for having the asshole pay his medical bills, including most of the physical therapy he required.

Raven, with Cappi. That could only mean some sort of trouble. And of course, after leaving a healthy roll of bills with Papa-Shan, the bartender, Busta Cappi placed eight quarters at the end of the table that I had been hogging. Well, to be perfectly honest there is only one pool table in the Salty Dawg. My winning streak, however, had already brought me enough problems and an unscheduled trip to Seldovia was beginning to sound good.

The fisherman from Kenai, Joe, looked at me from the corner of his eye and called the two ball in the center pocket, once he prepared for the shot. Even though he missed, the ball bounced off three banks and slowly rolled up to the mouth of a corner pocket on the far side, quietly falling into the hole.

"Shit, man, still the same . . . you are at the peak of your game. Papa-Shan, put a beer for Sloppy Joe on my tab, will ya?" shouted the big-boned man, filling the air above the pool table with the warm stench of moonshine.

Fortunately the cue ball ended up all the way on the other side of the table, more or less lined up with the nine, which I would soon enough sink into the opposite pocket. It was a long shot, with lots of green in the way, but it's also my specialty and at that moment my only source of income; whoever dominates that particular shot could easily bet on the game without actually risking much. Those long shots spanning the entire length of the table are decisive, the classic coup de grâce. Joe and the other three fishermen sighed simultaneously and the third one spit on the floor—

they had already seen me make every one of those shots and were not able to hide the anger they felt at the mere thought of me winning four tables in a row.

Once the nine ball fell into the rawhide pocket, the black eight went down even easier after it, almost on its own, after having spent the latter half of the game hovering over the other center pocket. Ignoring the routine shake, Joe made his way through the crowd to the phone at the end of the bar and stared at me nonstop for the few minutes, I presume, he was talking to someone.

"You're not leaving, not yet," Constantino—the one who'd spat on the sawdust and lost the first game—informed me. "I got next dibs, I'm playing you again. All or nothing. . . ."

"That depends," I returned with forced humility, "on whether or not I beat Cappi."

"You're not getting off that easy. If fatso wins," he explained sarcastically, "you'll wait your turn like a regular joe schmoe, get it?"

The exchange was brief. Cappi was quick to butt in and displace us with his huge twentieth century Viking body mass. "Don't scare him off, Con, you'll make him miss his mark," he offered the other fisherman in a familiar way. "No sweat against these lower forty-eight trash, uh?" he said once he stood facing me. "Let's see how you do against the real thing, one hundred percent Alaskan thunderfuck."

As it turned out, I did surprisingly well, better than anybody there could've guessed, including myself: I sank the eight ball on the break. Pure luck, no doubt. Everyone was stunned, nailed to their places, burning a hole into the table with their wide-open eyes. Silence spread swiftly, like a bad smell. Several of the regulars, glued to their usual stools, swung around looking for the source of the uncommon and momentary lapse of sound. *Who pressed mute?* asked an untraceable and inebriated raspy voice.

"Beginner's luck," I said, improvising, as best I could in so short a time and before such a suddenly captive audience, what innocence was available to my face at that time and place. "If you want I'll rack 'em now."

Cappi kept his silence. He frowned, as could only be expected, and pulled up to his quarters on the length of the table. He took two and introduced them into their respective slots. From his back, Raven whispered something in his ear and smiled. With movements much too quick and smooth for someone his size, Cappi turned around and slapped the girl loudly. Not real hard and with a closed fist, as he would do with me, for example, but rather with the entire palm of his hand, as if he was merely applying discipline to a naughty child. It still cracked like thunder.

Silence returned, but this time accompanied by layered rumors and a rising background murmur.

I, on the other hand, did not experience the sharp sense of indignation I would've most likely felt had I been more at ease. Instead I was overwhelmed by the rush of relief granted by the newly found anonymity. No one was eyeballing me any longer because I had been replaced as the center of attention. Most of those there were now staring straight into the star-shaped rosy bruise Cappi's hand had left on Raven's cheek. A few of those present even threw sideways glances infused with genuine disgust at Cappi.

And it wasn't ten yet. Night, I mean darkness, would not come until much later, until well past midnight.

As Cappi placed the balls inside the triangle on top of the table, a glob of gossipers slowly formed around us. I imagine they anticipated Cappi losing a second time and their curiosity drew them closer. Fatso was a terrible pool player, but everybody knew he was a worse loser, very sore. Sometimes Cappi got so drunk he took over the table by force, by sheer size, and nobody would play him, nor would they even put quarters on the table. They would all leave him alone, waiting, for the next hapless foreigner, or tourist, to wander in without a clue. It was not unusual for the locals to get a good hefty bet going on which outside asshole lasted the longest with the fat man. The unfortunate traveler would end up running for his life, leaving a cloud of sawdust hanging in the air behind as he scurried like a rat beneath the boardwalk and in between the tents on the beach.

At least a lot of them had seen me playing quite a bit that night. Perhaps I should've called it quits as soon as I had doubled my money, as I used to do to avoid drawing attention or being remembered. But leaving Homer, Alaska—population peaking at four thousand in the summer—was not easy or cheap, especially if you were standing on the side of the road to hitch a ride for whatever reasons. As I wondered whether it was worth it to simply and quietly just hurry the hell out of that bar, the fishermen materialized nearby—smiling, snickering, as if they could taste the blood Cappi would extract from me once I beat him again—along with a group of the hardest drinkers around, in for the show I guess, among which I recognized Ben, Izzy and a few others I knew only from a distance. Some nodded or acknowledged me discreetly by lifting their eyebrows and dipping their chins, almost like telling me *fuck him, he deserves it.* Or at least that was what I thought, rather than thinking their sudden interest was sparked by that morbid curiosity we humans feel whenever we smell misery on someone else.

It was all happening too fast anyhow. I needed fresh air, definitely. I needed to think. And to smoke, goddamn it. "Mind if I take a cancer break before beating you again, eh Cappi?" was my attempt at a joke.

"As long as you come back," he said. He sounded bullish, strangely forced. Too obvious.

"Whatever . . ."

## II. The End of the Road

After spitting that word out, I moved through the crowd toward the bar, but without forgetting to elbow Ben discreetly on the way. "Take out three brews, from this Papa-Shan," I said, handing over two twenties and a ten, "for me, Benjamming and Dizzy. Keep the change, but please make sure Uma gets a shot at the end of the night."

The bartender slurred something sounding like *thanks*, acting like it was only loose change and not a thirty-odd-dollar tip lying on the bar. Then Ben was standing next to me and the three bottles of beer were brought over.

"Please tell Uma to meet me outside," I pleaded.

"Consider it done," was the answer I received from someone I hoped was a friend.

Leaving the Salty Dawg was not too hard. Everyone got out of the way even before I got to where the four were standing, blocking my exit. Where could I escape to in Homer? I was right at the end of the road, literally on the westernmost point in the U.S.-Canada interstate network of highways, because after all, Alaska's interstate system would not connect to the lower forty-eight states if it weren't for the Canadian highway leading to Alaska, better known as the Al-Can.

Standing outside of the Salty Dawg, you can see the two lanes of the road pass in front of the bar, divide, and each wind its way on opposite sides of a shared parking lot until they both meet again over by the entrance to the Land's End Hotel, the last building on the spit. Homer wasn't really the end of the road. Technically it was some miles down the road, heading east, in Kachemak City, which is not even on most maps. In any case, from where I was standing I could only go back out of town the same way we all came in, the Sterling Highway, which found its way out of the peninsula through Anchor Point, Ninilchik and Soldotna, the only place that connected to Anchorage, hundreds of miles northeast, straight behind me.

When you thought about it, strategic evasive action—or better, a good old plan of escape—could not be executed on land. The best thing really was to set sail, take the sea route, perhaps the ferry

out to Seldovia or Kodiak, and from there take an air taxi the rest
of the way to Cordova.

I lit a cigarette and was distracted by the book of matches.
Salty Dawg matches. Matches I'd had for almost a whole week,
since the *Horizon* fiasco. On the inside of the cover, someone, obviously a woman, judging by the calligraphy, had scrawled the
phone number of the Fisherman's Lounge and signed with a single letter, capital *R*, period.

"What the fuck, Uma," I snapped as soon as I sensed her near
me. "What's going on?"

Uma placed her forearm across my lower back, as she had
grown used to doing, but her demeanor was not the same as before. She was more tense, reserved, than usual. She took her time
looking through her pockets until she produced her own filterless
cigarette—*wherever particular people congregate*—and bided her
time as she brought the tip of it to the burning match, which she
had lit along a length of her jacket's zipper.

I said nothing, awaiting her response in silence. I focused my
eyes on the far side of the beach and beyond, where the sun still
bathed the ocean and the Kenai mountains on the other side of
the bay with a peculiar light. The sun's rays produced a weak reddish glow that fell over the dozens of fjords and rocky, fractured
promontories between Poot Peak and Neptune Bay, and also
shone its warm tones over the entire Sixty Foot Rock to the west
and the rest of the stone-faced sentinels that had watched over
those waters for thousands, maybe even millions of years. Without
ever straying too far from the horizon, the humble yellow star
saved its bloodiest and most intense red to smother Doroshin
Glacier, all the way to my left, west of Gull Island and opposite
the solitary snow-capped volcanic peak of St. Augustine, on the
other side of Cook Inlet, to my right. Every time my gaze wandered upon that isolated floating coastline, I felt something stir inside, unable to resist the magnetism that lonely volcano cast over
me like a spell. I would watch it for hours, watching it nonstop

through Leña's field glasses, fixing on it dreamily, carried away by its apocalyptic airs. It erupted with unexpected violence back in '87, its ash covering miles and miles of coastline, woods, and all the immense solitude of Kenai Peninsula. People in town often referred to it as the "gray snow," and the more talkative ones enjoyed recalling the event to scare tourists and other recent arrivals to the spit, reminding them that the smoke that could usually be seen coming out of the volcano meant an imminent eruption was most likely moments away. It was actually one of the few topics of conversation the town's permanent residents did not mind touching upon freely and frequently in front of us drifters and travelers. In the end there weren't that many who entertained conversation, most kept quiet—in Alaska the rule was silence, zero past talk, nobody would ask where were you coming from or where the hell you hailed from. The things they carried were their own business, period.

"Did you ever hear the con of the couple and a stranger?" Uma asked as she took a drag of her cigarette.

It seemed like the right moment for St. Augustine to really blow its top and wake up from its slumber. Two weeks ago it had belched forth a single solid column of black smoke, quite different from its daily discharges. It calmed down after a while, but not before it had raised every human hair on the spit as we all watched in horror from the beach. The jokes and the scaring of tourists stopped, if only for a few days. I like to think it was a real enough warning, but that's just the way I am. "What? The couple and a stranger?" I said and faked discomfort as best I could.

"It's me, Uma, your main squeeze. Remember? You don't have to play dumb with me. Anyways, you've got the shot nailed down, to perfection."

"What are you talking about?" I insisted in vain, unable to fully repress a crooked smile.

"I don't know either, to tell you the truth, so don't worry about it. Relax. Raven explained it all to me quickly, in the bathroom, but I didn't understand jack, mostly the stuff about the shot, and only because I just saw you doing it against Sloppy Joe and his goons."

"Raven?" I thought out loud.

Uma approached me closely, pinning me against the wooden wall of the Salty Dawg Saloon. "I know you like her, you men are all the same. If you could, you would trade me for her like that," she said, snapping her fingers. "Any day of the week, right?"

"I'm not all men," I snapped back and kissed her lightly on her neck. She got closer, letting her cigarette fall to the ground, and kissing me with a concentrated, fleeting intensity.

"You're supposed to miss," she said after exchanging saliva with me and wiping her lips clean with her tongue. "Of course, first bet everything you got, she'll take care of Cappi. That's about all I really understood."

"Do you have any idea of what you're saying? It's not that easy, no matter what Raven told you. And what's all this about she 'taking care' of Cappi, how? Didn't you see how that asshole slapped her across the face in front of everybody," I reasoned, although I couldn't say whether I was talking to her or to myself.

"I'm just the messenger, Raven said you would know what to do," she added, questioning me and lifting an eyebrow. "How do you explain that one to me? Why is she so sure about what you'd do? Have you two met? That's what's weird, at least for me."

"There's nothing strange about it, Uma, it's the oldest trick in the book," I said and offered to explain it as a way to create the illusion of being honest; it was impossible to know how she'd react if she found out about me and Raven. "All right, you got a couple, not unlike that idiot, Cappi, and the redhead. And then you have a stranger, say a guy like me, a good player, the quiet type, and of course, alone."

She did not interrupt me. She opened her eyes and listened to me without blinking. It's not an easy con to explain, much less to set up. However, with Cappi and Raven already in character, act-

ing out their roles, Uma had no trouble following the inner work-
ings of the trap, which was to foster the basic hatred—in this case
against a brute like Cappi—that is needed for people to lay their
money on the table without thinking twice about it. At the same
time, the stranger, drifter, loner or foreigner, et*fucking*cetera, well
of course he needed to win the confidence, the trust, of the crowd,
dazzling them with his precision, with the way he sinks each ball
in a different pocket decisively, almost without fail. As the stranger
shows off his pool skills, the man in the couple, always full of ill
will, makes the collective blood boil. He must tap into dormant
emotions like resentment, jealousy, which is why slapping his female counterpart is so effective in spreading that maliciously male
envy like an accursed disease. That's why Raven and Cappi were
perfect as well. When at last it gets too tense and unbearable,
the flashy pool player uses the trump hidden in his sleeve: with the
long shot perfectly set up, he suggests a wager to the couple. The
crowd, completely at home in the group mentality mode, digs
deep in its pockets and almost tastes the killing they are about to
make. No one has the slightest doubt the strange loner is about to
pull it off comfortably, as he would've been doing all night. Then
again, you could easily overdo it and risk looking too obvious. The
face, right when he misses the shot, is key, it's the mask that will
help him escape when the shit hits the fan. At this point it is also
vitally important that the wife-beating creep's proportions be big,
physically, not unlike Cappi's, and that his appearance be menacing, since he'll have to find a way out through the thick of it with
the money, the woman and, preferably, the keys to a fast motor
vehicle.

"Now," I said, wrapping it up, "tell me, how could Raven take
care of Cappi?"

"She said she would give me something to put in the old crab-
ber's drink."

"And that's it, just like that she talked you into it . . . this
stinks, Uma. If I miss I'll never be able to leave and, needless to

say, I won't find anybody who'd bet me a clean dollar a game unless I go to someplace like Nome in the Polar Circle."

Uma looked at me with those dark big eyes of hers and shook her head. "You're not telling me something, I can feel the hole in your story, but we'll have plenty of time for that later. Don't worry, I'll catch you when the time comes. Now it's my turn to tell a story, so prepare yourself, because mine is much better than yours."

She was right, her story was better. Much better. It so happened that Raven was not freely participating, of her own volition, in the events of that night in particular. Although she expected only to satisfy a debt her old man had with Cappi, she was beginning to regret it.

"Do you remember the fishing boat that ran aground on the sandbar about two weeks ago? Well, that was Raven's father, drunk, in Cappi's cruiser."

### III.  Hook, Line and Sinker

I let her talk, so she could tell me the story the way she wanted, without me bothering or interrupting her. At the other side of the street I could only see the tops of tents and a few spit rats silently moving among them, with their eyes wide open. To think that I left all my stuff in there, protected only by a mere zipper, and no one ever stole them. Dead weight, I suppose the more daring ones decided, the ones that were like birds of prey and moved around the improvised village as if they were truly part of the group of unhappy, unemployed men who considered this cold and remote part of the coast their home. Everyone learned pretty fast to carry what they considered essential with them. Although there were always one or two spit rats who spaced out and left their passports, money or some other important document in the tent while going for a cup of coffee on the boardwalk. One could see them after a while walking around, with an empty look on their faces, as they repeated "they stole it" over and over again, like a scratched record.

Welcome to Homer Spit. Who told them to be so stupid and think that solidarity among spit rats is real. It's a miracle that they've made it so far.

While Uma continued with her story—which had turned very interesting by now, when she's telling the part about how Raven's dad lost to Cappi at poker—I got distracted looking for the sun. The old star is not the same up here, it's a poor imitation. It gives off no heat and it never rises more than thirty or so degrees, always hovering just above the horizon as it travels around back east, to sink where it had risen a tad longer than twenty hours before. (The night, which does not bring darkness until after 1 A.M., lasts perhaps only three lousy hours.) At four-thirty A.M. the sun comes out again and begins once more its slow, long crawling parallel to the horizon. But I didn't find it, it was already behind the Salty Dawg's tower.

Instead of the old yellow star, what I saw was the bald eagle that lived on the beach. It's an enormous bird, with a wingspan more than a couple of meters long. It usually glides slow and low as it approaches Cook Inlet, then rises suddenly when it goes over tent city. It always heads straight to the boardwalk, where the seagulls hold their daily fight over the halibut leftovers that are thrown off from the boardwalk's kiosks. It arrives and takes the day's unwanted fish easily, leaving in its wake a handful of mad, screaming seagulls. The seagulls huff and puff, as if cursing as they take to the air in vain. Finally the eagle beats its wings, but only once, and soars above the gray clouds always covering the sky. And this goes on every day, because this northern region belongs to the bald eagles, the elks, and all other wild animals hiding in the bush. We're only clumsy explorers or fugitives. Or both.

"Uma, do you really want me to believe what you are telling me?" I finally interrupted her. "I have to go back, I don't want to leave Cappi waiting. . . ."

"He's already playing."

"You don't say."

"With Big Mac. He said he wants to warm up, to even things out a little."

I had no option but to look into her eyes. I couldn't discover in them anything out of the ordinary, no nervous tics, not one sign of treachery. She looked at me with her same old eyes, with her eyebrows raised innocently. She was somewhat anxious, that I could see. "So let me see if I got it straight. You are telling me that Raven is out with Cappi tonight because she wants to make up for her father's dumb-ass mistake? That's what you are saying, isn't it?"

"Well, pretty much, yeah. . . ."

"I can't understand why she'd do something like this. I mean, really, I'm not sure I'd believe it. To top it off, she just told you all of this minutes ago, in the bathroom."

"Not all of it. Most of it I heard in Addie's the other day. It's been the week's most talked about topic of conversation, knocking out the previous week's St. Augustine smoke out."

"So then everybody in town is hip to the facts . . . I dunno, seems like gossip to me."

"And like I said, I'm just the messenger."

"Yeah, well, and that message, where does it come from? Who's sending it?"

"I'm only supplying you with information, nothing more, you are free to draw your own conclusions."

"All right, just gimme one of those filterless cancer sticks, I need something strong. . . ." I really would've loved to see Leña and honor the origin of his nickname.

As soon as she handed over the cigarette, Dan showed up in his beat-up old car, a veritable and rusty pharmacy on wheels. "Wassup?" he said, throwing off careful glances all around him. Uma smiled, but the guy did not catch the subtle camaraderie in her gestures.

"Percodan, it's me," she had to say, stretching out her hand.

The traveling pill man smiled back and whispered something I could not understand, although to her it seemed like plain English. Dan placed something in her hand and put the car in gear. As he sped away, without even waving good-bye, the screeching of worn-out engine belts filled the parking lot. Yet even through the noise we could still hear the electronic beep of a pager or cell phone, the true sign of every successful capitalist.

"Well," she said at last, "you'll know what to do, I suppose."

"That's what everybody seems to think tonight, except me of course."

"So now it's like Raven's everybody." She sighed and paused. Then, "Anyways, what happened with the *Horizon*? Are you on it?"

"No," I said, paying no mind to the cynicism of her previous comment, and told her all about the *Horizon* fiasco. After he interviewed me, this guy by the name of Leslie, the boat's captain, asked me to tag along to the store and help him with the stuff he needed to get for the trip. Once there he ordered twelve cases of Jim Beam, a .357 that was behind a glass cabinet, half a dozen boxes of ammo, and then he grabbed a stack of porno mags, which covered the entire wall in front of the gun cabinet. In no time he'd spent hundreds of dollars on things that I hadn't thought of as necessary for a trip at sea. A big gun, dozens of porn magazines, bourbon and five hairy men out in the middle of the Bering Strait. "No thanks," I resolved.

"So now what, what's your plan?"

"What I told you before. I'm getting the hell out of Dodge."

"But—I thought . . ." she said and fell quiet for a brief moment. "Come with me, please."

I feared turning corny for an instant, because I knew she would never accept my offer. It was also a good way to conceal what had happened, and what I, despite my love life with Uma, wanted to keep happening between Raven and me. Raven had already agreed to come with me if I asked her to. On the other hand, Uma had made it clear from the beginning that she couldn't leave

Homer at least until the end of summer. Maybe in the fall. However, she'd been pretty vague about her reasons. Family issues, she'd said on occasion without much conviction.

"You know, maybe it's a possibility after all."

I opened my mouth in quiet disbelief.

"Oh, c'mon, don't look at me that way. It can't be that much of a surprise."

"But . . ."

"If it's really that important to you, I could cook something up."

"Of course," I said, surprised and stunned. "Thing is, that's what the cash I was taking from the fishermen was for."

"Don't worry, I've got some money saved. We can stop at the bank on our way out, in Kenai. That is, if we leave at dawn, of course. What time did they say you have to be on the *Horizon*?"

"Five."

"Wow, that's in just a little while," she observed. "You're crazy . . . well, at least Raven's implying she'll split the jackpot with you, right?"

"Sure, but do you trust her?"

"She seems to trust you," she spit out sarcastically. Spitefully, one might say.

Now it was my turn to be silent. There was no doubt in my mind that Uma was expecting some kind of explanation. But it wasn't the right moment—if I tried to make sense out of something that hadn't an iota of logic, or reason, I'd only jinx the scam we were brewing that night at the Salty Dawg—and plus, she didn't insist. She just agreed to meet me at daybreak, around four-thirty, at Addie's Big Paddies. Seemed like a perfectly normal suggestion, it's on the boardwalk, after all, and it's always open. Twenty-four seven. Of course.

Don't sweat it, she actually said. Because she would get the car. "Not to worry, Uma's on it," were the last clear words I heard her say.

Then she kissed me.

## IV. Raven

How to describe her? Impossible. No matter how accurate the words may be, they could never do justice to the smoothness of her curves, to the hidden fire between her hairs or to the nocturnal texture of her eyes. I don't care if Benedetti himself came to Alaska and wrote her a poem, nobody could capture her with just words. I must insist, impossible.

That, of course, doesn't mean I won't try. I am no different from any other guy who's washed up on this beach. You couldn't step anywhere here without bumping into some wino-sore surrounded by a captive audience of newcomers while he's all wrapped up in his own description of when he first saw her. It's almost a mandatory rite of passage: you arrive, listen to the alpha males gesticulating endlessly about Raven and then you see her for yourself, live, with the faded jeans practically painted over her skin, the bulging blouse threatening to burst any minute and send its buttons flying off. From there you pass on to the next level, in which you must find a recent arrival and proceed to describe her, to fantasize about her out loud and possess her in your mind. And that's how you become a true spit rat in the Homer's Phlegm. Alaska would not be the same without her, period. There's no other woman, no person, who could comfortably compete with the natural majesty surrounding the peninsula. There could be bears in the middle of the street, but if Raven is nearby crossing the road, forget it, the tourists' cameras stop snapping as the Homer Tongue holds its breath and silence falls, covering everything from coast to coast. Or at least all around Raven in a widening circle.

Perhaps the best thing would be to describe what I saw when I got close enough to her for the first time, as I walked out of the store with the captain of the *Horizon*. I had already decided I would not sign up with that boat and its demented seaman and his deep-sea crew. Nevertheless, I couldn't leave just like that, without reason; after all, I had been hired to cook on the boat and there was only one week left before it set sail on its first run of the salmon season. The hiring had all been done long distance, thanks to a friend on the inside, back when I worked as the sauce man in a Whitehorse dive. A fellow pots-and-pans colleague of mine, although really a sommelier by training, had hooked me up with the boat's owner, a true gourmet pothead who placed a strategic phone call in appreciation of a quarter pound of seedless G-13 weed I got him for a very affordable price. It took him less than five minutes to instruct Captain Leslie to hire my services and accommodate me in the *Horizon*'s galley for the duration of the salmon season. Quitting would no doubt be seen then as a borderline and brazen, not to mention delinquent, act of treachery. It would definitely be hard, if not impossible, to find a substitute at the very last minute, two days from the start of the season, and with at least basic culinary skills of some sort.

I had no choice but to run under cover of night, like a thief. And to do so I had a daily window of opportunity not longer than a mere three hours, at most. Regardless, all I wanted to do was get up and go, leave that place without looking back or calling any attention to myself. There was nothing left for me to do in Homer anymore, perhaps even in the entire northern territories. My mistake had been arriving three weeks before the boat was ready to go to sea. On top of it I got into town with no money in my pockets because I thought I wouldn't need any cash in the middle of the ocean. My fault, really, for listening to the old alcoholic who gave me the wrong date for the beginning of salmon season before leaving Whitehorse.

Now, after more than twenty days scavenging for food, unloading cod from the huge ships moored by the docks behind the Salty Dawg, taking advantage of drunk fishermen and betting them at pool, all I had to look forward to was a nightmare peopled with lonely white sailors, hungry sperm whales circling the boat, frenzied gunshots coming down from the bridge and, last but not least, some serious booze, all confined in a private floating hell, a personal, claustrophobic cell of my own choosing. That's what I was thinking about as I walked out of the Country Store with the captain and a store clerk in tow pushing a dolly stacked high with boxes of whiskey, porno mags and bullets. In the meantime, the old seaman played with the brand-new .357 in his hands. Dying to find an excuse to leave the captain's side, I looked around desperately.

There was Raven, standing against a car and dressed not with her usual pair of black jeans painted on, but with a long, dark and somewhat transparent skirt and a black blouse that hung loosely, like a shadow over her body. Every hair on my body, every pore on my skin was suddenly electrified and every body cavity dried out, while inside the flowing blood conspired to amass below my waist. There were no words then, as there are none now. How to explain the effect her stare had on me, the gamma-ray quality of her big round eyes? (The last days of Eddie Lopez, I could call this chronicle of a failed ruse. And yes, that is my name.) She grabbed the excess cloth of her skirt with both hands and folded it between her thighs, so that the length of her legs became perfectly silhouetted by the fine fabric. One thing was obvious now that she didn't have her jeans on: she wore no underwear. From her knees all the way up to her derrière resting on the vehicle, the folded fabric traced an uninterrupted, smooth line and then bunched up between her legs, falling to hide the details of her feet. She had stretched the skirt along her legs with distracted motions, while she looked first away and then slowly brought her stare to where I stood glued to the sidewalk.

"Captain . . ." I began to say but was unable to finish, forgetting the excuse I had thought of only seconds before. Desire had always made my creative juices flow freely. But Raven had, in an instant, managed to steal my voice and my thoughts.

"Yeah, yeah . . . whatever. Just be there, behind the bar, at dawn on the solstice," the captain said, zeroing in on her crotch. The clerk also stopped and stared.

"On the eve?" I asked.

"No, I meant the morning after. I don't give a damn if you go to the Farm, really, I don't give a shit. As long as you are there at five A.M. you can do whatever the hell turns you on."

No one said anything. We were three starved men before the most delicious meal we'd see on a day like that. Captain Leslie pointed the Magnum automatic at the stack of whiskey cases and managed to break away from her spell by way of the gun. "I'll be there, waiting for you," he threatened before reaching for the bullets.

Silence again. "Whether you are or not," he added immediately and as a matter of fact.

Raven hanged until the old seaman edged on, clerk in tow with the stuff, and then walked over to where I was. The wind was blowing briskly, hitting her head-on, so that her breasts were also clearly outlined and crowned with hard, protruding nipples, thanks to the cold. She saw me staring and crossed her arms in front of her, lifting a single eyebrow.

"Hurry, we're going to have to burn your clothes," she said in a warm tone, almost intimate.

I mumbled pieces of words, but they made no sense.

"We're going to build a fire," she ordered a little later. "Please don't disappoint me," she added after she realized I wasn't moving, that I wasn't reacting at all.

Of course she had taken me completely by surprise. At best, I expected maybe some vague nodding of the head, or even a half smile, as she moved her sights on around the beach. Her presence and her words, on the other hand, came out of left field. Needless to say I mumbled some more of the same gibberish over and over again, not unlike a babbling newborn.

"Easy there, don't think yourself to death," she observed, carefully placing one hand on my shoulder. "Don't get me wrong, but you stink. Your clothes reek. I mean, it's pretty cool, not being afraid of work, that's always a good sign in a man, but this . . . a bit much, don't you think?"

All of a sudden the stench of forty thousand pounds of black cod slapped me across the face with the force of a freight train. Two days before I had been one of the handful of wretched souls hired to unload the *Paiper Maru*, which had just tied down at the docks. The fish were packed so tightly that the bigger ones had the smaller ones rammed down their throats. Me and another unlucky bastard were thrown down into the ship's refrigerated bowels, where we found ourselves chest deep in black cod, and the rest were given derricks and cranes to lower the big metal containers we were to fill all day long as we swore off the unforgiving north at the top of our lungs but to no avail. Ten hours later I was drenched, with my hair matted against my temples, fish guts splattered on my clothes and globs of entrails stuck all over my face.

"Of course, you will also need a bath," she explained. "Or a shower, with lots of soap."

"I don't know where you expect me . . . ." was all I managed to verbalize with any degree of success.

"Shhhhh." She was always so eloquent. "Look, just so you know that I am not taking you for a ride, I'll give you the combination. Here, it's written right here."

Not only did I have the Homer goddess talking to me about taking my clothes off and hopping in the shower, but she also wrote, on the inside of a book of matches, the group of words and numbers most coveted by every unemployed, homeless spit rat on the beach. Raven was referring to the Fisherman's Lounge, a room full of shower stalls, washers and dryers equipped with television, a Ping-Pong table and an assortment of vending machines. It was located above the cannery on the other side of the spit, near the Land's End Hotel on the far end of the road. It was the only real luxury afforded to the fishery's employees, which counted among its members several spit rats. They in turn would turn a profit by selling the sought-after alphanumeric code, which was changed every couple of days. At the time I had only heard stories about it and it definitely seemed to me that the Lounge was more of a legendary, mythical place. 'At one point I had dreamt about its accommodating luxuries and facilities. In the dream I always bought a small cereal box in one of the vending machines, but when I put the coins in to buy milk, the machine would malfunction and keep my money.

"C'mon, we don't have much time," she told me, taking me by the arm.

"Why?"

"Because the second shift is finishing up soon."

"No, not that. What I mean is why me?"

She looked me up and down. "Because you need it badly."

"I'm serious."

"So am I. I like watching you steal halibut from the seagulls. It breaks my heart."

"Aha, it's out of pity. . . ."

"I don't think so. More like an ache."

I tried, unsuccessfully, to say something.

"I already told you not to think yourself to death. But if you prefer, I'll leave."

It was my turn to grab her arm. "No," I said, a tad too quickly.

"What's your name?" she asked later on, as we climbed the spiral stairs leading to the Lounge on the outside of the building. They were made of steel and our steps made an incredible ruckus.

"Eddie. Are you sure we're safe now?"

"If you want we could leave and come back tomorrow. It's your choice," she answered, standing still, letting me creep up behind her. "That is, if my numbers still work. . . ."

I decided to keep quiet; after all, I had never been the articulate type. I followed her up the stairs with the wind on our backs. Violent gusts blasted us upward and pressed her skirt neatly against her body, silhouetting her ass wonderfully and making me want to jump all over her right then and there. Once we got up to where an electronic keypad held the door locked tight, she turned around and smiled shyly, very different from what I had imagined Raven's playful smile would be like.

"Hold your horses," she said when I tried to take her into my arms, putting her hand flat on my chest. "There'll be plenty of time. You're not going anywhere soon, no one in this town is going anywhere until after salmon season."

She then turned around and pressed several numbers on the keypad. The security gadget whirred and wheezed for a mechanical moment, and when Raven pulled the door swung open to reveal a row of handsomely cushioned recliners inside. A draft of warm air wafted out of the doorway and enveloped us for an instant, caressing our exposed skin. She grabbed my shirt and pulled me inside, locking the door behind us. There was nobody around. We were alone.

Heaven, I discovered, was located in Alaska, on the upper floor of a nondescript warehouse on Kenai Peninsula.

## V. Solstice

*The sexual act is the parody of a crime.*
—GEORGES BATAILLE

In the contiguous lower forty-eight states, people go crazy in New Orleans in February, when they celebrate Mardi Gras; in the Southern Hemisphere Latin Americans converge in Rio de Janeiro for the most famous carnival in the world to commemorate the fattest Tuesday of the year; in Puerto Rico my fellow *boricuas* have their good old San Sebastian Street Festival in Old San Juan, which went from a two-week affair years ago to its current, pathetic single-weekend lifespan. And in Alaska, people save the best party of the year for summer solstice, the longest calendar day.

Year after year Homer has celebrated it in the same place, on the spacious grounds of a farm outside of town. People come from all over the peninsula and beyond. They come by plane, boat or by car, they come on foot, on bicycles and even on horses. In fact, they come any way they can to the Farm; they come with cases of booze, with plenty of weed, with LSD, mushrooms, mescaline and everything else they deem timely to introduce into their bodies while they worship the sun, the same star that one way or another makes life a little bit easier during the summer months for the inhabitants of the far north. Maybe that's the only way you can weather months of winter darkness, when the sun hides below the horizon and the moon colludes with the evening blackness to take over the night as only satellites and deep space can do.

During the weeks leading to the festivities, everybody in town works together to make sure that there is nothing missing on the longest day of the year. Animosity, feuds spanning generations and general hostilities toward foreigners are put aside until the last week of the month. The farm grounds are segregated and certain unseen lines are drawn between the chosen spaces, so that those who cannot stand to see each other can attend without risking unforeseen stress due to chance encounters.

Even us spit rats will have our very own solstice soirée in a space reserved for us behind the stables, and we are reviled by everyone in town because all we do is go for the fast buck during the commercial fishing season. It had its price and we had to make a collection so we could bribe the farm owners. Still, even though we hardly raised the agreed amount, the owners took what we had and sanctioned the gathering. At least that's what Leña told me, and he was a volunteer on the Saturn Committee, which was the self-appointed name of the group of vagrants in charge of tent city diplomatic efforts regarding the solstice celebrations. There was also a two-dollar cover charge, and while everyone else could walk into our little party behind the stables, spit rats could only partake of the fishermen's fete on the other side of the stable.

Leña said they had planned it like that because they knew the fishermen hated the beach bums. That way they could count on some action out of the friction, or at the very least some prime bareknuckle entertainment.

"You can always count on a fight," he continued. "Whenever you put together thousands of drunken fools and fugitives, you can count on a fight breaking out. Precolombia was saying they are trying to keep it out of doors this year. Apparently some time ago a bunch of crabbers did a pretty good number on a collection of porcelain birds belonging to the lady of the house."

"You're going, right?"

"I dunno," he answered, grimacing. "I told the guys on the committee I was going, but I met this squaw, you see, and she's real hot and sexy and I want a piece of her. We agreed to meet that day and she's the type who avoids the Farm at all costs. If she won't let me go all the way home, well, I guess you'll see me drunk out of my mind somewhere in the neighborhood of the stable. You never know. . . ."

Several days before the solstice, ships from all over the peninsula began filling the Homer docks. Many of them would only be moored for a few days, long enough for their crews to get laid a couple of times and drunk at the Farm before returning to sea in search of fish. There were also those who came to stay, after spending weeks on the open waters, fishing for cod, salmon or whatever else was in season. Crew members cashed their checks as soon as possible, hoping to spend as much as they could before heading home to their families. They'd spend days drunk out of their asses in and out of bars and then they would finally get those long, sober faces as they made their way back home. Those were the kind I needed to bet against in pool at the Salty Dawg if I expected to make enough money to get away someplace where Captain Leslie couldn't find me. Even before I saw Raven standing outside the Country Store I had decided not to sign up. It was a question of methods, a matter of logistics, of resources.

Although I had found paradise between Raven's legs, there was something strange in the way she had seduced me. Well, I'm not sure I could really call it a seduction. In the end all she did was push me against the Fisherman's Lounge door, pull my pants down and put my cod-stinking manhood in her mouth. She almost didn't have to do anything, I came within a couple of minutes and she surprised me by swallowing the product of that premature pleasure. Something completely peculiar, I decided, in the way she licked her lips clean with her tongue and asked me: "You ever heard of the con 'the couple and a stranger'?"

Of course, that's what I decided now, as I wait for Cappi to finish his warm-up game with Constantino. (At the time, of course, I thought it was the most romantic blow job I had experienced in my life.) Or maybe what was strange was the fact Raven showed up with that gorilla of an asshole. *Quizás cojones*, that makes me feel, as they say on the island, like a cat licking motor oil. That sneaky fox did not have to involve Uma in her own mess. At the same time I have to admit that after hearing the bit about her father's debt with Cappi, Raven's behavior seemed somewhat more logical. She was so smooth she knew that once I had tasted the forbidden fruit, the sweet nectar hiding underneath her hairy, triangular secret source, I would've done anything to continue enjoying her charms. I could already hear Leña saying "a hair from a cunt pulls way more than a plow drawn by oxen," as he watched a pot of coffee on the coals and fired up a nice spliff of Northern Lights with a burning ember.

The last time I saw Raven at the Lounge she asked me not to go to the Farm on the solstice. She told me Constantino, Joe and the others were boycotting the party outside of town because of some problem they'd had with Sullivan, the proprietor. A misunderstanding, it seems, which had left Con without heat last winter, when he was renting a place from Sullivan. Instead, they had organized an alternate blowout at the Salty Dawg with a case of bourbon already prepaid for the first adventurous souls on the scene.

"They can't stand Sulli. And they're not alone, almost everybody who has rented from him has ended up in court. He's a prick of a landlord, won't fix a faucet even, but if you are late with rent he sues your ass the first month," Raven explained to me as she opened the Lounge door. "Papa-Shan was going to close the Dawg, but between the four of them they got a hundred bucks together for him to keep it open. It's the only pool table around, unless you wanna go into town, to Pioneer Ave. The four of them really love their pool," she added as she peeled her clothes off.

Her voice was rain falling on my tent in the mornings, cold and constant. Regardless, I could not ignore her, she would blow softly in my ears when she whispered into them. "This could be the chance we've been waiting for to make enough money to get outta here, together. . . .

"They're terrible players, but they are in denial. Conman even thinks he's Minnesota Fats," she told me while she kissed my neck, as she sat naked over my lap and swallowed me whole with her moist lips between her legs. "Know what? They'll be loaded, three of them fish on the *Kryptonite*, which is not only one of the best-paying ships, but has also finished one of its most lucrative seasons. We are *the* couple, hon, don't you forget it."

I kept quiet. I hate talking business while I'm making love.

"Oh daddy, baby, you're so big, ooh I wanna feel you in deeper, all the way inside me . . . feels so gooood," she'd say and I'd hold her with my arms under her thighs, so I could lift her up and then let her fall on top of me ever so gently. "Yeah, yeah baby, like that, like you mean it, harder, I want you to fuck me over and over, so you get real good at it and you can fuck them too, take their money and take me far away from here, baby. I wanna feel you inside of me all over Alaska, down south. . . . You'll take me, won't you, Eddie, won't you, take me and come inside me when we are gone, when we're on the other side of the world?"

"Whatever you say, *mamita*," was all I could say at times like that. I was never the talker, I'm more the silent type. Sometimes I hold my breath when I'm in bed with someone, I like feeling that tingling sensation spreading through my entire body.

But now, with Cappi slapping Raven around and the four fishermen eyeballing me with that demonic look in their eyes, I had no idea of what was going on. Yes, Raven had planned the whole bit about the couple and a stranger, poring over all the details again and again until she made sure I understood to perfection the illusion the con depended on, but I never thought she was serious. Instead, I thought she would tell me those things because she couldn't help it, because she was responding to some irrepressible wish she had nurtured for years. Raven had been dreaming about leaving Homer with a handsome outsider, I assumed pretentiously, and it so happened I came along. She seemed to have chosen me, not anyone else, but me, whatever reasons there could be.

That's how one gets when one is high up, when everything is going terrific and it all goes to our heads without warning. I don't care if it only proves my simple-hearted nature, but I actually convinced myself I was helping Raven realize her arctic hillbilly dream of falling in love with a traveling foreigner and following him to see the rest of the world with her own eyes.

I asked for it, by being careless, because nobody else would've made such a gross miscalculation. Only me. It might sound far-fetched, or naïve, but since the day I met Raven I'd never expected any surprises. I don't know why, 'cause women like Raven usually aren't anything but full of surprises.

## VI. Amores *Sub Rosa*

An automobile pulled up in front of the bar and a heavyset bald man wearing dark sunglasses got out of the car.

"You're Eddie," he said and buried both his hands in his pockets. "I come to offer you a ride to the Farm."

I wasn't positive, but I knew he had to be the nefarious Colombia character, better known as Precolombia by some spit rats due to his well-documented kind of ruthless disposition. As I saw him standing in front of me, he was an exact replica of the description Leña had given me half a dozen times.

"To the Farm?" I said, acting aloof. "Thanks, but I'm not looking for work today."

The bald man laughed. He then spit to the side and took off his sunglasses. "I'm not waiting for you, that you already know. What you don't know, on the other hand, is that someone . . . well, appreciates you, obviously too much. And they're doing you a favor. Let them."

I couldn't help frowning a little. He was a total stranger to me, yet I confess I wanted to get in the car and ask him to light up a bug jay, Jamaican style, but it was too late. No doubt Cappi had racked the balls and was already waiting for me. (I could picture him anxious, chalking up one of the warped house cues.)

I shook my head and laughed hoarsely. I didn't say anything either, I didn't want to start making new enemies over nothing. Colombia got back in the car, a blue Mustang evenly corroded by the sea air, and put his sunglasses on. "Last call for the Farm express," he added before taking off, snickering loudly.

Colombia could not have been referring to Leña when he spoke about his "friend," I had no doubts about that. He would be, most likely, still somewhere on the beach making his move on that Eskimo woman he had met, practicing his lame ladies rap on her. No, it definitely was not a reference to Leña. All of a sudden, as I watched a reddish light covering St. Augustine's solitary crater, I had an idea, a notion, and for a few seconds I was sure, more than sure, that Colombia had offered me a ride at Uma's request. Or had it been Raven's? Those two alternatives, with the ominous implications they presented, cracked open the proverbial can of worms and the mere thought of them resulted in the onset of a mean migraine, which was, fortunately, brief in nature.

If either of them had sent the dreadful Colombia, then only tribulations or transgressions would come out of it. It was all downhill from that point forward, I realized as the Mustang's taillights vanished around the curve past the boardwalk. Most vehicles, and any form of transportation in general, gained an importance that was readily taken for granted in more civilized regions, in more developed areas, where how to get from point A to point B never presented any real difficulty or hazard. Not here. In Alaska a VW Bug could've just as easily been the space shuttle or the *Titanic*, or both at the same time, depending on the circumstances and what you expected to get out of its use.

Fuck it, one of these days I would have to explain the whole thing to Uma, preferably through a long-distance telephone call. It had been her, and not Raven, who was responsible for the recent twist of events, I surmised at long last—wishful thinking, really, and not an act of deduction. Or even better, I could make something up instead of trying to explain it. It wouldn't be the first time, though someone was falling for it finally.

Raven needed help, were my thoughts, believe it or not, before going back in the Salty Dawg to face Cappi at pool. *She* needed me, I told myself. Damn the twenty hours of daylight. What I needed was a long, dark night, not unlike the tropical nightfall, to provide the cover of the malfeasances scheduled for the solstice. Goddamn it, I told myself and walked into the bar, completely thinking I had Raven's fate in my pocket.

Our eyes met when I opened the heavy wooden door and she turned halfway toward the front, watching the entrance. Something smiled inside her eyes, some small sparkle beckoning me, urging me to come, to go as far away as possible you and me, c'mon . . . I'd never felt anything like it in my bullshit life, I had never found myself in the leading part like that before, never in my short walk through the world, and not only that, but I could also taste what it was like to have someone's life on my hands, as if I could truly control what happened around me the way I can control a pool game.

Cappi mumbled something and sat down on a stool next to her.

Those present still kept paying attention to me and the table, but from a safe distance, with ample space in between so the players could shoot comfortably, without obstacles. Uma passed by with two shots on a tray. I killed the first one bottoms up, straight to the bone, and the second one I drank in two gulps one after the other. Tequila, the everlasting stimulant, the quickest pick-me-upper among the strongest spirits.

Every dog has its day, I thought and broke. However confident I was, I could still say, in retrospect, that at the time I was not ready to go through with the con and in fact, I even thought at one point that I simply wouldn't do it and nothing would happen, one of us would win uneventfully and nobody would have anything to say about it. Of course, as long as we both slipped out of there first. That fool's coolness, that cocky naïvete, I suppose, was what allowed me to relax, to loosen my muscles and ease into my initial run, in which I sank the fifteen, twelve and nine in the two opposite pockets and the eleven in the side pocket. Now, that was after sinking the ten ball in the other side pocket on the break. The thirteen and fourteen balls stayed close to where they were originally racked, keeping company with most of the solids clustered nearby.

When Cappi got in place to make his first shot, the nosy and curious converged suddenly around, elbowing each other to see the fat man's opening shot. He sank three of them, heavily sweating, the ones closest to the pockets. Later he had no choice but to

break the mess of balls in the middle, hoping to carom some slop
into any pocket. But no dice, he simply left the cue lined up behind the fourteen. It was an easy shot, just a matter of following
the bank all the way to the far pocket down the line of the table.
The trick was to give it enough english to make the cue ball fall
back near its point of departure. That way I set up the next shot
rather comfortably, the thirteen on the side pocket a short way
across.

I didn't hit it with the necessary push, however, and the cue
stayed spinning in its own orbit, drifting some ways down.

The long shot, the hard one, the one everybody was waiting for
except me.

Raven raised her eyes to mine, smiling ever so subtly without
giving it away, a smile exclusively for me. Coincidentally, the jukebox was between songs and only the static of the needle on the
vinyl of a different 45 was heard. Some people began to murmur,
and wager as well.

Cappi stood up and grabbed his cue with his left hand and
with his other one scratched his goatee. He exhaled loudly and
lifted his eyebrows.

A ripple traveled through the crowd near him for a few seconds, until a space cleared up to let Uma appear with a tray full of
drinks. She handed them out to those immediately around her in
the perimeter, and when she got to Cappi, handed him the bottle
of beer he'd asked for. She soon lost herself in the crowd, without
collecting payment, but not without first throwing me a quick
sideways glance, somehow conspiratorial.

I felt everybody's eyes prodding me, sizing me up and analyz-
ing me. Some of the more expressive ones covered their mouths
with one hand while they leaned over to say something into their
neighbors' ears. The damn 45 seemed to have no song on it and
the smoke from so many cigarettes burning at once watered my
eyes, making my sockets itch. Incomplete pieces of conversations
wafted near me, mixed in with lone words of the most varied in-

ference. Sorry . . . her . . . out back . . . you're kidding . . . that kind
of thing, constantly buzzing in my ears, making me hesitate, while
everybody stared, frisking me with their eyes in my own personal
space. There was no way to block it out, to retreat into myself.
Neither could I give in to the luxury of coming across as mysterious, which would only raise unnecessary doubts in the audience
and complicate things, create problems.

At long last the jukebox overcame its technical difficulties and,
somewhere behind the faceless mass, the insane first violin of
Charlie Daniel's Band burst into life, crackling with static. The di-
version was good to me, it allowed me to blow off some steam,
some stress, and gave back the scene its cinematographic quality;
it now had a soundtrack. But how could I do what Raven expected me to? How to interfere with the flow of things and from
one instant to the next transform it all into a matter of money, of
cold hard cash? It wasn't the same thing as spending a relatively
quiet evening, fiving it until I reached seventy or eighty dollars,
taking breaks here and there and always keeping the risk factor
comfortably low. The planet had suddenly shifted, as if it had begun spinning in its imperfect orbit but in reverse. The enormous,
and evident, dimensions of my stupidity were immediately magni-
fied. Moments before I had dismissed Uma like any other billiard
ball, like it was really in my hands to dispose of her, and now I
wondered whether she would deem myself worthy of being on
speaking terms with once she discovered it had been a crass mis-
judgment to place her trust in me.

The song was reaching its grand finale, the violin duel between
Johnny and the Devil, when a womanly wail filled the small quarters of the watering hole. It was Raven, cowering before Cappi,
who was twisting her arm violently while he spoke right into her
ear with a clenched jaw. Someone behind me said something
about a "motherfucker" and spat. What's with the people of these
seaports spitting anytime and anywhere they please.

Cappi let go of the girl and walked over to the table. He just fixed his sights on me on the spot. I could sense him trying to look past the surface, to see things eyes could not, as if my outside appearance spelled out the answer to an essential question he needed to know. I didn't like it at all, but I quickly forgot about it when the big man threw down a roll of bills on the felt. The wad of twenties hit the green and it detonated a sudden silence inside the Salty Dawg. The jukebox, true to form, began again the time-consuming task of switching vinyls, according to its stubborn mechanics, its incomprehensible tune selection techniques the moment it chooses the next number. Constantino came up to the table, sighing, grabbed the money and with resignation announced: "All right, watch the door, it's on. . . ." Right after he said that the group assembled around us, splintering into a myriad of pieces and began immediately to recombine, to conspire and to convene privately with each other, discreetly, and during which, I suspected, the pool was divided only to break so many hearts soon after. The throng of lushes placed their bets, while others swarmed and dug money out of their pockets, cursing at those who interrupted them or got in the way.

That small Alaskan bar was transformed into a surreal grunge-style stock market, a flanneled commodities exchange reeking of raw fish and an inclination toward hard liquor. The hollering was short-lived, couple of minutes of chaos at the most, but enough to draw everyone's attention away from the interesting interaction unfolding between Raven and Cappi. The fat man looked in my general direction and laughed, obviously thinking I couldn't see him. But not Raven; Raven indeed looked right into me through the throng and lifted her eyebrows, something like her eye equivalent of shrugging her shoulders and spreading the palms of her hands.

It seemed pretty clear to me Raven had told Cappi about what I was supposed to do. I don't know if she had said something due to the fact that she understood, very perceptively, that I would've never been able to get the betting going and she would've missed the chance to put Cappi in his place, or if maybe she'd just tried to deflect the hardships headed my way. Of course, looking at her I saw her as in the past—naked and powerful on top of me, swallowing me whole with her body, chewing me with her arms, devouring me between her legs—so I simply saw my lover, throwing in the towel for me at the very last minute, making my life easier like women are expected to do for their men.

What I didn't notice, although I actually saw it, but not carefully enough so as to take stock of its true meaning, was Uma throw a glance over to Raven, a harmless one no less, but a glance I was unable to interpret at the time.

Whatever, the thing is that soon enough the jukebox's needle finally made contact with the wayward vinyl and a Lynnyrd Skynnyrd song came to life, though I can't remember which of their songs became the background music for the final act of the night. I imagine the vast majority of those there bet against Cappi, more than any of us could imagine, because when I missed, the collective despair was much more widespread than anybody really expected. Even Joe, who already had lost ten dollars to me and was good friends with the old sea wolf, sighed his disappointment when the thirteen ball kissed the corner bank and bounced back up the table.

A deathly silence momentarily took over after the initial shock. Then I felt their eyes tearing away at my masks as through layers of an onion, but I must confess I took a certain joy, a conceited pride, in my acting. I had won hands down, in my acting, I mean, opening my mouth and eyes wildly, dilating the nasal cavities, like a cornered beast. And, as the final touch, I closed my eyes and sank my head between my arms, which were still stretched out on the table's edge, cue stick still in place.

I could hear and see the spit falling like rain around me, restoring the real gravity to the heaviness of the situation. I kept shaking my head, cursing myself. I then grabbed the cue and swung it against the table. Almost snapped. If the Academy could see me now.

"That's it, it's all over," were Papa-Shan's words, aimed at regaining his reins over the sawdust, over the entire precinct. "Bring him. . . ."

Uma took a shot glass and pushed and shoved her way among the pack of idiots. Very soon they would begin to realize they'd lost all their money and all hell would break loose, no way to know how it would end. Uma bit her lower lip and handed me the glass with the golden liquid and with the strong scent of tequila filling the air. Her eyes were telling me a million different things, not that I paid any mind, focusing my concentration on the shot, the heat flushed down my body as I kept an eye out for my future there in the defeated, fuming audience.

Raven, thousands of miles of road, a perfect story to laugh at en route. But I couldn't see her, no matter how hard I tried to penetrate the wall Constantino and the other collectors erected around Cappi and her, of course.

"Go through the back, we haven't got much time," Uma said, forcing me out of a trancelike state.

"There's no way out through the back," I corrected.

"Please, stop it. Go talk to Papa-Shan."

And I did, right after Uma knocked her full tray down on purpose, knocking off a couple of drinks and a load of cash, one Franklin at least in small bills. It wasn't that bad, the back door was hidden by the details of the wood, like a false door. Behind it I found myself inside a strange space, too small to require its own name, and with an opening to the parking lot on the other side of the bar's watchtower. I leaned into the frame of a nonexistent door, torn off from its hinges as the rusty evidence seemed to suggest, and felt my life hesitate two seconds within my limbs. I was completely out of it, and never even knew it. My line of vision doubled, and doubled and tripled in rapid succession.

I saw Raven fill that strange mini-foyer and smile. I was *soñando despierto*, dreaming awake, without the slightest clue, that far ahead in the game, even as my eyes wandered aimlessly. My knees then gave in from beneath me, as if they were made of the wettest, gutter-soaked bread. Drugged, physically melting away entirely, I insisted on believing what I wanted to. The countless miles of blacktop, her smile, her luscious hair grabbing me, her lips sucking me dry, extracting from me the very nectar of life, the dream that was coming undone right there in front of her.

And in front of . . . Uma?

Yes, Uma, frowning, unable to disguise her discomfort as she did this to me. Nevertheless it was a steady hand that tucked the plastic bottle of pills under my buckle. I felt her hand softly on my face, my cheek, just as if I was a boy, just like I remembered from times long past, the same way every woman in my remote child-hood always ever caressed me. The kiss on the forehead, repeating over and over again that it is only another day breaking. One more time, tiger.

Now, the long kiss she gave Raven sent painful pangs through the deepest regions of my chest cavity, where all my raw emotions emerge and converge. I resented that kiss, I envied it, I burned it forever into this rock-hard head of mine, which is rendered use-less whenever a woman walks in front of me. It was murder, the kiss, apocalyptic.

Papa-Shan's shadow laughed behind me. "I'm jealous," he said in his usual hoarse whiskey voice, showing off his yellowed teeth. "I'm gonna miss you guys. And I guess Cappi will too," he added, and as I saw it, he winked at the two young women.

They talked amongst themselves, I know, but it went right over me. I thought I heard something about the law, maybe police, but I was relieved by the animosity I sensed toward the authorities when they decided to keep them out of the deal. I knew I was had by then, however I sensed hostility toward Cappi in the exchange. Yet I was too drugged, tossed like a sack of potatoes in the back of a bar at the end of the world. I still could feel the affection flowing between the three of them, in their gestures, as they held counsel with each other. I remember a final round of good-bye kisses and then silence, directed toward me. I knew it was Uma, still carrying all that guilt. I thought I heard someone say, "Don't let them get too rough."

Car doors were slammed shut and an engine was started loudly. I don't know why but it sounded American, like a Mustang or a Camaro, something like that, the last little piece of my dream. "Oh, Eddie, I still like you, don't take it too personal. I'll help, you'll see," said the barman before raising his fist and knocking me out twice, just to make sure. Papa-Shan was now in the role of avenger. *Look who I found trying to sneak out the back way* . . . , I could perfectly imagine him saying after dragging me back into the Dawg's interior again, and throwing me there on the sawdust-covered floor.

Last thing I remember hearing was Papa-Shan's voice, as I drifted in and out of consciousness, talking to another shadow that had materialized in that strange small space. "The fat man must've already fallen, listen to the racket those people are making. . . ."

# Junot Díaz
## (Dominican Republic, b. 1968)

Junot Díaz was born in Santo Domingo, Dominican Republic. He is a graduate of Rutgers University and received his MFA from Cornell University. His first story collection, *Drown*, was published in 1996 to enormous critical and popular acclaim. It has since been published internationally in more than a dozen languages, including a Spanish edition in the United States entitled *Negocios*.

Díaz's stories have appeared in *The New Yorker*, *The Paris Review*, *Time Out*, *Glimmer*, *Train*, *African Voices*, and anthologized in *Best American Fiction 1996* (edited by John Edgar Wideman), *Best American Fiction 1997* (edited by Annie Proulx), *Best American Fiction 1999* (edited by Amy Tan), *Best American Fiction 2000* (edited by E. L. Doctorow), and in the 1999 "The Future of American Fiction" issue of *The New Yorker*. He received a Pushcart Prize XXII for his story "Invierno," which was later also selected for *The Pushcart Book of Short Stories*, a compilation of the best fiction from the first twenty-five years of the Pushcart Prize.

The recipient of numerous fellowships and awards, including a Eugene McDermott Award (1998), a Guggenheim Fellowship (1999), and a Lila Wallace–Reader's Digest Writers' Award (2000), Díaz teaches creative writing at Cornell University.

# Edison, New Jersey

The first time we try to deliver the Gold Crown the lights are on in the house but no one lets us in. I bang on the front door and Wayne hits the back and I can hear our double drum shaking the windows. Right then I have this feeling that someone is inside, laughing at us.

This guy better have a good excuse, Wayne says, lumbering around the newly planted rosebushes. This is bullshit.

You're telling me, I say but Wayne's the one who takes this job too seriously. He pounds some more on the door, his face jiggling. A couple of times he raps on the windows, tries squinting through the curtains. I take a more philosophical approach; I walk over to the ditch that has been cut next to the road, a drainage pipe half filled with water, and sit down. I smoke and watch a mama duck and her three ducklings scavenge the grassy bank and then float downstream like they're on the same string. Beautiful, I say but Wayne doesn't hear. He's banging on the door with the staple gun.

\*      \*      \*

At nine Wayne picks me up at the showroom and by then I have our route planned out. The order forms tell me everything I need to know about the customers we'll be dealing with that day. If someone is just getting a fifty-two-inch card table delivered then you know they aren't going to give you too much of a hassle but they also aren't going to tip. Those are your Spotswood, Sayreville and Perth Amboy deliveries. The pool tables go north to the rich suburbs—Livingston, Ridgewood, Bedminster.

You should see our customers. Doctors, diplomats, surgeons, presidents of universities, ladies in slacks and silk tops who sport thin watches you could trade in for a car, who wear comfortable leather shoes. Most of them prepare for us by laying down a path of yesterday's *Washington Post* from the front door to the game room. I make them pick it all up. I say: Carajo, what if we slip? Do you know what two hundred pounds of slate could do to a floor? The threat of property damage puts the chop-chop in their step. The best customers leave us alone until the bill has to be signed. Every now and then we'll be given water in paper cups. Few have offered us more, though a dentist from Ghana once gave us a six-pack of Heineken while we worked.

Sometimes the customer has to jet to the store for cat food or a newspaper while we're in the middle of a job. I'm sure you'll be all right, they say. They never sound too sure. Of course, I say. Just show us where the silver's at. The customers ha-ha and we ha-ha and then they agonize over leaving, linger by the front door, trying to memorize everything they own, as if they don't know where to find us, who we work for.

Once they're gone, I don't have to worry about anyone bothering me. I put down the ratchet, crack my knuckles and explore, usually while Wayne is smoothing out the felt and doesn't need help. I take cookies from the kitchen, razors from the bathroom cabinets. Some of these houses have twenty, thirty rooms. On the ride back I figure out how much loot it would take to fill up all that space. I've been caught roaming around plenty of times but you'd be surprised how quickly someone believes you're looking for the bathroom if you don't jump when you're discovered, if you just say, Hi.

After the paperwork's been signed, I have a decision to make. If the customer has been good and tipped well, we call it even and leave. If the customer has been an ass—maybe they yelled, maybe they let their kids throw golf balls at us—I ask for the bathroom. Wayne will pretend that he hasn't seen this before; he'll count the drill bits while the customer (or their maid) guides the vacuum over the floor. Excuse me, I say. I let them show me the way to the bathroom (usually I already know) and once the door is shut I cram bubble bath drops into my pockets and throw fist-sized wads of toilet paper into the toilet. I take a dump if I can and leave that for them.

Most of the time Wayne and I work well together. He's the driver and the money man and I do the lifting and handle the assholes. Tonight we're on our way to Lawrenceville and he wants to talk to me about Charlene, one of the showroom girls, the one with the blow-job lips. I haven't wanted to talk about women in months, not since the girlfriend.

I really want to pile her, he tells me. Maybe on one of the Madisons.

Man, I say, cutting my eyes toward him. Don't you have a wife or something?

He gets quiet. I'd still like to pile her, he says defensively.

And what will that do?

Why does it have to *do* anything?

Twice this year Wayne's cheated on his wife and I've heard it all, the before and the after. The last time his wife nearly tossed his ass out to the dogs. Neither of the women seemed worth it to me. One of them was even younger than Charlene. Wayne can be a moody guy and this is one of those nights; he slouches in the driver's seat and swerves through traffic, riding other people's bumpers like I've told him not to do. I don't need a collision or a four-hour silent treatment so I try to forget that I think his wife is good people and ask him if Charlene's given him any signals.

He slows the truck down. Signals like you wouldn't believe, he says.

On the days we have no deliveries the boss has us working at the showroom, selling cards and poker chips and mankala boards. Wayne spends his time skeezing the salesgirls and dusting shelves. He's a big goofy guy—I don't understand why the girls dig his shit. One of those mysteries of the universe. The boss keeps me in the front of the store, away from the pool tables. He knows I'll talk to the customers, tell them not to buy the cheap models. I'll say shit like, Stay away from those Bristols. Wait until you can get something real. Only when he needs my Spanish will he let me help on a sale. Since I'm no good at cleaning or selling slot machines I slouch behind the front register and steal. I don't ring anything up, and pocket what comes in. I don't tell Wayne. He's too busy running his fingers through his beard, keeping the waves on his nappy head in order. A hundred-buck haul's not unusual for me and back in the day, when the girlfriend used to pick me up, I'd buy her anything she wanted, dresses, silver rings, lingerie. Sometimes I blew it all on her. She didn't like the stealing but hell, we weren't made out of loot and I liked going into a place and saying, Jeva, pick out anything, it's yours. This is the closest I've come to feeling rich.

Nowadays I take the bus home and the cash stays with me. I sit next to this three-hundred-pound rock-and-roll chick who washes dishes at the Friendly's. She tells me about the roaches she kills with her water nozzle. Boils the wings right off them. On Thursday I buy myself lottery tickets—ten Quick Picks and a couple of Pick 4s. I don't bother with the little stuff.

\*　　\*　　\*

The second time we bring the Gold Crown the heavy curtain next to the door swings up like a Spanish fan. A woman stares at me and Wayne's too busy knocking to see. Muñeca, I say. She's black and unsmiling and then the curtain drops between us, a whisper on the glass. She had on a T-shirt that said *No Problem* and didn't look like she owned the place. She looked more like the help and couldn't have been older than twenty and from the thinness of her face I pictured the rest of her skinny. We stared at each other for a second at the most, not enough for me to notice the shape of her ears or if her lips were chapped. I've fallen in love on less.

Later in the truck, on the way back to the showroom Wayne mutters, This guy is dead. I mean it.

The girlfriend calls sometimes but not often. She has found herself a new boyfriend, some zángano who works at a record store. *Dan* is his name and the way she says it, so painfully gringo, makes the corners of my eyes narrow. The clothes I'm sure this guy tears from her when they both get home from work—the chokers, the rayon skirts from the Warehouse, the lingerie—I bought with stolen money and I'm glad that none of it was earned straining my back against hundreds of pounds of raw rock. I'm glad for that.

The last time I saw her in person was in Hoboken. She was with *Dan* and hadn't yet told me about him and hurried across the street in her high clogs to avoid me and my boys, who even then could sense me turning, turning into the motherfucker who'll put a fist through anything. She flung one hand in the air but didn't stop. A month before the zángano, I went to her house, a friend visiting a friend, and her parents asked me how business was, as if I balanced the books or something. Business is outstanding, I said.

That's really wonderful to hear, the father said.

You betcha.

He asked me to help him mow his lawn and while we were dribbling gas into the tank he offered me a job. A real one that you can build on. Utilities, he said, is nothing to be ashamed of.

Later the parents went into the den to watch the Giants lose and she took me into her bathroom. She put on her makeup because we were going to a movie. If I had your eyelashes, I'd be famous, she told me. The Giants started losing real bad. I still love you, she said and I was embarrassed for the two of us, the way I'm embarrassed at those afternoon talk shows where broken couples and unhappy families let their hearts hang out.

We're friends, I said and Yes, she said, yes we are.

There wasn't much space so I had to put my heels on the edge of the bathtub. The cross I'd given her dangled down on its silver chain so I put it in my mouth to keep it from poking me in the eye. By the time we finished my legs were bloodless, broomsticks inside my rolled-down baggies and as her breathing got smaller and smaller against my neck, she said, I do, I still do.

Each payday I take out the old calculator and figure how long it'd take me to buy a pool table honestly. A top-of-the-line, three-piece slate affair doesn't come cheap. You have to buy sticks and balls and chalk and a score keeper and triangles and French tips if you're a fancy shooter. Two and a half years if I give up buying underwear and eat only pasta but even this figure's bogus. Money's never stuck to me, ever.

Most people don't realize how sophisticated pool tables are. Yes, tables have bolts and staples on the rails but these suckers hold together mostly by gravity and by the precision of their construction. If you treat a good table right it will outlast you. Believe me. Cathedrals are built like that. There are Incan roads in the Andes that even today you couldn't work a knife between two of the cobblestones. The sewers that the Romans built in Bath were so good that they weren't replaced until the 1950s. That's the sort of thing I can believe in.

These days I can build a table with my eyes closed. Depending on how rushed we are I might build the table alone, let Wayne watch until I need help putting on the slate. It's better when the customers stay out of our faces, how they react when we're done, how they run fingers on the lacquered rails and suck in their breath, the felt so tight you couldn't pluck it if you tried. Beautiful, is what they say and we always nod, talc on our fingers, nod again, beautiful.

The boss nearly kicked our asses over the Gold Crown. The customer, an asshole named Pruitt, called up crazy, said we were *delinquent*. That's how the boss put it. Delinquent. We knew that's what the customer called us because the boss doesn't use words like that. Look boss, I said, we knocked like crazy. I mean, we knocked like federal marshals. Like Paul Bunyan. The boss wasn't having it. You fuckos, he said. You butthogs. He tore us for a good two minutes and then *dismissed* us. For most of that night I didn't think I had a job so I hit the bars, fantasizing that I would bump into this cabrón out with that black woman while me and my boys were cranked but the next morning Wayne came by with that Gold Crown again. Both of us had hangovers. One more time, he said. An extra delivery, no overtime. We hammered on the door for ten minutes but no one answered. I jimmied with the windows and the back door and I could have sworn I heard her behind the patio door. I knocked hard and heard footsteps.

We called the boss and told him what was what and the boss called the house but no one answered. OK, the boss said. Get those card tables done. That night, as we lined up the next day's paperwork, we got a call from Pruitt and he didn't use the word delinquent. He wanted us to come late at night but we were booked. Two-month waiting list, the boss reminded him. I looked over at Wayne and wondered how much money this guy was pouring into the boss's ear. Pruitt said he was *contrite* and *determined* and asked us to come again. His maid was sure to let us in.

What the hell kind of name is Pruitt anyway? Wayne asks me when we swing onto the parkway.

Pato name, I say. Anglo or some other bog people.

Probably a fucking banker. What's the first name?

Just an initial, C. Clarence Pruitt sounds about right.

Yeah, Clarence, Wayne yuks.

Pruitt. Most of our customers have names like this, court case names: Wooley, Maynard, Gass, Binder, but the people from my town, our names, you see on convicts or coupled together on boxing cards.

We take our time. Go to the Rio Diner, blow an hour and all the dough we have in our pockets. Wayne is talking about Charlene and I'm leaning my head against a thick pane of glass.

Pruitt's neighborhood has recently gone up and only his court is complete. Gravel roams off this way and that, shaky. You can see inside the other houses, their newly formed guts, nailheads bright and sharp on the fresh timber. Wrinkled blue tarps protect wiring and fresh plaster. The driveways are mud and on each lawn stand huge stacks of sod. We park in front of Pruitt's house and bang on the door. I give Wayne a hard look when I see no car in the garage.

Yes? I hear a voice inside say.

We're the delivery guys, I yell.

A bolt slides, a lock turns, the door opens. She stands in our way, wearing black shorts and a gloss of red on her lips and I'm sweating.

Come in, yes? She stands back from the door, holding it open.

Sounds like Spanish, Wayne says.

No shit, I say, switching over. Do you remember me?

No, she says.

I look over at Wayne. Can you believe this?

I can believe anything, kid.

You heard us didn't you? The other day, that was you.

She shrugs and opens the door wider.

You better tell her to prop that with a chair. Wayne heads back to unlock the truck.

You hold that door, I say.

*       *       *

We've had our share of delivery trouble. Trucks break down. Customers move and leave us with an empty house. Handguns get pointed. Slate gets dropped, a rail goes missing. The felt is the wrong color, the Dufferins get left in the warehouse. Back in the day, the girlfriend and I made a game of this. A prediction game. In the mornings I rolled onto my pillow and said, What's today going to be like?

Let me check. She put her fingers up to her widow's peak and that motion would shift her breasts, her hair. We never slept under any covers, not in spring, fall or summer and our bodies were dark and thin the whole year.

I see an asshole customer, she murmured. Unbearable traffic. Wayne's going to work slow. And then you'll come home to me.

Will I get rich?

You'll come home to me. That's the best I can do. And then we'd kiss hungrily because this was how we loved each other.

The game was part of our mornings, the way our showers and our sex and our breakfasts were. We stopped playing only when it started to go wrong for us, when I'd wake up and listen to the traffic outside without waking her, when everything was a fight.

She stays in the kitchen while we work. I can hear her humming. Wayne's shaking his right hand like he's scalded his fingertips. Yes, she's fine. She has her back to me, her hands stirring around in a full sink, when I walk in.

I try to sound conciliatory. You're from the city?

A nod.

Where about?

Washington Heights.

Dominicana, I say. Quisqueyana. She nods. What street?

I don't know the address, she says. I have it written down. My mother and my brothers live there.

I'm Dominican, I say.

You don't look it.

I get a glass of water. We're both staring out at the muddy lawn.

She says, I didn't answer the door because I wanted to piss him off.

Piss who off?

I want to get out of here, she says.

Out of here?

I'll pay you for a ride.

I don't think so, I say.

Aren't you from Nueva York?

No.

Then why did you ask the address?

Why? I have family near there.

Would it be that big of a problem?

I say in English that she should have her boss bring her but she stares at me blankly. I switch over.

He's a pendejo, she says, suddenly angry. I put down the glass, move next to her to wash it. She's exactly my height and smells of liquid detergent and has tiny beautiful moles on her neck, an archipelago leading down into her clothes.

Here, she says, putting out her hand but I finish it and go back to the den.

Do you know what she wants us to do? I say to Wayne.

Her room is upstairs, a bed, a closet, a dresser, yellow wallpaper. Spanish *Cosmo* and *El Diario* thrown on the floor. Four hangers' worth of clothes in the closet and only the top dresser drawer is full. I put my hand on the bed and the cotton sheets are cool.

Pruitt has pictures of himself in his room. He's tan and probably has been to more countries than I know capitals for. Photos of him on vacations, on beaches, standing beside a wide-mouth Pacific salmon he's hooked. The size of his dome would have made

Broca proud. The bed is made and his wardrobe spills out onto chairs and a line of dress shoes follows the far wall. A bachelor. I find an open box of Trojans in his dresser beneath a stack of boxer shorts. I put one of the condoms in my pocket and stick the rest under his bed.

I find her in her room. He likes clothes, she says.

A habit of money, I say but I can't translate it right; I end up agreeing with her. Are you going to pack?

She holds up her purse. I have everything I need. He can keep the rest of it.

You should take some of your things.

I don't care about that vaina. I just want to go.

Don't be stupid, I say. I open her dresser and pull out the shorts on top and a handful of soft bright panties fall out and roll down the front of my jeans. There are more in the drawer. I try to catch them but as soon as I touch their fabric I let everything go.

Leave it. Go on, she says and begins to put them back in the dresser, her square back to me, the movement of her hands smooth and easy.

Look, I say.

Don't worry. She doesn't look up.

I go downstairs. Wayne is sinking the bolts into the slate with the Makita. You can't do it, he says.

Why not?

Kid. We have to finish this.

I'll be back before you know it. A quick trip, in out.

Kid. He stands up slowly; he's nearly twice as old as me.

I go to the window and look out. New gingkoes stand in rows beside the driveway. A thousand years ago when I was still in college I learned something about them. Living fossils. Unchanged since their inception millions of years ago. You tagged Charlene, didn't you?

Sure did, he answers easily.

I take the truck keys out of the toolbox. I'll be right back, I promise.

My mother still has pictures of the girlfriend in her apartment. The girlfriend's the sort of person who never looks bad. There's a picture of us at the bar where I taught her to play pool. She's leaning on the Schmelke I stole for her, nearly a grand worth of cue, frowning at the shot I left her, a shot she'd go on to miss.

The picture of us in Florida is the biggest—shiny, framed, nearly a foot tall. We're in our bathing suits and the legs of some stranger frame the right. She has her butt in the sand, knees folded up in front of her because she knew I was sending the picture home to my moms; she didn't want my mother to see her bikini, didn't want my mother to think her a whore. I'm crouching next to her, smiling, one hand on her thin shoulder, one of her moles showing between my fingers.

My mother won't look at the pictures or talk about her when I'm around but my sister says she still cries over the breakup. Around me my mother's polite, sits quietly on the couch while I tell her about what I'm reading and how work has been. Do you have anyone? she asks me sometimes.

Yes, I say.

She talks to my sister on the side, says, In my dreams they're still together.

We reach the Washington Bridge without saying a word. She's emptied his cupboards and refrigerator; the bags are at her feet. She's eating corn chips but I'm too nervous to join in.

Is this the best way? she asks. The bridge doesn't seem to impress her.

It's the shortest way.

She folds the bag shut. That's what he said when I arrived last year. I wanted to see the countryside. There was too much rain to see anything anyway.

I want to ask her if she loves her boss, but I ask instead, How do you like the States?

She swings her head across at the billboards. I'm not surprised by any of it, she says.

Traffic on the bridge is bad and she has to give me an oily fiver for the toll. Are you from the capital? I ask.

No.

I was born there. In Villa Juana. Moved here when I was a little boy.

She nods, staring out at the traffic. As we cross over the bridge I drop my hand into her lap. I leave it there, palm up, fingers slightly curled. Sometimes you just have to try, even if you know it won't work. She turns her head away slowly, facing out beyond the bridge cables, out to Manhattan and the Hudson.

Everything in Washington Heights is Dominican. You can't go a block without passing a Quisqueya Bakery or a Quisqueya Supermercado or a Hotel Quisqueya. If I were to park the truck and get out nobody would take me for a deliveryman; I could be the guy who's on the street corner selling Dominican flags. I could be on my way home to my girl. Everybody's on the streets and the merengue's falling out of windows like TVs. When we reach her block I ask a kid with the sag for the building and he points out the stoop with his pinkie. She gets out of the truck and straightens the front of her sweatshirt before following the line that the kid's finger has cut across the street. Cuídate, I say.

Wayne works on the boss and a week later I'm back, on probation, painting the warehouse. Wayne brings me meatball sandwiches from out on the road, skinny things with a seam of cheese gumming the bread.

Was it worth it? he asks me.

He's watching me close. I tell him it wasn't.

Did you at least get some?

Hell yeah, I say.

Are you sure?

Why would I lie about something like that? Homegirl was an animal. I still have the teeth marks.

Damn, he says.

I punch him in the arm. And how's it going with you and Charlene?

I don't know, man. He shakes his head and in that motion I see him out on his lawn with all his things. I just don't know about this one.

We're back on the road a week later. Buckinghams, Imperials, Gold Crowns and dozens of card tables. I keep a copy of Pruitt's paperwork and when the curiosity finally gets to me I call. The first time I get the machine. We're delivering at a house on Long Island with a view of the Sound that would break you. Wayne and I smoke a joint on the beach and I pick up a dead horseshoe crab by the tail and heave it in the customer's garage. The next two times I'm in the Bedminster area Pruitt picks up and says, Yes? But on the fourth time she answers and the sink is running on her side of the phone and she shuts it off when I don't say anything.

Was she there? Wayne asks in the truck.

Of course she was.

He runs a thumb over the front of his teeth. Pretty predictable. She's probably in love with the guy. You know how it is.

I sure do.

Don't get angry.

I'm tired, that's all.

Tired's the best way to be, he says. It really is.

He hands me the map and my fingers trace our deliveries, stitching city to city. Looks like we've gotten everything, I say.

Finally. He yawns. What's first tomorrow?

We won't really know until the morning, when I've gotten the paperwork in order but I take guesses anyway. One of our games. It passes the time, gives us something to look forward to. I close my eyes and put my hand on the map. So many towns, so many cities to choose from. Some places are sure bets but more than once I've gone with the long shot and been right.

You can't imagine how many times I've been right.

Usually the name will come to me fast, the way the numbered balls pop out during the lottery drawings, but this time nothing comes: no magic, no nothing. It could be anywhere. I open my eyes and see that Wayne is still waiting. Edison, I say, pressing my thumb down. Edison, New Jersey.

# Jorge Volpi
## (Mexico, b. 1968)

Jorge Volpi was born in Mexico City, where he majored in law and in literature at the Autonomous University. Eventually he would travel to Spain to pursue a doctorate in Hispanic philology at the University of Salamanca. Volpi had determined from an early age that he was destined to become a writer, and he soon published a first novel, *Apesar del oscuro silencio* (1992). In the meantime, he started a career in law, and from 1992 to 1994 he worked as secretary to the chief magistrate of justice.

It was not until 1994 that he decided to devote himself entirely to literature. In the next two years he joined with other writers of his generation, including Ignacio Padilla and Eloy Urroz, to found the "Crack" group, whose movement signaled a return to the roots that had engendered the great writers of the sixties' Latin American "boom." With Padilla and Urroz he published *Tres bosquejos del mal* (1994), which included his short novella *Días de Ira*. This was quickly followed by three more novels, *La paz de los sepulcros* (1995), *El temperamento melancólico* (1996), and *Sanar tu piel amarga* (1997), as well as a nonfiction work chronicling the volatile intellectual history of 1968—all of which now figure among the seminal works of "Crack."

The "Crack" writers were, of course, a disparate group, but united in their rejection of North American neorealism and a facile magical realism. They cultivated a more ambitious form of the novel, with a complex structure that invites the reader's complicity. In 1999 Volpi received the distinguished Biblioteca Breve Prize for just such a work, *In Search of Klingsor*, a baroque literary thriller detailing army lieutenant Francis Bacon's singular pursuit of the mysterious scientist known as Klingsor, who had masterminded the Third Reich's effort to build the atomic bomb. A groundbreaking novel in which the author transgresses the traditional barriers between essay and fiction, the work quickly became a literary sensation and won its author an international following. Volpi lives in Paris, where he is cultural attaché and director of the Mexican Cultural Institute. He is working on the second volume of a proposed trilogy begun with *Klingsor*.

# Ars Poetica

I'll begin the story with a statement of principles: I am a character and I am prepared to speak (badly) of the author of the books in which I appear. I am well aware that this approach is a little novel—the difference being, I don't wear glasses with tortoise-shell frames, or linen vests in order to make myself look like a genius—but it's not my fault that I've been created by a little whippersnapper less than thirty-five years old who, after having won who knows how the Sphinx of the Short Novel Prize (short on insight is my guess), thinks he can resort to the techniques of a Cervantes or Unamuno simply because they figure in Woody Allen's latest film.

So you know what class of individual I'm talking about, you only have to take a quick peek at his resume (touched up each day before he showers):

*SANTIAGO CONTRERAS (Texcoco, México, 1971). Completed studies in Medicine, Law, and Anthropology before deciding to dedicate himself solely to literature. He has participated in more than a hun-*

dred national literary competitions; nevertheless his first recognition came from a foreign country, when in 1995 he received honorable mention in the Alcorcón City short story competition, the first Latin American to receive such notice.[1] He followed up this accolade a year later with the Juan Rulfo Prize for his story, "Conjectures About Doctor Aristides Kapuchinski," published recently by Out of Ink Press (Toluca, 1997).[2]

He is the author of the following books: I Will Spit on Your Grave (Parrot Books, Texcoco, 1994) and Can I Please Go to the Bathroom? (Interwoven Notebooks, Xalapa, 1995), which belong to his first stage of fiction, and the novels The Muse of the Game (Joaquin Mortiz, 1996) and Theory of Women (Earth Inside, Mexico City, 1997), which signal the beginning of his mature creativity. Editorial Alfaguara will soon publish, in Mexico and in Spain, Zeno Perplexed, contender for the Sphinx Prize for Short Novel.

Four times he has received scholarships from the National Foundation for Culture and the Arts. Although he has declared himself to be the enemy of categories and doesn't think he owes his success to being a "young writer" but rather to his persistence over many years, he is considered the most promising novelist of his generation. He is currently writing his autobiography and a script for the film based on The Muse of the Game.[3]

On the other hand, I don't even have a name. In another sense I have more than I want: even if the names are different, Santiago has put me in three novels and a dozen stories. When showing off his ingenuity, he baptizes me as Aristides Kapuchinski, or Gilbert

[1] Alcorcón City is one of 527 contests listed in Guide to the Competitions and Literary Prizes in Spain (Fuentetaja, Madrid, 1996). Its first year was 1995. As for the other, there exist so many prizes in Mexico that use the name of Pedro Paramo's author in order to perpetuate magical realism.

[2] On this subject, it is worth pointing out that we are talking about the Juan Rulfo Prize for Stories about Airplanes, supported by Mexicana Airlines and Corona Distillery. (C.N.)

[3] Six books before his thirty-fifth birthday! And two "narrative stages." The commentaries are coming out all over the place. Even so, I have one question: where it says, "He is considered the novelist, etc."—Who wrote those words? (C.N.)

O'Sullivan—in a book on medieval Ireland—but most of the time I've had to play the role of Sylvester Cabrera, Saturnino Corominas, Saul Camacho and other witty variants on his initials. But that would be the least of it. The worst is, naming me however he names me, I always stand out with the same personality: a not very happy combination of the man Santiago is and the one he will never be. You might conclude that an author, when he portrays himself in his books, lives various roles forbidden him, fulfills his most arbitrary fantasies and overtakes those goals that are always out of reach; so I don't understand what the reason is that in story after story I'm always the same dope.

Santiago's insignificant career ended the day he found the lifeless body of Juan Jacobo Dietrich spread out on the rug of the house they shared. In spite of the fact that in his *opera omnia* there can be counted more than forty violent deaths—among them a dismemberment (which made his sister vomit and led her to two years of psychoanalysis), various duels, Chinese torture in homage to Salvador Elizondo, and even a meticulous autopsy undertaken by the fearless Doctor Kapuchinski—in reality Santiago has never seen a corpse, much less that of one of his colleagues. Later on in *Zeno*, he forced me to reveal his impressions in cold and unsavory language, influenced—or so he says—by Raymond Carver: "I saw him. He was spread out on the floor like one of my sister's Barbie dolls. His bare navel made me think of the frogs in college. I didn't go closer to look at him because I hate staining my argyle socks" (p. 14). In real life the scene was less glamorous: Santiago ran out of the house and once in the street fainted into the fleshy arms of Susana Ruvalcaba, famous author of *Pricks*. Immediately after his decease, the press discovered that Juan Jacobo Dietrich was using a pseudonym: in his wallet was a driver's license for Juan Jacobo Reyes, with a photo that proved that that unusual surname was nothing more than another of the dead author's Germanophile manias. Meanwhile the quarrelsome North American doctor who attended him didn't waste two seconds before venomously confirming that his next book—if there was one—would have to carry a seal with the inscription "posthumous."

Santiago and Juan Jacobo had been companions since high school. They had known each other since the first literary competition in which they participated. Their school, run by Marist brothers, wasn't known for its love of literature but for some reason still displayed a short story prize said to have been won by Carlos Fuentes. The legend was in fact even more inflated: the young Fuentes, who turns up in the yearbooks with big glasses, no mustache, and a saintly look he would lose in no time, hadn't been content with winning first place, but using three distinct *noms de plume* he had carried off all three medals. Even if Santiago was in those days a timid young man, the type who sits in the back of the class, inside he was proud and arrogant: he wasn't going to limit himself to emulating the author of *Aura*'s feat—he planned to ridicule it. He sent ten different stories, arranged to win, like a novice, the first ten places. He almost pulled off his plan: the day the prize was announced he learned that his narratives had taken second to eleventh place; an unknown by the name of Juan Jacobo had snatched first prize.

In "The Virgin and the Serpent," one of those primitive sketches, Santiago brought me into the world with the intention that I should incarnate, in a beautiful allegory, all the historical sufferings of the Mexican people (shamefully, there seemed to be too many for a somewhat neurotic adolescent). I quickly forgave him this slip in spite of his innocence—or perhaps because of it—in these pages, written by hand until his fingers hurt, I possessed a passion that, sadly for me, I've watched fade away little by little. Don't misinterpret me: the story was a bad one, very bad; the sad part is, in my opinion, the ones that came after weren't any better.

Be that as it may, from then on Santiago and Juan Jacobo became inseparable. In an environment dominated by boys who triumphed in football, they felt like the last survivors of a long-gone civilization: the two were ugly—Juan Jacobo a little more so—and they were both virgins—Santiago a little less so—and both shared a strange affection for books of alchemy, filthy nails, unpolished shoes, and jokes at the expense of the *straights*. Left out of the gossip, the parties, and cutting class, they quickly realized that their destiny was to turn themselves into *intellectuals*. The task took to them like a ring to a finger: all they had to do was to memorize unpronounceable Russian names—of writers, film directors, and poets' lovers—and have the capacity to discern, without a moment's hesitation, between the *phenomenal* and the *putrid*. In those years, the muralists, Nicaragua, Fidel, and above all, the chubby tropical god who had invented Macondo were *in*; gringos, the PRI, and most of all, that chubby and arrogant devil named Octavio Paz were *out*. (In following years the list switched with an awesome rapidity.)

"Is he really dead?"

"More dead than a Chiapas Indian in a military camp," Susana told him, without taking a break from chewing her gum. "And uglier than your bitch of a mother." (If you feel that the celebrated author of *Pricks* was being overly crude, simply take a look at her latest book.)

In *Zeno Perplexed*, the rest of the scene is transfigured in the following manner: Susana was named Gloria, and instead of her cheese-grater skin, she looked like Maribel, a neighbor who never recovered from her nausea after kissing Santiago; overnight I was changed into a music critic and Juan Jacobo into an opera singer. (Inserting the structure of a lyric drama into a noir novel seemed very postmodern to Santiago.) Other details: the meeting of Latin writers (*Hispanic* writers in North America) organized by the University of Utah became a montage of Puccini's *La Fanciulla del West* in a natural stage set (the Arizona desert) and, of course, Susana had lost half her preferences, resigning herself to the usual—although somewhat reckless—heterosexuality. What comes next is not only predictable but frankly absurd: in that moment, I, a simple music critic who never lifted my head up from my scores, transform myself, as demanded by the canons of contemporary taste, into a levelheaded detective, ready to solve the enigma of the slain tenor.

Thanks to my conversations with characters from other young authors, I've learned that in their repertory there are only three types of narration: detective (every time more sophisticated so that nobody will compare the author to Agatha Christie rather than Umberto Eco), self-referential (only idiotic young people appear, people similar to the writers themselves, instead of young idiots disguised as adults, as in the other two genres), and feminine (whatever this last may be). If you were going to compile statistics on Santiago's work, detective stories turn up most often, at 67%, ahead of 31% for self-referential—especially stories influenced by the New Wave when it was *in*, now revitalized by *pulp* fashion— and finally, 2% with various themes. (He has so far lacked the courage to tackle feminine themes, but who knows?) The sociologists explain this phenomenon in many ways: TV, movies, street violence, general disenchantment, the Fall of the Berlin Wall, etc., but I think that if there are so many noir novels it's due to the law of minimal effort: it's enough to fill the mold, as bad poets do with a sonnet or the ice cream man does with a cone. Be that as it may, after the death of Juan Jacobo, Santiago decided to invert the roles and imitate that which he had done so many times before with me: he himself would become the levelheaded investigator, in spite of the opposition of the scandalized chairperson of the Romance Languages Department. In *Zeno*, he obliges me to explain *his* motives with Dostoevskian profundity: "He had to do it."

"He seemed like a fag to me," Susana added, while petting the snail she had tattooed on the nape of her neck.

"And what does that have to do with anything?" Santiago asked.

"Half of all crimes in the United States have racial motives and the other half are sexual. You make the choice."

Susana's logic was overwhelming. Not for nothing had she been able to write a hilarious catalog of penises—many of them belonging to famous writers and some not so famous—that had made her into the best-selling artist of the year.

In his first novel, *The Muse of the Game*—written in two feverish weeks after his discovery of Paul Auster—Santiago obliged me to play the role of an inexperienced Sherlock Holmes, this time using the identity Seymour Compton, with a stage setting that, for a work of more than capricious chance, carried me from Brooklyn to Ciudad Neza. In the novel I follow a carefully outlined plan: (*a*) identifying the corpse (a black marketeer who—what a coincidence!—had studied with me in grade school; (*b*) reconstructing the scene of the crime; (*c*) drawing up a list of suspects among whom is found a femme fatale who, by chance, becomes my lover; (*d*) interviewing them one by one until, thanks to a final stroke of luck, I find the criminal.

When he decided to investigate his friend's death, Santiago didn't recall this series of events; but his literary instinct brought him to repeat it to such a degree that even Auster himself would have been surprised. The first two steps were almost completed—no one doubted that Juan Jacobo was very dead and the crime had been committed, as everyone knew, in the apartment he shared with Santiago during a Latin Writers Congress organized by Ohio University—so that he had to begin with step (*c*), the creation of a detailed list of suspects.

Although it was the intention of the chairperson, Ms. Ellen Cunningham, to bring together the cream of the crop of Latino intellectuals, the tiny budget obliged her to make due with fifteen authors less than thirty-five years old who, altogether and in spite of endless rounds of bourbon, cost her less than a single conference dedicated to Isabel Allende. Furthermore, she could feel proud of counting among her staff of professors Doctor Elida Garciabonilla, a perfectly legal American citizen who, though she could barely stammer the Spanish of her parents, was the world's greatest authority on the material at hand, that is—you won't believe it—Latin American writers under thirty-five.

The list of possible guilty parties wasn't really very long. But if you had the chance to look at the faces of the invitees to the conference, you would doubtless have imagined a collective crime. The thirteen participants who were still alive were criminals in waiting: two Peruvians who wrote only about murders (the killer was always Asian); an Argentine playwright; three Venezuelan short story writers; three Colombians; a snobbish group of poets composed of a Uruguayan, a Chicana, and a Dominican; two critics and a novelist (Susana) from Mexico; and a Costa Rican oral storyteller. Of course, neither Ms. Cunningham nor Doctor Garciabonilla could be excluded.

Santiago's and Juan Jacobo's literary trajectories had begun to separate when they left high school. Dietrich (he'd already begun to sign his name in German), more adventurous or more irresponsible, decided to study philosophy while Santiago, with more common sense, flip-flopped for several months between the professions of his father and that of his grandfather: the dissecting rooms of the School of Medicine and the even messier classrooms at the School of Law. The outcome was obvious: while his friend surrounded himself with a circle of impenetrable, pure poets and lovers of Central European literature, Santiago transformed himself into a precocious exponent of dirty realism, the second arrival of the Wave, the undertow of the Spanish *Movida* and Sick Literature, with the respective doses of sex, drugs, and rock 'n' roll that all of these tendencies demanded of its adherents.

But by that time their friendship was stronger than their aesthetic differences, and despite all the predictions, they decided to launch a new literary movement, which they called Generation Kaboom. After some intense proselytizing efforts—including the writing of the celebrated "Manifesto Kaboom"—they brought two other promising young writers into the group: Paco Palma

(Ectapec, 1973), at present a prisoner in the Cerro Hueco, Chiapas, jail; and Clementina Suárez (Jiquilpan, 1974–Morelia, 1996) who died prematurely in a car accident (crack brought her to the point of proving that light poles aren't friendly objects at three in the morning). In spite of the incomprehension of the critics—especially Jacinto Tostado, who referred to them as a "literary golf club," their watchwords were clear: to struggle, in hand-to-hand combat, against literature *light*, or in other words, to try to steal away some of the readers of *Like Water for Chocolate*.

After drawing up his list of suspects, Santiago decided to start making inquiries, always helped by gentle Susana.

"You're useless, kiddo, " she said to him. "Why don't I, the big flirt, the cock of the walk, do the investigating and you bitches keep your mouths shut. You ain't coming up with nothing, little guy. These fucking gringos aren't going to let you stick your butt into their business. We aren't in Joligú anymore."[4]

But Santiago had made up his mind. Imitating my role as a tough guy, he turned up unexpectedly in one of the bars that ringed the campus and as he hoped, found himself face-to-face with the sickly silhouette of Jacinto Tostado, who hadn't shown up for even one of the conference meetings. "If I already know that they're full of shit, why do I have to listen to them?" he said to the two inebriated black males with whom he shared his erudition. "A tall glass of bourbon has more brains than whatever those junk collectors have written." Intrigued, the bartender asked him if he had read any of the junior Latinos' books. "Not even on pain of death," Jacinto responded. "If I already know they're a pile of shit, why do I have to read them?" and in a sudden fit of generosity, he called for another round. In *Zeno Perplexed*, the dialogue between the two characters develops as follows: "'Haven't you stopped yet?' I asked Giacinto Brucciato simply to make him un-

---

[4]Exact transcription of the writer's words, just as she would later put them to use, with a remarkable linguistic fidelity, in her characters' dialogues.

comfortable. 'Go to hell, Cameron,' he shot back, his eyes like an eel's. 'Did you hear about Turchini?' 'Sad, no? The unlucky little tenor. Another piece of shit, Cameron.' 'Can I ask you where you were yesterday in the afternoon?' 'Right here, drinking this shit. Ask my friends—' And the big, crafty mouths of the blacks opened together as if they were the very gates of hell" (p. 56).

As you can imagine, Santiago limited himself to correcting the original episode a little. " 'Haven't you stopped yet, Jacinto?' 'I'm not crazy, pal. This is the only way to make a roundtable at which you're reading bearable.' 'You've heard what happened to Juan Jacobo?' 'Too bad, isn't it? The poor dead scribbler. And a piece of shit, Contreras.' 'Can I ask where you were yesterday afternoon?' 'Fucking Susana. Ask her if you like. . . .' " (If he had written that he would be running the risk of seeing it in the seventh and expanded edition of *Pricks*, so he let it pass.)

The critic was to blame for the heavy shadow of rivalry that had sprung up between Juan Jacobo and Santiago. Sure enough, he had written in a review that the prose of the former was "like a mixture of Joyce and that fag Lucas" (a decidedly ambiguous commentary), while referring to Santiago, he hadn't left any doubt: "What we have here is without question the worst writer of 1996." After this statement the Kaboom Movement died forever. Although they tried to hide it, the friendship between its founders was never the same.

"I heard that you were fighting with the Nazi"—Juan Jacobo's nickname, given him by jealous types like Susana, and at times, Santiago himself.

"Nonsense."

"Then why are you obsessing over this, Santi?"—He hated her calling him that, as much as I hate his metaphors. "Why get involved?"

As if making a reply directly imported from *Zeno Perplexed*, Santiago responded once again, "I have to do it." (In *I Will Spit on Your Grave*, the phrase that gives the book its title is repeated forty-eight times, in the end lending it a style similar to that of Javier Marias.)

Despite his expectations, the two baboons from the Ohio State Police in charge of the case prevented him from entering the scene of the crime (not that he was thinking to change anything: it was his house too and he needed clean socks); they wouldn't let him take prints and they said to him, in a screwy dialect, that the other *artistes* were very nervous and weren't going to tolerate Santiago bugging them with his absurd interrogations.

The distance between Santiago and Juan Jacobo had widened even further when the latter received a scholarship to study in Germany, where he planned to write stories about the soldiers of the SS. Santiago turned his jealousy into ethical condemnation: "How could you? Nazis. Good lord, Juan Jacobo, you've got to give that up to save your dignity. . . ." But Juan Jacobo didn't give it up: he wrote a brief treatise of thirty-eight pages, *There Were Heroes Too*, which won the applause of Mexican critics—Santiago was in the habit of saying that its success was owing to the fact that the critics never read anything longer than forty pages—and a translation into English. (It was banned in Germany.)

The brutality of the real world quickly introduced itself into Santiago's investigations. It wouldn't have occurred to him in his worst story: two days after the murder, in front of the astonished faces of the members of the conference, the two police officers arrested Jacinto Tostado, handcuffed him, put him in a patrol car (but not before reading him his rights) and carried him off to the county jail. The image called to mind the worst Hollywood movies but no Tarantino was available to come up with witty dialogue to save the situation.

"Like the butler, the critic is always guilty," Susana whispered after the event.

In reality she was the least likely to say it. While the greater part of her generation had to stoically endure the insults and diatribes of the reviewers—generally it wasn't a question of frustrated authors as is commonly thought but of something worse: working writers desirous of exhibiting their analytic abilities— Susana invariably received flattery and indulgence. And the strangest thing was that this wasn't owing to her beauty (which was negligible) or to her innate disposition to bestow sexual favors (although she did so often) and much less to her gifts as a writer (which were, everyone agreed, null and void). Her critical reception was one of those small mysteries that nestled in every small literary community.

"And why was he going to do something like that?" Santiago asked.

"Doctor Garciabonilla found his motive. In a story that Juan Jacobo was going to read the night of his murder, the homodiegetic narrator is, according to her, the image of Tostado."

"I don't follow you at all."

"The professor is sure that Juan Jacobo was going to mock the critic."

"But I read that story myself and the narrator is Heinrich Himmler!"

"What do I know!" Susana shot back. "She's the expert, and she says that when you deconstruct the character, Jacinto's traits appear."

"Well, she's wrong." Santiago chewed his nails. "And you know it! Jacinto couldn't have done it because he was with you when the crime was committed!"

"With me?" At times she succeeded in being enchantingly roguish.

"He told me he was . . . OK, that you two were . . ."

"So I'm his alibi?" The writer laughed like she hadn't since the chapter of *Pricks* that she reserved for Camilo José Cela.

"Come on, let's go to the police station," Santiago pressured her.

"What for?"

"You have to prove his innocence."

"Me?" She smiled again. "If I did, the literary community would never forgive me. I'm sorry, but no. It's word against word. And can I tell you something? He's much better as a critic . . ."

I don't need to add that in *Zeno Perplexed* this discussion has been altered until it became unrecognizable—but it's so poorly written it's not worth repeating. Santiago hadn't felt so anguished since he finished reading Paco Palma's first novel (he had realized, with horror, how much better it was than his, and he had prudently recommended that Paco file it away for later. Deciding to save Tostado—Susana thought that later he might want to make use of the favor—Santiago deceived one of the guards, broke the police tape, and snuck into his house on the sly in search of proof that would demonstrate the critic's innocence. From what he was able to see the American cops weren't like their Mexican counterparts: everything was in its place—that is to say, in the same mess it was in before the murder—and the only new element was the adhesive tape that drew Juan Jacobo's silhouette on the floor. Perhaps because they didn't understand Spanish, or because they were as indifferent to literature as Ms. Cunningham was, the police had neglected to take a look at the dozens of papers signed by Juan Jacobo that could be found on every shelf. Looking for a clue, Santiago went through them one by one until he was sick of black uniforms, swastikas, Charlot's tiny mustache hairs, and the iron crosses that ran riot through the now-dead man's final production. At last, he found what he needed sitting on top of the toilet: a loose page, written by hand in Juan Jacobo's chicken-scratch calligraphy. There was no question that it was a suicide note.

*To Whom It May Concern:*
*When you read this note it will be too late for me. I will already inhabit the silent territory of the void. I myself took charge of administering the poison. Why? This is precisely the problem: there is no why. I simply realized that I prefer silence. No one thinks about the silent old age of Rulfo or Areola anymore. They quickly realized*

*that they had nothing more to say. On the other hand, I have dis-
covered that I never had anything to say. As I said in an interview, I
write because I don't know how to do anything better. But that
doesn't mean I do it well. No one is to blame for my death.[5]*

J. J. *Dietrich*

Santiago copied the paragraph literally in *Zeno Perplexed*, only
substituting the verb *sing* for *say* and Maria Callas and Giuseppe
di Stefano for Rulfo and Areola (p. 77). He had done it! So many
years of reading and writing detective novels had served a purpose!

That same morning, Santiago went to the police station. Susana accompanied him (unwillingly, but putting on a show in a
magenta outfit with plunging neckline), as did Ms. Cunningham
and the rest of the Latino writers. (Only Doctor Garciabonilla ex-
cused herself, perhaps because she believed that Santiago wanted
to discredit her philological investigations.)

"My lord," Santiago started by saying in English although he
was only speaking to a simple guard. "I've come to stop a terrible
injustice from being committed. That man"—and he pointed at
Tostado, who from before he had been thrown in jail was on a
drunk and didn't even realize he was behind bars—"is innocent.
Indeed he is, ladies and gentlemen, *innocent.*"

And some say that serious literary types aren't influenced by
John Grisham.

"What the hell are you talking about?" the guard shot back.

"Juan Tostado may be a miserable fifth-rate critic, a man who
has sold his pen to the highest bidder, a mercenary and a dog
without principles but he, ladies and gentlemen, did not kill Juan
Jacobo Reyes, a.k.a. Juan Jacobo Dietrich."

"O no?" the chorus sang pompously, as if this were an opera
that Santiago put in his novel.

---

[5]He couldn't even be original in his last moment? (C.N.)

"No. I have the proof here"—and he began to wave a piece of paper in a police officer's beard.

"What is this?" asked the security guard with newfound interest.

And at that moment Santiago responded in a voice energetic and firm, the voice that Emile Zola must have raised when he brandished his *J'accuse*:

"My signed confession," he said, and after a long pause, added, "I killed Juan Jacobo Dietrich." If in that moment I could have broken out from the moldy books that imprison me, I would have slapped him mercilessly. Why did you do it, you son of a bitch? I would have said to Santiago like a character out of *I Will Spit on Your Grave*. Unfortunately such undertakings are forbidden me. I'm a simple character, and as they teach you in the first literary theory class, never confuse the narrator with the author.

Only now, at the end of this story—and through this story having shared Santiago's doings and his dreams—I believe that I at last understand. Perhaps only this story made the trouble he took worth it. The dialogue that follows is, then, doubly impossible: it has nothing to do with my reality or Santiago's, and above all, nothing to do with *his* fictions or *mine*. It is nothing more than a dream. The eternal dream of literature.

"Why, Santiago? Why did you do it?"

"Killing Dietrich?"

"We both know it wasn't you. You found his note, isn't it true?"

"Maybe yes and maybe no. As you said, only you and I know."

"They've thrown you in jail for thirty years, Santiago."

"The same as you, dear friend. From here on you will share your days with characters in Revueltas and Solzhenitsyn. Doesn't that seem thrilling to you?"

"I don't know."

"Just look at yourself. Look how you've grown in the last weeks. Before you were a stupid young punk disguised as Doctor

Kapuchinski, or a music critic, or as me myself. Now on the other hand you're a great character. Autonomous, rounded, full of nuance. Jacinto Tostado has written that you possess the richest character in contemporary literature."

"That's owing to you. You can't trust any of his opinions."

"I agree. But for the first time you have valuable things to say. Isn't that what you wanted? Didn't you complain about being stupid and empty? Now you are intelligent, perverse, brave, subtle, sad, innocent and criminal, like all human beings. . . ."

"Why did you do it? In order to go through an experience that would really make you into a writer?"

"I appreciate your confidence but you overestimate me. I never thought that this would occur. At least I didn't have it planned. It has been a last-minute consolation."

"So?"

"You don't know me any better? I couldn't let Juan Jacobo be turned into a legend. A young author who commits suicide at an American university before he's thirty-five years old? What did his note say? *The silent territory of the void.* Doesn't that kill you? A Jorge Cuesta, a Raymond Radiguet, a Latino Kurt Cobain. . . . What more do you want? No, my friend. Nobody remembers him now. Nobody. You hear me? And do you know how many theses are being written about my work? How many news reports, biographies, essays, movies, books? I couldn't give him that pleasure. I just couldn't do it."

*Translated by James Graham*